# PIRATES
## of the
# ASTEROIDS

### the belter series: book one

# E.S. MARTELL

Printed in the USA
Second Initiative Press

ISBN: 978-0-9989805-9-1

**Editor**
Adriana D'Apolito of 3P Editing
**Cover Art**
Aleksandra Klepacka
**Typography**
Kelley York of Sleepy Fox Studio
**Interior Design and Typeset**
Melissa Stevens of The Illustrated Author Design Services

This book is dedicated to Hayden, Oscar, Elliot, Rowen, and Hazel
– May you retain your curiosity always.

# PIRATE SPACE: BEWARE!

All Adam wanted was his advanced degree and a girlfriend. What he got was betrayal, kicked out of University, and exiled to the Asteroid Belt.

The Asteroid Miners have just about had their fill of the oppressive Federal bureaucracy, and some of them are ready to take steps towards freedom.

Adam arrives just in time to find himself involved with a budding revolution. Unfortunately, he had been working on a physics degree, and it wasn't as if there was a course of study on Practical Pirating offered at the University.

How does one become a pirate? Adam is about to figure it out.

This story is set against the background of the asteroid belt and filled with a mixture of existing technology and new inventions. It is a near future, wild and woolly journey around the solar system that provides what every reader wants: entertainment, adventure, humor, tragedy, and a little romance.

# CONTENTS

# ACKNOWLEDGMENTS

I rely on my wife, Sally, for critique and feedback. She also makes sure I eat while I'm writing and that makes things convenient. Without her help, these stories would never have made it out of my head.

This book benefited immensely from the editorial expertise of Adriana D'Apolito of 3P Editing.

Special thanks to Aleksandra Klepacka for her cover art. As always, she has captured the essence of the story in her art.

Kelley York of Sleepy Fox Studio added her expertise to the cover by providing typography.

Interior typesetting by Melissa Stevens of The Illustrated Author made the book much easier on the reader's eye.

# 1

# ON THE LAM

"THAT'S A STUPID name. Cue? What? Did your parents play a lot of nine-ball or something?" The new marines, just out of Boot and with a couple of drinks warming their insides, were obviously feeling good about themselves. The biggest one apparently had decided he was a good target.

Adam had needlessly used his full name in response to the marine's question. He habitually recited Adam Q. Maxwell in an attempt to separate himself from his famous father, Adam J. Maxwell. Why his dad hadn't included Junior or II after his name was a puzzle to him, but so were many of the things his genius father had done.

The marine, seemingly sensing some weakness, had focused on his middle initial, choosing to make fun of it. Adam looked around the seedy bar. No help there. Most of the other occupants were preoccupied with their drinks. The bartender glanced at the marines, then turned away. He'd seen a few thousand fights in his career and didn't look interested in what was potentially going to happen. The sergeant in charge of the newbies had gone to relieve himself, leaving the unsupervised boys free to play.

Regretting his naivete, Adam wished he'd remembered to use a made-up name. He needed to learn to be more careful since he was on the run. It was too late to correct his response now.

"No. My dad is a physicist, quantum-type. When I was conceived, he refused to allow the doctors to determine my sex. Then he decided that since there were only two possibilities, he'd name me Qubit."

He spelled it, something that had become habit after twenty-two years. "The letter Q then u followed by bit. It is short-hand for quantum bit. My mother pitched a fit, so he settled by naming me Adam and using Qubit for my middle name."

The big one looked puzzled. "What kind of name is that? What's a quandum whatzit, anyway?"

He sighed. It was usually like this. "It's the chance that Schrodinger's cat is living when you open the box."

"Huh? A cat?"

"The other option is the cat is dead. There are only two choices, and the status of the Qubit determines the outcome."

The big guy looked like he was coming out of his flummoxed mode and moving into an angry one. "What the hell? You kill cats? I suppose you kill dogs, too? Maybe you'd like to clean the deck with your tongue!"

The skinny sergeant appeared just in time to hear the challenging tone. "Leave him alone, Lonzo."

"Aw, Sarge, he's looking for a fight, and I think he wants to lick the deck."

"Leave him alone. I'm serious. I didn't see what started this, but I'm not going on report for letting you idiots beat up the first civ you see."

The four others looked disappointed. They'd been ready to back Lonzo and jump him as soon as the first punch was thrown.

Adam leaned back in his booth and closed his eyes. It wasn't likely they'd continue now that the sergeant had told them to lay off. The marines' conversation was muffled. The constant noise of the band made it difficult to hear unless the speakers were face-to-face. He could still hear the discussion, but now it seemed to be more oriented towards the stripper and her lackadaisical attempt to pole dance.

He had a few hours left to waste until he was due at the ribbon. The bar had seemed like a safe place. It was too cold in the high altitude to hang around outside. Besides he was tired and wanted somewhere to sit down.

The last few weeks had been filled with frantic action. The Revenue Department's case against him had been built with frightening efficiency and speed. Most people thought that government bureaucrats were inefficient. Ha! They certainly moved quickly enough when they were directed to get somebody. He'd done nothing illegal. There was nothing to find. He'd broken no laws, but they used a combination of fake leaks to the press to create enough buzz that he seemed guilty. Given that perception, they were able to convince a judge to issue a warrant for him.

He had figured out how to find a lot of free money in the last couple of weeks. After the disillusionment with Elseth, he absolutely had to keep his mind occupied, or he'd go insane. Few people knew that there was such a thing as a zombie bitcoin. He couldn't help it that some people were so careless that they lost their keycodes. He'd figured out an algo that recovered some of the lost coins.

At last count, he'd been worth a couple of million. That was before the Senator had gotten the FBI after him. Now all he had was a stolen credit card that would probably bounce the first time he tried to use it.

That thought brought him back to full attention. The marines were still gawking at the unfortunate woman dancer. The bartender was mixing for another group of men who looked like regulars, maybe ribbon maintenance workers.

Adam tilted his drink and sipped. The booze was poor quality and raw, but it warmed his stomach. *Have to make this last.* He was nearly out of cash, and that credit card shouldn't be used until there were no other options. He leaned back again, glanced around, then closed his eyes.

It was a rotten situation. He'd been happily studying physics during his second year in grad school. He thought he had a chance with Elseth. His train of thought wavered, and he repeated her name softly. The sound of it on his lips was still moving. He'd fallen for her, not knowing that it was all a lie. In retrospect, he saw he had been incredibly naive. No way an upper girl like her would stay interested in a dep with his background, even if his dad did have a prestigious teaching and research job.

Still, miracles do happen. One thing led to another until he was prepared to ask her to marry him. Then there had been the faint smell of cologne on her pillow. He'd been suspicious, but she had kissed him, and he'd forgotten about it in the heat of the moment.

He felt sick about the situation for two weeks, hoping that everything was okay and that she really loved him, but afraid that he was wrong. It was a miserable feeling.

The whole charade came crashing down five weeks ago. He'd caught Elseth and Serge in bed, and it hadn't been a pretty scene. It was so far from his expectations that he had difficulty understanding what he saw at first. His next thought was that he wanted to kick Serge around, but that turned to panic when the skinny Swede had pulled a pistol on him.

For a moment he had thought that he was going to die, then Elseth had intervened. She had told him that she did love him, but one man just wasn't enough for her. She wanted him, but to earn her love, he'd have to help the two of them in a project.

It was a ludicrous concept, but he was so far gone that he actually considered trying to show her that he was worthwhile by agreeing.

The project, when he'd found out about it, was so horrendous that he'd gone straight to the police. That was where Elseth's father, Senator Worthington, had stepped in. The police had ignored Adam's statements, and he'd ended up sitting in front of the Senator.

He played the scene over in his mind.

Senator W: "Adam Maxwell, hmm?"

Adam: "Yes, Sir."

Senator W: "Seems familiar. Didn't your father come up with a variant on the em-Drive device?"

Adam: "Yes, Sir. That was his idea. It increased efficiency by--"

Senator W, waving his hand to shut Adam up: "I know. I know. It was a masterstroke and all that. What's your opinion of the Government, boy?"

Adam: "Uh, well, maybe things have gotten a little too restrictive lately. The speech codes and that kind of thing."

Senator W: "Yeah. We plan to do something about that. I understand that you're not going to help. Elseth told me you were against the idea."

Adam: "I, uh, well something needs to be done, but blowing up the capitol building seems, you know, extreme or something."

Senator W: "Don't worry about that, it was just a fantasy of Elseth's. She was supposed to recruit someone to help, someone who knew physics, but her imagination ran away with her. No one is going to blow up anything. However, young man, we still need to gain control. The other party has lost their collective mind as has the President. I intend to rectify things. We could use a physicist, even a student physicist."

Adam: "I don't think I'm the type of person who would be any good at this kind of thing. No. Besides, I voted for the President, and this seems to be a betrayal of my confidence. Working against him, I mean."

Senator W: "I see. Well, that won't be a problem. Now, I've got to meet with some important people, so you should get back to whatever you were doing. By the way, don't bother trying to go to the police. If you embarrass Elseth again, I'm going to have to take action. I can't have any scandal associated with my daughter, and by extension, me. Do you understand?"

He understood only too well. He was in deep trouble, despite the fake friendly demeanor of the Senator. He'd been right about that. His problemshad multiplied quickly. First, the social media debacle that led to his losing his scholarship and being placed on suspension.

He ground his teeth in frustration. He'd been framed. He'd never been to that party, and he'd never be so stupid to refer to a woman in that way. The grievance committee didn't care. Men weren't given much credibility. The supposed victim got all of the sympathy. He'd--

What seemed like an explosion struck his cheek, knocking his head back and to the side. He slid down into the seat, raising his hand to block. Lonzo's arm was raised for a follow-up, but the big idiot was looking over his shoulder at his mates with a grin. His legs were spread invitingly, too.

Adam gritted his teeth in frustration. Getting in a fight and attracting attention wasn't part of the plan, but the other marines were moving to get in on the fun. Apparently their sergeant had disappeared again, so they felt free to indulge themselves by picking on him.

Best to stop this mess right now. The target was obvious even to someone who hadn't studied martial arts as long as he had. He shrugged, then kicked upwards as hard as he could.

Lonzo groaned, bent double, and grabbed at his crotch, then fell sideways on the floor. One down and four to go..

Adam raised his head and deliberately incited the marines by sticking out his tongue and making a ptttbh sound.

One member of the back-up group shouted, making an outraged, but incoherent noise. The four rushed forward to attack, the desire for revenge showing on their faces. Adam quickly slid under the table as they reached over trying to grab him. As he did, he kicked the middle marine's legs out from under him. That resulted in a satisfying 'thunk' as the guy slammed down on the tabletop. From the sound, he must have landed hard on his face.

Adam scuttled into the gap, crawling under the tabletop man's thrashing legs. Two of the marines were leaning over the table, trying to see where he'd gone. It was the fourth that was going to be a problem. He was just in the act of swinging his foot forward in a kick aimed at Adam's face.

That required a quick jerk back. The leg went by, a miss, but too close for comfort. Adam wasn't quite sure what to do next, but the problem was settled for him. The kicker gave a surprised grunt then collapsed. The bartender was standing behind the man's prostrate body holding a club that appeared to be made from a sawed-off Little League Bat.

Before the others regained their bearings, the bartender stepped closer and whacked the standing two, dropping both on top of the one that was still lying on the table.

"Ok, kid. Hit the door behind the bar, straight through the storage room and out. There's another door across the alley. Go in, lock it and stay there till I come to get you." His voice was low and rough. When Adam didn't move quickly enough, he added, "Git!"

That was all he needed. Adam jumped up, dashed around the bar and through the first door. He glanced back as he exited. The patrons and the dancer were studiously ignoring the bartender and the marines. The stripper gave him an unidentifiable look as he shut the door.

There was a dim light in the storage room, and it was a good thing. Otherwise, he would have tripped over a case of beer lying directly in his path. The back door was unlocked, as was the one across the alley.

For a moment Adam thought of ignoring the opposite alley door and running, but something in the bartender's attitude had convinced him that the man knew what was what. He opened it and slipped inside. It was dark, except for some light that filtered through a window.

The place seemed to be an old clothing store. There were a few disconsolate mannequins interspersed among wheeled racks of hangers that stood in close ranks. The door sported a deadbolt, and he turned it, being careful to follow the bartender's instructions.

Since he'd decided to rely on the man, it was probably better to count on him entirely, rather than to try and second-guess him.

There was a stack of boxes near the wall and, after looking around again, Adam found a comfortable seat between two of them. He leaned back and relaxed, then jumped as a siren sounded in the street nearby.

The cops! He needed them like he needed a hole in the head. If they caught him, they'd lock him up as soon as they realized the FBI wanted him. Senator Worthington had done a thorough job in setting him up. He'd be lucky to make it to prison the way things were going.

Worthington probably had the influence to arrange for him to be killed in a staged escape attempt or something. He grimaced again.

Falling for Elseth had been a bad mistake. Yet, he still wanted her. She was cute, smart, and amazingly sexy. Adam sighed, resigned to the fact that it was never going to happen. He had been blind to the fact that she was promiscuous as hell. He was confident that Serge wasn't the only one she'd seen behind his back. Then there was the plot. That was what she'd really wanted him for. That was probably the only reason she'd come on to him in the first place. It wasn't like the two of them traveled in the same circles at school.

The siren got closer, then he could see flashing lights through the dusty window. He slumped lower between the two boxes as someone tried to open the locked door. It was lucky he'd decided to believe the bartender.

A flashlight shined through the window, partly illuminating the mannequins and making the room seem even spookier. He held still, hoping that, if they could see his feet between the boxes, they'd think he was just another mannequin. It apparently worked. After a few seconds, the light disappeared. The doorknob rattled again as someone tried it once more, then it was quiet.

Adam drew his legs up and tried to think. Elseth and Serge's plot to bomb the Senate seemed to be related to the current hearings that were going on. He didn't follow politics, but there had been something in the news that he'd noticed as he scanned his social media account. It had mentioned some other country that was presumed to be ready to attack.

Worthington had been mentioned as calling for a preemptive strike. That was what had caught his eye. He was fine-tuned to notice anything that related to Elseth. Maybe Senator W had decided to take out the opposition directly since he apparently couldn't convince them to go along with him.

Adam shook his head. Maybe focusing on research alone wasn't such a good idea. It would help if he knew what was going on with the country. Well, it didn't matter so much now. There was no one he could tell that could do anything.

His only option was to try and get away. That was why he was here, in the mountains of Equador. The space ribbon was the only way off Earth and space seemed to be the only safe place for him. It didn't hurt that he'd always wanted to go to Mars anyway.

That desire had been the reason for his physics and math studies. People didn't just randomly get selected for the colonization effort. They had to qualify. He thought he would be approved now, but the warrant complicated things. He'd just be arrested if he went through the standard procedure. The obvious thing then was to stow-away on one of the ribbon elevators. They were as large as cruise ships, and there were plenty of places to hide. At least he thought there would be places.

That was the hope, anyway. He'd used the last of the bitcoin money, the part they hadn't confiscated, to get down here. It remained to figure out how to get on the elevator, how to hide, and then how to stowaway on a Mars transport.

Once on the transport, he'd have a little over six months to convince them that he could earn his keep. They couldn't just turn around in mid-flight. If they wanted to turn him over to the authorities, they would have to ship him back from Mars. They were too civilized to space stowaways. At least, he hoped they were. Senator W had a lot of influence.

It was still a good bet that he'd find a position on Mars. Shipping him back would be a waste of fuel and having him off the planet was just about as good as having him dead as far as Senator Worthington's plans went. He'd pose no threat if he couldn't get back. Interplanetary communications were expensive and were reserved for official business. There was no way Adam would be able to send a message. Besides, there was no one to tell.

He jumped again. The door lock had clicked. The door swung open slowly, and the stripper's head poked through the gap. She looked around, then whispered, "Hey, where are ya?"

Adam thought about it. Chances were, the bartender had sent her. He struggled up, making the boxes rattle. The dancer jerked back, then reappeared.

"C'mon out of there. Jack says it's all clear. Ya gotta get out of here. We can't take any chances with the cops. Jack says ya gotta leave."

She looked wary as he approached. He held up his hands showing her the palms.

"Look, I'm not going to hurt you. I don't have anywhere to go. They're after me."

"I know. The PO showed your pix to Jack. I saw it. Not a good likeness, but then, they never are. Ya gotta go."

"I really don't have anywhere to go. I---" He stopped abruptly. Was it a good idea to tell her his plan of stowing away? He shrugged. What option did he have?

"Look, I want to get on the ribbon, get off-world, and head for Mars. They most likely will leave me alone, if I do."

She backed up. "I don't know anything about that. Wait here while I ask Jack ta come talk ta ya."

JACK WANTED MONEY. He implied that he could help, but it would cost. In fact, it would cost more than Adam had. Jack didn't want the credit card. He thought it would be trouble. Using it would alert someone somewhere, and the risk was too high.

Adam searched his mind, then inspiration struck. "How would you like a way to make lots of money?"

"Depends. Is it legal?"

"I've got an algorithm that finds zombie bitcoins. There are millions of dollars worth of them. All you have to do is to find them, then cash them in."

To his credit, Jack seemed to know about zombie bitcoins. "That's interesting. I don't have any crypto myself, but, if your algo really works, I can sell it." He paused for a moment, thinking it over.

"Alright, I'll get you on the el. You got to take care of yourself after I get you on and hid. That's as far as my contact will go. If that works for you, then we gotta deal as long as your algo really works."

"It really works alright. It's just that Senator Worthington sicced the FBI on me because..." Talking too much again. He wished he could learn to keep his mouth shut.

Jack growled, "Worthington? Look, kid, I'll still take your algo, but I'd help for free, if it'd hurt that slime ball. He's going to destroy this country, if he can."

# 2
# THE RIBBON

WHO WOULD HAVE thought that going into space was so boring? The trip up seemed to be designed by a master torturer, forcing Adam to grit his teeth as he struggled through long periods of enforced inactivity, punctuated by brief moments of frenetic work as he labored to patch the inefficient air scrubbers.

Jack had done much better by him than he'd expected. Instead of merely smuggling Adam on board and leaving him to hide on his own, the bartender had called in a debt or rather several debts. The stripper, Susan, had arranged for a fake ID, while Jack had gotten Adam signed on as crew. His job was nominally waste facility coordinator for C deck, which meant that he was responsible for the small team that cleaned the toilets in that area.

This was not an inconsiderable job, since the journey up the ribbon involved gradually decreasing weight, then weightlessness, then steadily increasing weight. When the elevator reached the null point, the pull of gravity was counter-balanced by centrifugal force producing a short period of weightlessness. Then weight gradually increased as the elevator began to brake on its way to the departure station. The station swung at the end of the ribbon and acted as a counter-weight, in addition to providing a docking point for the Earth-Lunar shuttle, commonly called the trans-shuttle or just the trans.

The fake ID passed the test and Adam, now known as Richard Headly, made it onto the elevator with no questions asked. He had a small room that he shared with another C deck supervisor, Frank Lowery. Frank was in charge of the janitorial crew for the section. He was experienced crew and knew his job. After a little conversation, he took Adam on a brief tour of the heads.

Adam took a look at the waste facilities and immediately understood what he was up against. The toilets were similar to airplane toilets with a vacuum flush. The primary difference was due to the weightlessness requirement.

Using the things during that period required sitting with a plastic wrap around the user's waist. The vacuum was continuous, and the plastic was needed to keep the user sucked against the seat so that the waste didn't escape.

Generally, the toilets sucked most of the waste down the sewage line, but some always got on the user's bottom and occasionally other places. The seats had a tendency to get quite dirty, and this kept the cleaning crew busy.

Adam didn't have to clean, but he did have to keep his crew's morale up. He did this by bringing them pizza on their breaks and generally trying to be a good boss. They joked with him and gradually became proficient at their jobs. The jokes sometimes became a little rowdy, but Adam didn't care as long as they did their jobs.

IT WAS BREAK time, and Adam was on his way to meet his crew at C Deck, Section 9. He had three pizzas and was being careful to hold them tightly since the experienced gravity pull was now quite low. Weighing twenty pounds made it more difficult to walk. He had no desire to get off balance, crash into a wall or a passenger, and possibly lose control of the pepperoni and sausage pizzas. That had happened once and the resulting mess made for a time-consuming cleanup.

The elevator was large and carried twelve hundred passengers on the four decks. Adam had restricted himself to C Deck and kept his head down, staying busy at his assigned job.

He had just passed the deck-to-deck elevator bank when he heard something that sent shivers up his spine.

"C'mon, Lonny. We'll get in trouble if Sarge finds us down here."

Adam glanced back at the elevators. The same five marines were just coming out of one of the doors. He swiveled back quickly, so all they could see was his back, then increased his pace.

Lonny was apparently leading the group. "Naw. Sarge will never find out. He's busy with paperwork. Let's go. There's gotta be someplace to get a drink on this heap. I think it must be on this deck."

It was like being caught in a nightmare. The faster he tried to walk, the less efficient his walking motions became. It was best to glide at a slow pace, but trying to get away from the Marines led him to rush his steps. One of them noticed.

"Lookit, that guy. He can't walk too good."

Another one shouted at him, "Hey, landlubber! Don't ya know enough to go slow?"

Adam didn't respond, except to keep on going. Fortunately, Lonny thought the bar would be in the opposite direction.

"He's carrying food. That had to come from a bar. Let's go back that way."

The five shuffled in the opposite direction.

This put things in a new light. He didn't want to meet them again. They'd be sure to recognize him and want to continue the fight. That would likely blow his ID. What would happen next wasn't difficult to imagine. He'd be clapped in irons and sent back on the return trip. Unlike the Mars trip, it cost little to send a man back on the ribbon. The elevator had to return, and it rarely carried a full complement of passengers on the way back to Earth. Most people continued on to the Moon or beyond. Few returned.

He quit shaving. If he met the five again, maybe they wouldn't recognize him with a beard. Frank warned him that large beards weren't regulation, but admitted that a small one would probably be ignored.

THE WEIGHTLESS POINT had come and gone. They were now living on what had effectively been the ceiling of the elevator when they left Earth. The beard hadn't been needed. Adam hoped the Marines had gotten in trouble for their unauthorized jaunt to another deck, but even if that didn't happen, he hadn't seen them again.

He was on his way to meet his crew at the first restroom when the emergency siren began to sound.

The rule for passengers was the siren signaled that they should get in their cabins, seal the doors, and wait for the all-clear.

After a moment's hesitation, Adam decided that he was closer to his crew than his cabin. They would have to lock themselves in the restroom and wait. He hurried on.

There was excited talking around the next corner. Adam came ahead and walked into a group of officers who were looking through a narrow hatch.

One of them saw him as he passed.

"You! What's your job? Why aren't you in your cabin?"

"Going to my crew, Sir. We'll lock down in the restroom."

"Are you familiar with the air-scrubbers? You wouldn't be some kind of engineer, would you?"

"Uh, yes, Sir. I am actually a physicist, but I know something about engineering."

"The air recycling mechanism on this deck is signaling that it's failed to reset itself. Think you can figure it out? The main engineer is sick, and his assistant is working on the recycling system on Deck B. There's nobody to work on this one."

"Yes, Sir. If I had a manual for the system, I could probably do something." That would put a halt to their attempt to Shanghai him. They likely didn't have a manual."

"Great, I've got the manual."

Adam reluctantly turned and took the book. It wasn't too thick, and that was reassuring. He hoped the book was a very basic one.

"Go through this hatch. The mechanism is about a hundred feet away. Chances are that it has a fried filter, but we don't know how to fix one of those."

He leafed through the pages, then stopped at the ones about the electrostatic filters. "Says here that a replacement needs to be installed within thirty minutes before waste gasses build up to a toxic level."

"Yeah, we know. Can you take care of it?"

Adam wondered at the group of three officers. They seemed lost like they had no idea how to proceed. They were also young, about his age. He shrugged. How they'd become officers on the elevator was not his business.

The hatch was tight and led to a narrow passageway with turns that wound in the general direction of the elevator core. He worked his way along, squeezing through some narrow points where the walls were closer than comfortable. It was lucky that he wasn't much over middle-sized.

The passageway ended in a small room with an open tube transecting one side. Adam looked down and then up the tube. Sound echoed up and down what seemed to be hundreds of feet of tubing. The noise was a low frequency grinding caused by the elevator's driving mechanism pulling it along the ribbon.

The air-scrubber installation was a large panel of controls and latched compartments mounted against the wall at the far side of the tube. He'd have to lean over the opening to reach anything. That didn't seem like something anyone in their right mind would want to do. A suspicion began to dawn that the officers had known about it and passed the task to him because of the fear factor.

Adam looked at the panel curiously. A light was flashing red. He wasn't entirely sure, but the flashing probably meant trouble.

The manual confirmed it. He'd have to open filter bank 12 C, extract the breaker unit, manually reset it, then reinstall it. Filter bank 12 was...he looked. It was practically unreachable, as far away across the tube as it could be, then up near the ceiling of the compartment.

A FEW MINUTES later, Adam exited from the hatch.

"Did you get it?" one of the officers asked, anxiously.

"Yes. It was difficult, but I reset the thing. It should be working normally now unless something else is broken too."

"No. That was it. If you actually got it, that is."

He didn't like that. It was an insult to his vanity to be doubted. He started to open his mouth in protest when the background sound of the warning siren stopped.

The older officer said, "Great! The O-Sat warning has quit. You actually fixed the thing."

Adam nodded. There had been some doubt about his fix, and his success was a little surprising. The thing hadn't reset the way the booklet said it would, but if the siren was off, then his effort had worked.

THERE WAS AN unexpected and undesirable outcome of the event. The Captain decided to award him a commendation.

From Adam's perspective, it didn't seem like much of an award. The first he knew about it was when security arrived at his door and handcuffed him.

They wouldn't answer any questions. It was maddening, but after trying once, he bit his lip and waited to see what was in store. Meanwhile, his mind was racing through the possibilities. Every path led him to a single reason for the arrest. His identity had come out, and the government had requested his return.

The Captain was apologetic. He had intended to reward the man he knew as Richard for his heroic action. Adam didn't think it had been brave, but he hadn't known the entire situation.

The scrubber he'd reset was linked to the rest of the ship's scrubbers, and there was a design flaw that no one had known about. When the one scrubber failed, it stopped all of the others. Adam had restarted it just in time. A and B decks had been nearly out of breathable air. That was because the entire air conditioning system flowed from D deck. With the C deck scrubber out, the only deck had adequate air was D. C deck was just starting to get bad, but B had reached the point where people were having trouble breathing. A deck was worse. Two hundred and seven people had lost consciousness by the time the system was back up. There were still thirty-four passengers in medical, some of whom were going to have brain damage.

Captain Abrams was upset about the result. This was a direct result of his well-intentioned desire to reward Crew Supervisor Richard Headly. He'd sent a news release including Adam's crew id picture. The return instructions to lock up the internationally wanted criminal Adam Maxwell and return him to Earth for trial were not the result he'd been expecting.

There was nothing Abrams could do. Adam found himself sitting in a barren cell. They'd been kind enough to give him a blanket and a pillow, but the room had no other features. It had been designed as an overnight holding cell for drunks, and they were customarily released as soon as they were sober enough.

The elevator had three more days to go before it reached the docking station.

Then there would be a twenty-four-hour wait before it started back down. The second elevator was already on the way down on the opposite side of the ribbon. Adam was glad of that because it gave him a day before he had to start the return trip. He didn't know what he would do during that time, but any time at all was desirable since it pushed off his return.

THERE MUST HAVE been a bit of rebel in Captain Abrams. Twelve hours before the elevator arrived, he had Adam brought to his stateroom.

The escorting guard knocked on the closed door with his free hand while he held Adam's upper arm with his other hand. It was ridiculous. There was nowhere to run, and he had no intention of struggling.

"Come." The captain was in, and his voice echoed out of the small speaker in the doorframe.

The guard opened the door and ushered Adam inside.

Captain Abrams looked Adam over, then waved the guard outside. "Wait by the door. I doubt that I'm in serious danger from this young man. I'll call you when I'm ready to send him back."

The guard let out a heavy breath, then released Adam and stepped out.

Captain Abrams seemed embarrassed.

"I'm sorry about this situation. I intended to reward your service. The scrubber failure was something that wasn't supposed to be possible. You saved a lot of lives by your brave action."

It was upsetting, partly because he was facing prison at the least, and partly because it wasn't right. He hadn't been brave.

"Anyone else would have done the same thing. I just happened to be available."

"Not true, young man. The three officers who were at the site have been demoted. They could have taken action, but they knew the layout inside the service corridor. They were fearful of falling down the shaft, so they made you do the dirty work. I'm recommending that they are terminated from the elevator service with prejudice."

All Adam managed to say was, "Oh."

Abrams nodded but didn't speak, so Adam added, "It was a bad layout. Whoever designed the thing with the breaker over the shaft should be fired, too."

"The breaker was designed to reset automatically, so the planners must not have considered the possibility of someone having to climb over the shaft to reset it. But, that's beside the point. I brought you in here to discuss your future. Do you mind explaining to me why the FBI, IRS, CIA, and just about every other government agency wants your hide? What did you do, anyway?"

This was going to take a bit of time, but time was all he had right now. "I guess the main thing I did wrong was fall in love with Senator Worthington's daughter."

Abrams' eyes narrowed. "Worthington, huh? Tell me more."

"In retrospect, I was stupid. She didn't love me. In fact, I caught her in bed with someone else. The other guy was going to shoot me, but Elseth convinced him that I'd be useful. Then she told me she really loved me, but I'd have to prove myself by helping them." He stopped. Telling the captain might not be a good idea, but he had little to lose.

After a few seconds of deliberation, Adam resumed. "They are plotting to bomb the Senate to disrupt the hearings. I think they want the country to go to war. Senator Worthington interviewed me, and when I told him I was loyal to the President, he dismissed me. He didn't make any threats, but right after that, I was accused of making sexist remarks. It was all over social media. I lost my scholarship, got kicked out of university. I was going nuts, so I did some research on my own. That must have been a mistake because the IRS claimed I owed thousands of dollars in back taxes. I never earned that much in my life. They got after me, but I'd had enough. I ran. I found out that the FBI was after me, too."

Abrams nodded slowly. "You don't do things by halves. Getting on the wrong side of someone like Worthington was a big mistake. What led you to get on my elevator?"

"I'd always wanted to go to space. Everything on Earth was going wrong, and I thought that I might find a safe place on the moon. I'm a quantum physicist, but I also have experience with engineering and electronics. Have to. I designed and built all my own experimental setups."

Abrams leaned back in his chair and sighed hugely. "That is an unfortunate situation. I suspect that it won't turn out well for you when you get back to Earth. What about the bombing plot? Do you know more?"

Adam shook his head. "Worthington said it was Elseth's fantasy and nothing more. I guess he's probably right. No one would do that in the real world."

"Don't be too sure. Worthington has a reputation of doing whatever needs doing to achieve his goals. I wouldn't put it past him to come up with something like this. By the way, don't tell anyone I said that. I can't afford to have him after me."

Adam grinned. "I'll keep my mouth shut. There's no point in my dragging you into my problems."

"I like you, Mr. Maxwell. Under other circumstances, I'd promote you to officer level. I think you have promise. Here's what I intend to do. It's not legal, and it may get me in a lot of trouble, but what's happening to you isn't fair. I've got a connection that I'm going to call. He'll get you on a mining ship. Sorry, I know that miners don't have a very good life expectancy, but it's the best I can do. I can't place you on a Trans-shuttle. You'd be caught when you disembarked on Luna, and I'd be dragged into it. If you disappear totally, though, no one will know exactly what happened.

I'll report that you escaped your cell and tried to exit the elevator to the docking station, but you used the wrong airlock. That's possible. We have several airlocks that can link to the docking station but normally aren't connected. If you popped one of those, you'd be sucked into space. The only way we'd know something had happened would be that the airlock warning light would come on. You'll be gone, and I'll be in the clear. Considering how many people you saved, I think that's the least I can do."

Adam was speechless for a moment.

Abrams added, "You've got to go back to the holding pen. Be ready in twelve hours when we dock. I'll send someone for you. Follow their instructions precisely. Good luck."

Without pausing for Adam to speak, he pressed the button to summon the guard.

Back in the cell, Adam tried to sleep. It was well into his night period, and the combination of stress, fear, and lack of sleep was terrible. It seemed like he couldn't get to sleep, but when the cell door opened, he blearily realized that he'd been dreaming about asteroid mining.

The crewman led him on a long, circuitous route, avoiding populated areas. Finally, they reached an obvious airlock.

"Get in, wait for five minutes to let me get to another part of the ship, then open the outside door. There'll be someone there to take you on to your destination."

Adam suddenly had a frightening vision of betrayal purchased by Worthington's money. What if the airlock really wasn't connected? He'd be sucked out. That would suit everyone just fine, except him. He turned to the crewman, wide-eyed and prepared to fight the man.

While he'd been thinking about the possibility, the crewman had strategically retreated and was now pointing a laser pistol at Adam's middle.

"Get in. I don't want to shoot you, but I will if you don't get in there right now. And, don't try to come out again. I'll be locking the door so it won't open from inside. Wait a few minutes, then go out. You'll be okay. I know you probably think it's a set-up, but it's not. Captain Abrams is a good man. I owe him big time, and trust me, I know. He's set everything up to get you on a ship. Now go!"

Adam backed to the door, fumbled for the handle, then retreated inside. If he was going to die, he wanted to delay as long as possible. The laser looked painful. Of course, being sucked out would be too, but it would probably kill him more quickly. That meant less pain, so...he struck his forehead with his palm. Stop thinking about it, it just makes it worse.

After five minutes, he took a deep breath, held it, and opened the door.

# 3

## ON THE D-R

THE AIRLOCK DOOR seal cracked open. Adam waited, but there was no sudden evacuation of air. Instead, the pressure seemed to be constant. He pulled the door fully open and stepped out.

"There you are. I'd just about decided to leave. This isn't a safe place to be hanging around. The guards will be by eventually. C'mon, let's go."

The speaker was a slight woman who looked to be at least twice his age. Maybe more. Adam took a deep breath and relaxed. She didn't appear to be a threat. At least he wasn't going to be killed out-of-hand.

She repeated, "Let's go. What's a matter with you? Don't understand English?"

"No. I'm a little disoriented, I guess."

"You can't afford that. Start putting your feet on the deck." She turned down the passage. "I owe Jim, but sometimes he asks too much." This last was muttered under her breath as she strode away.

"Jim?"

"Jim – James Abrams. The guy who's going way out on a limb for you. He's got me going out on the same one, and I don't want it to break off. Now, let's go. I'll get you to the D-R. Safely, I hope. What happens next is between you and Suarez, and his crew."

It didn't seem to be the right time for questions. The woman was already ten meters ahead of him and walking quickly. He trotted to catch up. The passage was narrow, too narrow for both to walk side-by-side, so Adam followed quietly, keeping his mouth shut.

What Captain Abrams had told him was going to happen and what she'd said implied that the D-R was some sort of ship. A miner, if Abrams had been telling the truth. Suarez must be the captain.

The country had a lot of Spanish speakers, and Adam had never had any trouble getting along with them. In point of fact, his mother was a Latina, but she never spoke the language in front of him. Still, that fact gave him some confidence that he might prevail on this Suarez's sympathy if things got difficult.

The crew, however, was another matter. They might be friendly or not. As a budding academic, he partly expected blue-collar workers to be hostile. He didn't talk the same way they did, and they knew he was likely to make more money than they did. Not good grounds for friendship, in his limited experience.

The woman turned a corner, then another then doubled back along another long, narrow passage. Three more branching intersections and he was totally lost. The passage was faintly lit by red LEDs every ten meters. It was a great place for someone to jump him. Adam looked over his shoulder. No one back there, but he couldn't see too far.

They turned another corner, and he could see a brighter light glowing up ahead. He snickered to himself. It was the proverbial light at the end of the tunnel. Maybe that meant his troubles were over. More likely they were just starting.

She turned her head and said, "Shut up. There might be some staff on the docks, so keep quiet and follow me. I'll do all of the talking if we get stopped."

The light abruptly became bright as they exited the passageway. The docks spread out in both directions. Adam looked along the vast expanse of metal decking. It receded in the distance, but he could see it curved upwards along the arc of the station's hull.

High overhead was a maze of pipes and wires winding through girders and air system vents. Drops of condensation fell sporadically from the rims of the vents, creating small puddles on the rough deck surface underneath. He fastidiously avoided walking through the puddles. The water might be contaminated in some way, and he didn't want a drop to land on his head.

There was loading machinery, electric tractors, and fork-lifts moving back and forth near one of the big air-locks in the near distance. They continued, dodging between two of the fork-lifts.

One of the drivers yelled as they walked in front of his machine.

"Watch it. Idiots."

The woman raised her arm to display her middle finger. He swore but didn't say anything else directly to them.

Adam walked faster. No sense getting involved in some stupid dispute.

They'd walked several hundred meters when his guide turned towards one of the big air-locks. She led him to a smaller human-sized lock nearby, pressed a button, then waited, her arms crossed.

Adam fidgeted, trying to decide if he should try to talk to her or just keep quiet. Her expression was faintly hostile, so he didn't say anything.

Nothing happened. She pushed the button again. "Answer, dammit."

Something poked him in the back, and he started to turn.

It poked him harder.

"Hey, that hurt!"

"It'll hurt more if I pull the trigger. Keep still." It was a man's voice.

The woman turned towards the speaker. "Just like you, Jem. Sneak up behind someone and poke them in the back with a shotgun. I want Suarez, not you."

"Suarez is busy. You got me. Who's this kid?"

"New crew for your flying coffin."

The gun barrel quit poking the small of his back, and he cautiously turned around, holding his hands very still, just in case. Jem was a medium height man with dark skin. He'd lowered the barrel to an intermediate position pointing at the floor.

"Don't look like no crew. He's too slicked up. What are you, kid? Running away from Daddy's plans for you? Maybe you got some girl pumped up, and you're running away from her daddy? Ha Ha Ha."

The words were spoken in a joking tone. The guy seemed somewhat friendly. At least, he wasn't obviously hostile.

"No, I--"

The woman cut in. "I told you to keep it shut. He's got trouble, Jem. It might be more than Suarez wants. That's why I want to see him."

Jem shook his head. "No. I told you Suarez is busy. I'm in charge of boarding. What's after the kid?"

"Feds, maybe others. Don't know. Don't wanna know. I'm just the delivery person. If you're good with him, I'll tell Abrams. There will be some cargo credit for the D-R, but he says it'll be piecemeal. It's easier to slip it in a bit at a time."

Jem nodded. "Okay. Yeah. I'll take him in. Can't say what the Captain will think, but if Abrams is offering credit, that'll go a long way towards making it work out."

He slung the short-barreled gun around to his back, then stuck out a hand. "Welcome to the D-R, kid. Hope you don't regret it. It might be worse here than what's on your tail."

JEM LED HIM to the crew quarters. A cursory glance informed him that the accommodations were not luxurious by any stretch of the imagination. The D-R was designed for mining. It had big engines and lots of fuel storage, but the crew seemed to be an afterthought.

The room had a bank of hammocks along one side, lockers on the other, and a door with a light over it at the opposite end from the entrance.

"That's the head. Best to read the manual before you have to go, kid. Might suck your thing clear off, otherwise. It ain't real user-friendly. Old."

Adam nodded. "I'm trained in physics, but I'm a pretty good engineer and mechanic, too," he said, trying to be helpful.

Jem laughed, "Well, well. The kid can talk. Maybe if you're as good as you think, Suarez can use you for something besides shit details. We'll see."

"When will I see him?"

"Ah, he's busy right now. In his cabin with the door closed. You don't ever open it less he calls you in. Last guy that did that got shoved in the recycler."

Something else had been bothering him. "What's D-R mean? Is it the ship name?"

Jem leaned back against the door jamb, sighed, and said, "Nice to have a little stronger force. D-R's rotation is okay, but it's barely Luna gravity level. This here's a lot stronger. Being swung on that long ribbon has its advantages."

"My mass feels almost normal. You're saying that it's a lot less when this ship undocks?"

"Yes. Hope you don't get sick. Be a miserable few days till you get over it unless you don't. We won't turn around to let you off, either. You'll have to suffer through it."

"Okay. I don't think I'll have a problem. What's D-R mean?"

"I was getting to that. It means a lot of things. It'll be a while before Suarez sobers up, uh, I mean gets done with his business. Just disregard what I said or keep your mouth shut about it, understand?"

"Okay, but D-R?"

"Alright, alright." He sounded bored. "Suarez is from Patagonia, and he's got a classical education. Studied lots about Greeks and Romans and stuff. He's got a mean sense of humor, too. That's part of it. He named the ship after those big birds that live in South America, Rheas they call 'em."

"Okay, R equals Rhea. What's D?"

"You ain't so smart after all. D is obviously Dire. Welcome to the Dire-Rhea, kid."

That was crazy. Adam shook his head in disbelief, prompting Jem to explain a bit more.

"That's it alright. But it's not so simple either. Sure the ship is dire as in dismal, oppressive, causing horror, urgently in need of assistance. It's also dire as in ancient Roman mythology. See, I bet you didn't know this. The Romans believed that there were avenging goddesses called the Dirae who tormented criminals. You aren't the only wanted man here. Just about every crew member has something they'd rather forget."

"Dirae, huh. You mean the ship torments the crew?"

"Well, it's about like that. She's a good ship, but she has her problems. When something goes wrong, it's almost always a life or death situation, so she keeps us busy. Now, there's still another classical part and, if you quit fiddling with your hands like that, I'll tell it to you."

He had been absentmindedly picking at his fingernails while he listened. "Oh. Sorry. Go ahead."

"It's like this as best I can remember. Rhea was the daughter of the Greek earth goddess and the sky god. She was also the wife and sister of Cronus or time. Cronus ate most of their kids, but she saved their last kid, Zeus, from him. The Greeks thought that was important. Anyway, she was the mother of the Olympian gods and goddesses, so she was important. The best part is that her parents were named Gaia and Uranus. That's apt since the D-R travels from Earth almost out to Uranus. See, I told you that Suarez was well educated."

Adam was beginning to wonder if the man would ever get done, but he was spared any additional discussion by a voice that echoed down the passageway.

"Jem, you in the wardroom? Suarez wants to see the new crew member."

"Yeah, Flynn. I got him here. We'll go up now."

Suarez' door was open. Jem poked his head through. "Got the new kid here, Captain."

"Send him in, then close the door."

It hadn't been so bad this far. Jem was friendly. However, his fate rested on the upcoming interview. Adam felt nervous, something he didn't want. He had a bad habit of responding to stress with sarcasm. It was one of his worst faults.

CAPTAIN SUAREZ LOOKED like hell warmed over. Adam had seen a lot of hangovers, especially in his first couple of years of university. This looked like one of the worst he'd seen.

"Sit. Sit down, dammit. Why do you all insist on standing? Looming over me. Damn! Sit, I said." Suarez motioned weakly at the chair on the opposite side of his compartment. He was half lying on the folded out bunk. At least three empty bottles were lying on the mattress behind him.

"Yes, Sir." He took the indicated seat, then looked down, trying not to stare at the Captain. Even a psychopath with zero empathy would find looking at Suarez' state painful.

"Mr. Maxwell." Suarez paused to massage his temples. "Abrams told June what you did. He said that we should be glad to get you. You have anything to add?"

"No, Sir. I did what needed to be done. That's all."

"That's the most hopeful thing I've heard all day. You might notice that I've been drinking. Running this ship isn't a bad job, except when the Feds start giving me crap about my loads. They always want more from us. Somebody somewhere got the idea that we were holding back the most valuable metals and just dumping iron on them." He ran his palm over his forehead, pushing his grayish hair back.

"They're right, of course. I've got to make a profit somehow, and the D-R needs a lot of work. You're supposed to be an engineer, right?"

"Not actually, Sir. I'm a quantum physicist, er student. Haven't graduated yet. I'm a pretty good electronics engineer, though." He paused, then thought of something else. "I make all my own experimental equipment. I guess I probably know enough engineering to get by."

"Not precisely what I wanted to hear, but maybe you'll do. You'll have to do. We can't get any more crew. Feds are holding back, and I found out this morning that they'd blacklisted us. No more crew and supplies are twenty-five percent higher. I'm beginning to wonder if a crew member leaked some info."

"Uh, should you be telling me this, Sir?" Adam didn't like the idea that he was being given what seemed like private information. He was already in enough trouble.

"Don't worry. Everyone on the ship knows we've been dropping a packet of precious metal to my people in Patagonia." Suarez frowned, then rubbed his hands on his neck.

"It's the only way they can survive. Buenos Aries has increased taxes three hundred percent in the last two years. Damned socialists always run out of money. They're starving the countryside to pay for their crazy plans. The least I can do is drop what gold and silver we find to my brother. Feds don't like it. Well, too bad. I needed an engineer. They wouldn't find one for me. Now I got you, so you have to be the engineer. Understand?"

"Yes, Sir. I'll do the best I can, but I probably won't be too fast. I don't know the ship's systems."

"That's another thing. You get yourself down to the Em-drive bay. There's a bunk and a head down there. It's not too nice, but it's private. Engineer's privilege, see. Somewhere down there, you'll find a manual. The last guy used it a lot. You can probably figure out what kinds of trouble we usually have by looking for the most worn pages."

This was better than he'd thought. "Yes, Sir."

Suarez wasn't done yet. "Now, I know you don't know squat about running a ship, but I'm going to make Jem get you squared away. He's been here so long, he probably can't remember ever being on Earth. Engineers are officers, sort of. You get to order the crew if you need help, but only if you need help. Don't go trying to boss them around just for the hell of it. Especially To'afa. He's a big Polynesian. His idea of fun is to get punched in the face, but he always gives back at least twice what he gets. Steer clear of him."

"Seems clear. I can ask for help, and they're supposed to help me. Don't be bossy and leave To'afa alone. I can do that. What I'm worried about is the Em-drive. I know a little about them, but I've never worked on one."

"You know microwaves, right?"

"Yes, Sir."

"The drive is basically a big microwave oven, but it doesn't cook anything. The microwaves bounce around in a shaped container, and they create thrust."

"Yes, I know that. I know basically how it works. I don't know the specs and settings though."

"You'll learn that from the manual. Don't be so worried. My last engineer did okay, and he'd never graduated from high school."

"Yes, Sir. What happened to him? Did he transfer to another ship?"

Suarez made a laughing sound but then grabbed his head in pain.

"Don't make me laugh. It hurts too much. There's no transferring out here. Once you're on a miner, you stay on her. Hewitt got cooked. He was out on the hull at the wrong time messing with the shielding antennas. There was a solar flare. We'd heard about it, but no one had bothered to tell us that there had been a preliminary spike before the main flare. Hewitt made it back in, but he was badly burned. We brought him here, and they're supposed to get him in hospital. I don't know that he'll make it though." He looked down at the floor. "It's dangerous work. The ship has some shielding that's supposed to be effective against radiation, but it's not really worth much. I expect that we'll all die of radiation poisoning eventually."

There was nothing to say about that. Adam nodded his head in understanding. The issue was closer to his academic interest than microwaves. Some of the concepts were things he'd already been thinking about. As a result, he had some ideas about solar radiation and plasma systems. Maybe that would provide a solution.

"Mr. Maxwell, welcome to the Dire Rhea. If you don't die from fright in the first few weeks, you'll probably live to get your first paycheck. Sorry, that's the most inspirational speech you're going to get from me right now. You're dismissed." He raised his voice, "Jem? Get in here."

JEM KNEW MORE about the Em-drive than seemed likely. He'd helped the ill-fated Hewitt extensively, even though his job was in cargo. He showed Adam the engine room, got him oriented about the ship, helped him find the Em-drive manual, then left him alone to study.

Adam unfolded the bunk, sat down and leaned back to think. After a bit, he opened the manual, sighed deeply, and began reading.

# 4

# NEAR EARTH

IT HAD TO be time to eat. His stomach was so shriveled, it was thinking about crawling up his throat and prowling around to find food on its own. It had been several hours since Jem had left. In that time, he'd finished half of the manual, comparing it with the device in front of him.

The system was, just as the Captain had said, basically a microwave oven. The main difference was that there was no door. The microwaves bounced back and forth in a resonant chamber. Something about its shape generated force without emitting any detectable particles.

Adam's father had worked on the original device and was responsible for greatly enhancing its efficiency. He'd installed waveguides that funneled the waves back to the magnetron end in such a way that they didn't interfere with the emitted waves. This resulted in a fifty percent increase in propulsion. The modified drive was often referred to as the Em-Max in honor of Dr. Maxwell. Adam never mentioned this to anyone.

As far as he was concerned, he needed to stand or fall on his own merits.

In point of fact, he'd never worked on one of the things, although he knew more about them than the average physicist. He couldn't help picking up some knowledge from his father since that was about all the old man had talked about before his untimely death.

He stretched and headed for the door, expecting the passageway to be vacant. It wasn't. There were two men there with their heads together. From the way they jumped, they were doing something illicit.

Adam smiled and asked, "You guys mind telling me where I can get something to eat?" As he did, he noticed that one of the men still had some white powder on his lip and around his nostrils.

Great. They're doing drugs. That doesn't make me feel any better about this tub. If the captain's a drunk and the crew are druggies, the chances of survival are probably slim. I can't imagine how they got back here in one piece.

"You the new engineer? You look too young to know anything."

From the size of the speaker, Adam figured he had to be To'afa. He tightened up inside. The guy was huge.

"Yeah. That's me. Looks can be deceiving. I'm pretty well qualified, I think." He didn't want to say it, but he needed credibility. "My father was Professor Maxwell. He created the Em-Max drive."

The smaller man's eyes widened. "So, you're his kid? That right?"

"Yes. I'm Adam Maxwell. Don't ask about my middle name. It's odd. Just call me Adam. I'm about half done checking the drive, but I'm too hungry to continue. Got to get something to eat now."

The smaller man said, "Great! I'm Tom Murphy. I'll show you the mess." He looked up at To'afa. "Why don't I meet you in the cargo hold in about thirty? We can work on those ore samples like the captain said."

To'afa had a surprisingly deep voice. "'K. See you there, brudda."

Adam slipped by, turning sideways to avoid crowding the big guy. Tom led him along the passage.

"The big ox is To'afa. He's alright, just don't get him riled up. He likes to fight, and it takes a lot to get him to quit. Last time, Cap'n Suarez had to hit him in the neck with a pipe wrench. Laid him out for all of an hour. He don't hold no grudges, though, so that's good."

Adam thought about that. "That is good, but I wouldn't want to have him after me. He's too big."

"Yeah. I stay on his good side. You saw, didn't you? I scored a little blow on the station. Surprising how much of that stuff gets up here. To'afa likes it, so we do a little now and then. Keeps him happy with me and also seems to calm him down. Strange, I know. Anyway, Suarez knows about it, so no need for you to think you have to report us."

"Well, I wasn't sure what you were doing. I won't report anything unless it's dangerous to the ship. I guess as long as you can work, it isn't dangerous."

"That's the right idea. I can do my work just fine. You know about our cargo issues?"

"Uh, no. What about them?"

"Look here. The Feds got it in for us. Miner crews don't have an easy go of it. The ships can't carry much armor, and the radiation is high enough that most miners get cancer or radiation poisoning. This is my third trip out to the belt. Probably be my last. We're pretty safe here cause of old Earth's magnetic field, but when we leave orbit and start out, we'll hit a point where the radiation goes way up. It's even worse if the sun is throwing off flares."

They turned into the kitchen. There were four tables with attached benches.

"This is where we eat. Ship spins so's there's enough g-force to keep things mostly in place. The edges on the tables and the cup holders are mostly there for Coriolis force. Things can creep off sideways on you if you're not careful."

Tom showed him the food storage and helped him assemble a sandwich, then made another for himself.

"Snorting that stuff stimulates my appetite. Not time for me to eat, but I'm going to have a bite too. Now, where was I? Oh, yeah. Feds want us to bring in valuables. Stuff like minerals, precious metals, uranium ore, whatever. Suarez has a brother that can move stuff, so not everything we find gets turned in to the Feds. We drop some of it when we enter orbit. Suarez got it figured perfectly. Always drop at the same point, same time after insertion into the same orbit. Lands where his brother can get it. We're all going to benefit. Suarez has got it set, so the proceeds go into bank accounts, one for each of us. When we get sick, that's what we use to survive."

Adam swallowed the mouthful he'd been chewing. "So, the Feds figured out they weren't getting everything, and now they're charging more for supplies?"

"That's right. You aren't so slow at figuring things out. They won't get us any additional crew, and they're holding up on supplies. Makes the Captain drink. He hates them, you know. He's taken to bringing in only iron. It's valuable enough to keep us going, but they don't like not having other things too."

Suarez walked into the room and Tom immediately quit talking.

The captain said, "Mr. Maxwell." He paused, as if that was enough, then continued. "I see you found the kitchen. We work three shifts here. Eat before you go on and after you get off. I'll excuse you this time since you're new. Tom, you need to get on your cargo business. Feds might take a notion to inspect before we undock."

"Yes, Sir. I'm going now." Tom stood, took a last bite, then wandered out.

"I trust you've been using your time productively." Suarez looked much better. He seemed to have fully recovered from his hangover.

"I've been going through the manual and cross-checking the drive as I finish each section. I'm not an expert, but I do know a bit about the equipment."

"I thought you might. Keep at it. We're leaving in eight hours. I know that will make a double shift for you. I can give you twelve hours off, once we're undocked and moving. That work?"

"Yes, Sir. I should be through with my check. Twelve will be fine. I'm not tired now, just hungry. Uh, Tom was talking about the shielding. Says there's not enough. Is that true?"

Suarez looked like he'd bitten into a bitter apple. "We don't have enough shielding because the Feds want the ship to be able to move more ore. The less shielding we have, the more power we have to move valuable stuff. Crew isn't considered valuable enough to worry about."

"I didn't know. That's horrible. Why do people work on these ships?"

"Most don't have any choice. You think you've got problems? Just about each of these men here has equally bad ones. Besides, there's always the chance we will hit it big and be able to retire rich. Except the Feds will probably take everything in that case."

"Understood. I'll get back to work on the drive. I, uh, I was working on plasma phenomena in school. There might be a chance I can do something about the shielding. I never had discretionary funding in school. I only worked on my assigned research, but there's a possibility I can cook up something that might help with the radiation."

"Get the engine checked out first. I want you familiar with it. If there's a problem, you'll need to know enough to fix it, or we're all dead. After you're happy you've mastered the drive, you can do whatever you want, until I need you to fix something."

"Ok. I'll get back to work, then."

THEY UNDOCKED WITH no problem. Adam had finished checking the drive when the intercom broadcast the take-hold signal.

"Undock in thirty. Safe positions, strap in. Count will begin at ten."

He climbed into the acceleration chair, buckled in, and waited. At ten seconds, a voice he'd never heard before started the countdown. The magnetic grapples released with a clunk at five seconds. At zero, the attitude jets fired, creating a hissing sound that seemed to come from the bones of the ship.

Adam could feel acceleration, then they were weightless. His stomach flopped. Dizziness seemed to rule the world for a bit. Then the crew section began to rotate and g force gradually accumulated. That settled his inner ears.

After a short time, the intercom clicked, then Suarez came on.

"Clear to unbuckle. We'll be on this course for the next ten hours. Be aware. I'll give as much warning as possible before maneuvers, but emergencies do happen. Over."

# 5
# OUT-BOUND

"CLEAN UP AFTER yourself, why don't ya?" Flynn was standing by the table, hands on hips, and looking at the remnants of Tom's meal.

Tom and Adam had just finished eating. Adam had taken to eating with Tom before going on-shift. They'd been accelerating in the general direction of Mars for two weeks, and everyone had settled into patterns.

Unfortunately part of Tom's pattern was to be a slob. Adam usually prompted him to put his dishes in the sanitizer, but he'd been eager to get back to the little workshop that lay adjacent to the Em-Max.

Flynn was one of the three alterday crew members, a little Irishman with flaming red hair and a temper to match. He was nominally nav, as was Jem on day shift, but every one of the eight-person crew had multiple jobs.

Flynn was in charge of cooking and cleanup of the mess room today. It wasn't his favorite task, and he was irritable as a result.

Each man was responsible for returning his own utensils and dishes to the sanitizer. The cook had to clean up the cookware and wipe the tables.

Tom looked embarrassed. "Sorry. Forgot. I got to get to cargo. We're still sorting samples from the last three rocks."

"That's no excuse. If ya wasn't such a weakling, I'd be tempted to wipe the floor with ya." Flynn waved his hands in the air. "What's the use. I might as well try to teach old man McClatchy's sheep to stay out of the garden. Just go on. Get to your rock sorting. I'll take care of it. Ain't like I got nav work to do."

Adam stifled a snicker. The ship was largely computer controlled. Once the course had been input, it kept to it, barring unforeseen hazards.

Tom skipped on down the passageway, heading for the hold. Adam continued on past and entered the small shop.

He'd been working on an idea since he'd become aware of the radiation problem. It was worse than he'd known. He'd heard about it, of course, but his instructors at University had implied that it wasn't too dangerous. Certainly not bad enough to kill people.

He'd gradually come to the conclusion that there was a lot of stuff that the Feds lied about. They must have realized that it would be difficult to get volunteers if people thought they were going to die a painful death as a result.

Adam had done some preliminary work on plasma research. It wasn't approved by the department, so he'd gone on to virtual particle theory. Now the plasma research had given him an idea, and he was closing in on a system that might screen out some of the radiation.

It was going to be difficult to install on the surface of the ship since it required a series of small generators to be spaced equally on every meter of the hull. Last shift, he had just about completed fabricating his second generator. Two were needed to run a successful test.

Today, he would finish the little device, sync the two using a high-frequency radio, then see if together they created the plasma field he'd theorized was possible.

He worked quietly for a couple of hours, then took a break to check on the Em-Max. It was humming softly to itself, its drive end pointed directly towards the rear of the ship.

It was funny that the drive didn't need to be on the outside of the hull. It could be mounted anywhere in the ship, as long as it was mounted solidly and had space to turn on a universal joint. The thrust pushed the ship ahead despite there being no observable emission of reaction mass.

It certainly beat rockets and ion-drives for convenience. It might lack in acceleration, but the continuous force gradually built up into a very respectable fraction of light. They'd have to turn around to use it to decelerate, once they reached the halfway point.

The intercom came on with Suarez' voice. "Take hold warning. Maneuvering in fifteen." He proceeded to count down.

Adam sat and buckled in. At zero, he watched the Em-Max move slightly on its mount. That was it. The ship's thrust vector had changed. He could feel it, but the sensation of odd acceleration quickly faded as Suarez adjusted the D-R's axis with the jets to parallel the new vector.

Now it was time to test the two generators. He'd mounted them on a framework that would fit through the cargo hold person lock. It wouldn't be a good idea to fire them off in atmosphere. The plasma field needed a vacuum to form correctly.

Adam carried the frame to the cargo hold. To'afa and Tom were there, sorting through rocks, pausing every now and then to run a sample through the spectroscopic assay unit. To'afa was doing the bulk of the work, while Tom dictated entries to his tablet.

"Find anything interesting?" Adam asked.

To'afa shrugged and continued sorting. Tom laughed at the expression on the Samoan's face.

"He's pissed, so don't ask him. We're running low on dust. Always do, but it isn't fun. Got to ration now. What is that thing you've got?"

To'afa looked up again, then frowned and returned to moving rocks, striking at likely places with a standard rock hammer.

Adam answered, "It's an invention I want to test. Got to put it in the airlock and evacuate the air. It's got to run in vacuum."

"You get the Captain's permission for that? We don't just go opening up the locks like they were screen doors in the summertime."

"He knows. You mind opening up for me? You've got the code for the hold. I don't know it."

"Zero, two, four, eight. Powers of two. Now you know, so open it yourself. I'm busy."

Adam placed the framework on the airlock floor, secured it, then closed the door. The frame lit up red as the air was gradually pumped into the storage tank. He watched through the thick glass window in the interior door.

When the display showed no pressure, Adam cracked the outside hull door. It worked remotely, and he stopped it when it was just a couple of centimeters open.

Taking a deep breath, he activated his generators. Nothing was visible at first, and he swore under his breath for a moment. Then there was a pale glow that extended from each generator to meet between them. The light spread out in a thick layer. It looked similar to an oval-shaped pancake.

Adam was bouncing in excitement. It worked!

"What the hell is that?" To'afa loomed over him, then pushed him aside to look more closely out the glass.

"That is what's going to keep the radiation off us, my friend."

The big man grunted in surprise. "I don't usually get friendly with officers, but if you're right. I'm your friend for life."

Tom said, "You made some kinda plasma field, didn't you? Will it stop radiation?"

"Should. Might not stop the really hard stuff, but it should lower the levels in the ship. The problem is building a generator for every square meter and installing them."

Tom shook his head. "That could be a problem. Do we have enough components to make that many?"

Adam nodded. "I checked. To cover the ring, we'll need just shy of two thousand of the generators. I think we have enough stuff to make what we need. If we don't, maybe we can trade for more supplies somewhere."

"Not likely. The chances of seeing another ship in the belt are slim to none, and slim just left town. We could intercept one of the Mars supply ships, likely. But it's ten to one they won't let us have anything. It ain't like there's a hardware store out here, kid," Tom said, shaking his head.

The thought of radiation, striking them all the time, had been driving Adam in the endeavor. He'd become so worried about it, he thought he could sense his cells dying when he was in bed. An idea took hold.

"Tom?"

"Yeah?"

"Are there any duplicate parts for non-essential systems?"

"Ah. Now that's a thought. Yes. There are two back-ups for just about everything. We could cannibalize some of the least important. Course, they're all important, if something unexpected breaks, but it's unlikely. Captain would probably let us take some parts from the back-ups. Especially if you could guarantee no radiation."

"This shield will work. There's no doubt about it." Adam hoped that he wasn't lying. He thought it would work, but there was always some unexpected factor that impacted performance. They'd have to set up a real shield, to be sure.

"Let's call the Captain down here and show it to him." Tom turned to the intercom.

SUAREZ WAS MODERATELY enthusiastic. "Mr. Maxwell, I'm impressed. If you're correct, this shield will revolutionize mining. Go ahead and get started building the generators. Tom and Jem can help you when they're not busy elsewhere."

IT TOOK TIME, but they worked diligently. The alterday crew heard about the idea, and they started showing up before they went on shift. That helped. In four shifts, they'd built enough to provide partial coverage.

Adam calculated that he could install one per every four square meters. The field strength would be weak between the generators. It dropped exponentially with the square of the distance, but it would still cut out much of the radiation.

AFTER MUCH LABOR, the entire crew gathered in the ring to watch Adam flip the generators on. Flynn was hovered over the radiation counter, reading it out loud.

Adam turned his invention on. Flynn continued to read the same numbers, fluctuating by only a little.

Jem shook his head. "Well, it was a good try. I just wish we hadn't worked so hard on the generators."

Flynn's voice suddenly shot up almost an octave. "It's down! I can't believe it. It works! The kid's idea works."

"Let me take a look." Suarez pushed the little man aside. "Damn! He's right. Total radiation is down sixty-five percent, and it's still dropping."

The others rushed up to look, but Suarez turned, anger on his face, and set them back.

"Back off, you fools! How many times have I warned you about crowding me? That's right! More than you can count. I won't have it, here or anywhere else. Now back off. You can satisfy your curiosity on your own time when I'm not around."

The men fell over themselves backing up. Adam hadn't seen this side of Suarez. To this point, the man had been overly polite to him, even when in the throes of a hangover.

Suarez spun and left the room and Adam glanced around at the others. They looked abashed.

Jem made a small face, then looked at Adam and said, "He don't like to be crowded. Really hates it. He actually hates people, that's why he's here. Can't stand it on Earth. Hates the Feds. They killed his daughter, you know. Now he's out here with us losers. Most of us are facing arrest back on the ground. He goes back, it'll be for one thing only."

Adam asked, "What's that?"

Jem paused, thinking about the idea. "It'd be to take revenge on Senator Worthington for raping his daughter. The girl was only eighteen. She tried to walk home." He paused to shake his head with an exaggerated motion. "It was twenty miles. She'd been drugged. Probably couldn't think clear enough to know what she was doing. Car hit her. The Feds refused to do anything. Buried the investigation cause of Worthington."

"That's horrible. I didn't know." The idea that Worthington had done something so heinous didn't surprise him. His experience with the man and his daughter—that thought still hurt—had convinced him that the old saying about power corrupting was true.

The others crowded close to the counter to look at the reading. They'd recovered quickly, now that Suarez was gone.

Adam backed away, content that his invention was actually working. The idea of Suarez taking revenge on Worthington played through his mind.

That was an activity in which he'd happily take part. Elseth too. He'd come to a new understanding of that in the past few days. Maybe it was the distance from Earth, or perhaps it was just that he'd come down of his hormonally-induced confusion about her. Either way, he now understood that she had never really wanted him for who he was, only for what he could do to further her plans.

Worthington had said that the bomb was her fantasy, but it might not be. The senator was ambitious enough, by all accounts. He might actually think he could take over if the majority of the government were out of the way.

He shook his head, amazed at both his own puppy-eyed stupidity over the girl and at his new perspective. Maybe he was actually capable of understanding human motivation a little bit. That's all he wanted: a little bit of understanding. To actually understand others at the level he understood quantum physics was a possibility beyond his ambition.

During the next week, Adam created more generators. It got so that the other crew members took to running away from him when they saw him coming. He'd repeatedly asked each of them to donate personal electronics to cannibalize for parts.

Despite their reticence to deliver any more of their toys to him, he'd managed to get the entire hull protected. He'd also fine-tuned the system. The addition of the other generators had caused the system to reach some kind of critical mass. Once he'd adjusted it, the radiation penetration had dropped to less than three percent.

Outside, in the vacuum, the cold plasma field flickered around the ship, creating an eerie blue glow that seemed to hover a few centimeters above the surface. It flashed at times when a solid bit of dust struck and was annihilated.

# 6
# INSPIRATION

ADAM SLEPT BETTER, as a result of the shield. His dreams of cells dying had disappeared. Now, thoughts of a new modification of the plasma field flitted through his mind, disturbing his sleep, but in a pleasant way.

He toyed with the idea of patenting the shield and becoming fabulously wealthy from the royalties. Everyone would want it. That was a given.

However, his new insight into the human condition prompted him to realize that the government would just steal the idea. It was too valuable. They'd claim it was a matter of national security or something like that and that would be all she wrote as far as him getting paid for the idea.

More likely, Worthington or someone like him would benefit financially. Some corporation would pay billions or more to have the exclusive right to manufacture and license the equipment.

THEY'D PASSED THE turn-around point, and the ship was decelerating, approaching their first target. It was a pity the Em-Max didn't provide more thrust so that they could reach their destination quicker. Miners couldn't explore too many rocks before they ran out of supplies. It took too long to travel from one object to another.

The power supply was another limiting factor. Most of their electricity was generated by a small reactor; a device that he hoped he'd never be called on to service. It used plutonium and was deadly as hell if the container was ever breached.

A solar array provided backup when they were close to Earth. Farther out, it's output declined, and the nuclear system was the only source of power.

The plutonium mass was too small to allow them to stay in space for more than a few months before they had to go back and refuel, in addition to taking on more supplies. The ship couldn't simply accelerate to a distant asteroid, then stop. It took too long to get from one point to another. As a result, the average mining ship surveyed fewer than ten rocks on each trip.

Most of the rocks were just that: rocks. But, there were enough that contained iron and other, more exotic, more valuable metals and minerals, to keep the mining effort going. Besides, no one knew when, or if, they would stumble on something really valuable. Astronomical surveys were useful, but not accurate enough to be really helpful. Nothing was as good as actually getting close to an asteroid, getting samples, and assaying them.

Adam had built another plasma generator system, but this one used a magnetic focusing ring that allowed him to launch blobs of plasma into space. The projectiles didn't move very quickly, just a few hundred meters a second, but they had considerable range before they attenuated.

Suarez didn't mind him experimenting as long as the engine, and other critical systems ran as required. In between maintenance jobs, Adam busied himself with his research.

He was now working on increasing the velocity of his plasma blobs.

He'd tried several things, but none worked very well. The thing he needed was probably unlimited power, but that was not possible. Power was in short supply. He couldn't command the entire output of the reactor. The ship needed almost all of it to keep them alive.

THE EM-MAX CREATED a minor emergency that kept him from his research for a day, but it turned out to be a good thing because it generated a new idea. After he'd fixed the drive by replacing and tuning the internal waveguides, he woke up in the middle of the night. He'd been dreaming, and there had been something that made sense. What was it? After some thought, Adam found himself focusing on the Em-Max mystery.

To date, no one was quite sure how the thing created propulsion. The device worked, and no one could argue that fact, but explanations fell short. It was a simple thing to say it shot microwaves at the target end of a resonant chamber and that created thrust, then quickly change the topic, but that was neither a complete explanation nor accurate.

The dream had shown him something that he'd never thought of. The Em-Max used microwaves contained in a chamber. His father had become famous by adding internal waveguides to redirect the rebounding waves along the sides of the chamber. This reduced interference while delivering the waves to their point of origin in a manner that kept them from pushing backward.

The whole system seemed to violate ordinary physics. Nothing was emitted from the working end of the device to create thrust. In his dream, he'd seen an invisible flow of particles pushed by the microwaves. They'd been visible because he seemed to be able to look through matter in the dream.

What if the microwaves were capturing, entraining, and pushing virtual particles through the end of the Em-Max? The more he thought about it, the more likely it seemed. There were plenty of virtual particles, even in deep space. Quantum theory held that each meter of space was full of virtual particles continually appearing and disappearing. Would it be too much of a stretch to think that the microwaves provided a quick shove to some of the particles while they were present? He couldn't see why that would not be the case.

If it was, the Em-Max might be able to operate on a plasma field also.

With that in mind, Adam set out to attach one of his generators to a small model of the Em-Max that he'd built. The crew wasn't going to be happy with him if the kitchen microwave broke down. He'd used the replacement oven parts for his model.

It took some fiddling to get the plasma injected into the chamber without allowing the microwaves to leak. He couldn't have that happening. It would be dangerous to anyone nearby.

After a few days, he'd managed to complete the setup. Now it needed testing. He was delaying asking the captain if he could go out onto the hull to test it. Suarez had been in a bad mood since he'd yelled at the crew and Adam was reluctant to disturb him.

Despite his reluctance, his device was ready to test, and he had been working on his courage, screwing up his nerve to ask the captain for permission. He'd reached the point where he was ready to chance it when the intercom came on.

The slight crackle followed by Suarez' voice startled him.

"All hands to the bridge. Repeat, all hands to the bridge."

He wondered what was so urgent that Suarez would wake the alterday shift. Still wondering, he strode down the passageway, turned the corner and headed to the ship's bridge.

The bridge was a misnomer for what was really a smallish room containing the nav computer and maneuvering controls. No large port looked out at space. There was usually nothing to see. A bank of video screens provided better views than a single port could.

Adam arrived at the tail end of the crew. They were all viewing the vid screens. Suarez was off to the side as far as he could get due to his reluctance to be crowded.

Adam craned his neck to see over Malquiel's broad shoulders. The alterday cargo chief was built like a short, but very strong wrestler.

Malquiel glanced back at Adam, his teeth white in his dark face. "Hey, Engineer. Scoot forward here and take a look at that. Pretty as a picture," he said, pointing at the screen.

Adam looked and nodded in agreement. They'd arrived at an asteroid, and it was pretty in a bleak fashion.

THE ROCK HAD been part of the original cloud of circling and swirling debris that had given rise to the birth of the star. It was larger than average and had orbited the new sun for millennia, peacefully minding its own business. The dust cloud had gradually coalesced, forming additional mass points, some large, some small. A few million years back, one of the rock's companions had intersected its orbit at precisely the right time.

The two had collided spectacularly. One of the asteroids had ricocheted away, ending up orbiting Jupiter. The other was reduced in size. The collision had knocked off a lot of mass on one side of the rock. The removal uncovered a cavern that had existed inside the asteroid.

The video showed an intriguing opening in the rock as it spun lazily by the spaceship. Every time it came around, the crew leaned forward, trying to see into the dark hole.

"It might have something inside, huh?" To'afa asked the group in general.

Suarez replied. "We'll need to land on this one. I've got an idea about it, and I want to check it out. Some of you know that I picked this rock based on our observations on our last resupply trip. We couldn't stop just then, but there was enough evidence to make me curious about it. I checked on it while we were resupplying. It's not on anyone's list as being interesting. It is barely detectable from Luna. We're a little past Jupiter's orbit, and there's a lot of closer stuff between this point and Earth. They've focused on the easy pickings so far. We've been doing as well as we have because we take more risks. I need Jem and To'afa suited up. The three of us will jet over there and take a look. The rest of you are on standby, in case we find anything worth exploiting."

Suarez started for the door, and Adam pushed through the crowd to intercept him.

"Mr. Maxwell. What is it? I need to get suited up, so be quick."

"Yes, Captain. I've got an experiment that needs to be tested in vacuum. Would it be alright if I got suited up and ran my test while you three were over there?"

"Hmm. Ordinarily, I'd say no. There's a small chance that we may encounter a problem and need help. The ship might have to move closer. However, if you're already suited up and stationed on the hull, you could provide back-up for us, if necessary. I'd want you out there until we start back. Is that acceptable?"

"That'll work fine, Captain. I'll start moving my equipment to the cargo bay lock. I can have it set up and tested in an hour or so, once I'm outside."

"Okay. Make it so."

# 7

# THE ROCK AND THE WEAPON

ADAM GOT HIS stuff staged in the hold, then suited up. It took a bit to cycle everything through the airlock. By the time he had all of his equipment secured outside, Suarez and the other two were working their way across the surface of the asteroid.

Jem reported that the rock had something heavy inside. There was a slight, but definite gravity field. It was stronger than it should have been for a rock of this size, so the asteroid had metal in its composition.

Adam was involved in setting up his test and paid little attention to the chatter back and forth from the ship to the rock. He worked diligently, mounting the pieces on each other, securing them to the hull, then carefully aligning the generator and the little Em-unit, tested the seal, and connected to ship's power through the auxiliary connection mounted beside the cargo door. Finally, he was ready to test his idea.

He cast around for something in sight. The large asteroid had a smaller companion, apparently a chunk that had been knocked off in the collision. The smaller piece was several hundred meters away, orbiting in front of the main stone, like a pace car leading the mass of race cars in the starting lap.

That would work. He aligned the bore of the equipment with the small rock, held his breath, and triggered the apparatus. What happened next astounded him. He'd thought he'd invented a way to accelerate the plasma blobs he'd been projecting through the magnetic field. He had, but it worked far better than he'd thought.

There was a blinding flash at the business end of the equipment as a bolt of blue plasma shot out, covering the distance to the small rock instantly. It hit the rock, and the result was spectacular. The stone exploded into superheated fragments that flew in all directions.

Adam ducked behind his equipment as some of the small pieces rattled against the hull nearby. The sound provoked Flynn to transmit a query.

"What the hell was that? Sounded like rocks."

Adam answered, "It was some debris. Wasn't moving too fast. Everything is fine out here. No damage that I can see."

Suarez came on at that moment. "Whatever it was, it hit near us too. We're inside the hole and something just bounced by."

Adam didn't want to claim responsibility for bombarding the captain, so he kept quiet. He was busy thinking about the plasma bolt. It was unexpected, but he could see that it could potentially be useful as a mining tool. Then the idea of a weapon came to mind. It would be easy to scale up the Em-unit and the generator also. Given enough power, he could shoot a plasma bolt that would vaporize a big rock."

He was reluctant to think about other targets, but after a moment, he whispered. "I could vaporize a ship just as easily. I've invented a plasma cannon."

Suarez came on the radio. "This is incredible. There's an iron-lined cave in here. I think that there's a lot of iron in this rock.

Somehow, it formed a big bubble. It wouldn't take much to install a lock at the entrance. We could have a secure base here."

Jem had apparently been busy also. His voice came on next. "There's water ice here. It's just outside the bubble. Captain, we've got the makings of our own private base."

EVERYONE HAD GATHERED in the bridge again. The noise was considerable since they were all talking at once. The idea of a private base was something new. It would allow them to store precious metals before returning to Earth. The presence of water ice meant that the bubble could be filled with an atmosphere. The cavern needed a workable airlock, and a power supply and the D-R would have a secret base.

Adam couldn't get a word in edgewise. He was dying to tell about his invention, but the cavern dominated everyone's thoughts. After a few minutes of listening, it occurred to him that maybe the cannon should be kept secret until he had the opportunity to present the concept to Suarez. The captain was irrational at times, but he had earned Adam's respect.

TO'AFA AND MALQUIEL worked the next shift unloading mining equipment while four of the others transported it to the rock. It was apparent to Adam that they'd done this kind of thing before. The work went smoothly.

Suarez was busy planning. They had taken laser measurements of the opening, surveyed the stone and metal, and had found a point suitable for the lock. There was an iron outcropping on the other side of the asteroid. The mining laser was moved there first. The plan was to cut off enough metal to build the airlock.

This was a massive undertaking, but the mining lasers combined with the two augmented-strength lift units allowed the crew to cut the metal into precisely designed pieces, transport the parts around the asteroid, and begin installing them. The job proceeded much faster than Adam had anticipated.

Suarez came to him with a project. "We need an apparatus to separate the hydrogen and oxygen in the water. We can't have a pure O2 atmosphere in the bubble, but we've got the nitrogen tanks that power the maneuvering jets. We'll need to save enough to dock at the orbital station to resupply, but the rest can be mixed into the atmosphere. The issue is going to be getting enough gas to create something breathable."

Adam had been thinking about that. "I can build the separator, but finding additional gas is going to be a problem. Is there anywhere we can resupply aside from the orbital station? I don't think the Feds need to know about our base."

Suarez had been in good humor since the discovery. "Oh, that's for sure. They'll never know anything about it if I can help it."

Adam prompted, "Resupply?"

"That might be a problem. We'll have to bring in something pretty good to get the bureaucrats off our back. I've been thinking that we should head straight for an asteroid that we found on the last trip. It had a large copper deposit. Remember? We could extract that, then head directly back. That should give us enough credit. The problem is that extra bottles of nitrogen aren't usually part of outbound cargo. Maybe I could convince them we need to maneuver more than we normally do."

The captain paused a moment, then continued. "There is another possibility. We could conceivably intercept one of the Mars supply ships. We might say we had an emergency and needed supplies. There's some precedent for that. We couldn't just take what we needed, though. That would put us on the wrong side of things."

Adam thought that over. "Mmm. Maybe we could intercept one of the unmanned ones."

Suarez nodded. "Mr. Maxwell, maybe I'm off-base for suggesting this, but would that really be so bad? We're already on the wrong side of things with the government. You're wanted. So are some of the others. Customs thinks we've been holding out on them, and they're right. The next time we hit the orbital station, they could confiscate the D-R, throw us all in the brig or worse and that'd be the end of that. I've been trying to figure out how the Mars shuttle could have some kind of accident and disappear."

Adam nodded. The idea made sense. He had little loyalty to the government, considering what he'd been through. It was true that he'd be imprisoned if they got their hands on him. After a bit, he asked, "How hard would it be to take one of the unmanned ones?"

"Not too hard. We'd have to rendezvous with it under some pretense. The onboard system would report to the authorities before it would let us dock. If we docked without permission and took what we wanted, we'd be criminals, pirates."

"What if the ship couldn't transmit?" Adam felt guilty, but his pent-up anger about his treatment had suddenly found a path for revenge.

"What? Do you mean you can jam their transmission?" Suarez looked startled.

"No. But, we can shoot off their antenna array," Adam said.

"How in the hell can we do that? The mining lasers only focus at short distance. Nothing else can...wait a minute. What were you experimenting with while I was in the cavern?"

Adam grinned a wolfish grin. "Oh, nothing much. I just invented a plasma cannon that has a range that, well, let's say that I don't know how far it will shoot. It can be made with enough power to vaporize a space ship. We'll have to build some additional equipment, but with this as a weapon you have got a warship, Captain."

Suarez' jaw dropped. "Mr. Maxwell, you surprise me. I took you for one of those peaceful types, too fearful to do anything that wasn't approved. Now you've turned the thing around. You're trying to convince me to become a pirate. Correct?"

"Well, maybe not anything that radical, but with my invention, we can enforce compliance. If we don't get it, we can blow them out of space."

THE AIRLOCK DOORS were completed while Adam worked at creating a simple machine to electrically separate hydrogen from oxygen. Once the doors were able to seal, To'afa filled the cavern with all the extra nitrogen. Adam set his invention to disassociating water ice that the alterday crew had mined and stored. The solar-powered device worked steadily, if slowly, and the bubble began to accumulate the start of an atmosphere. The solar panels came from the ship's back-up array. If all went well, the D-R wouldn't need them again.

Once the equipment was in place and operating, it could be left to run automatically. It would stop when it ran out of water. There was plenty of ice on the rock, but the separator could only access enough to bring the O2 component into breathable balance with the nitrogen. The pressure was going to be too low to breathe until they could add more gas. If they were successful in getting more nitrogen, it wouldn't take to long to make the atmosphere dense enough to support life.

THIRTY DAYS AFTER the D-R had reached the asteroid, it departed, heading for the Mars-Earth shuttle orbit.

# 8

# CROSSING THE LINE

SUAREZ, JEM, AND Adam were discussing strategy in the captain's cabin. They were nearing the regular Mars route, and it was time to make final plans. Adam had worked the other members of the main-day crew hard during the transit. They had created a more powerful plasma generator and paired it with the third back-up Em-Max, then mounted the odd-looking result on a remote-controlled gimble at the front of the hull.

The system could be aimed by the computer or manually. Adam had insisted that it could only be fired by hand. He didn't want the computer to be responsible for making a kill decision. Its limited AI wasn't good enough for that.

The route varied depending on the relative positions of Mars and Earth when the supply ship started its journey. The supply ships spiraled out from Luna or the ribbon station, taking about six months to reach Mars. They could have been constructed to go faster, but it was deemed too expensive to equip them with more powerful engines. The ships got to Mars on their own time.

If the colonists needed supplies, they would just have to wait until the ship arrived in orbit.

Ships carrying colonists were marginally faster. That was due to the limitations imposed by radiation effects on the human body. It was easy to tell the two kinds of ship apart. The passenger ships had much the same shape as the miners, except their rotating habitat ring was much more substantial.

Jem said, "The supply ship is just within range of our optical system. The profile is that of an unmanned vessel. This should be easy."

Adam said, "I'm worried about the accuracy needed to knock out the comm system. The ships have two different ones, a modulated laser, and a narrow-band radio. If we fail to destroy them both quickly, a message will get out, and within about thirty minutes the Feds on the ribbon station or Luna will know something's wrong."

"Sure, but they won't know what. Your gun has enough range to scorch the hull and burn off both the laser pod and the radio antenna before we close. The supply ships' cameras only monitor dead ahead anyway. We can keep off to the side and approach from the rear. That will keep us out of view of the camera. When we're close enough, we hit the pod and the antenna. Then we dock and load up," Suarez said.

Adam commented, "You've been thinking about this, haven't you, Captain?"

The captain nodded, and a smile crossed his face. He hadn't shaved recently, and the contrast of his white teeth shining through the dense black beard was startling.

Adam continued. "I think that will work, provided we can get close enough. I've calculated and recalculated the joules the gun can deliver. The energy does attenuate a bit, due to dust. Presuming we're in a relatively clear area, the attenuation can be ignored. Velocity of the shot is about one-quarter light. I thought it was faster, but that's still so fast that it's almost instantaneous at reasonable ranges. Accuracy is still the limiting factor. The gimbal mount has some limits in the fineness of its movement. That means that we need to be within five hundred klicks to be sure of hitting our target. Any farther and the margin of error becomes too great."

Suarez nodded. "What about the energy level, the joules delivered to the target? I don't want to blow the whole ship, just burn off the antenna."

"That is something I'm still trying to calculate. The hull is mostly carbon and steel. The antenna and laser pod are aluminum alloy as are their mounts. If I adjust the generator to a little over twenty percent output, the plasma blob will be light enough to melt the aluminum, but not damage the carbon. Well, not too much, I hope." Adam grinned and shrugged.

"Mr. Maxwell, that doesn't give me much confidence. Can you make sure we don't destroy the cargo, at least?" Suarez grinned again. He was apparently enjoying the idea of becoming a pirate.

"I'm confident that I can do that, Sir."

THE MARS SUPPLY ship looked somewhat like a hot dog. It was a long tube, rounded on front and back. Its drive was inside the rear quarter, and the antenna and laser pod were both mounted along the rear hull near the end. They were positioned out of direct line of the engine. This wasn't strictly necessary, but some engineer somewhere had apparently felt that the Em-drive might be ejecting something that would interfere with communications, despite all evidence to the contrary.

The D-R approached slowly on a quartering path, gradually pulling closer to the oblivious supply ship. Suarez waited until they were within two hundred kilometers before he allowed Adam to activate the plasma cannon.

The result was disappointing to Adam. He'd somehow expected more fireworks. The pale blue plasma bolt looked weak as it streaked across the intervening distance. The strike was unimpressive. No flares, no fire, no smoke, save for a mist of melted aluminum. The antenna slumped and then floated free from the hull. The laser pod was untouched.

"Damn it!" Suarez exclaimed. "The hull is rotating too slowly. Wait a bit then shoot again when the pod appears."

Adam glanced at his computer. "The system is charging. It might take to long before it's ready for another shot."

"The supply ship computer has to know that something took out the radio. It might run some diagnostics, but eventually, it will use the laser pod to send an error message. What's the chance we can slip up to it and then use one of the mining lasers to burn it off?" Jem asked.

Suarez replied, "That might work. What do you think, Adam?"

Adam noticed in passing that this was the first time the captain had addressed him informally.

"Uh. Yeah. It could work, but by the time we're that close, the plasma gun will be ready to fire again."

"Ok. We're moving to approach." Suarez was piloting the D-R himself. Nav crew usually took that job, but the captain wanted to handle the attack himself.

Adam kept tabs on the charge progress. When they were within fifty klicks, the cannon was ready. "Okay, Sir. We can shoot whenever you want."

Suarez kept his eyes on the screen, watching their closure rate.

"Wait til the pod comes around again. Ah, there it is. Got it?"

"Yes, Sir."

"Fire when you're sure of a hit."

The plasma cannon pulsed again, again shoving the ship with recoil. This time the supply ship's laser comm pod flared a bit, then burst into pieces. Something inside exploded with a puff of gas and debris.

"Wow!" came from someone in the assembled crew.

"That would be the laser system blowing. The bolt delivered more energy than we really needed, but it got the job done," Adam said.

THE DOCKING TOOK some time since the supply ship's computer wouldn't cooperate. They had to grapple the rotating ship and pull themselves close. The angular momentum transferred to the D-R and gave the crew the sensation of movement parallel to the deck with a violent initial kick.

The cargo crews, both mainday, and alterday were already suited up. They exited the cargo bay, made their way to the supply ship's cargo door and hooked the emergency port to the D-R's power. The supply ship computer had no answer to that. When they turned the power on, the cargo bay door obediently retracted. They were inside in a few seconds.

Moving the supplies was a lengthy process. Jem found a lading bill, which was delivered to Suarez. The captain selected the items they needed. He'd made the decision not to take everything. The Mars colonists were dependent on the supplies, and Suarez didn't want to be responsible for them starving.

Eventually, the D-R's cargo bay was loaded with nitrogen cylinders, enough of the food supplies to last the crew six months, and a case of rum that Jem swore the Martians didn't deserve.

They sealed the supply ship's bay, released the hull, then backed off. The computer controlled ship, on finding itself free of the extra mass, fired its maneuvering jets to reinstate its stately rotation. It carefully adjusted its vector to the predetermined direction and moved away slowly as if nothing had happened.

Everyone gathered in the bridge on a common impulse. They were talking quietly and watching the vid screens as the supply ship departed.

"It's probably screaming for help, but nobody can hear anything it's sending," Jem said, then added, "Must be frustrating."

"Or terrifying, but it's just a computer, so maybe not," Flynn responded with a grin.

The crewmen were silent for a bit, thinking about what they'd done and what it meant for their lives. None laughed at Flynn's weak attempt at humor.

Captain Suarez came into the room. He'd been in his cabin doing something. Probably having a drink, Adam thought. Suarez looked serious as he addressed the crew.

"Men, the Dire Rhea has taken an irrevocable step. From this point on, we're pirates. Not that we were really on the right side of the law before. Now, we've got something to show for having the Feds on our backs and, if I have anything to say about it, we're going to get rich and live well in our own base. Are there any questions?"

Flynn asked, "Seeing as how we're now pirates, shouldn't we be celebrating with the rum?"

The rest of the men hooted in agreement. Suarez grinned and answered, "I think we can afford a few hours of celebration. There's nothing and no one around here that's going to bother us. If there are going to be repercussions, it will take a while before the proverbial fecal material hits the fan."

Adam was careful not to drink too much. He'd suffered from hangovers in the past, and he was worried about Suarez. The captain seemed to have his drinking under tight control, but Adam had seen him with that terrible hang-over. Someone needed to be able to respond in case Suarez was wrong about his time frame, or if some other problem materialized.

# 9

# CHANGES

THE BUBBLE, AS they came to call the asteroid cavern, made a good base. It was large enough to provide living space for a few thousand people along with adequate supplies to keep everyone healthy for years.

The new pirates worked at building the start of a settlement. It was a daunting task. Not only did they lack supplies and building equipment, they also lacked the knowledge. Not one of them knew anything about construction, architecture, or municipal planning.

After a month, they had finished a combination kitchen and mess hall with some adjacent sleeping rooms. Adam found himself getting irritated more and more easily by the enforced closeness. Somehow it was worse here than on the ship. Perhaps because one expected no privacy on a ship, but the immense unused space inside the Bubble seemed to taunt him. It seemed crazy to pack into tiny rooms when there was an option.

He took to going to the opposite side of the cavern for privacy. It was usually too noisy to think in the mess hall, and that was what he needed to do.

The plasma cannon was fine, but it needed some improvements. For one, it couldn't fire rapidly. It took too long to recharge the power capacitor. He wanted to fix that before it became a serious issue. If the D-R were attacked, it would be good to have rapid-fire ability. The mining lasers could be used at close range, but Adam had the suspicion that space conflict would be at longer range.

He was forced to work out tactics and strategies on his own. To this point, there had never been a space battle. Sure, the Fed space force had dropped some KEWs to destroy targets on Earth, but there had never been the necessity to enter combat with another space ship.

He had read somewhere that the five existing space cruisers, which comprised the Fed space navy were armed with both KEWs and a few missiles. They had planned on countering missile fire with some point defense pods, but those were simple variations on computer-targeted mini-guns of a type that was common on ocean-based vessels.

The other thing that bothered him was their need for resupply. The Feds had figured out that the supply ship had been raided. It had taken a couple of days because the colonists had taken their time about contacting Luna to report the damage. Apparently, the missing antenna and laser comm pod had been attributed to a collision until someone had pointed out that the rear half of the supply ship's hull showed signs of ablation. That was suspicious, and had led to them concluding that the discrepancy between the lading list and the supplies wasn't due to incompetence on the part of the cargo loaders.

The upshot had been that Vice-Admiral Nashua of the Federal Space Navy had dispatched the cruiser Knoxville to Mars. The

Navy intended to follow the supply ship's orbit as if that would tell them something.

Adam snickered to himself. It wasn't like anything was lying around in space. The missing parts had been mostly vaporized, although the laser pod explosion had blown some larger chunks into space. Those were moving fast enough that there was zero chance the cruiser would find them.

It was more likely that Nashua thought that whoever had robbed the supply ship would tackle the Knoxville. There was no point in that. The cruiser had a compliment of marines that was three times the size of the D-R's crew. Unless they burned a hole in the hull and killed everyone on board there was no way they'd be able to off-load supplies. There was just too large an opposing force.

Something else was gnawing at the back of his mind. After a little more thought, he realized that he really didn't want to kill any navy personnel. He didn't know them and had no quarrel with them. Now, if Worthington were on board, that would be different.

He sighed, collected himself, and returned to the mess hall. There were two of the alterday crew eating, but no one else in sight.

"Hey, Jake. You know where the captain is?"

"Yo, Adam. Yeah. He's outside looking at the Bubble wall trying to figure out where to build the next part of our luxury apartment. Ha!" Mal looked disgusted, then turned his head back to his meal, terminating the conversation.

Adam went outside and worked his way around the building to the metallic wall of the chamber. He saw Suarez after a bit. The captain was moving at the end of a tether inspecting the attachment points of their construction.

"Oh, it's you," the captain said as he approached. "Do you know anything about building? I know, I know. We've been through this before, but I'm at a loss about how to proceed."

"Same answer as before, sir. I'm a quantum physicist, not an architect or a civil engineer. I do have an idea, though."

"What would that be, Mr. Maxwell?" Suarez had remembered his formal manners.

"It seems to me that the Mars colonists have to include some people with the skills we need. Maybe we should go visiting and see if any of them want to be a pirate."

"You know Mr. Maxwell, I've been thinking something like that myself. They have builders and the type of engineers we need. True, they've been trained for light gravity work, but some of them might be interested in helping us."

"Two things, Captain. First, we could add some spin to this rock. It would make it a little more difficult to dock, but the benefit would be to give us angular momentum. We could walk on the Bubble walls, rather than half float. That would definitely help with our building effort. Second, aren't there some of the Mars people who were conscripted? I heard somewhere they were sending political undesirables there."

"Ah. I see what you're getting at, Adam. The gravity might make it easier to find some people who resent their treatment. That would be good since we can't send anyone who knows about our base back to be interviewed by the Feds. Anyone we get will have to join us permanently."

"That's what I had concluded, sir. How about the Knoxville? Is it still hanging around?

"At last report, it left Mars and is partway back to Luna. They must not believe they have anything to worry about considering the way they broadcast their plans all over. We've been able to keep close tabs on them simply by listening to the radio.

"They could turn around and come back if the Mars people start screaming for help."

"That is a problem, but if we use our laser comm to call Mars, the Feds won't know. We can offer them some ice. I know they need that. Once we get a dialog established, we can probably bargain for the help and supplies we need."

"No more piracy?"

"Well, maybe a little. If we're working with Mars, we don't want to antagonize them, but we could intercept colony ships and take off people who want to join us. I don't think that would upset the Mars people too much. They have a percentage of colonists who want off the planet in the worst way, too. With any luck, we can get a decent number of people here. That would give us the labor we need to really make progress on the base."

"I agree, sir. It seems like a good idea."

AS A RESULT of that conversation, the D-R headed for Mars on a recruiting mission. The Bubble was closer to Jupiter than to Mars, so the journey took days. The D-R didn't have to begin deceleration at the halfway point since the ship would use Mars's gravity to slow them. They would enter an orbit that intersected with that of Deimos. The Martians used that moon as a docking and cargo unloading point. Phobos was unusable for that purpose due to its speed and gradually decaying orbit.

On the way, an event occurred that proved Elseth hadn't been merely fantasizing. The first Adam knew of it was when Flynn began shouting excitedly from the nav station. Adam had been trying to get some sleep, and the noise echoing down the passageway jolted him to full wakefulness.

He got dressed and headed to the bridge. Everyone else was already there when he arrived, and Flynn was explaining.

"The government has been decimated. Someone set a bomb off in the Capitol building. It killed almost everybody, including the President and Vice-President. The military has clamped down on the country, and Senator Worthington has taken control. The capitol has moved to New York. Worthington has extended martial law and no one's moving around. They don't know who was responsible, but Worthington is promising he'll find out and whoever it was will pay."

Adam's jaw dropped slightly. He could have been involved in that if he'd been stupid enough. Right now, being a wanted pirate out in space seemed to be highly desirable.

After a bit, the crew calmed down. Suarez, always quick to decide, said, "If Worthlesston is in charge, I have no problem playing pirate. We'll see if Mars will help. If they won't, we'll raid every supply ship including the manned ones. This is our chance to get back at the people who threw us out here. Does everyone agree?"

Flynn insisted that they swear a dread oath, binding them to each other and pirate life. "Look, men. Those scum drove us out here, then Worthington took over. I don't automatically hate every Earther, but that fat senator is responsible for the Captain being here, and I think Adam had a run-in with him too. We can revenge ourselves by making him look bad. Now, pirates always swore an oath, and we should do it too. Everybody, here are some syringe needles from medical. Let's all poke our thumbs and mingle our blood."

The needles were distributed, and the crew swore the Oath of the Bloody Thumb.

"May our blood bind us together. We vow revenge on the Feds who cheated us and those who sent us out here. Brothers forever in life and death. May vacuum take anyone who betrays our base and our operation."

It was corny, but they repeated the words as Flynn wrote them on paper. Afterward, they held their thumbs against the white sheet, leaving thumbprints in blood and DNA attesting to their oath.

Adam reflected that he hadn't started out to be a pirate, he'd never even had a passing thought about pirates in space, but the idea seemed appealing. Besides, it offered a chance at striking back at Worthington, and maybe Elseth.

No, scratch that thought. He rubbed his face with his hand. When would he grow up and get over that woman? She didn't care about him. He'd seemed to be an easy mark. Someone she could convince to help in what he now recognized as her father's plan. They probably would have arranged for him to take the blame, also. That would be about par for his luck. If he was ever going to meet a woman and build a relationship…He paused. That was highly unlikely since there were no women within several million miles. Maybe he could meet someone on Mars. She would have to be a spacer, though. He'd been out long enough that he knew he'd never be comfortable on a planet again. He'd found his place building a community in the Bubble. True, there were only the eight men, but maybe they'd find people who wanted to join them in creating a new life, one free from government interference.

THE D-R MADE a slow approach to Deimos. The moon was little more than a small, irregular asteroid that was fifteen kilometers at the widest. It was a little over twenty-three thousand kilometers from Mars' surface. That was quite close compared to Luna and Earth. The small moon made a complete orbit in a little over thirty hours, which was a speed that made it far more suitable for a base than the second Martian moon. Phobos was much closer to Mars than Deimos and had a correspondingly faster orbital period of seven hours and thirty-nine minutes.

The colonists had set up a shuttle base in one of the two named craters on Deimos. The supply ships unloaded at the Swift crater base.

The ships weren't designed to enter a deep gravity well. Their thrust was so minimal that, once in the well, the ship could never climb out again. Deimos had an escape velocity of 5.6 meters per second, which was about as much as the supply ships could manage.

The shuttle from the moon to the Martian surface was minimally aerodynamic, but that wasn't a problem with the minimal atmosphere of Mars. It could lift from Mars with no problem, although it would not have been able to reach space from the surface of Earth.

A small crew whose primary job was transferring cargo from the supply ships to the shuttle operated the Swift base. They also acted as immigration officers when the crewed ships brought another load of colonists. The government had taken to banishing their worst criminal offenders, those with no hope of reform, those who had committed capital crimes, and worst of all, political enemies. Being sent to Mars was considered to be equivalent to a death sentence.

The crew at Swift interviewed and oriented new arrivals. They also made sure that particularly undesirable individuals never made it to Mars' surface. If a colonist-to-be was judged to be a potential problem to the close-knit Mars colony, they were given a tour of Deimos' surface—without a space suit.

THE D-R DREW near, coming up on the little moon from behind. The Captain had called the Swift base a day before to announce his intent to visit. Now they were engaged in a moment-by-moment communication stream as they moved in to dock.

The supply ship docking-cradle was too large to fit the much smaller mining ship, but Swift sometimes dealt with the asteroid miners, serving as a repair station. The miners usually paid with water ice, something that was in short supply on Mars.

There had been a brief effort to drop an ice comet on the planet, but it was written off as too difficult and too expensive. The existing surface water was concentrated in polar ice. The Martians were planning on using it, but there was a lot of work to do to liberate the small amount of water in the poles.

Consequentially, they were anxious to get what ice the miners brought.

The Feds frowned on that trade, though. The miners were expected to bring ore and minerals back to Luna or the ribbon station. Even a small mining ship was expensive to operate, and the chartering companies had to pay their shareholders along with a steadily increasing tax burden.

AFTER THEY DOCKED, Suarez had them establish an airtight seal with a personnel tube. Shortly after that, two Swift base staff came across. Suarez had insisted that they have a face-to-face meeting. He didn't want to use the standard communication system since it was automatically recorded. There was too much risk in that. He didn't want the Feds to find out what he had planned until it became apparent.

The older of the two Martians was the base commander, Citizen Oliver. The younger was a guard, brought along for security, although against what threat was not clear to Adam.

Suarez had seen fit to include Adam in the discussion, although the other members of the D-R's crew were not invited.

The four men crowded into Suarez' cabin, facing off over the captain's desk.

"Welcome, Citizens," Suarez said. "We're pleased to be here."

Citizen Oliver made a curt nod. "Captain, our time is valuable. Mars has adopted different customs than Earth. We like to get directly to the point without social pleasantries. What do you need from us?"

Adam grinned a little. The man reminded him of an overly officious beaver.

Suarez nodded, just as curtly. "I understand. We want to establish a working relationship with your colony. We believe that both sides can benefit from this."

Oliver didn't mince words. "Are you responsible for raiding one of our supply ships?"

Suarez glanced at Adam, then said, "Yes. We took some needed supplies from you. We acknowledge the act and intend to make it up to you. If we can work together, we will do more than make it up to you."

"Tell me more," Oliver folded his arms.

"The Feds have been mistreating us. We've had more and more difficulty getting authorization for supplies at the ribbon. It has reached the point where we've decided that we don't need them any longer. In short, we intend to create our own asteroid colony."

It was Oliver's turn to glance at his companion. "Where do you intend to build such a colony?"

"That's restricted information. We obviously don't want the Feds to come visiting. You know their expectations for miners. They want to exploit us until we die from radiation poisoning, and that's it. If it got around that we had an operational base, other miners would be tempted to join us, and the Feds would miss the inflow of minerals and metals. They'd come after us."

"That's a given," Oliver nodded. "So what is your proposition?"

"We will trade ice for supplies. We can deliver ice to any part of Mars, as long as you have a clear space for us to drop it. We should be able to establish a value schedule so we can build up credit with you. We will then use the credit to purchase what we need from you."

Oliver thought about it, then apparently decided to negotiate. "I'm not sure that will work. As you said, the Feds will resent it."

"Citizen, we already have our base. We need supplies. If you do not trade willingly with us, we can always intercept your supply ships." It was apparent from his expression that Suarez was determined.

Oliver frowned. "Is that a threat?"

"No, it's a reality. However, we would much prefer to trade with you. The Feds already see us as pirates, but even pirates need resupply, and these pirates can pay with something you desperately need: water."

"When you put it that way, it seems that we really haven't a choice. I think we can work out the details, but I'll need a few days to return to the surface and meet with our governing council. For the record, we don't like the Feds any more than you do. Most of us aren't here because we came for the salubrious climate."

Suarez nodded. "We are in much the same situation. They don't want us back on Earth. If we returned, most of us would not survive the experience. We might even be sent to you as prospective colonists. We would like a response quickly, but we have time to wait for you to meet with your council."

Adam felt that Suarez was overlooking part of their needs. "Citizen, one of our immediate needs is for additional pairs of hands. In short, we need volunteers. We have a lot of work to do developing our base, and we need help. Will you ask your council to search for volunteers for us?"

Suarez nodded, "That's important. We can't create a new society with only the crew of the D-R. We especially need architects, builders, tradesmen of all kinds as long as they can work in low-g and vacuum."

Citizen Oliver nodded. "I'll raise the issue. We need our builders and engineers for our own projects, but we pride ourselves on allowing our citizens to make their own decisions. If some of them want to help you, they will probably be allowed that option. Meanwhile, we are expecting the Knoxville to return in forty-eight hours for refueling and supplies. Given your circumstances, it would be wise if they didn't see your ship. You'll have to distance yourself."

Suarez glanced at Adam, then said, "Ah. We'll be leaving as soon as you return to your base."

Adam added, "It occurs to me to wonder if you want the Knoxville here."

Oliver looked sharply at him. "Young man that should be obvious to you. We do not want it. They take our supplies and give us nothing. They say they are ensuring our security, but, given your successful raid on our supplies, their ability to keep us secure is dubious. It's more likely they will eventually serve as a force to enforce Federal demands on us. To repeat, no. We don't want them here. However, we have no means to keep them off. They can destroy our base with a single missile. Our surface installations are no more secure. A few well-placed rocks dropped from orbit would kill most of us."

The two pirates looked at each other. Suarez said, "Well, it might be possible for the cruiser to have an accident. A fatal one."

Oliver's eyebrows went up. "You have that ability? What about their missiles? They have good point-defense also."

"Citizen, as much as I respect you, I have no intention of disclosing our capabilities to you. Suffice it to say that we might be able to keep them from visiting."

"If you do, I believe I can guarantee that we'll work with you. You can have some of the supplies they have demanded. We've already shuttled them up. Just keep them off our backs for now. Maybe they won't send another cruiser for a few months."

"Citizen Oliver, I believe that they will send another one. If the Knoxville disappears with no trace and no warning, they will probably want to investigate. The long-term question is what will Mars do in the future. Will you try to work with both the Feds and us, or will we be able to devise a means of working together that does not include the Feds?"

Oliver rubbed his chin and said, "That is the crux of the matter. I'm not the one who will make that decision, fortunately. I'll bring it before the council tomorrow. Now, I must go, as must you, if you're not going to be seen by the Feds."

He turned and marched officiously out, followed by his guard.

When they heard the airlock cycle, Suarez said, "This might be the start of something good for us."

Adam replied, "Or something terrible if we've misjudged how tough that cruiser might be."

"Well, I'm not averse to a fight. God knows I've wanted revenge on those people long enough. Let's get uncocked and moving, then you and I will plan a battle strategy that makes the most use out of your cannon. If we can, it would be good to take their ship without destroying it. We need supplies, besides having a military ship will give us additional options."

Adam left to get the Em-Max warmed up.

# 10
## THE FIRST SPACE BATTLE

THE D-R DRIFTED quietly. All non-essential systems were shut down, scan was passive only. The solar array was tilted so that no accidental flash of sun on its surface could be seen. Adam kept checking power usage, nervously hoping that his checking would help to keep their profile minimized. He'd even shut off the air regenerator system. The crew could survive on stale air for the few hours necessary to spring their ambush. If the Knoxville took longer than expected to arrive, he would grudgingly release pure O2 into the ship. That would give them a few extra hours, but would also necessitate regeneration at the first possible opportunity. It wouldn't do to go into battle with an atmosphere that was high in oxygen. A random spark could ignite any number of flammable components, including the crew themselves.

With the cooperation of the Swift base, the pirates had carefully prepared the field of battle. Adam had worked for thirty hours straight building as many proximity mines as he could. The things were relatively simple but time-consuming to build. He had come up with a radio trigger that would be woken up by the Knoxville's initial contact with Swift.

Once primed, the trigger monitored normal comm signal strength. This was the dicey part. Adam had relied on his best guess of how strong the Knoxville's signal would be at close range.

Suarez had crosschecked and announced that he was satisfied that the trigger would work. Their intention was for the trigger to hold off until the Knoxville's signal strength was so high that the cruiser had to be within a few hundred kilometers. When the ship was close, the mine's computer would orient towards it, fire a miniature jet pack and go scooting towards the target. The triggering system would wait until the mine was within a klick before firing its explosive charge.

The mine was really a mobile cannon with an explosive charge packed in a tube full of miscellaneous scrap metal. The scrap would scatter somewhat and hopefully damage the Knoxville's sensor array and its point-defense turrets. The bulk of the damage would be self-inflicted due to the higher velocity of the cruiser as it flew through the slower scrap field.

Adam was worried. Things could get bad if the mine idea didn't damage or distract the enemy. Plowing through an unexpected debris field should be enough to focus the Knoxville's helm on the hazard. With any luck, they would not notice the D-R's approach until the smaller ship was well within plasma cannon range. Suarez wanted to hit the Knoxville with every available joule of power. He'd come to the conclusion that capturing the cruiser was going to be too difficult. He and Adam had discussed the situation and agreed that their most likely result would be total destruction, assuming they prevailed at all.

Adam had unsuccessfully tried to rest, but pre-battle jitters kept him from relaxing. He'd finally dropped off for a few hours of nightmare-filled sleep when the intercom broadcast an alert, startling him out of a disturbing dream where-in the D-R was about to be struck by multiple missiles. He jumped to his feet, nearly hitting the overhead. Suarez came on.

"Attention. Target is approaching our minefield. Projected time till mine detonation is fourteen minutes and counting. All hands prepare for impending battle." The system clicked as he placed the mike down.

Adam got to the engine room, got suited up, then prepared to turn on the plasma shield. The cannon capacitor bank was pre-charged; however, some of the charge would have leaked by this point. Once the shield was on, he'd divert some of the power to the capacitors to top them off.

The Em-Max wasn't involved in the attack for a simple reason: it accelerated too slowly. They would use the maneuvering jets. Their Martian allies had provided them with extra nitrogen tanks, and they had gas to spare. Flynn had mounted several of the tanks on the hull. When released, the gas would be directed through pipes to act as rocket exhaust. That would boost their approach speed.

The captain counted down, his voice quivering with excitement and strain. When the first mine accelerated towards the cruiser, Adam could hear an echo of cheering voices down the passageway to the bridge.

Suarez was back on the intercom, keeping Adam informed. "The rest of the minefield is moving, jetting directly towards the Knoxville. They don't look as if they notice the mines!"

Adam was gratified at that. The mines were small, and their gas jets were relatively undetectable. He had planned for the cruiser to trigger them as it proceeded towards what was supposed to be a routine docking.

The first mine blew closely followed by three more. Adam knew because the cheering grew in volume.

He turned on the plasma shield, then directed power to the cannon. It hadn't lost much, so it topped off quickly. He had mounted a duplicate fire-control system in the engine room. The plan was for Suarez to make the firing decision, but Adam was prepared to take over in the event something happened. He turned to the monitor for a closer view.

THE KNOXVILLE HAD fired its portside jets, but it was too late to sheer off. It entered the debris field. All at once there was a series of flashes along the cruiser's sides as the metal chunks impacted. Another mine exploded directly in front and added its mass to the cloud.

The Captain abruptly spoke on the intercom. "Adam, take hold. We're accelerating in five."

He grabbed the fire-control system mount, saying a quick prayer that the improvised gas jets would work. Then there was the sensation of acceleration as Suarez opened the external tanks. The D-R didn't precisely leap, but it definitely began to move. Adam had no problem holding on through the gentle acceleration. He gulped, swallowing a taste of acid. They were accelerating into combat.

When he looked at the monitor, Deimos was appreciably nearer. Somewhat behind the moon, the silver cruiser could be seen crossing the reddish disk of Mars.

He increased the magnification. The cruiser had now passed through the minefield, but there was a glittering string of debris floating behind it. The mines had worked better than he'd planned.

The Knoxville still hadn't noticed their approach. The ship's captain was on the radio demanding an explanation from Swift, but getting no satisfactory answer. The colonists were acting as if they didn't know what was going on.

That was a reasonable strategy. If the D-R's attack failed, the Swift base would need to appear innocent.

There was something on the Knoxville's hull. He looked closer and saw that the idiots had sent out a repair party. Those were spacesuits floating around out there. Now he could see the suit strobes flashing against the darker body of the planet below. The plasma cannon would evaporate those poor guys if the captain shot now. He reached for the intercom.

Before his hand reached the microphone, there was an electrical snap, then a buzzing as the capacitors fired. The screen showed an intense blue flash, which almost instantly struck the Knoxville.

Adam gulped. This was distressingly real. It had seemed like a child's game, playing at pirates with no real damage done. Things were abruptly different. His hand shook as he routed extra power to the capacitor bank. The cannon must be ready to fire again as quickly as possible.

The Knoxville's profile looked different. The point-defense pods had disappeared as had the entire antenna array, the solar power array, and the missile pod that had been prominently visible on this side of the ship. There were some jets of atmosphere shooting out of holes in the hull.

The plasma had done a lot of damage, but not enough to render the cruiser helpless. It wallowed into a clumsy turn as the maneuvering jets on the far side were fired. Someone on the Knoxville had finally seen them. The cruiser came about slowly until it was oriented approximately at the D-R.

The missile pod on the starboard side fired. Adam reacted instantly, firing the cannon from his station. It hadn't completed charging, but there was enough charge to generate a faint azure ball of plasma that expanded as it left the ship. The missiles struck the ball with a silent flash as three of the warheads exploded. The fourth missile missed both the plasma and getting caught in the explosions. It was barely visible as it continued towards their ship.

Adam braced and then the missile was on them. There was a violent jolt, and a burst of light that left the monitor washed out for a second. When the view returned, it looked just as it had before. The Knoxville was still pointing at them with a trail of debris off to one side.

The cruiser's maneuvering jets had ceased firing, and it hung still in space with the red mass of Mars behind.

Adam controlled his shaking hand and grabbed the microphone.

"This is engineering. Damage report?"

Suarez's rough voice came back. "Mr. Maxwell. I've got to hand it to you. That was good shooting to get those missiles. The fourth one struck us a glancing blow, but your shield did something completely unexpected. I think it destroyed at least part of the warhead before it exploded. The main force of the missile was deflected away from our hull. I've got cargo looking for damage. The pressure isn't dropping, so we've still got an intact hull. Charge the cannon, in case we need it, but don't fire. We are going to close with them, burn a hole with the mining laser pod, then go over and see who's left to fight. We may yet get a second ship. I want it, even if it's severely damaged.'

He automatically switched the power to recharge the cannon. Then he pushed back a bit and sat still, breathing deeply and trying to calm down. The fight was still on, but there was going to be a period of inactivity as they closed.

A moment later, Suarez came back on. "There was a hull breach in the cargo bay, but To'afa threw a cargo pad on it. The pad is stuck in the hole, effectively plugging it. We're not losing much pressure, but get your helmet on, in case it pushes on through. We'll patch up after the action."

The D-R braked with its jets, then glided into position beside the injured Knoxville. The cruiser was rolling slowly. Adam watched curiously. There were several leaks in her hull shooting faint jets of moist air. The water immediately froze, forming white plumes of ice crystals.

The enemy continued to roll until the undamaged point-defense pods on the starboard side appeared. They immediately opened fire.

The D-R shuddered a bit with the impact of the projectiles. He could hear Suarez cursing clear down the hall. The plasma shield was as effective against the relatively slow projectiles as it was against the missile. Although there was some vibration, there was no rattle of bullets impacting the hull. Adam sighed with mixed relief and satisfaction that his invention was working.

Then the mining laser fired. A point on the middle of the enemy hull heated, instantly glowing red, then white. A flurry of molten metal boiled off, leaving a dark hole with glowing red edges. Whoever was aiming the mining lasers, probably Jem retargeted quickly and began to melt the visible point-defense installations. They went down just as quickly, then the lasers quit firing.

Everything seemed to be moving in slow motion to Adam, and the sudden cessation of action disoriented him. He moved his hand to the plasma cannon button but pulled back at the last second. Suarez would space him if he destroyed their prize after the battle was won. What was he thinking?

Suarez came on the intercom. "Mr. Maxwell, please come to the bridge. I want you to take command. We're going to board her, and someone needs to be here."

He ran down the passageway and met Suarez and Jem heading towards the cargo bay. Suarez yelled, "Get in there and take the helm. If we don't come back, blow them out of space. I'll be on the radio, so monitor me, but don't interrupt. I'm going to be busy."

The two men continued towards their destination. He dashed into the bridge, then sat at the nav station. He could hear the crew speaking in short bursts as they exited the airlock and jetted towards the disabled cruiser.

# 11
## AFTERMATH

THINGS SEEMED UNREAL. Adam watched his friends as they used compressed gas jets to make their way over to the cruiser's hull. Most of the men were carrying conventional pistols and knives. The two notable exceptions were the captain and To'afa. Suarez had strapped on a large curved sword that he'd gotten from somewhere. Adam hadn't seen it before and knew little about such things anyway. From the curved shape, he assumed it was a cutlass or something like that.

To'afa's weapon was easy to identify as an ax. The thought of the injuries it would produce made him shudder. The big Samoan would chew through a mass of space-suited men with a few swings.

Vacuum magnified any small injury. Once a suit was punctured, the occupant was effectively out of the fight. If they didn't immediately patch the leak, they were dead in a few minutes. If the leak was too big, they died faster. The ax would create huge holes. Adam shuddered.

The crew disappeared around the hull, and he could hear Suarez snapping orders as they prepared to blow the outer airlock. Apparently, the lock did not have an emergency override like the D-R's lock. It would have to be forced open.

Suarez ordered the men to move back. Shortly after that, Adam saw some debris fly off the Knoxville. They'd blown the lock open.

The inner lock required the same treatment. Suarez didn't hesitate to blow it also. If there were unsuited men inside, they were now dying from explosive decompression.

The radio chatter became difficult to follow as the men entered the ship. The signal strength was less than before, and the crew seemed to have forgotten radio discipline. They were all shouting at once as they fought the enemy.

He listened intently, trying to understand what was happening. The resistance weakened for a few minutes, but then the fighting regained its strength. Time seemed to flow as slowly as mercury on the moon.

Adam didn't know how long he'd been hunched over the radio, trying to follow the fight. It was similar to listening to an Earth football game where each player had a microphone in his helmet, but without the play-by-play announcers. The audio consisted of grunts, yells, screams of anger or pain, and curses.

The transmission quieted, and he sat back and wiped his forehead in relief. It was covered with sweat.

Suarez' voice came crackling through. "Ahoy the D-R. We've successfully taken the ship. No prisoners. Tom's gone, though. See if you can move closer. We're going to transfer supplies. Flynn and To'afa are taking this hulk back to the Bubble."

He answered, "Yes, Sir. Moving shortly."

Suarez added, "Observe radio silence from this point on."

Adam queried the sensor array. The Knoxville was just short of ten klicks away. A few keystrokes into the nav comp and the maneuvering jets fired gently. The ship began drifting closer to the prize.

The jets fired again, stuttered, then fired to stop the approach. The two ships were only meters apart.

Some of the crew came sailing around the cruiser's hull. He could hear the thump of the cargo bay airlock as it cycled. A short time after that, Suarez came into the bridge.

"Good work, Mr. Maxwell. We've taken our first prize. I'm not happy with the price, though. Tom was a good crewman as well as being a friend."

"I'm sorry," was all he could think to say.

"We'll have to find a replacement as soon as possible. I sincerely hope those Martians have a few discontents who want to try something else."

"Well, yes, but what if they are troublemakers?"

The captain grinned unpleasantly. "I've thought of that, too. They won't last too long. If necessary, I'll set To'afa on them. If that's not enough, we can always space the really bad ones."

Yes. That was a possibility. Adam shook his head slowly. His understanding of his life was changing. He'd been angry and cheated before. He'd been persecuted and hunted, but he'd always had a kind of naive outlook that led him to expect things to turn out fine in the end. This battle and its aftermath brought home the reality and deadly seriousness of what they were doing in a way that he hadn't been able to process before. He was tempted to tell Suarez that he'd changed his mind. He didn't want to be a pirate. He wished he could go home and start again.

That wasn't even a remote possibility. He was committed. There was no choice, but to make the best of the situation. If he were a pirate, he'd be the best one he could be. Only, maybe not as bloodthirsty as Suarez seemed to be.

THEY GATHERED IN the cargo hold for a service honoring Tom, then launched his frozen body into space on a course that was at right angles to the ecliptic. With any luck, Tom would float forever, gradually moving farther and farther into deep space.

The Knoxville's Em-Max had escaped damage in the attack. The plasma cannon had wiped everything off one side of the hull, but the other side was undamaged, save for the point-defense systems that had been slagged by the mining lasers.

Unexpectedly, the cruiser had a secondary sensor array on the undamaged side. That meant Adam had less work to get the ship ready to travel.

He rigged a temporary yagi antenna for communications between the two ships, then tested the link. It worked. Jem and To'afa took all the spare oxygen tanks over to the cruiser. They'd have to remain suited for the voyage to the Bubble.

Once at their base, the ship could be brought inside. It was a tight fit through the lock, but there was plenty of room in the asteroid. There, they could commence repairs without having to work in vacuum.

The Swift base hailed them, wanting to know what was going on. The Martians had been watching, but without enough magnification to see details.

Suarez handled their query smoothly. From his transmissions, a third party would have to assume that the Deimos base was not involved in the battle and had no interest in the outcome, except for the concern that the pirates would turn on them next.

Listening to him, Adam reflected that the man was full of surprises. He was far more than he'd appeared to be at first. If the Feds heard the conversation, they'd blame everything on the D-R and assume the Martians were on their side.

Suarez glanced at him and said, "A few more raids like this, and the Martians will be forced to support us openly. Right now, they're undecided, but our taking the Knoxville is going to get them thinking. We need trade with them, and the only way to ensure it is to show them that we're a force that can contend with the Feds. We've just done that, and I'll bet some minds down in their council chambers are concentrated as a result."

He turned back to the radio to inquire about possible volunteers. Tom had to be replaced.

No Martians were willing to join them at such short notice. However, their success had convinced the council to publish their request. Suarez thought that it would only be a matter of time before they had crew to spare. Adam hoped that he was correct.

THE RETURN VOYAGE was slow. The Knoxville continually drifted off course. Jem was kept busy steering the cruiser, a task that was complicated by the damaged maneuvering jets. He had to roll the larger ship to position the undamaged jets correctly before firing them.

Stress levels were high, even on the D-R and it was a relief when they reached the Bubble. They left the Knoxville drifting outside for a day while they rested.

Twenty-four hours later, the crew began warping the big cruiser into the Bubble. It didn't exactly go smoothly, but they somehow managed to get it inside without damaging the airlock doors. The secondary sensor array was trashed when it grazed the metal wall of the cavern.

That didn't improve Adam's mood. He was going to be busy for several weeks fabricating parts and patching the leaky hull. If the Knoxville didn't have enough spare parts, they'd have to go looking for more.

That meant another raid on a supply ship unless the Mars colony had decided to work with them.

They'd started a minor war with the Federal Space Navy, and that meant raids would become more dangerous. Getting the Knoxville operational was a high priority. Having two ships armed with plasma cannon and protected by what the men were now referring to as the Q-shield would go a long way towards making them more difficult to defeat.

Adam set to work with as much energy as he could muster.

"CAPTAIN, WE'VE GOT to have more carbon-composite. I'm about three-quarters of the way done patching the hull, but I'm out of material. I also need components for sensors. They had replacements, but one of our lasers burned through the hull in precisely the right location to ruin all of them. Aside from those two issues, all we need to fly the cruiser is more trained crew." Adam was sitting in the captain's cabin, watching Suarez as he opened a folder.

The captain held up a photo. "See this girl. That's my daughter. She was the light of my life. Worthington, may he burn in hell, took her from me. Adam, you have my promise that I'll get you whatever you need to get that ship flying. With two ships, we can come at them from opposite sides. That will make it far more difficult for them to defend."

Adam reflected for a moment, then said, "Better make it so that we don't approach from exactly opposite directions. The plasma cannon blast might miss the enemy ship and damage one of our ships if we're directly in line with each other."

The captain nodded, his eyes intense. "We have to develop our own strategy. The Feds probably have experts planning battle maneuvers for them. We don't. It's only you and me." He put the picture back in the folder, then added, "And our experience. That's something they don't have. The crew of the Knoxville got some, but they didn't survive the lesson. We have to make sure that we continue to win."

Adam nodded. Suarez was driven in a way that he was not. The captain made good sense.

Suarez continued, "If we can capture a third ship, we'll become undefeatable. If the Mars people give us some crew, we can have our own space force. We've got the perfect base for it. I've been planning, and I think we could easily house ten thousand people here."

Adam hadn't considered that he'd been too busy with repairs. However, it seemed about right. He nodded, silently.

Suarez said, "Look. Here's what we'll do. We will collect some water ice, then go back to Swift and try to talk them into giving us what we need in exchange for the water. If they still aren't convinced, we'll intercept the next supply ship. It's going to arrive at Deimos in a couple of weeks."

He pushed back from his desk, signaling the discussion was at an end. "Buckle up your work in the next twelve hours, then shut everything down. We're leaving tomorrow."

"Yes, Sir." Adam stood to go.

"Oh, and Adam?"

"Yes?"

"I haven't said this before. I was initially worried that you'd be a liability. I was wrong. You have become an indispensable part of the crew. The D-R depends on you." His skin darkened a little with a flush of blood. "I depend on you. Now get busy."

# 12

## THE SECOND RAID

THE DIRE RHEA was closing in on the Mars supply ship's projected orbit. They'd been in transit for a week. Rather than hit the ship in the same position relative to Mars, Suarez wanted to attack early with the intent of making it appear that the pirates weren't frequenting the space adjacent to the red planet.

During the transit, Flynn had taken paint tubes outside, and with the aid of a pre-cut stencil, he had placed an irritated-looking bird's head on both sides of the front hull.

He'd gotten quite offended when To'afa had accused him of painting a chicken on the ship.

"No. You big oaf, that's a rhea. You know, the big flightless bird from South America."

To'afa hadn't taken offense at being called an oaf, but he wasn't ready to drop the discussion yet.

"Oh, so now you're saying the D-R is flightless? Is that it? Maybe I'd like a chicken better. At least they're good to eat." He rubbed his stomach suggestively, then smacked his lips.

Flynn was reduced to sputtering incoherence at this absurd non-sequitur. To'afa left the wardroom with a grin on his broad face. It wasn't often that he triumphed over the Irishman in an argument. He strode out before Flynn could recover enough to think of a suitable retort.

The art wasn't that bad. It looked more or less like a rhea, but one with an upset stomach, rather than a dire threat. Still, the painting gave the ship a sort of piratical air. At least it wasn't the standard skull and crossbones.

THEY ARRIVED IN the area that the shuttle would transit, then shut off extraneous power to wait. The D-R drifted, trying to keep a low profile. The supply ships weren't equipped with state-of-the-art military grade sensors. The pirate ship probably wouldn't be noticed until they began their raid.

The plan was to duplicate the first raid. They'd approach from the rear quarter, utilizing the supply ship's sensor array's weak spot. Once they were close, they'd fire the plasma cannon to burn off the antennas and sensors. Then they'd match up. The previous raid had gone smoothly, even though it was improvised. Suarez wanted this one to go down in the same manner.

The D-R coasted closer. Adam was watching the approach on the duplicate fire-control monitor in the engine room. His fingers twitched over the trigger button, but he restrained himself. The captain would make the call at the correct time.

As he thought that, there was a click as a heavy relay kicked in, then there was a deep humming sound from the capacitor bank as the cannon fired. The bluish plasma bolt shot towards the supply ship, then licked over its hull. Droplets of white-hot metal sprayed off into space as the antenna and sensor arrays burned off.

The supply ship hung off their starboard side, seemingly unmoving, although both ships were hurtling through the void. Suarez' order came through to the engine room.

"Engineer to the bridge. We're go for boarding."

Adam turned to the passageway, threading his way through the interior maze to take over at the nav station. The captain was waiting.

"I expect this to be like the other raid. Keep your station until we start staging supplies outside the hull. Then bring her closer so we can load without a long traverse. Understood?"

"Yes, Sir. I'll be here if you need me."

"I'm counting on that, Mr. Maxwell. Now turn off the shield so we can get out there."

A few minutes later, the cargo bay airlock thumped. Shortly after that, the crew could be seen jetting over to the supply ship's hull. They worked their way to the main bay and activated the external lock mechanism.

Adam watched passively. This was precisely how they'd done it the last time. There were no surprises. The men would shortly begin moving supplies out to stage on the ship's hull before pushing them across to the D-R.

The supply ship's lock opened, and all hell broke loose. Adam jerked upright, horrified.

They'd been ambushed. There was a force hidden inside the supply ship. The first volley struck both Flynn and Suarez, leaving their space suits streaming vapor. The rest of the crew ducked away from the open door and began to shoot back. The pirates were at a disadvantage, though. They were trying to shoot around the edge of the door, while their enemy was positioned in among the boxes and tanks in the hold. The Feds simply had to cover the door. The pirates had to look over the edge, risking being shot in the process, take aim, then shoot and duck.

Adam evaluated the situation. Prospects did not look good for them. Flynn was patching his suit while drifting away from the fight and Suarez was moving sluggishly. There was no telling from the bridge what his status was.

The other five were firing sporadically and apparently with little effect if the number of muzzle flashes in the darkened cargo bay was any indication. They hadn't reduced in volume at all.

He suddenly realized that the Feds would come pouring out at any minute. Once the superior force was outside, the pirates would be annihilated quickly.

Adam toggled the radio. "Rhea crew! Clear the door now!"

The crew moved as if it was Suarez' ordering them. Someone, it looked like To'afa, grabbed Suarez and dragged him away

Adam made some adjustments on the cannon, then waited, gritting his teeth in frustration and anger.

The force inside stopped shooting, save for a couple of shots at the D-R. They bounced off the hull, doing no damage.

The pirates moved cautiously away from the door, keeping their pistols pointed at the opening. After a minute, Adam could see movement inside. The Feds were organizing for a sortee.

The shapes of space suits gradually became clear in the darkened hold as the enemy approached the airlock. When they were just at the verge of exiting, Adam triggered the plasma cannon.

It hadn't nearly achieved a full charge. Nevertheless, the attenuated blue beam instantly ablated the enemies' armored suits. A huge puff of gas mingled with rapidly freezing blood and some pieces of something blew out of the open airlock, spraying into space.

Adam waited, hoping that a second shot wouldn't be needed. The cannon would take nearly fifteen minutes to recharge fully.

Things in the supply ship were quiet. The only radio chatter he could hear was that of his crewmates. Flynn was cursing in a steady low monotone. To'afa was dragging Suarez back towards the D-R, moving as quickly as his jetpack could pull their combined mass. The others lingered with their guns pointed at the door. If any enemy came out, they wouldn't get far.

The cargo bay airlock thumped as To'afa and Suarez came through. Adam got on the intercom to ask about the captain's status. He could hear nothing except some muffled thumps as To'afa pulled their suits off.

That noise continued for a couple of minutes, then there was nothing.

Silence.

Adam queried again. "Report the Captain's condition."

There was an intermittent sound that he couldn't identify for a moment. Then he realized with horror that To'afa was sobbing. The big man choked out an attempt to speak, then got himself in better control.

"He's...the Captain is dead. They killed him without any warning."

Adam felt the blood rush from his cheeks. It seemed unreal. They'd been pirates together, but now...what would happen. He'd relied on Suarez. The older man always seemed to know what to do.

Something changed in him at that moment. It was almost like the cannon firing relay clicking. His mind switched from confusion and doubt to a crystal clear vision of what to do.

"Understood. To'afa, secure his body in the hold, then open the airlock and prepare to receive cargo."

The next minute Adam switched to the radio.

"D-R crew. Clear the enemy hold, then begin moving supplies outside for transportation to our cargo bay."

The figures on the hull of the supply ship hesitated a moment, but then began to follow his orders.

The plasma burst had obliterated the enemy force. It had been weak, but there was enough power in it to vaporize them and burn through the interior wall of the supply ship and vent it.

Cargo began to flow across the gap between the two ships. Adam had approached carefully, and the surviving men were simply tossing boxes and packages at the D-R's open airlock. Most of the thrown goods sailed through and bounced off the far wall. To'afa was kept busy fielding the rebounding items.

After a bit, the pirates moved some more massive objects out. It looked like metal stock from the effort it took to move the mass. Then someone brought out a roll of composite carbon fiber sheeting. That was what he really needed to work on the Knoxville's hull.

The stream of items gradually thinned, then the pirate crew jetted back across the gap.

The airlock thumped. Adam flipped the take-hold warning, waited five seconds then fired the maneuvering jets to gain some distance between the two ships.

The D-R moved away, leaving the supply ship with its cargo bay gaping open.

The plasma cannon charge indicator suddenly glowed blue. It was ready to go again. Without thinking, Adam aimed and triggered off a full power blast.

The supply ship shuddered, then broke apart into three large pieces along with a hail of debris. Some part of the ship had still been pressurized, despite the first breach. That atmosphere blew out in gouts of sparkling crystals that pushed the ruined supply ship farther away.

Adam watched grimly. It wouldn't make up for the loss of the Captain, but there was a certain satisfaction knowing that they'd triumphed over the ambush. The Feds would understand that the pirates of the asteroid belt were not to be trifled with.

He turned to the Em-Max controls. The drive began to push the ship gently. It didn't accelerate with much force, but it kept at it. They would be moving at a respectable speed within hours. At the moment, he had no plans other than to return to the Bubble.

Once home, they could regroup. He thought about finishing the repair on the Knoxville. If it was armed and shielded like the

D-R, they could extend their operation and seek revenge on the Feds.

A space suit helmet that suddenly appeared on the fire-control monitor interrupted Adam's reverie. One of the Federal ship's crew was outside on the D-R's hull, looking at the plasma cannon. The helmet bobbed and then disappeared.

# 13

## A HITCHHIKER

HIS HAND QUIVERED over the shield button. A simple press and the person outside would be gone. He thought about it for a minute, and that was a mistake. Perhaps it was because the concept of death by vacuum had been remote and watching Suarez die had been too close. Whatever it was, the idea of the shield vaporizing someone's feet and lower legs, then vacuum draining the blood out of their thighs as they screamed soundlessly made him feel nauseated.

His hand activated the intercom instead. "To'afa. Jem get outside and get that marine off our hull."

Jem answered almost immediately. "The guy is outside the cargo bay lock, knocking. I think he wants in."

To'afa rumbled in the background, "I'll open up. You shoot him when he comes into the lock."

Adam's stomach flipped. "No. There's been enough death out here. Let him in. You'd want in if it were you and your friends had all been killed. Let him in. Make sure he's not armed first, though,

101

then strip him and bring him to the bridge. Maybe he'd like to be a pirate."

Flynn answered with a curse. "Damned effn Fed. Let's throw him out the airlock with no suit. Shoot me, will they?"

"No, let's bring him in and see what he has to say. Maybe we can get some useful information out of the guy. We'll head back to Swift and drop him there with a message for his masters. If they can't figure it out on their own, they need to be told that we rule out here."

There was the sound of discussion on the open intercom channel, then Flynn came on. "Are you sure about this, Maxwell?"

He pulled back. Was he sure? Not by half. Suarez was dead and, as the only other officer rank on the ship, that meant he was in charge. He'd been acting like everything was up to him. Was that a good idea?

Flynn was too impulsive for command. To'afa too slow to make decisions. Jem...maybe, but he wasn't self-motivated. With him in charge, they'd get little done.

The other two crew? Jake was full of hot air and self-indulgence. No, and Ryan Lembuster couldn't, as his father used to say, pour piss out of a boot with the instructions written on the sole.

It had to be him. He took a deep breath, then leaned forward. "That will be Captain Maxwell, now that Captain Suarez is gone. Yes, I'm sure. Now follow orders."

The intercom clicked definitively. After a few seconds that seemed like hours, he felt, more than heard the thump of the cargo bay door. If the fed tried to fight and was killed, well, that was too bad. If he was peaceful, then he might survive to get back home.

Killing in cold blood might have been the norm for the sea pirates of old, but Adam wasn't cut from the same cloth. He wanted to be left alone to create what? Well, a colony based at the Bubble would do for a start. He had visions of a future filled with mining ships and shuttles exploiting the resources of the belt. They could gather gas from Jupiter and Saturn, water from comets. Just about everything needed could be made out here. All they needed was time and no interference.

That was what he'd work to accomplish. Meanwhile, he shut the Em-Max down. No sense heading for the Bubble before he dealt with their captive. Definitely no sense in letting the man see their home. They couldn't let him go after that.

ADAM WAS SEATED at the nav station. It had been fifteen minutes since the airlock had cycled and no one had reported yet. He had been ready to go down there to find out what was going on, but now he heard feet in the passageway.

Jem walked in, all smiles. "Captain. No problem with the prisoner. No weapons. Lost the gun getting out of the supply ship. She says she's a marine, but looking at her, I'd say she was scared to death."

He swiveled the chair around. "Wait a minute. You said 'she?'"

"Ah, yes, Sir. The captive is a woman. Jake wanted to get a little overly friendly taking her spacesuit off, but I and To'afa convinced him that wasn't polite. Here she is, now." He turned and waved his arm.

To'afa was close behind the smaller figure that was just coming into the bridge. He studied her closely.

The woman was young. Probably younger than he was. She was fit, but still managed to give off a feminine feel, but maybe that was just him. He'd been in space with only men for a little too long. Her hair was cropped short in a black mat that dropped down her neck an inch in the back. He looked at her expression. She looked frightened, and that made him embarrassed that he'd checked her out so obviously. That wasn't acceptable behavior on Earth.

A sudden wave of defiance rolled over him. He was a damned pirate. They were expected to be masculine. He had nothing to feel sorry for.

He deliberately dropped his gaze to her breasts, then down to her hips. When he looked at her face again, she looked angry and slightly flustered.

"Welcome to the Dire Rhea. I understand that you're not here willingly, but we happen to have the only ride in this sector, so you're stuck with us unless you want to walk home."

Adam was amazed at himself. Where in blazes had he come up with such a dramatic and cliched greeting?

She cleared her throat. "Hmmpf. I wouldn't be here if you followed the law. I demand to be taken to the Ribbon station."

Adam frowned. Her voice quavered a bit. She was frightened, but not enough not to challenge him. Her attitude angered him.

"No. Every one of us has been driven off Earth by the Feds. They don't follow their own laws, or rather their laws are for the bottom ninety-five percent and not for the top five percent. Did Worthington think up your nasty ambush by himself?"

She started to speak, but he continued. "No. He's not smart enough. Someone in the space force must have planned it. What's next? Are you planning an invasion out here?" He waved his hands in an expansive gesture that caused Jem and To'afa to laugh.

He waited a moment, then added, "There's nowhere to invade. Your ambush cost us one of our best. That's unforgivable, and I take it as a declaration of war."

She'd regained some composure as he spoke.

"It's not war, you jumped up criminal. We're engaging in a police action. Robbing the supply ships was a cowardly act. You deserve punishment, and if your man had been law-abiding, he'd still be alive."

"Ah. I can see that we don't agree. Continuing like this will have no productive results. Let's start over. I'm Adam Maxwell. I was chased off Earth because I knew too much about Worthington's plot to take over. His daughter tried to convince me to help with the bombing. I'm the Captain of the D-R. Now, who are you? I'd like to address you politely."

Her mouth dropped open. Apparently, she'd been prepared for an argument or threats, anything but his sudden change of attitude. After a moment, she said, "I'm going to assume that you don't really want my ID number."

He shook his head sardonically.

"As you've already observed, I'm a corporal. Nile Jackson, of the Earth Space Navy Marines."

He smiled. This was actually kind of fun. He'd never had the opportunity to be in a position of outright dominance before. He'd have to try not to let it affect him.

"Nile, would you please tell me what is currently happening on Earth?"

Her complexion darkened even more. "That's not something you need to know."

He replied, "That's not something you get to determine. I asked, and you answer. That's the way this works. Now, tell me about the political situation."

She looked right and left. Jem and Flynn were on one side watching her closely, and To'afa loomed on the other. Her shoulders slumped.

When she looked back at him, her expression was distressed.

"Things are not good. First, there is no political situation there. Worthington has unilaterally declared himself President for life. The members of Congress have all been killed or disappeared. Most of the population is confused and waiting for someone to tell them what to do. The few, bold enough to protest, were hauled off by the Feds. The Space Navy is under Admiral Johnson's control. He's a new appointee, chosen by Senator— uh, President Worthington. The navy has been making routine patrols. Once the word came about your raiding, we were sent out to stop you. You are the first challenge that we've had. Obviously, we underestimated you."

He grinned wolfishly. She drew back a little in response.

"Obviously. We intend to control our own destiny. Earth forces aren't welcome out here. I'd like to see Worthington dead or in prison. His lying daughter, too."

She shrugged showing her lack of concern for his preferences.

He continued, "I'd like to know exactly how many ships the navy has at this time. How many are being built, when they'll be placed in service, and what plans this Admiral Johnson has."

She started to speak, defiance showing on her face, but he spoke over her.

"However, we'll get to that later. Right now, I've got work to do. One last thing: If you cooperate, don't cause any trouble, and give me the information I want, we'll see that you're returned to the base at Swift. You can figure out how to get home from there. We're not going to raid every ship that comes and goes, so you can probably get a safe ride back to the ribbon or Luna. I will not stand for any more ambushes. If your navy doesn't leave us alone, I will destroy their ships. All of them."

Her face paled. "That's—that's unthinkable. There are eleven cruisers, not counting the one out beyond Mars. You couldn't defeat that many."

Finally, some information he could use.

He replied, "That means there are only eleven cruisers in your force. We took the Knoxville. It's ours now. Apparently, your superiors haven't told you everything."

She looked in shock. "You took the Knoxville? But, their missiles..."

He waved his hand, and she quit speaking.

"Yes. Their missiles didn't bother us. Nor the point-defense pods either. We're currently rebuilding the hulk to meet our needs. She'll be armed better than she was when we're done."

The girl looked stunned. "Was...was that the thing I saw on the hull? Is that the weapon you hit us with?"

That was disclosing too much. He just smiled. "I think we're done here for the time being. To'afa will escort you to one of our empty rooms. Don't damage anything. If you do, you'll go hungry. The door will be locked, at least until I can be assured you'll behave."

He leaned back and motioned to the Samoan.

SHE'D GONE. JEM and Adam looked at each other.

"Now what, Captain?" Jem asked.

"I think I'll drop her at Swift. Maybe the Martian colonists will have a surprise for us by now. I hope they've found some volunteers. We need hands more than just about anything."

Jem said, "We do need help. Do you think she might want to be a pirate?" The expression on his face indicated more than just the desire for an additional crew member.

"Jem, I'm Captain now. I wish that Suarez had lived, but he didn't. Now I'm in charge, and I say that, pirates or not, we will treat our captives humanely. There will be no attempts to rape or seduce her. I'm not in the mood to put up with that. Treat her well as long as she behaves. Understood?"

Jem looked somewhat offended. "Geez, Captain. I didn't mean it like that. I'll make sure she's okay. The others will leave her alone. Okay?"

Adam waited a moment to see if he had anything else to add, then said, "See that you do. Now on another topic, is the cargo hold secure?"

"No, Sir. We jammed stuff in there every which way. We'll need some time to sort it out."

"Please get started on that. I'd like to have the supplies we captured squared away and inventoried before we get to Swift. That way I'll know if we need to request anything additional from them, and I'll know if we have anything to trade. They had to be expecting that stuff. They probably need at least some of it, and I don't want to make them too angry. We'll see about working out a trade."

Jem nodded. "Makes sense to me. I'll go and get the crew started on the cargo." He turned, but then stopped and turned back.

"Sir, I want you to know that I'm behind you one hundred percent. There isn't anyone else on this ship that can run her. You have to be Captain, although I wish Suarez were still in charge."

Adam nodded. "I do too. I miss him, Jem. He always knew what to do. I'm not that experienced, but I'm a fast learner. Just give me your opinion when I ask for it. That will help."

Jem answered, "Yes, Sir."

ADAM SET THE nav system for the return to Swift. Deimos was a quickly moving target that required ships to catch up with it as it tumbled around Mars. Calculating the course took the computer a couple of seconds, then it displayed a graphic solution. He studied it, then sounded the take-hold alarm.

The D-R's jets fired, turning the angry-looking bird head on the hull back towards Mars.

# 14
## NILE

ADAM WAS WORKING out in the empty part of the cargo hold. The gravity was not earth normal, but it was sufficient for him to generate a sweat. He snapped a high front kick, blocked, then turned to throw a back fist at his imaginary target.

Ms. Jackson was standing just inside the passageway, watching. He stopped instantly, feeling a little embarrassed. He was in the habit of working out daily, and the other crew members mostly ignored him. Their methods of fighting varied, but could all fall under the heading of catch-as-catch-can and fast-and-furious.

He'd forgotten that two hours previously, he'd made the decision to allow her to wander freely. Only an idiot would sabotage the space ship that was transporting them to freedom. He didn't think she fit into that category.

Now that he'd noticed her, she stepped inside the bay.

"Keep going. I was watching your technique."

He bowed slightly, as he might to an opponent before a match. "I was almost done with the Kata. What can I do for you?"

"Your moves remind me of our instructor in basic. She was second dan in Kempo. You've studied some kind of martial art. What is it?"

"Probably nothing you've heard of. It's kind of a mash-up of Kyokushin and Shorin karate. It's useful against multiple opponents and reasonably effective."

He looked down at his hands, then back at her. "Actually, I learned both styles. I've kind of figured out my own way of blending them so you won't find it taught anywhere."

She looked impressed. "Both styles? How long have you been studying anyway?"

He shook his head, deprecatingly, then answered, "Too long. Since I was eight, actually. The kids in school kind of resented me. I had to learn to defend myself since my father insisted that I stay in that school."

That led her to another topic. Her eyes flashed with interest as she asked, "Are you really the son of the Adam J. Maxwell?"

It was the same old thing. People always seemed to be interested in him because of his father, not because of anything he'd done.

He said, "Yes, I'm afraid that right. I'm the pirate son of the late and famous Professor A. J. Maxwell, inventor of the Em-Max modification that cut months off space voyages. I'm guilty, and before you ask, I never benefited a gram from the relationship. He insisted that I make my own way."

She frowned as she asked, "Even as a pirate?"

That caused him to laugh bitterly. "Even as a pirate," he said. "Your friends killed our real captain. I was the ship's engineer. Still am, I guess, but we've got so few men, that I'm the only choice."

That shut her up for a moment. When she spoke again, her voice betrayed strong emotion. "You killed my friends. You and your real captain are murderers. I'd kill you if I had any way to survive afterward."

"You probably would try, but you don't have a chance. Besides, that ambush was your idea. Wait. Don't say it. I know it wasn't yours personally. Some desk jockey on Luna or Earth thought it up. You got stuck with the dirty work, but you and your friends were the ones who shot first. We were defending ourselves."

"You had no right to defend yourself! You have no right to be stealing other people's supplies. If you were on Earth, you'd be in prison."

That pushed his temper over the edge.

"Listen, you blood-thirsty little..."

He stopped abruptly, tried to calm down, then continued. "First, if I were on Earth, I'd be dead. I knew all about Worthington's bomb plot. His daughter tried to convince me to place the bomb. He was the one who got about a hundred three-letter agencies to persecute me. I had to escape as best I could, and it wasn't easy. Second, the other men in the crew are mostly here because Earth doesn't want them. Third, Earth has rejected us. We owe no loyalty to the government. We're here in Mars orbit, trying to build our own life. Do you think we'd have a snowball's chance in hell of trading for the supplies we need to live, let alone build a base?"

Before she could answer, he spat, "No! Earth would rather have us die. We haven't, and that's inconvenient for them. I'm sorry about your friends, but we've got the right to defend ourselves. It's a natural law. We've claimed this space, and by Jupiter, we're going to keep it. If Worthington and his buddies want to exploit the asteroids, they will have to deal with us on our terms, not theirs."

His speech had been so fierce Nile stepped back, alarm showing on her face.

Adam passed his hand over his eyes, then added, tiredly, "I'm not going to hold it against you. I know you were trying to do the job you'd been ordered to do. People like you always end up paying the price when people like Worthington want something done. It's the way the world works."

Nile moved forward, coming back into his personal space. "Maybe. You've shown me one thing, though. That there are two sides to the situation. I hadn't thought about it from your side."

He said, "Why should you? You had your orders. Kill the pirates. If you'd killed all of us, you'd be celebrating. Hell, they'd probably give you a medal of some kind. I shouldn't care. I'm dumping you at Swift so you can jump on the next ship back. With any luck, you can still get a medal or a promotion. You can tell your superiors how weak we are, how we've only got six men, one ship, and a hulk in need of repair. That should be enough to earn their gratitude."

Nile's face worked a moment. She said, "You know I'll have to do exactly that. That's my duty. I owe my loyalty to the space marines."

He nodded silently.

She looked at his face expectantly. When he didn't reply, she asked, "Why are you going to set me free? You know what I'll do. Once I tell them about you, they'll send an overwhelming force, and that will be the end of your little rebellion."

"Is that what you think it is? A rebellion? We might be rebels if the Feds actually owned the solar system. As it is, they only control space around Earth and Luna. They don't have the strength to control it out here. I could say that any intrusion into our space by the Feds is an invasion. We'll fight to defend our territory."

"Sounds reasonable, when you put it that way, but what about Mars. Surely you don't think you own Mars too? Don't the colonists there have any say in the matter?"

"Of course they do. I suspect that Earth will eventually learn that the Martians' loyalty will be to their own people on their own planet. You know that they've been a dumping ground for political undesirables. Why should they be loyal to the government that kicked them out?"

She answered, "They depend on us for supplies. Without supplies, they're not able to sustain themselves. They have to be loyal."

He suddenly realized that their conversation wasn't going to result in either party changing their outlook.

Adam turned his back on her to pick up the towel he'd thrown on a box.

Nile was apparently angrier with him than he'd thought. She kicked the back of his right knee than tried to wrap her arms around his throat for a choke hold when he dropped.

There was a natural counter for that move. He caught her wrist, torqued her arm, then spun to the right, throwing her against the nearby pile of supplies. She staggered and fell down.

"Ow. That hurts. I think you broke my arm."

"Not a chance. I'm better than that. I only used enough force to get you off my neck. What were you trying to do? Break my neck?"

She tried to stand, then gasped. "My back. You hurt my back."

Adam shrugged his shoulders. "Sorry, you should have thought about that before you kicked me. If it's any consolation to you, my knee hurts like crazy."

"I'm glad you feel it. I...I guess I lost my temper. You seemed so unreasonable. I mean clinging to an indefensible position. I'm not good at arguments."

She carefully used a convenient box to lever herself up to a standing position. "Maybe I'd better go back to my cabin before you get that big ox to drag me back there."

"To'afa is anything but an ox. Don't call him that. Especially where he can hear you. He likes to fight, and you don't want to offend him."

She nodded, curtly, then started towards the passageway. Her back was obviously in pain. She staggered a bit as she reached the door.

He responded instinctively. He'd probably regret being nice, but that was something he couldn't help. The sight of her suffering dragged him forward to put his arm around her waist to help her along.

She jerked her head up, startled. "What? Now you're making a pass at me?"

That made him laugh. "No. You look like you need help walking. I'm offering assistance."

Her eyes softened a bit. "Thanks, but I can make it on my own."

Their faces were close. Adam looked at her and saw someone other than an enemy. He pulled her closer and kissed her lightly.

She leaned against him for a moment, and her mouth softened a bit, just an infinitesimal softening. The next second she pulled back, her eyes flashing.

"That's just the sort of thing I'd expect from a pirate. I'll make it back to my cabin on my own. Thank you."

He let her go, then stood there, feeling confused as she walked away slowly.

Maybe he was a pirate after all. His hand moved up to his lips as he replayed the moment, trying to memorize the feel of her body and her mouth. Would a pirate do that? He didn't know. More likely a real pirate would have grabbed her and dragged her to his cabin.

He imagined that scene. No. It was something he couldn't do. If she came to him on her own, that was different. He stopped, dragging his mind back to reality with an effort. Fantasy was fine, but it would never happen. Nile had made it clear that she despised him and his fellows. They didn't have any right to exist as far as she was concerned.

He sighed and turned towards the captain's cabin.

# 15
# NEGOTIATIONS

THE SHIP WAS approaching Deimos. Adam had been alone on the bridge while the other crew members were resting. Apparently, Jem hadn't been sleeping. He had wandered in a few minutes prior and was watching Adam maneuver the D-R into orbit.

Nile had avoided him for the past two days, but now she came into the bridge. She sat down next to Jem, giving him a friendly smile. He tried to focus on the controls and ignore them, but it was difficult.

The two were carrying on a quiet conversation behind him as he worked on the orbital insertion. He thought he heard his name, then found himself trying to listen in. It was distracting. Moreover, it made him feel misused. He'd dreamed about their brief kiss for the last two nights. Finally, he turned and said, "Can you two keep it down? I'm doing something complex here."

Jem nodded, wordlessly, but Nile looked up at him, then said, "Maybe it's too difficult for you." It wasn't the disparaging remark, so much as it was the smirk on her face that set him off.

"That's enough. Both of you, off the bridge, now!"

Jem jumped up and left quickly.

Nile remained sitting. She frowned at him, then said, "If that's what you want, Captain."

Now that she was alone and the competition was gone, he was torn about his order. He wanted her to stay, but he'd given an order, and she wasn't following it. He opened his mouth but could think of nothing to say.

She added, "Hadn't you better keep an eye on the nav screen?"

"The screen? Oh, yes," he said.

He sounded like an incompetent idiot. Something about her had gotten to him. All he could think about was that brief moment in the passageway. The beeping of the nav computer dragged his attention away from her.

The ship was ready for orbital insertion and was requesting permission to begin slowing. They'd gradually creep up on Deimos from behind. The approach period always seemed to him to take a disproportionate amount of time.

He made the required adjustments, then sat back to watch the screen. As he did, he realized that Nile was standing beside him, looking over his shoulder.

"You really shouldn't stand like that. It's unlikely that we'll have to maneuver violently, but it is possible. An unexpected rock, or--"

She placed her hand on his shoulder, and he forgot what he was going to say. When he looked at her face, she was smiling with a sort of wistful expression.

"Captain...Adam, I want to get things straight between us. I'm not the hard-hearted marine that you probably think. When you get down to it, I don't approve of what's happening on Earth. Worthington's coup overthrew the legitimate government, the government that I signed up to serve. All I've got now is the Space Marines. I owe my loyalty to them."

He nodded, his eyes on her face.

She continued, "I thought about what you said. You know, about you claiming this area and wanting to start your own colony. If our own history offers any guidance, maybe you've got the right to do that. I'm not qualified to say. What I guess I am saying though, is that you've made me see your side of the situation."

He nodded again, still not saying anything. Her hand tightened on his shoulder, then relaxed and moved in a small rubbing motion.

He placed his hand on top of hers and pressed. Her pupils widened, and her eyes became dark pools inviting him to venture within.

The computer beeped again, and she jumped, then pulled her hand back.

"I owe my loyalty to the Marines, Captain." She turned and strode out of the bridge without looking back.

What the hell had just happened? It was confusing. For a moment, he'd felt like they were on the verge of getting closer, then everything had changed. That infernal beep had broken the mood. He started to call out, but she was already out of sight.

The computer beeped again, demanding attention. Adam sighed and turned back to his piloting. Deimos was close, so he activated the docking sequence, then sounded the take-hold. Docking usually involved some abrupt vector and momentum changes. Not violent, but strong enough to throw unsecured humans around.

Swift base came on the comm. They'd acknowledged the D-R's approach an hour prior and now were sending him last minute docking instructions. He wondered if the Martians were going to be difficult about the supplies the pirates had preempted, or if they would be reasonable.

THE MANEUVERS WERE completed successfully, and the D-R was resting in the docking cradle. Adam was adjusting his space suit. Citizen Oliver was back from the surface and had asked for a meeting in his office. The docking tube was nominally pressurized, but a meteoroid had struck it, and the hole hadn't been patched.

Nile was already dressed for transfer. She'd donned her service space suit under the watchful eye of To'afa. The military rigs had some built-in advantages over civilian versions. She now had slightly augmented strength. Her suit had artificial muscles that would boost her ability by about thirty percent.

Flynn had cautioned against letting her use the suit, but suits were personal property. They not only were sized to fit their owners, but after a few hours of use, they smelled like their owners. No one liked the idea of trying to use another person's suit any more than they favored the idea of exchanging dirty underwear.

To'afa insisted on keeping an eye on Nile. Just in case, he said. Adam wasn't worried about her trying anything, but he humored the Samoan. It was a good practice to keep the big guy happy.

He finished securing the interior straps and adjustments, then buckled up.

"Okay. I'm ready for vacuum. Nile, let's go."

The two entered the personnel lock, then waited as it cycled. When the door opened, the tube extended before them, leading a curving path from the hull of the D-R to the Swift base. He motioned for Nile to go first. She looked at him through her helmet, her eyes showing no expression. He waved again, and she started down the tube.

THE TWO OF them were in Citizen Oliver's office. The Citizen was detained by some unknown business, and they had been politely told to wait. Nile hadn't met his eyes since they'd stripped off their space suits.

At the moment, she was studiously gazing at a painting that graced the wall over the Citizen's desk. Adam had glanced at it, then dismissed it from his consciousness. It was unfortunately ugly; some variety of modernism, he thought. Not worth looking at.

What she saw in the purple and green blotch was beyond him. He tried to think of something to say. Something that wouldn't show her how confused he was. Something nonchalant and carefree. Finally, he cleared his throat.

Her head didn't move, but she glanced at him out of the corner of her eyes, saying nothing. It was maddening.

Adam said, "I suppose you'll be reporting all about us to your superiors."

"It's my duty. The definition of duty is something you must do."

Still no real response to him. She could be really irritating if she wanted to be. This was apparently one of those times.

"Nile?" Now she turned toward him, face expressionless.

"I, uh, I wanted to say..." He stopped. He wasn't actually sure what he wanted to say.

She asked, "What? What can you say? Things are as they are. No talking will change them. Understand?"

Adam's mood dropped a few degrees. He hadn't been happy before, now it seemed like depression would be a step up.

He nodded miserably. "I do. I'm sorry. I--"

She interrupted, "I was ordered to arrest or kill you and your men. I failed. If I can avoid a court-martial, I'll be lucky."

He hadn't thought of that. "Tell them all about us, if it will help."

"I will do just that, even if it won't help. It's my duty, as I've made abundantly clear to you."

He waved his hand tiredly at her. "I know, I know. That's enough of the duty story."

She flushed, looked angry, and started to respond, but he was saved as Citizen Oliver entered.

"Hello. Uh, Engineer Maxwell, isn't it? And, who is this beautiful young lady? I'm told she is a Federal Marine."

Adam stood to shake hands. "Citizen Oliver, I'm now Captain Maxwell. Captain Suarez was unfortunately killed when we intercepted a Federal supply ship."

"I'm sorry to hear that, Captian." Oliver was very smooth, but Adam could tell that he was suppressing anger.

Citizen Oliver continued, "I thought that we had an agreement."

Before he could say more, Adam motioned to Nile and said, "Oh, you asked about her. This is Nile Jackson, Corporal, USSN Marines. She was part of the force that killed Captain Suarez." He paused dramatically, then added, "The only part that is left, unfortunately. I've decided to send her back to Luna."

Oliver's eyes narrowed in response to the obvious threat. Adam had conveyed two messages. He'd implied that he could deal with any Mars force as easily as his ship had dealt with the marines, and had warned Oliver about disclosing their negotiations in front of her.

Oliver pressed a button on his desk. "In that case, I think I should offer her our hospitality. My man will take her to appropriate housing, where she can wait for the next personnel shuttle from the Ribbon."

The door opened, and the aide that Adam had seen before came in.

Oliver said, "Corporal, please escort this young woman to the visitor's block and see she has whatever she needs."

Nile didn't say anything. She walked over to the door and exited, followed by the corporal. Adam's last view of her was obscured by the aide's back. The door closed.

Oliver instantly turned into another person. "I thought we had an agreement. What did you think you were doing, taking our supplies? I've gone to considerable inconvenience for you, young man, and this is how you repay me."

Adam flushed, temper rising instantly. He drew a deep breath, then said, "Citizen Oliver, I see that we're not on the same page. It was my understanding that we had not reached a formal agreement.

If you had been able to promise that Mars would trade with us, we would have proceeded differently. As it is, we need construction materials for our base and ship-building materials to repair the Knoxville. The supply ship was a convenient opportunity to get some of what we need."

Oliver's face had turned red. "Now see here! I've got the council to agree to consider your proposal. They will debate the idea of trade and make a fair decision. They have to take into account the possibility of reprisal by Earth."

Adam replied, "I suppose that could be construed as a positive step, but it does nothing for us in an immediate sense. We need supplies now." He decided that he had better concede a little. "I'm prepared to trade you the materials I don't need. We could use both food and medicines, along with volunteers."

Oliver grunted. "Those are rightfully our supplies that you are proposing to trade to us. This isn't how a legitimate trading partner would act. You've committed an act of piracy. Now you're trying to sell our possessions back to us."

"That's right. We are pirates, but by circumstance, not choice. Citizen Oliver, the Feds may kill us. I'm sure that's what they want and what they're going to try to accomplish. Trading with us might not be to your advantage. It certainly won't, if they find out about it. However," He held up his index finger. "However, if you don't, we'll have to get what we need by raiding your supply ships. Which would you rather have? A guaranteed trade with us that will benefit both sides or the guarantee of missing supplies?"

Oliver paused, thinking. "Obviously, I'd prefer trade over stolen supplies. The question is, how to keep the Feds from knowing."

A sudden inspiration struck Adam. "First, you need to report the supply ship as missing. Let the Feds find out from Nile, er, Ms. Jackson, that we're responsible. Tell them that you still need supplies. We'll take as many of the supply ships as we can. We can deliver the surplus to you. You can claim you never received it. I guess that the Feds are charging you for every gram of mass they ship, right?"

This supposition was on target. Oliver cursed. "Yes, damned leeches! They charge us triple what the stuff is worth."

"Ah. Worthington and cronies are getting rich at your expense, then. If you don't get the supplies, they can't reasonably expect you to pay, can they?'

"That's a point, young man. Then you're saying, you'll intercept the supply ships, give us what you don't need, and trade water and minerals for the things we can produce on Mars?"

Adam said, "That's basically the deal. We don't need everything in the supply ships. Not even a quarter of it. We do need more metal, carbon fiber, food, and medicines, along with men. We need workers desperately." He paused, then continued before Oliver could speak.

"Look. You have nothing to lose as long as you keep this under the table. You don't get the supplies from the Feds, you don't pay. Then when we give you the supplies, you keep it secret. They won't know. Besides, we trade you things we can get that you need. Sure, there might be a conflict, if we need something they've shipped to you and you need it just as urgently. In that case, we'll try to sacrifice in your favor. I don't know what else we can do to make this easy for you, though. I do know that we'll take what we need, trade with Mars, or not if you and I can't make an agreement right now."

Oliver nodded slowly. "I thought you'd take that position. In fact, I've got the authority to cut a deal with you. You've made a good case. We'll work with you as long as we feel you're dealing fairly with us. And, as long as we can keep it secret from the Feds. If it appears that the Feds might find out, we'll scream for their help as quickly as we can. Mars cannot afford to alienate Earth. At least, not at this time."

"I suppose that's reasonable," Adam said. "What about men? Is there any chance of volunteers?"

"Will you take undesirables? Even in our group, a group that has been ostracized by Earth, there are people we don't want. I've got six of them here on Swift. You can take them if you want."

"What have they done to be kicked off Mars?"

"There are three that have been convicted of burglary, theft, and felonious assault. One who misappropriated official funds, and two convicted murderers."

"The murderers. Are they insane, dangerous to everyone, or were they provoked in some way?"

"One was definitely provoked. He caught his wife with another man. Killed her lover, and beat her seriously. The other is just plain mean. Knifed a man over a glass of spilled beer. What do you say? Take them or not?"

"Uh, I think we'll take them. The only one I'm worried about is the mean one, and I think I've got someone who can ensure he behaves, so yes. We need help. I'll take them. Now, do we have a deal on the trade thing?"

"We do. Mars will deal with you. Now, tell me about this marine you've dumped on me. What do you want us to do with her? I can send her to the surface and make sure that the Feds never hear from her again. Actually, that would be best for both of us."

That was not what he had in mind for Nile. "No. I'd prefer that you put her on a return ship. That's what I promised her."

Oliver shrugged. "That's a needless step. She's breeding age. Mars needs children. We'll just keep her."

Adam started to speak, but the door flew open. His mouth dropped open. Nile was standing there, pointing a pistol at him.

"Nile, what?"

"Shut up, Adam! I'm taking you prisoner. You're going to fly the D-R directly to Luna where you'll stand trial for piracy."

# 16

## A SURPRISE

CITIZEN OLIVER MADE an abortive movement toward his desk drawer. Nile switched the weapon's muzzle to him without saying anything. He lifted his hands slowly and leaned back in his chair.

"You won't get off this station, young woman. You have nowhere to run. Put the gun down, and we'll just forget about this unfortunate lapse in judgment."

"Not likely!" she said. She waved the gun at Adam. "Get on through the door and head for the docking tube. Don't try anything. I'm going to be far enough behind you that it won't work. I mean it! Now move."

Adam shrugged at Oliver, then turned and moved slowly towards the door. Nile stepped aside into the Citizen's cabin, just far enough to be slightly out of reach.

He wondered what she had in mind. Surely she didn't think she could hold him prisoner and hold off the crew of the D-R for the entire voyage to the Ribbon. A part of his mind was evaluating his chances of taking the gun away from her. The odds were low. The rest of his mind was surprisingly calm.

He looked over his shoulder. She wasn't following. Instead, she'd stepped over to Oliver and was whispering something to him. He nodded. She turned to Adam and motioned with the gun. "Go on. I'm right behind."

What in a methane hell was that about? He half turned, but she snarled and said, "Don't stop. Move it. Jog."

He picked up his pace, moving in the nightmare slow-motion that the light gravity required. There was no sign of anybody in the passage until they reached an open door about half-way to the docking port. He glanced in, surprised. Oliver's aide was lying on his side on the floor, unmoving.

Adam half turned again in inquiry. Nile snapped, "He's just unconscious. Let's go."

They burst into the staging area. He looked at his suit.

"Grab it. The tube is pressurized," she said.

He lifted the unwieldy mass, slung it over his shoulder, and grabbed his helmet with his free hand. Nile had done the same thing, but she somehow had managed to keep her gun hand free. He grinned in acknowledgment of her ability. She made a face, and said, "I'm a Marine. I can handle myself."

There was something to be said for her training, even if the suit weighed only a fraction of its earth weight. It still massed thirty kilos.

The airlock cycled, and they moved through, half walking, half bounding down the snaking tube to the D-R. The hatch was closed, and he keyed the activation sequence.

Once through, Nile dropped her suit, then turned to him, the gun still in her hand, but pointing at the deck midway between them.

His eyes focused on the lowered muzzle, then climbed to her face.

She smiled. "We'd better disconnect and move off. It's not safe here."

This was not precisely what he'd expected.

"What? What's going on then?"

He tried to sound authoritative like a pirate captain in charge of the situation, but his voice wobbled. Probably due to the fact he was breathing hard from the exertion, he told himself.

Nile lowered the gun entirely. "The Federal garrison on the surface found out about your visit. They've sent some men up to ambush you the next time the D-R showed up. Shelby told me."

For some reason, this triggered a burst of irritation. "Who the heck is Shelby? Your boyfriend?"

She gave him a look that he didn't understand, then she said, "Really? No. Shelby is Oliver's aide. He's a little too talkative for his boss's plans. He started bragging about how he would have first dibs on my services when they sent me down to the surface. I said you wouldn't allow that. That's when he came up with the information about the feds."

That would take some thinking about. He shoved it back in his mind for later consideration. "Well, what did you tell Oliver? He did let us go without sounding an alarm."

She sighed in exasperation. "Can't we get this hulk moving? They might try to break in or shoot at us. Are you that confident in her hull?"

"The hull? Uh, I'm not too worried, unless they have something heavy. Oliver?" he reminded her of his question.

"I told him that I'd tell the Feds that he was working with you if he didn't let us go. He's going to say that we were down the hall when we escaped, and he never saw us. The feds are waiting for his signal. I'd say from what I've heard that he's trying to play both sides at the same time."

"That would make sense. He's in a sensitive position. Mars can't afford to break with Earth. They need supplies. They also can't rely on us. We've been all talk and little action as far as trading goes. That reminds me."

He clicked the intercom on. "Jem, get everyone down to the cargo hold and unload the supplies we've separated out for the Martians. Do it fast. Jam their inner cargo lock, so it can't cycle and throw everything in there. We're leaving in ten."

"What the? Don't you need those supplies?"

"Yes, but two things. The Feds will wonder why we left the stuff. Oliver will have his hands full trying to convince them he's innocent. The other thing is, I told him we'd trade, so, by Pluto, we're going to make good on that."

"What if the Feds start shooting?"

"The hull will probably handle that. We can push the stuff outside with the grappling arm, and it won't take too long. If they shoot, I hope they miss. If they keep on shooting, I'll have to shoot back. They won't like that."

Nile frowned. "Don't push me. I got you out of that because it was in my own interest. I still haven't forgiven you for my friends."

He wanted to snap at her, but restrained himself and spoke calmly. "I regret your friends. And, I regret my friend, Captain Suarez. We've been over that. Look, I'm sorry, okay?"

She looked to see if he was serious, then nodded slowly. "Okay, I'll try to give you some credit for that."

THE D-R'S MECHANICAL grapples broke free of the Swift station's dock. There was a jerk as the ship pulled away from the dock, vectoring off at right angles. Adam hit the maneuvering jets hard, sending a strong push away from the little moon and turning on the Em-max at the same time.

Using the primary drive that close was strictly forbidden, but he didn't care, and he figured Oliver wouldn't say anything. There would be no damage, in any event.

The D-R wallowed a bit, then gained speed, moving away from Mar's ecliptic on a heading that would take them out of the solar system. He'd wait for a few hours before he re-vectored. Now that the Feds knew about them, it was important not to fly directly to the Bubble. They might be visible if one of the Earth radar systems happened to be looking, but the ship's albedo was so low that it would take a one in a million chance for them to be optically detected.

That consideration got him to thinking about possibilities. What would they do if they were found? They weren't ready to defend the Bubble. Maybe he'd make some additional plasma cannons, besides the one that he had in progress for the Knoxville. There was no reason they couldn't be mounted on the asteroid's surface.

Maybe it would be a good idea to begin searching for an alternate base, too. Nothing like the Bubble had ever been found, but they might select a more massive asteroid, say somewhere at the far reaches of the belt, or maybe a small moon. Saturn or even Uranus might offer something that they could use. That's what they needed. The Bubble could then become the forward base for raiding. They could retreat to the second base if it became necessary.

AFTER THEIR ESCAPE, Nile seemed to have decided that the D-R wasn't such a bad place. Her training had given her the skills and attitude to get along with the crew without allowing them any liberties. She made it clear that her self-enforced boundaries were to be respected.

As far as he was concerned, this was hopeful. She didn't go out of her way to see him, but she didn't avoid him, either. He was still dreaming about that kiss, though. It often took the form of a fantasy that she was in love with him, but trying to suppress her feelings out of a sense of duty.

He sought her out and tried to make it appear as if their meetings were by accident. Whether or not he fooled her, he didn't know, but she played along with his clumsy attempts to be near her.

THEY WERE FIVE days from Mars. Adam had sent the D-R back into the plane of the asteroid belt, and they were now moving towards the Bubble.

He was resting in his cabin when the intercom sounded. It was Flynn.

"Better get up here, Captain. We've got a faint emergency signal."

Adam grunted, sat up, and pulled on his pants. Having a woman onboard had changed some of the crew's habits. Before he might have responded in his underwear. Not now, though.

The alterday shift was clustered around the vid when he arrived.

"What is it, Flynn?"

"I thought it was way off in the belt, not near us, Captain. I was wrong. We got optics on it. It's too soon to tell, but I think it's a damaged mining ship."

He looked. It was too soon to make out any details, other than an intermittent faint flash as some moving thing reflected a tiny bit of sunlight.

If they went over there and there were survivors, they'd have to rescue them. Salvage law said that survivors had the option to keep their ship if they could pay for the rescue attempt. He jerked, then relaxed. He didn't need to worry about that. They were pirates. They could just keep what they found. Anyway, he was going over there. He wouldn't want to be stranded in space, and he didn't think anyone else deserved that fate if something could be done about it.

The D-R re-vectored, The Em-Max thrust was directed to slow their considerable speed. It was a complex nav problem, but the computer handled the bulk of it. All he needed to do was to okay the course correction.

They began to move toward the signal.

Nile arrived in the bridge. He didn't notice until she leaned over his shoulder to look more closely at the vid screen. She swayed and brushed against him, and his mind went blank for a moment.

She must have sensed his reaction since she straightened quickly. When she spoke, her tone was business-like and formal, putting a damper on his rising temperature.

"Captain, hadn't you better detail a boarding party. They need to be armed too. It's possible that this is a trap. You'd better be ready."

She was right. He hadn't thought of that. They needed to be ready for quick action.

THE D-R APPROACHED the signal slowly. Once they were close enough, they could see that it was unlikely to be a trap. The other ship was rotating slowly, turning end over end. As the hull came around, they could see a large gash in its side.

Jem said, "That rip would have dumped her atmosphere instantly. I'd be amazed if there are any survivors."

Flynn agreed. "They wouldn't have lasted as long as a pint o' stout at a teetotaler's wake."

# 17
## SALVAGE

THE D-R COASTED near the tumbling hulk. The damaged ship was well worth salvaging. The Knoxville needed parts to bring it back into service.

Barring the Mars colony trading parts for ice, there was no alternative. They had to board the hulk and stop its rotation.

Adam considered the problem. There were two alternatives, and he was hoping that the first one was going to be possible. If the damaged ship still had power and if the drive was usable, they would bring it along with them. If it couldn't be flown, there was really no alternative except to remove what they could.

The second alternative was less desirable for two reasons. Their cargo hold was already over half full, so they'd have to take only the most valuable parts, and some of those would be difficult to remove. The other problem was that the disassembly would take a long time. They'd be hanging in space, working on parting out the hulk for days.

He shook his head. It would be simpler to work inside the Bubble. It would be much easier to do the job in atmosphere rather than vacuum.

He stood. He'd come to a decision. The crew, experienced as they were, couldn't be relied on to evaluate the hulk's status properly. That was a joke. Neither could he if he were honest with himself. His pretension of being an adequate ship's engineer had worn pretty thin during the Knoxville's renovation. Still, he was the only one with some of the more specialized knowledge.

Flynn was left to guard the bridge.

"Just keep an eye on us. You probably won't have to maneuver, but if you do, try and keep close, in case we have to come back in a hurry."

"Understood." The little man eased into the vacated nav seat.

Nile looked at him curiously. "How about me? You should make me go with you, right? I can't be trusted here unless you lock me up again."

He studied her face to see if she was serious, then said, "I don't believe you would do anything bad, but you can come along if you like."

She shook her head at his obtuseness. "Adam, you have got to get over that attitude if you're going to survive out here."

This was embarrassing. Flynn was smirking. On the other side of him, Jem was nodding in agreement. Even To'afa was trying to suppress a grin. What was she thinking, lecturing him on his attitudes?

Nile waited until he was about to speak, then added, "I'm telling you the truth. You can't afford to take anything or anyone for granted. I could easily shoot Flynn in the back and take the ship. I know enough to get it back closer to Earth and call for help. I'd get a big reward for getting rid of the pirate problem."

Flynn wasn't smirking now. He was glaring at her.

Jem reinforced her statement. "She's right, Captain. You always look on the bright side of things. It's like nothing bad ever happened to you."

He took a deep breath, preparing to start yelling, but his hurt feelings faded and he exhaled slowly.

"Yeah. I guess you're all correct. Despite all the stuff that's happened to me, I still want to think that everyone will be nice. I don't know if I can change that. I'll try to remember in the future."

Nile smiled at him, and the rest of the crew faded into the background in his mind.

She said, "I don't want to change you totally. That streak of optimism is one of your nicer qualities. It's just that you have to think of all the things that can go wrong if you're to keep this enterprise boldly going where no man has gone before."

He flinched. Did she really have to add that silly phrase? Then he nodded, his eyes fixed on hers. If only she were more disposed to smile at him in that way.

Flynn cleared his throat.

Adam dragged his gaze away from her. It took him a moment to think coherently. Then he told himself that he was really far gone. The men were smirking openly at him. He reached deep for all the professionalism he could find.

"As I said, Flynn keep watch here. Everyone else suit up. We're going over to see what we can do. That includes Ms. Jackson."

He started towards the hold without waiting for responses. That should show them he was capable. Unfortunately, he was so intent on his goal, that he partly missed the door, hitting the jamb with his shoulder. He cursed under his breath. He couldn't even exit a room properly. Why they expected him to lead them was a mystery.

He straightened and strode as quickly as he could. After a moment, there was the sound of the others following him down the passageway.

THE HULK WASN'T rotating rapidly, but its motion was fast enough to make a landing on the hull difficult. The only place to land was at the center of mass where the angular momentum was least. If they tried to take hold near the ends of the ship, they'd be unable to hold on and would be thrown into space. While Flynn was probably capable of picking them up again, it wouldn't be fun, and it would take far too long.

The center of the hulk was their target.

The problem with that strategy was that there was no access to her insides there. The closest opening was the gash in the hull, and it had jagged looking edges. Adam didn't like the looks of that. It would be easy to get snagged and rip a space suit.

He was hovering in space about twenty meters from the rotating mass, studying the problem. There was no easy solution. He waved his arm in frustration.

To'afa took that as a command. The big man accelerated and landed at the center. He bounced, adjusted his jets, came back against the rotating hull and snagged an eyebolt. These were commonly found on the outsides of most ships and served as tether points for maintenance workers. He unclipped his leash and snapped the carabiner into the loop.

He waved, and the others followed, one at a time. To'afa fielded them, and they were quickly tethered to the hulk.

The cargo bay door was closer than the personnel hatch. That was the obvious place to enter. Adam set off, letting out his leash as he cautiously moved towards his goal. It was a slow process. He had to keep one hand on the hull at all times. That wasn't terribly difficult since there were evenly spaced eyebolts around the hull. The problem was keeping his tether under control. It wanted to tangle, and that made it hard to keep it tight.

The centrifugal force increased quickly. It became harder and harder to support his mass. He'd started toward the hold door headfirst, but he had turned around. Now it was like he was lowering himself down a rope over an infinitely deep cavern.

Adam felt disoriented. The perspective combined with the sensation of weight activated the ancient primate reflexes against falling. He clung tightly to the line for a moment, eyes closed.

He knew this couldn't continue. Sooner or later, he'd slip. The leash should hold him, but climbing back up it would be nearly impossible. He opened his eyes, slid down a bit farther, then paused again. He looked up at the others. They were silhouetted against the darkness, clumped up together at the center of the hull.

He drew a deep breath, then looked down. The cargo hatch external access was even with his waist. He'd made it! He slid down until he was facing the hatch control. It was the standard system, a lever to pull out and rotate. There was no coded locking system. That was thought to be unnecessary. There had never been any reason to secure a ship. There were no burglars in space.

He pulled the lever, rotated it, and the hatch began to retract. A bit of fumbling and he had secured the leash to the nearby eye. It was now stretched between the original eyebolt and the hold door, leaving him dangling on a short length that remained free. He worked his way into the hold and slid down to the end of the rope. He'd have to detach from the rope and drop about a meter to end up standing on the wall.

That needed to be done with caution. If he landed badly and fell backward, he'd topple out the door and go sailing off. That was not something he relished thinking about. He hung there, waiting for the ideal moment to let go.

Jem's voice came through the radio. "Are you in, Captain?"

It startled him, and he let go, hit hard, and fell sideways along the edge of the opening. His body was safely inside, but his face was looking out the opening at the bow of the ship. He jerked back into the hold.

"I'm in. One at a time down the leash. The first one in, secure your rope to the eyebolt outside the hatch, then someone at the center of mass can unhook it. Pull it inside and secure it on one of the wall tie-downs. We'll need to go back the same way if we can't get this merry-go-round stopped. We can't exit from here.

Too much angular momentum. Flynn would have a devil of a time catching up to us."

A few minutes later, they were all safely inside. There was no point in closing the hatch. The interior had to be hard vacuum with that hole in the outside. Jem opened the interior hatch, and they moved cautiously through the dark ship.

The interior showed the effects of explosive decompression. Bits and pieces of debris floated everywhere. The bridge was horrible. People had died messily in there.

Adam tried not to look at the frozen, bloated bodies. The place was full of frozen drops of blood that had come from the two corpses as they died. The fact that space was an inhospitable vacuum was burned into his mind.

They moved the bodies to a cabin where they could stay until the immediate problem of getting the rotation stopped could be solved.

The nav computer was undamaged, but there was only a little power. Adam cross-checked it again. There might be just enough to activate the jets. The controls were different from those of the D-R, and that added an undesirable level of complexity to the problem.

He touched the controls, hesitated, then said, "Take hold. I'm going to give it a shot."

He looked around. The others were holding on, so he fired the starboard bow jets at the same time as the port stern jets. The hulk shuddered as the momentum began to slow. The jets continued to burn, but the power indicator on the nav screen dropped quickly. The system was using battery power, and it was fading fast.

The jets stuttered, then died. The nav screen was unresponsive, and there was no way to see out. The only good sign was their apparent weight had decreased. The ship's rotation had to be almost stopped.

"Okay. I think we've got it slowed down. Can't get any more out of it anyway. Check the cabins for more crew. Take the ones we find to the cargo hatch and send them outside. That's the best we can do. Nile, you come with me. We're going to the engine room to see if the reactor can be restarted."

The rotation was almost all stopped. They traversed the passageway to the engine and reactor with minimal effort. Once in the engine room, Nile kept her light on the reactor controls while he inspected the system.

It had shut down automatically. Reactors had a fail-safe that was activated by a hull breach, and this one had worked perfectly. The batteries had been at about seven percent. That implied that the accident had happened about seventy hours ago. That was assuming that the battery pack here discharged at the same rate as the D-R's. He wasn't sure about that.

There was an override. The designers had wanted to ensure the reactor didn't go critical when the hull lost its integrity. A rock strike, passing through the hull in the wrong place, could damage the reactor, allowing it to super-heat. The over-ride was there for precisely the situation in which they found themselves. The surviving crew would need the power back on, as would a salvaging team.

Adam made a few adjustments. There was a sudden humming sound, transmitted through the floor into their feet. It deepened, then disappeared. The lights came on at the same time.

He could hear someone cheering through the radio system.

"Alright. That's enough celebration. We've still got a lot to do," he radioed back. He turned to Nile. "The engine should be okay. Let's go and check the rip in the hull."

She nodded, the movement barely visible in the darkness of her helmet.

They turned and headed toward the damaged section.

# 18
## SURVIVORS

THE RIP IN the hull looked like it had been caused by a glancing high-speed collision. Whatever had hit them had glanced off after ripping an eight-meter by one-meter hole in the outer hull. The presence of now solid beads of molten metal was proof that it had been something fast. A slow strike would not have melted the hull metal; it would have simply torn it.

Three of the crew cabins were open to space. The cabin doors were pressure tight so the hole would not have automatically killed everyone on the ship.

That had been caused by something else. The atmosphere supply tubing was mounted against the hull in the cabin walls and had suffered some damage. When it had been opened to vacuum, it somehow resulted in the entire ship losing pressure. That wasn't supposed to happen.

Adam inspected the damage. It appeared that a single check valve was responsible for the pressure loss. The valve was designed for a maximum pressure of twenty psi, which was twice the normal for spaceships, and it should not have failed. The check valve was generally located near the atmosphere regeneration equipment, so he went down the passage to the closet near the cargo hold.

He swore under his breath when he saw that someone had removed the guts of the valve. Perhaps it had been sticking, and the ship's engineer had pulled it, gambling that there would never be a pressure leak. It didn't matter now. What did matter was that he could manually turn off the supply line to the ruptured cabins. Once the leaking line was shut off, they could pressurize the rest of the ship.

He looked at the gauges. Naturally, they all were pegged at zero. The entire system had drained. Most ships carried extra O2 and nitrogen tanks.

The nitrogen was also used for the maneuvering jets and was stored in several tanks located around the ship. The O2 was always close to the regeneration system. He found a bank of tanks in another room that contained enough O2 to do the job. The atmosphere would be thin, but breathable.

THE DERELICT WAS beginning to come alive. The atmosphere had reached eight psi. It was breathable, but cold. The reactor was running again, happily at work charging the batteries. With the resumption of electric power, the heating system had come alive. The ship was going to be habitable shortly.

Adam, Nile, and Jem were in the bridge while the others worked at making some order out of the mess. The nav comp was running, and the ship's sensors were reporting that they were dangerously close to a large mass. The D-R was within one hundred meters, so the sensors were working as they should.

Adam searched the database automatic flight log. There was nothing for the past seventy-eight hours, then he found the collision record. He backed up past the event, then began to replay the recording at high speed.

"By Jupiter's seventh hell. Would you look at that! They weren't hit by a rock. That was a missile."

The other two bent over as he replayed the sequence. The mining ship had apparently been minding its own business, approaching a smallish asteroid when they'd detected a missile launch at extreme range. They had tried to position their ship so the asteroid would act as a shield against the incoming threat.

It had worked—partially. The missile had exploded when it struck the asteroid, but part of the projectile had ricocheted off and caused the damage to the ship. There was no indication of who had fired the missile.

ADAM BACKED UP the replay several hours to check the earlier records. Five hours before the fatal event, the mining ship had been approached by what appeared to be a Federal cruiser. The cruiser had requested they transmit the ship's id and log. They'd complied, and the cruiser had left.

For lack of a better theory, he concluded that the cruiser's captain must have turned around and fired the missile. He knew of no reason for the attack unless the cruiser had decided that the miners were pirates. The alternative was that the Feds were simply bloodthirsty and enjoyed killing innocent people. That was a little too much to believe.

The thought spooked him. What if the cruiser were hanging around nearby waiting for another victim? Here they were floating at almost a dead stop, making a perfect target. They needed to get moving.

Flynn came on the comm. "We've got two survivors down here."

Jem radioed back. "Where are you?"

The comm clicked. They could hear Flynn talking, apparently giving someone an order.

"Stay back, blast your eyes. I'm not your enemy. We're salvaging the ship."

The alterday chief suddenly answered. "I'm in the secondary hold near the stern. Two people made it into an emergency bubble back here. I'm bringing them to the bridge."

"Bring them up as quickly as you can," Adam said.

THE TWO WERE a man and a woman. They'd been checking mineral samples taken from some of the ship's finds. The hold they were in, was at the end of the atmosphere tubing and didn't evacuate instantly. When the ship was struck, the two had climbed into the emergency bubble and sealed it before the pressure had disappeared.

The rescued crewman said, "It's been days. We were sure we weren't getting rescued, so we've been sitting in the dark trying to get the courage to kill ourselves. We were out of water and only had a few hours of air left. It's lucky that you came when you did."

The woman wasn't speaking. She was pale and breathing rapidly. Shock of some kind, perhaps.

The man took a deep breath. "Air. Ah. That is so good. Smells clean, too. Believe me, the air in that bubble was bad. Ugh."

He looked at them, his eyes straying up and down Nile's figure. She'd removed her suit while Adam was searching the comp. The tight thermal outfit that was worn inside the space suit fitted her like a second skin and left little to the imagination.

Adam mentally bristled as the man's eyes lingered on her body.

To cover his anger, he asked, "What's your name? Her's, too. What's the ship called? And, what did you do to make the Feds take a shot at you?"

The crewman held up his hands, palms towards Adam. "Whoa. Whoa. Take it easy, mister. The Random Chance is our ship. It looks like Shirley and me are the only ones left, so that makes us the owners. You don't get to come on my ship and ask me questions like that."

Adam gritted his teeth in frustration. The fellow was going to be a problem.

"Okay. She's Shirley. The ship is the Random Chance, and who are you?"

"I'm Jason LeFleur. Alterday nav."

The guy appeared to be rethinking his confrontational attitude.

"Sorry. We've been through hell. To answer your final question, I don't know what we did for them to shoot us. It was cold-blooded murder if you ask me. We're not armed and couldn't possibly be a threat to a cruiser like that."

That had been obvious. The mining ship was an early model, one of three different types that were exploring the belt. None of them were armed. Adam mentally grinned, except the D-R.

He asked, "Did the Feds say anything that might give you a clue to their attack?"

"They said they were looking for pirates when they stopped us. Our ID package was in order, so they told us to go on about our business before they made an example of us. I guess that's what they thought they were doing. Making an example. But, who would even find us? It doesn't make sense to me." Jason shook his head in puzzlement.

Adam said, "It makes some sense. The Feds are trying to secure Earth, but they've been having some difficulty near Mars. Some pirates have raided the shipping."

Jason looked puzzled. "Why would anyone raid the shipping? All we really want is to get out of this ship and back to Earth. We're on our third mission and close to being maxed out on radiation exposure. Pirates don't make any sense."

When looked at that way, he was right. Pirates didn't make sense. However, his shield invention changed that. If space suddenly wasn't a death sentence, he was sure that more and more people would leave earth for space. It hadn't been good for a long time, between corruption and corporate capture of legislators. Now that Worthington had implemented a fascist dictatorship, things would get worse quickly.

He said, "The Feds were right. There are pirates. I'm sorry to tell you that the Random Chance is our ship now. We need it. We also need crew members. If you join us, I can promise you that radiation won't be a problem. As for living arrangements and food, we're doing pretty well without the Feds. You really don't have any other choice, but to work with us."

Jason didn't like that. His face grew red as he spoke. "You have no right to this ship. We're going to take it back to Earth."

Suddenly the woman spoke. "Shut up Jason. Can't you see? These are the pirates. You're not going to be able to bluff your way out of this, the way you usually do."

She turned to Adam, and said, "I assume that you're the Captain. I'll be quite pleased to work with you. I'm the Chance's main-day nav. Jason here isn't alterday nav. He's cargo and a total screw-up. Captain Boyd was looking forward to getting rid of him as soon as possible."

Jason glowered at her but said nothing.

Adam nodded. "What's your last name?"

"Shirley Nelson. I've been on the Chance for two voyages. This is my third. You say that radiation isn't a problem? How do you propose to make that fantasy come true?"

"I have my own ways. We need to get the Random Chance back to our base. We can work on the hull in comfort there. There are a few modifications we'll make. One is to install our shielding system, and the other is to arm the ship. The Chance is going to be the third ship in our fleet."

THE TWO SHIPS arrived at the Bubble within a few seconds of each other. They'd traveled nearly side-by-side, separated by only kilometers.

The D-R's alterday crew had taken over the Random Chance. Shirley had quickly agreed to join them as nav. She now sat at her old seat on the damaged ship.

They'd brought Jason over to the D-R and assigned To'afa to keep an eye on him. If he tried anything, the Samoan would probably pound him good, then put him right back to work. Whatever happened would be Jason's fault. One had only to look at the size of To'afa's biceps to realize how powerful he was.

Things were looking up. Now they had three ships and a base. The main issue was finding more people. There was too much to do and not enough hands to do it.

# 19
## BUILDING A FLEET

REPAIRING AND CONVERTING the Knoxville had been a long and challenging project, but it was done, except for final testing. The cruiser floated in space near the Bubble, reflecting only a tiny bit of light.

They'd first covered the hull with mirror-bright silvering, then hidden that under nano-carbon particles.

The group had come to view Adam as not only the Captain but as the ultimate authority when it came to rebuilding the ships. He, on the other hand, was consumed with doubt. Despite the success with the cold plasma shield, he was reluctant to rely on it during a battle. As a back-up, he'd had the silver-plating installed. That would reflect high-power laser strikes. It probably wouldn't work forever against a potent attack, but it might give the ship enough time to mount its own attack.

The old statement that the best defense is a good attack was one that he had taken to heart. The silver-plating had one major drawback. It made the ship stand out like a beacon in a coal mine.

Even though the silvering was designed to diffract light and looked white, every stray photon bounced off the hull, making it highly visible from a distance. That would never do, so the obvious solution was to cover the silver with a low emission coating. The carbon nano-particles were perfect. The surface could be sprayed on quickly, and the material was usually available.

The carbon made the hull almost invisible against the blackness of space. The only way it could be seen was if the ship passed in front of a light source or was illuminated at close range.

In a battle, laser fire would burn off the carbon but then be reflected by the silvering. Once the carbon started to burn off, the ship would become clearly visible. At that point, the plasma shield would have to provide the bulk of the defense.

The active plasma shield was installed. Adam had made an effort to treat the generators with the same silvering and carbon. That would make it harder to damage the shield with lasers. They built and mounted two plasma cannon one on the bow and the other mounted amid-ships. He had run some calculations and, although they weren't definitive, he thought that the plasma cannon blob would be deflected by the Em-Max drive.

Mounting the second gun on the middle of the ship didn't entirely solve that problem. It was installed on gimbals so that it could cover over half the sphere surrounding the ship. The bow gun had an even greater field of fire. It could reach anything on any side of the ship, except directly aft. Together the two provided almost full coverage.

After some debate, they'd renamed the Knoxville. It was now the Phoenix. It had died, then been reborn from the fires.

Whenever he glanced at the silent ship, Adam was filled with pride. He'd done an excellent job on it. They had a distinct advantage as long as the Feds didn't figure out his plasma systems.

The next project was to upgrade the D-R to the same level as the Phoenix. The silvering was in place, as was the waist gun.

They were now engaged in adding the carbon particles. After that was done, there would be time to work on the Chance.

Everyone except Jason had agreed to rename the second mining craft. He'd argued that the Random Chance was a fine name that they had no right to change. They'd thought about it for a while, then compromised by naming the ship Hell's Chance.

Everyone liked the implication that any enemy meeting it wouldn't have a chance in hell of prevailing. Even Jason agreed after sulking for a day. The Chance was still waiting for the rip to be repaired. That task was next in line, but they were short of materials again.

The nice thing about having the Martians who had been "volunteered" was they could operate two ships, or man one and continue the renovations, albeit at a slower pace.

The rapid depletion of shipbuilding materials provided the motivation for the decision to take the Phoenix out. There had been no signal from Citizen Oliver that the Martians were prepared to trade. Adam had hoped that they could make a common alliance. Based on the lack of communication, he suspected the Feds had stopped that idea cold.

There were two possible targets for this raid. The Mars supply ship was the obvious one, but he was reluctant to try it again. The Feds would undoubtedly be planning on another pirate raid. This time, the results might be far worse. Even so, they'd eventually have to hit the supply ship again, unless the Martians suddenly got rid of their overlords and became trading partners.

The other possibility was the one that he was leaning toward. The majority of the asteroid exploration and mining activity was closer to Earth. There was no reason to go as far out as the Bubble for most miners. There were plenty of asteroids with likely mineral concentrations much closer to Earth orbit. Without Adam's shield, the miners were anxious to avoid any more time in space than necessary.

Even with the shorter voyages, few of the miners made it to retirement age. Most suffered radiation damage that resulted in fatal cancers. If insurance underwriters were any gauge of danger, being a spacer was the most dangerous occupation.

The fact that the miners were mostly conscripted by the Feds and had little choice didn't matter. Not one company would provide life or health insurance for miners, and neither did the government. If a miner didn't strike it rich and manage to keep enough to take care of himself when he inevitably became ill, his best option was voluntary euthanasia.

Adam decided that the Phoenix would move sunward, into the center section of the belt. They would be more likely to intercept mining ships there.

For the most part, the miners were secretive and kept to themselves. There was not a lot of radio chatter in the belt. It made no sense to let others know where you were when you found a rich ore deposit.

There were stories that many ships had made their fortune by jumping another ship's claim. This idea was reinforced by the undeniable fact that there were always ships going missing. Some of these, at least, might have become victims of another mining crew's greed.

If they could find a mining ship, they could intimidate it into letting them board. Adam didn't feel good about taking everything away from a mining crew, but a few supplies wouldn't be missed terribly. Besides, he thought that some of the miners would jump at the idea of joining them.

Earth didn't offer much to the miners. They had been forced into the job, and they weren't treated well when they were no longer able to work. Another alternative would be met with serious consideration.

The radiation shielding was something that would convince a lot of them to join. He'd have to figure out how to provide medical care for the ones that had been exposed to too much radiation. It suddenly became critically important to him to locate and convince a doctor to join them.

A SKELETON CREW of six could fly the Phoenix. The rest of the pirates remained behind to finish the D-R and then start repairing the Chance. The "undesirables" they had gotten from Mars were left to work at the Bubble. Adam and Nile had agreed that having an unreliable crew on the current mission would present an unwarranted risk.

They left the Bubble in Flynn's control. The Irishman had an abrasive personality, but he could get people to work. He was also motivated by a dislike of the Feds and the urge to become rich. There was no doubt in Adam's mind that he'd get as much done on the ships as possible.

# 20

## THE FIRST FLIGHT OF THE PHOENIX

THE CRUISER MOVED through open space, sensors straining to detect asteroids. The belt held close to two million chunks of rock that were at least one kilometer in size. The largest ones had been visited first and were now claimed by the Feds. The government had kept miners from making bases on the large rocks, and there was some buzz that the Space Navy planned to build a base on Ceres.

Ceres would be large enough to have more gravity than the Bubble, but Adam was sure that it wasn't as hospitable. Finding an almost perfect habitat was unheard of luck. The Bubble made the ideal base, and its near-Jupiter orbit location made it even more desirable.

It would be a long time before anyone else discovered it unless they were unlucky.

The asteroids were divided into various types. The C-type asteroids provided a good source of carbon, and in fact, that was where they'd mined the raw material for the nano-carbon coating for the ships. Of the others, most miners looked for the M-type. These were mostly nickel-iron and had a high albedo and were predominantly found in the middle of the belt. A mining ship's fortune could be made by a particularly good M-type asteroid.

Contrary to popular opinion on Earth, the asteroid belt is mostly space. There might be millions of asteroids ranging from the dwarf planet, Ceres down to rocks a few meters across, but the volume of space in the belt is so huge that they are generally quite far apart.

The Phoenix had inserted itself into a solar orbit that was roughly in the middle of the belt. They were keeping a close watch on the sensors for other ships, although none had appeared.

Jem's voice came over the comm. Nile and Adam were talking quietly over cups of soup in the mess hall. Adam was pleased about the chance to speak with her in private.

It was not that she was unfriendly to him. It seemed that she was spending more and more time in his presence. They were main-day crew along with Ryan. Jem, To'afa, and Jake were alterday.

"Do you really think that you have a chance at recruiting Miners?" Nile asked.

He sipped his chicken noodle soup, then answered. "I think that many of them don't like Earth. They should jump at the chance of working on ships that have radiation shielding. I believe they will be happy to help build a new colony as long as they can count on living a better life than they'd have on Earth."

She made a snorting noise, then began to cough. It looked like she'd swallowed the wrong way. She gasped, then coughed again. Suddenly alarmed, he stood and pounded her back.

Nile gasped, "Water!"

It took him a moment to understand. He passed her a glass, and she drank, coughed again, then took another sip.

"I nearly choked to death when you said that."

"What did I say?" he was puzzled.

Nile had recovered. She smiled, then said, "That bit about having a better life than on Earth. You realize how bad that makes Earth sound? We're trying to live in a vacuum, a place with hazardous radiation, occasional rocks that might hit you at high speed, no amenities for humans, and the Earth authorities want to hang us. For this to be a better life, you must think Earth is horrible."

He nodded slowly. "I guess I do think that. Look, I don't know your history, but mine wasn't that good. I'm a dep. None of the uppers would give me the time of day, even if they knew who my old man was and what he did. Worthington is going to loot every penny he can, rip what personal freedoms still exist to shreds, and generally make life miserable for the vast majority of humans. I'd say that living out here, even with all of the problems, is far better. At least we're free."

"That's not really accurate. We may be free in some ways, but everyone has to obey orders, or all of us might die. Do you think you're better than Worthington?" She looked serious. Her eyebrows were knit, and her face was a little flushed.

He found himself breathing faster. It felt like he'd just been attacked and he was about to snap back at her. Then things fell in place. She was trying to be helpful. He hadn't seen that aspect of their situation.

Obviously, he felt free, he was running the show. What about the others? Jason, for instance?

"I understand, I think. You're saying that in some ways I'm no better than Worthington. Right?"

Nile shook her head. "No. You are better than Worthington. You are trying to get all of us in a position to have a better life. He's just stealing everything he can get and exploiting the population. He doesn't care about people. I've been watching you. You do care."

Adam tried to smile and make a joke about it. "Well, it's because I watched that video. What's its name? Oh, yeah. Ten Steps to be a Pirate Captain for Dummies."

"No. I'm serious, Adam. I can see that you do care. You don't know everything, but instead of bluffing, you ask for help. You listen to the crew. They would do anything for you."

The smile faded from his face. "Would you? Do anything, I mean?"

She unexpectedly flushed. "I'm a Federal Marine. If I were any good, I'd have killed you or be taking you to Luna to face justice. You're wanted, you know."

"Yeah, I know. But you didn't kill me, so would you?"

She leaned closer, smiling now. "Don't feel too safe. There's still time to shoot you in the back if you start throwing your weight around. Seriously, though, I've been thinking about it. You've treated me well. I know you're unhappy about Suarez. It wasn't me. I wasn't in the hold, and I never got into the fight. I got there too late. All I could do was jump to your hull." She stopped talking.

He leaned toward her. Her eyes seemed to grow larger, dark pools that invited him to look deep inside. He placed his hand along her cheek and pulled gently. Just the friction of his palm against her face.

She pulled away, stood up, and came around the table. He had risen when she did, expecting her to be upset. He didn't know what he'd do if she were.

As soon as the table was out of her way, she practically flung herself into his arms. They kissed.

Adam forgot about the ship, the crew, everything. Kissing Elseth had been a non-event compared to this. His mind was whirling. He held her, refusing to even think about letting her go.

She pulled back slightly, breathing fast. "Captain, I think you've got a Space Marine on your crew."

"I don't want you for my crew." He pulled her closer, and their lips met again.

When they broke, she placed her head beside his and whispered in his ear. "I'll be crew, as long as I can serve under you."

It was his turn to pull back and look at her face. She looked slightly embarrassed, but she nodded.

He pulled her tight again. "I've got a job I want you for. Are you available to work on it?"

"If it's what I think, I'm more than ready. I think I've been ready for some time."

The walked down the passage hand-in-hand to his cabin.

THE SENSOR SUITE detected a ship after another two days. Adam and Nile were lying in each other's arms. Their relationship had been met with quiet amusement by the crew. Jem had remarked, "I was wondering when you two would get around to seeing what we all saw. You're not real good at hiding your emotions, Captain."

Adam had stored that observation away for later reflection. He hadn't realized that he was so transparent. Nile must have known how he felt from that very first kiss in the hall. He thought he'd be embarrassed, but maybe later. Right now, he was too interested in exploring the miracle that was Nile.

She lifted her cropped head from the pillow when Jake came on the comm. "Adam, you need to get to the bridge. It sounds like they've detected something."

He groaned, stretched, then said, "I always thought it would be nice to be needed. Now I'm not so sure."

"They need you to tell them what to do," she said, getting up and pulling on clothes. She looked down at him. "So do I."

That statement was followed by a kick to his behind.

"Gods, woman! That's taking liberties with a superior officer."

"You've been taking liberties with me, so it's only fair."

"Okay. Okay. You're right. I'm getting up."

THE THREE ALTERDAY crew were huddled over the comp. Jem turned as the two came onto the bridge.

"Captain! We've got something along the Ceres vector. It doesn't mass enough to be a cruiser or supply ship. It must be a miner."

"Let me check the data, please." He pushed at Jake's shoulder. Jake moved, letting him get close.

"You're right. It isn't massing nearly enough to be a Fed. Must be a miner, but what is it doing coming from Ceres. That vector must mean that they've been visiting the Fed base there."

Nile said, "Unless they came in from another direction, then re-vectored. They might not have been at Ceres. Still, we'd better expect them to be Feds or have a Fed or two onboard."

Adam nodded. "We've got two hours and twenty minutes until we're close enough to use the short-range comm system. If they see us and hail before then, don't answer. I don't want to broadcast our location all over the belt."

The main comm was easily powerful enough to reach Earth. The short-range system signals would go just as far, but they were so weak, that it was highly unlikely they'd be noticed against the background noise. Now, if the Feds were smart, they'd assign an AI to the job of analyzing all the signals from the belt. That would be a problem for them. They'd have to go to modulated laser pulses for communications.

That was line-of-sight and had little scatter unless the light beam happened to hit a reflective surface. It would be better to use that mode for inter-fleet communications. Very few ships used the method, even though it wasn't beyond their capabilities. If he shot a laser at the oncoming ship, they either wouldn't notice, or they'd think it was a hostile act, perhaps a targeting trace for a missile.

"Nile and I are going to get some food. I suggest that everyone else take the time to eat and rest a little. The next few hours could get quite interesting."

THE SMALL SHIP continued moving towards them, showing no sign that it had detected the Phoenix. They were now close enough to use the comm system.

Adam was inwardly nervous, but outwardly, he felt he should show the confidence that would mark a real pirate captain.

"They haven't seen us yet. That means that our low-emission coating is working. That's an advantage the Feds don't have yet."

Jem answered, "They might have seen us, but think we're Feds. Nothing else in space that masses this much."

Whether they'd been seen or not, it was time to spring the trap.

"Hail them. Tell them to cease accelerating and stand by for boarding, please." Adam turned to the others. "Suit up. Get to the hold and get your jetpacks on. Full weapons."

It was gratifying to see the men turn and sprint down the passage. Somehow, and without his actually realizing it, they had become a crew; his crew.

The small ship used the close-range system to respond, thankfully.

"Unidentified ship, this is the Nautilus II. We're a chartered scientific research mission. Please identify yourself."

Adam thought quickly. He'd failed to plan for a false identity. He thought it was a little too sneaky for his preference, but it would also allow them to board without resistance. Expedience and safety came before his moral qualms. Using the Knoxville name was out.

He randomly grabbed for another city name in the same general geographic area, then answered, "This is the USSN cruiser, Memphis. Nautilus II. Confirmed. We're going to board you. No worries, just a routine check."

The captain on the smaller ship answered immediately. "Memphis. That's not a name I've heard. Please confirm identity."

He responded, "We're the USSN Memphis, just out of the Luna yards. This is our shakedown cruise. You haven't heard of us due to security reasons. Please comply with our orders. Stand-by to be boarded."

After a moment, which betrayed the other captain's hesitation, the sensor suite showed that the Nautilus II had ceased to accelerate. It was coasting, waiting for them to match up. Adam checked the comp. It had the solution ready. He sounded the Take-hold warning. There would be some solid thrusts as they re-vectored.

After fifteen seconds, he initiated the maneuver. There was a jolt as the first jets fired. The vidscreen view skewed in response, then corrected itself. They were on their way.

Thirty minutes later, the two ships were within one hundred meters of each other, apparently hanging still in space. The fact that they were moving rapidly towards Jupiter didn't concern them. They were matched in speed and vector.

The boarding crew jetted over. Adam had made Nile wait on the Phoenix, much to her disgust.

"I'm the only trained marine you've got. I know how to board an enemy ship. You need me over there, Captain."

Her use of his title showed her irritation.

"I need you here. If anything goes wrong over there, use the cannon. Then take the Phoenix back to the Bubble. Take control and try to have the best life you can."

"That sounds like you're expecting to get killed. No, you don't! Not when I've just found you, you idiot."

That wasn't quite what a crewmember should say to her captain in public. He looked around. The other members of the boarding party were trying hard not to laugh.

He shrugged wryly at them. "You know how it is, I guess," he said, addressing the other men. They snickered.

"Nile, I'm not going to get killed. Just do what I asked. Point the cannon at them. A little visual threat should go well as a back-up."

She grudgingly nodded, then turned to head back to the bridge. He lifted his hand to wave at her but stopped when she turned back toward him. She strode back to him, grabbed his face and planted a kiss on his lips.

"I mean it. Don't get killed."

This time when she left, she continued down the passageway.

THE NAUTILUS II was what it had appeared to be; nominally a mining ship. Captain Ngombe had chartered it to a group of astro-geologists. The lead scientist, Dr. Xipang, explained to Adam.

"We are studying type X asteroids. There's a theory that Tholen subgroup P-type asteroids, which as you must know, Captain, are darker than the main X grouping, and that implies..."

He continued to drone on with his exposition, something about possible chemical composition that might lead to conditions favorable for the formation of life if the asteroid landed on Earth.

The scientists hadn't questioned the lack of Federal markings on their suits. Captain Ngombe had been quiet when they'd entered his bridge, only greeting them briefly, then retreating to sit at the nav station and watch suspiciously, as he talked to Xipang.

Adam jerked. He'd almost been asleep. He felt sorry for Xipang's students. The man was boring. Now he'd stopped and was looking at Adam, presumably expecting some kind of answer.

"Uh, I'm sorry, Doctor. I was thinking about your research. What was the question again?" he improvised.

"Ah, it's good to meet someone who can appreciate how ground-breaking my theory is. I asked if you had located any small P-types. We know where many of the larger ones are, but small ones, smaller than a hundred meters, are not easy to find."

Suddenly, his patience wore thin. It was time to let these people know who they were.

"Dr. Xipang, that will have to wait." He turned to Ngombe. "I have business that will require the presence of your entire crew, Captain. Would you please call them to the control room? We can get this over quickly with a little cooperation. Thank you."

No sense not being polite. The old story about catching more flies with honey made sense.

Ngombe looked suspiciously at him, then issued the order. The crew began to straggle into the bridge. Adam waited until they were all assembled. The rest of his crew had remained in the Nautilus' cargo hold.

He called Jem. "This is the captain. Briefing started."

That was the signal for the crew to move to the critical parts of the smaller ship.

Jem answered, "Affirmative, Captain."

He turned to the mixture of scientists and crew. The Nautilus had six men plus Ngombe. The crew were the ones who might fight.

There were ten scientists; seven men and three women, none of whom looked to be capable of fighting in any way other than verbally.

"Scientists and miners. I'm sorry to inform you that pirates have captured your ship. We are from the Phoenix, and yes, it used to be a Federal cruiser. Captain Ngombe, before you decide to resist, please look at the vid. The Phoenix is only a hundred meters away. You can easily see the structure on the bow and the similar one on the waist. You're facing weapons that can destroy your little ship. My crew has orders to burn you out of space if anything happens to us. Your course of action should be apparent. Cooperate with us."

He paused, scanning the group for reactions. The scientists all appeared to be in a state of shock. The crew looked angry, but no one seemed to be ready to take a step that might lead to their deaths.

"I'm going to offer you a choice. We don't randomly kill prisoners. In fact, we go out of our way to accommodate prisoners' wishes. We do, however, need supplies. My crew is searching your ship for items that we need. Sorry, but that's the way it is. We're pirates, after all."

Captain Ngombe and Dr. Xiapang began talking simultaneously. Xiapang looked over his shoulder at Ngombe, anger on his face, then started shouting, trying to drown out the Nautilus II's captain. Ngombe stood, took two steps and swung his right hand. The punch struck Xiapang's temple with a thud, and the smaller man dropped in his tracks.

The Nautilus crew stirred restlessly. The violent act almost incited them to attack. Adam drew his sidearm, thumbed the safety off, and aimed at Ngombe.

"Anyone starts anything, Ngombe will be the first to die," he shouted.

Ngombe stood still, his eyes on the open bore of the pistol. He slowly raised his hands. As he did, the rest of his crew calmed down, then followed his lead.

Adam shook his head negatively. "Captain Ngombe, this is not the kind of behavior I want. Please do not do it again."

Ngombe said, "I've been wanting to punch that idiot for three weeks. He wouldn't shut up. He thinks he's too important to listen to us mere mortals. So, I knocked him out. It's my responsibility to keep my passengers and crew alive and safe, Sir. What are your intentions for us?"

Adam gave a deep sigh. He'd been afraid that he would have to shoot someone. The idea that he would actually contemplate killing someone boggled his imagination momentarily.

His mind churned over possibilities for a moment, but then came up with the only one that made sense. I've got to act like a hardened pirate. I've set us on this course, now play the part to the max. Now it's necessary to take command here.

"Understood, Captain Ngombe. I see that you felt your action was necessary. In the future, please allow me to make that decision. I'll take it poorly if you punch anyone else."

Ngombe calmly answered, "Yes, Sir. I assure you that I don't normally knock passengers on the head. Will you tell us what you intend to do with us?"

Not that again. It was a problem for which he had no easy solution.

"There are options for you. We are, as I said, in need of supplies and ships. The fate of your ship is, therefore, sealed. We also need men, recruits, to help build a life in the belt, free from Federal oppression. If you join us, I can promise nothing but hard work, occasional battles, and freedom.

How far you progress, how wealthy you become, how successful you are will be up to you. We are building a society based on meritocracy.

Every spacer already knows the necessity of self-responsibility. There is no big brother in space that will come riding in to save you if you don't do your job. Our society is the same.

If you join us, I see no reason why you should not retain your ship, provided you earn our trust.

Now, how about the rest of you? Experienced spacers are our priority. Scientists who can help establish a base will also have the opportunity for research. We intend to have our own working society eventually. Scientific knowledge and analysis will be a big part of our future.

Are there any volunteers?"

He drew a breath, then thought I've got to learn to be a better orator.

He looked at the group, scanning from left to right.

The crew all turned to look at Ngombe, waiting for him to tell them what to do. This implied that he was a good captain. They relied on his judgment.

The scientists looked at each other out of the corner of their eyes.

After a moment, one of the younger men said, "I will. I'll join you. I'm in debt on Earth. My wife divorced me, and I haven't got a chance of getting tenure. I'm an astrophysicist, but I know a little about building habitats in vacuum. I'm Lawrence Peters."

He glanced defiantly right and left as if he expected one of the others to disapprove.

Three of the other scientists slowly held up their hands. That made four. Better than nothing. If only Ngombe and his crew would join.

Something in Ngombe had changed. He moved slightly, then lowered his hands. "I can't speak for my crew, Sir, but I would rather join you than lose my ship. I completely agree with your objective. The Feds haven't treated me well. They don't treat any miner well, but I suspect that they have my name on a list of undesirables. I've been on the wrong side of politics in the past. Now with this new order, I believe they will try to confiscate all of the independent mining ships. I might find myself in worse condition, were I to stay with them, then I would be if I joined you."

"Captain Ngombe, I'm very pleased that you feel that way. You will understand that talk is cheap, and actions speak louder than words. You will still have to earn our trust. Anyone else want to join?"

All but one of the Nautilus' crew agreed. The hold-out was a man who actually wanted to join, but felt that his duty was to his aging mother. He'd only become a miner so that he could earn enough to support her.

The remaining scientists were reluctant to give up their positions. Xipang was sitting up, holding his head gingerly. He whispered to one of the women, and she relayed his desire to be returned to Earth to Adam.

It could have been much worse. All told, this was a good start. The problem now was how to return the ones who wanted to go back. It looked like they would have to head for Swift again.

That had its own set of problems. Sooner or later the Martians, as represented by Citizen Oliver, would have to make a commitment. They would likely elect to stay with Earth. They needed the supplies and the colonists too much to make a clean break.

THE NAUTILUS II would be a liability until it was armed. If it were present, Phoenix's ability to respond to an attack would be limited by the necessity to defend the smaller ship. Unless he decided to let Nautilus fend for itself. That was something that Adam couldn't do. He thought about it, but he was constitutionally unable to be quite that ruthless.

There might be some circumstance that made it necessary, though. It was better all around to send it back to the Bubble to refit. Once the Nautilus was armed and shielded, they would have a fleet to be reckoned with. They only had four ships, but with shields and the cannons, they would be able to attack a force at least twice their number.

After some deliberation, Adam assigned a skeleton crew of Jem and Jake to the Nautilus II. He didn't want to lose Jem, but Jake and Ryan couldn't be depended upon to get the ship to its destination. To'afa was going to be useful in keeping the new crew in check if they decided to be recalcitrant. He thought about sending Nile, but there was no way he was going to go anywhere without her. Maybe he was just selfish, but that was the way it had to be.

He solved the problem of the four scientists at the same time. It was sure that they wouldn't be much help on the Phoenix. However, they could reasonably be expected to fit into life at the Bubble. They had technical skills and would probably be able to help with either habitat construction or with refitting. The other scientists stayed on the Phoenix.

The two ships parted ways, the Nautilus headed to be refitted, and the Phoenix turned towards Mars. Adam would put those who didn't want to stay off at Swift. It would also give him another chance to negotiate with the Martians. He hoped that this time, they could work out an agreement that both could live with.

NGOMBE TURNED OUT to be a competent captain, having captained two prior, successful voyages. His crew both respected him and relied on his judgment. Once he fully understood the tactical advantage of the shields and the cannon, he became quite enthusiastic. He hadn't lied. He had almost as much reason to hate the Feds as had Suarez.

He was close-lipped about it, however. Adam couldn't get him to disclose any of his back story, other than he'd been so downtrodden that the idea of asteroid mining had seemed a welcome opportunity. Given the radiation-lowered life expectancy of the profession, that said volumes about his past life.

The two of them spent hours discussing strategy for the small fleet. If they could bring all four of their ships into battle at the same time, the strategy would depend on how many enemy vessels they faced. It was a given that none of the current generation of ships had an advantage in acceleration, turning ability or sensor suites. The Fed ships mounted long-range and short-range missiles with conventional warheads; at least they had heard of no nukes so far. The Fed's point-defense system was powerful, but it was old tech. It was a variation of the old sea-based Aegis system.

The point defense system used a combination of radar-guided short-range missiles to intercept incoming missiles and two to four modified Phalanx CWIS turrets. The radar domes for these turrets had been miniaturized. They no longer looked like the robot that had given them their nickname, R2-D2.

This generation was shaped like a thick pancake with the 20mm Vulcan cannons mounted to cover half of a sphere. They were dangerous weapons that could defeat both incoming missiles and boarding attempts.

The Vulcan's round was heavy enough that it could penetrate a space ship's hull, and its lethality was increased by the lack of ballistic drop.

Once fired, the round would continue on the same trajectory until it struck something or was captured by a gravity well. The main weakness of the system was that its velocity was ploddingly slow when compared to that of a space ship. This meant that its best use was to create a storm of projectiles that might intercept an incoming missile.

Given these two weapon systems, the obvious attack method was to use the plasma cannon at its maximum effective range. A direct hit would burn off all external antennas on the target. This would leave the Phalanx still operational, but its fire would be unguided. A closer cannon burst would take out the Phalanx systems, rendering them unable to fire.

As for the longer-range missiles, they could also be taken out by a plasma burst, as Adam had previously discovered. The shield system provided far more protection against incoming debris than the armor plate the Fed cruisers depended upon.

The two discussed their options. They wanted to avoid dogfights. Splitting their small fleet up to go one-on-one would minimize their advantage. They decided that their preferred plan would utilize a loose formation, where one of the mining ships led. It would fire the first plasma burst. The Phoenix would be next. Its hull was thicker than that of the mining ships so it could sustain more direct hits.

The other two mining ships would follow, using their cannon to destroy long-range missiles, while the Phoenix closed in. Once close, the cruiser would attempt to burn all point defense turrets and missile pods off the targets.

They thought that this attack would be sufficient, as long as they weren't faced with too many ships.

# 21

# ANOTHER TRAP

THE PHOENIX WAS approaching Mars orbit. The voyage had given Adam a chance to learn about and organize the new recruits so that he now had enough crew to have two full shifts. That was an advantage in one way, but a disadvantage in another.

The disadvantage was mostly to him, personally. Nile had moved to the alterday shift. While To'afa was intimidating, he wasn't suited to lead a shift. He could serve as muscle to keep any rebellion under control. Nile was both quick thinking and was trained to take on a leadership role. She took over as alterday lead in place of Jem.

This arrangement had the effect of making Adam feel more secure about fitting the new men in and simultaneously making him suffer due to the lack of time he could spend with Nile. It was nearly impossible to have a few minutes alone with her.

Ngombe stayed on main-day with Adam. He made no complaint about the assignment. He could have easily taken the lead on alterday, but he understood the necessity of earning Adam's trust.

It would be too easy for him to lead his men in a mutiny if he were not under direct supervision. He understood that and worked diligently to show Adam that he had bought into the vision.

They were working toward an independent settlement; one that was not controlled or exploited by – it amounted to the same thing, Adam thought – the Feds. They needed to become self-sufficient, but, without outside help, and being essentially at war with Earth's government, that was going to be a difficult task. Luckily, there were supply ships to raid and miners to recruit. He shook his head in amazement at his situation. He had never, even in dreams, thought he'd end up a pirate.

ADAM WAS AT the nav station, working on the fine adjustments needed to insert into high Mars orbit, then to decelerate and drop to intercept Deimos. He was nearly finished cross-checking the final solutions when the sensor suite alerted.

Nile was there before him, bending down to check the readings.

"It looks like a supply ship." She turned to look at him, an eyebrow raised. "I thought they were scheduled thirty days apart. It's only been, what...seventeen days since the last one got in?"

He shrugged, then answered. "I think that's about right. But, you know the Feds. They don't bother to ask our permission when they schedule a mission."

"It's puzzling and a little suspicious. Do you think Mars has been screaming for help against the evil pirates?"

That seemed unlikely, given that Oliver had given some indication that they weren't averse to a trading agreement. On the other hand, he hadn't warned them about the Fed trap. They'd been lucky to get away unscathed.

Oliver gave every appearance of a man playing both sides of the situation. It made sense for Oliver, but Adam didn't like the uncertainty.

The oncoming ship might have been sent at the request of the Fed garrison on the planet. They could have requested more supplies or even reinforcements.

It was impossible to tell. He considered radioing Oliver and just asking him, but decided against it. There was no sense broadcasting their presence to more people than necessary.

He came to a decision. Mars had tacitly supported the Feds by not warning them. Maybe a bit more pressure on the colonists would convince them that they needed a trade agreement.

He turned decisively to the nav comp.

"I don't care if they did or not. Let's take that ship. It'll show the new crew we mean business, and it will give them much needed experience. The other thing it will do is to keep Mars thinking about trading with us. I want them to understand that it's better to have us on their side and trading peacefully than it is to have us raiding and taking supplies they might need."

He flipped the intercom and gave the alert.

Nile moved to the gunnery station, sat and powered up the systems.

"System one nominal, system two nominal. We'll be at full charge in ten." She looked over her shoulder. "How about the hull shield? Is it ready?"

He glanced. The plasma generators were all on and working well.

"Yes, it's okay. How about the mining lasers? Status, please."

"They're charged and ready."

She looked at him and asked, "Do you think we should add some missile turrets and maybe an autocannon or two? The plasma cannons are nice, but they are almost too powerful. Maybe some conventional weapons would give us more flexibility."

He nodded. "I've thought a bit about that. Conventional weapons would give us the ability to scale our response, but the problem would be ammunition. The Phoenix has ammunition lockers, but we aren't going to get ammo by ordering it from the

Feds. I think we're better off working on our own weapons. They haven't got the plasma cannon yet, thank Jupiter."

NGOMBE REPORTED FROM the hold. "We're all suited. Everyone is armed and ready to go."

He answered, "We're on an intercept course. The supply ship is headed generally in our direction. They're going to get a nice view of us through the camera system. It might be a good lesson for them to see the old Knoxville serving its new masters."

Ngombe replied, "May it make them angry. An angry foe is one that won't think so clearly."

That was what they needed: enemies that were driven by emotion and a thirst for revenge rather than reason.

THEY USED THE by the now established tactic of moving in and burning off as much of the sensor array and antennas as they could with a single cannon shot. It worked just as well as it had previously.

Adam was wearing his suit in the cargo hold. The door had been opened, and the rest of the boarding crew was jetting over to the other ship which hung in space almost exactly beside them. He paused looking at the scene. From a distance, a third party viewing the two vessels would have thought they were resting at zero velocity, rather than speeding towards Mars.

He made a last check of his suit, jet pack, and weapons. He'd taken to carrying Suarez' curved sword, although he viewed it as more of a symbol of authority than a weapon. Somehow a pistol felt more comfortable to him.

Ngombe had grinned savagely at the sight of the sword.

"You use a cutlass, then, huh? That's a good pirate weapon and good for in close fighting too." He reached out to run a finger along the back of the blade as Adam sheathed it.

"Yeah, Captain Suarez carried it. I guess I view it as a tradition of sorts. Never used it though."

"It'll work fine. Just let your instincts go wild, and you'll see."

The dark skin of the man's face was hidden in the shadows of his space suit helmet.

"I guess it would at that. Lucky they don't crew these ships, at least most of the time. Probably won't be any fighting today."

At least, he hoped so.

Adam looked up. All of the boarders were clinging to the hull of the supply ship. He moved toward the open door, thrusting his legs against the cargo hold floor. They'd slowed the rotation of the Phoenix to make it easier to load the cargo bay. It made no sense to try to bring boxes of supplies and raw materials onboard with the ship rotating rapidly enough to create earth-normal weight. It was a lot easier to move and stack containers when they weighed only enough to hold them on the floor.

One last leap, thrust against the edge of the door with the right leg, and fly across the infinitely deep void to the island of safety that was the hull of the supply ship. The crew was gathered by the airlock already working on opening it.

The lock swung open slowly. Adam had a split second to look within at an oddly shaped something before a brilliant flash dazzled his vision. There was an exclamation over the comm system.

"They're shooting at us again, dammit."

He madly swerved. He'd been heading right at the open door, prepared to sail inside. That would be suicide. There was a brief burst of flashes as whatever automatic weapon was in there fired again. The rounds missed him, but not by much. He hoped the Phoenix would take no damage. The shots had to be going right into her cargo bay.

"Nile, rotate the ship and close the cargo door. Then turn on the shield," he shouted.

She responded, "Moving now." The cruiser started to roll more quickly.

The gun was still shooting. Most of the crew was huddled outside the door, but there was one drifting away. Whoever it was, wasn't moving.

He looked closer and saw a visible hole in the side of the suit. His mind blanked for a moment, then flushed with anger. Another ambush!

Adam landed near two of the crew, secured himself, then worked his way over to the edge. He chanced a quick peek over, and nearly got his head taken off by another burst of fire that struck the inner edge of the opening.

"What is it?" he asked.

"Some kind of autonomous weapon. There's nobody in there. It might be remote controlled, or maybe an AI. Don't know," Ngombe answered.

There was an answer to that. Adam unclipped an explosive pack from his belt, made an adjustment, then slung it through the open door. An answering burst of shots made a flickering light against the shadowed wall just inside. There was a pause, then a brilliant flash. The ship shuddered a bit under them.

"That should have done it. Let's go," he commanded.

One of the others, someone he didn't know, waved a rifle over the gaping opening. There were no answering shots.

Adam was furious. Losing another man was not what he wanted. He swung over the edge, moving quickly with the cutlass in his free hand.

The weapon system was mounted in the center of the door and inside about two meters. The explosion had damaged it somehow, but it was still active. As he swung in, the barrel of the machine gun began to traverse, moving to track him. It moved in a series of jerks as if the controller were having difficulty getting it to move.

Before it lined up, he bounced off the ceiling directly toward it and swung the cutlass as hard as he could. The force of the swing rotated him away, but the sword crashed against the sensors mounted just above the receiver of the weapon.

The barrel began waving back and forth. It paused as the thing shot a five round burst that bounced down the wall harmlessly. Adam rotated all the way around, swinging the heavy blade in a wide arc at the end of his arm. This time it didn't bounce off. The edge split the controller housing and buried itself in the circuitry inside. There was a blue flash followed by a brief shock in his arm.

The gun ceased firing in response.

"All clear. I've killed it. Let's start moving cargo," he radioed.

The others came over the edge tentatively at first, but then in a rush.

The robot weapon didn't respond. He had destroyed it with Suarez' Cutlass. Not a bad feat, he thought.

The back of the hold held the usual assortment of items, and the crew began to move them out as quickly as possible.

Adam tried to identify the men, but with no success. They'd have to paint numbers or unique insignia on their space suits. They were too similar to keep straight otherwise.

"Who did we lose?" he asked, after a minute.

"I think it was Phillip. He was beside me one moment, now he's gone. I didn't see for sure, though."

That was To'afa. He could see that the big man was looking directly at him as he spoke. So, it was one of Ngombe's crew. He didn't really know the man, but every loss hurt.

"He wasn't moving. Looked like a big hole in his side. We'll try to pick him up after we load, but it'll just be for a funeral." Adam moved towards the inner lock of the cargo bay as he spoke.

The inner lock opened easily with no puff of released gas, indicating there was no atmosphere inside the supply ship. That wasn't unusual. The only time there was atmosphere, was when the ship was occupied.

Ryan was beside him, waiting for the lock to open. "That's good, huh? Nobody on board," he said.

Adam nodded, but then realized that the other couldn't see the motion. "Looks clear to me," he answered.

They slid through the lock, heading towards the bridge, Ryan leading.

There was a movement in front of them. Something was in the darkened passage.

Adam grabbed at Ryan's foot, trying to jerk him back, shooting at the moving thing at the same time. There was a series of flashes, and the back of Ryan's helmet exploded.

A six-inch splinter from the helmet slammed into Adam's helmet. He screamed in pain. His pistol, set to full auto, fired twice more, sending rounds down the passage into the dark section, then he dropped it. It took all of his will not to grab at his face.

He clamped his teeth together, straining to keep calm. His left eye was full of bright flashes, and it hurt like hell. He forced himself to think. There was a hole in his suit. That was deadly. He needed to get back to the Phoenix.

He tried to look with his good eye, but that caused more pain in the left one. The pressure in his suit was holding. The shard must be plugging the hole. That was good, but it couldn't be counted on to keep the seal intact.

Someone grabbed his hand. To'afa said, "You got a spike sticking out of your helmet. I'm going to get you back. Try not to move."

# 22
## A PATCH

THE PHOENIX MOVED slowly away from the supply ship. When the two were a klick apart, the plasma cannon fired a full charge burst. It was so powerful that the Phoenix jumped in response. The supply ship glowed, then holes appeared, and it split into three pieces. Something inside exploded, sending one of the pieces spiraling away. The other two drifted onwards toward the red planet.

THE SPLINTER HAD ripped through Adam's eye, damaging the retina. All he could see with his left eye was distorted blurs of light. He remembered an unrelenting and intense pain, but now it was somewhat under control. He was drugged, but not so heavily he couldn't interact with people.

His last shot had disabled the mobile LAWS that had killed Ryan. The bullet had found its way to a tiny camera lens, and from there, a fragment had ripped through a critical bus on the small motherboard. The robot had ceased firing and turned towards the passageway wall. The last they had seen of it, it was still trying to crawl through the solid wall.

The boarding crew had taken all of the supplies from the other ship.

Ngombe and Nile had taken the two shifts and were waiting for him to recover enough to take command. Ngombe thought they'd be better off leaving Mars orbit, but Nile had insisted that they wait for Adam's opinion.

She had just entered his cabin and now was sitting beside him, a concerned look on her face.

"How do you feel? Is the pain any better?"

"It's still there. The pain, I mean. My eye apparently isn't."

He was trying to be humorous as if the loss of half of his vision didn't bother him.

She didn't help with his attempt. She didn't laugh, but only looked serious. "Yes. Well, it might be repairable, if we had a first class surgical robot and a trained operator. I'm only good for first-line repair of battle wounds. I got the splinter out, bandaged your eye, and drugged you. From the little I know, you'll be able to function with minimal pain, as long as you keep from pushing at your eye. The hole in your cornea wasn't very large, and it should seal completely in another forty hours or so. What caused the damage was the movement of your head and eye against the splinter. It sliced through your retina, and wadded it up to one side."

"Thanks for the graphic detail. I was feeling pretty good. Now I think I may have to vomit."

He was only half joking this time. The thought of the sharp splinter cutting through his eye was nearly unbearable. It taught him two things, though.

Despite the deaths of Suarez and the others, he'd been treating the idea of being pirates and revolutionaries almost like a game.

The pain had taught him that it was for real stakes. It left him wondering if he was ever going to grow up.

The second thing he had learned was that the enemy, the Feds, would now use lethal autonomous weapons systems, something that had been considered to be morally unacceptable. If they went that far, they must really want to get rid of the pirate problem.

That left him wondering what was next? Maybe a full squadron of cruisers would come hunting for them.

Nile answered, and he realized he'd spoken out loud.

"That's a reasonable supposition, but the last I heard, there were only four cruisers ready. We are sitting in one, so, unless they've finished more, they only have three. I don't think they'll risk sending them after us. They have to be worried about our advanced weapons."

He looked at her, wonderingly. She was a trained marine, yet she'd come over to his side.

"Any regrets?" he asked.

Nile leaned closer and lightly placed her lips on his. When he moved to put his arms around her, she pulled back.

"No. Let's not get you excited. It wouldn't do your inter-ocular pressure any good. That'll wait for a while." She settled back in her chair, then smiled. "No. You should know by now that I have no regrets. If you're a pirate, I'm going to be one, too."

That was too much for him. His good eye teared up and he drew a ragged breath. She looked alarmed and put her hand on his forehead.

"It's okay. I didn't really like the service anyway. It was the only way I had to get out of the crappy situation I was living in."

He shook his head. "It's not that, it's the idea that you care about...Oh, never mind. I think the pain medication has made me a little loopy."

She smiled again, a tender smile, he thought.

"Adam, I do care about you. I wanted to kill you at first, but you have something about you. You expect the universe to be goodness and light and kind to everyone. I don't think you would ever harm anyone else if you had a choice. The fact that you don't have a choice is what I hate. In one way or another, we're all victims on this ship. I think you will do what needs to be done to make our circumstance better. You have to understand that the Feds mean business. They will eventually bring all their force against us. We need to plan on that, and we need to be ready to fight or run."

He reached for her. She seemingly forgot about his blood pressure this time, prolonging the kiss until they began to breath harder. She pulled back again.

"That's enough for now. You'll have to take a rain check for later. I'm going to dim the lights and try to get some sleep. I'll be right beside you if you need anything."

He held out his hand.

"What's that for?"

"I'm waiting for the rain check."

"Silly. Now try to relax. I'm tired. I just got off main-day and need some rest."

"Okay. I do need one thing."

"What's that?"

"Some black cloth."

"Black...what for, may I ask?" She had straightened in the chair and was looking at him in a way that implied that she thought the drug dosage was too high.

"I want to make an eye patch. A pirate has to have one, you know."

She snorted, then said, "Get some sleep, you idiot."

HE THOUGHT ABOUT their conversation for a while, then drifted gradually into a restless sleep. His eye throbbed with the beat of his heart, but it was regular, and that made it easier to get used to.

He woke and looked hopefully at her chair, but she had left. The only sign of their conversation was a strip of black cloth hanging on the armrest. He picked it up and held it as he dropped back to sleep.

ADAM WAS BETTER. Well, not really better, but he was functional. He'd retaken command of the Phoenix, and both Nile and Ngombe were relieved. They hadn't been able to establish a smooth working relationship with him laid up. Each had wanted to go a different direction, and they were at loggerheads.

Adam listened to them for a bit, then said, "There's no reason to abandon our plans to stop by Swift. We promised the scientists that we'd let them off, and we will live up to our promise. Besides, I want to meet with Citizen Oliver in person. I've got something to say to him that I don't want to broadcast all over the galaxy."

He was sitting at the nav station on the bridge. He had made good on his promise and was wearing a black patch over his left eye. He'd come to terms with his loss and had actually reached the level of acceptance where he thought the patch gave him a rakish look. Maybe even handsome.

The ship had been idling along in the same orbit as Deimos, but lagging behind halfway around the planet. He activated the nav program, and the ship moved to overtake the small moon gradually.

Ngombe stood and said, "I still don't trust the situation there. From what Nile has said, they may try to ambush us again."

Nile nodded in agreement.

Why was it that the two couldn't get along when he was absent, but when he showed up, they both sided against him? He put that out of his mind. They were just being sensible.

"I know. I don't trust them either. We won't dock this time. We'll match velocity and then transfer over with jetpacks. The escape velocity is small enough that we can get back easily with their thrust. I'm going to want four armed crew to come with me. I'm not taking any chances of getting captured. If we have to shoot our way out, we will."

# 23

## DEIMOS, AGAIN

THE SCIENTISTS HAD been repatriated, not without some regret on Adam's part. He could have used their expertise.

Now, he and Nile were waiting to see Oliver. The other three men, Ta'afo, included, were waiting in the reception area. The aide who was watching them seemed fascinated by the big man's ax. His eyes kept straying to it, then looking at Ta'afo's face. He was probably wondering just what kind of barbarian would use so horrible and primitive a weapon.

The two of them turned to the door as Oliver came in.

"Hello, Citizen. It's a pleasure to enjoy your hospitality once again," Adam said, trying not to sound too sarcastic.

Oliver passed it off without comment. He was an experienced diplomat and probably had suffered much worse in the way of sarcasm and insult.

"Mr. uh, Captain Maxwell, nice of you to come over yourself."

Adam noted that Oliver could defend himself smoothly.

The Citizen continued. "We've spoken to the scientific personnel you've returned. It seems that some of their number elected to stay with your group. That speaks well for what you've proposed."

Adam responded, "I trust that no unpleasant surprises are awaiting us on this visit."

"My, my, young man. You get right to the point, don't you?"

"We've had our fill of ambushes, Citizen. We've survived all of them so far. The unfortunate thing about the continued attempts is that it's made it difficult for us to allow your supply line to continue relatively unmolested. That last supply ship was transporting two LAWS. I trust that was not your idea?"

Oliver looked shocked. "I...no, I knew nothing about that. I knew you had intercepted the unscheduled supply ship. I wasn't aware of the cargo. The Earthers don't see fit to inform us about every voyage."

He paused, then before Adam could speak, asked, "Was there really a LAWS on the ship?"

Adam nodded grimly. "There were two. The first killed one of our crew. The second killed another crewman and injured me." He motioned briefly at his eye.

Oliver was still pale. "I was going to ask what happened to your eye. Is it repairable?"

"Not without an advanced surgery robot. That's something we do not currently have."

"We have one on the surface. I don't suppose you'd like to go down and have your eye repaired?"

Adam shook his head. "Are the Feds still down there? Are they up here, for that matter?"

Oliver had recovered his composure. "They are still on Mars, yes. The group that had come up was taken off by the Lagos shortly after you left."

"The Lagos. That is a Federal Cruiser, correct?"

"Yes. It is the sister ship of the Knoxville, which I believe is paralleling us in orbit at the moment."

"Ah, no. Not the Knoxville. At least, no longer. You're looking at our cruiser, the Phoenix. Reborn to better use, I must say."

"That fits with what I've been given to understand. Look, Captain. I'm tired of this cat and mouse we are playing. I propose we speak clearly."

"That would suit me perfectly, Oliver. Please feel free."

"Hmmph. Mars cannot afford to anger the Federal government. We are at a delicate phase in our development. We still have some earth years to go before we are self-sustaining. If you had come along earlier, we might have gladly joined forces with you. Now our citizens and council are able to see that we will eventually be able to live here without relying on Earth. No Martian likes the idea of being a colony. We probably want self-determination as much as you, but, as I said, we cannot afford to break our relationship with the only place we can get the materials and supplies we require."

"That's clear enough, Citizen. I would feel much the same. However, have you thought ahead to the time when you are self-sustaining? Will you still be willing to accept Earth as an overlord then?"

"That is difficult to say. I suppose it depends on how onerous their demands become. Right now, they don't require much of us, except for scientific knowledge based on geological research. They also insist on sending ship after ship of marginally useful people, many of whom are political outcasts, others of whom are out and out criminals. But, you already knew that."

"Yes. By the way, the so-called undesirables you passed off to us the last time we were here have proven to be anything but undesirable. They've integrated into our crew and are performing admirably. So, if you have any more such people, give them to us."

Oliver looked somewhat astonished but then smiled, covering up his confusion. "Oh. I'm glad to hear that they're working out for you. We don't have any spare people up here right at the moment. I'm sorry I must disappoint you in that regard."

Adam had reached his limit. It wasn't that he wanted to be offensive, he felt that he was wasting time when it was a precious commodity. The Lagos could be hanging around anywhere or returning to Swift. It would be inconvenient to meet the cruiser while the Phoenix was hanging in orbit with five crewmembers off the ship.

"Look, Oliver. I'm going to be brief about this. We're leaving in five minutes, regardless. I've got to go see a man about a dog."

Oliver looked confused again. "A dog?"

Adam grinned. "It's a figure of speech. An old one. We're running out of time. Will Mars work out a trading agreement with us or not? Think carefully about this question. I want a firm answer, and I don't have time to wait around for diplomatic maneuvers."

The Citizen looked shocked, then angry. He was apparently unused to being spoken to in such a forceful manner.

"Captain Maxwell, I am unable to make promises without the full authority of the council. I believe I made that clear before."

"You did. You did. I had hoped that you'd be competent to communicate the advantages of such an agreement to your council and they would have agreed by this time. I ask you once again. Yes, or no?"

"What about the supplies you've been stealing from us? We need those shipments. How are we supposed to deal with someone who has shown they will rob us blind?"

"I've taken care not to take everything, save for this last ship. The ambush cost me too dearly. We took all the supplies as partial recompense, but we do not count the score equal. The Feds, and you, if you persist in equivocating, still owe us. I don't take the loss of my crew members lightly." Adam glared at the older man, wishing he could look threatening in spite of his eye patch.

From Oliver's reaction, he did. The Mars representative flinched slightly. That movement, more than anything else, went a long way toward increasing Adam's self-image. He instantly felt more confident.

He stood, looking down at Oliver. When the man looked up at him, he said, "We're leaving. If we leave orbit without an agreement, your supplies will not be safe. Understood?"

He turned and strode out, not looking back. Nile had stood when he had. Now she hastily followed.

"C'mon, guys. Let's blow this place." He waved at the others as he walked by.

They headed down the hall, moving slower than he wanted in the low gravity.

Nile pulled at his arm, and he turned to look at her. She was looking up at him, her face glowing.

"That was the most amazing thing! Adam, dearest Captain! I've never seen a diplomat so put in his place. Even if you might have gotten more agreement by being more polite, it was worth it to see his face when you turned away. His expression collapsed. He's probably crying to his council on the radio right now. The big, bad Pirates just threatened to take his lunch money."

ADAM DIDN'T RUSH his departure from Deimos. He took time to lay in three different legs for their trip back to the Bubble. They'd leave, apparently heading directly out of the solar system into vacant space, then turn towards Uranus. Once they were a few million miles away, and out of detection range, they'd head directly for home.

The shield would wait for a few hours. He had made it a practice not to approach Swift with the cold plasma shield active. No sense giving them a hint about his defense. He didn't like the resultant radiation exposure, but it couldn't be helped as long as he wanted to keep the system secret.

He'd thought briefly about giving the device to all spacers, but the Feds would probably clamp down on his idea, refusing to disseminate it to the miners, who really needed it, while using it exclusively for the naval ships. He didn't want to give his enemies an advantage.

He lingered over the nav system, hoping that Oliver would call, but there was no sign of a message from the base. There was, however, a considerable amount of encrypted traffic with the surface. Oliver was doubtless in touch with his council.

If he waited any longer, he'd give the impression that he was unsure about his ultimatum. He sighed, disappointed. It would be so much easier to trade. Well, safer, anyway. He gritted his teeth. They would get the supplies they needed regardless.

His finger stabbed at the touch screen. The Phoenix drifted away from the moon, then began to accelerate, heading at an odd angle to the ecliptic.

There was no signal from the Swift base. Adam reflected that Oliver had made his choice. They would find no assistance coming from Mars. The unknown factor was whether the Martians would actively move against them.

The pirates needed food, raw materials, and manufactured parts to continue developing their base. The supply ships were the primary source of these essentials, but the miners could be a secondary source of supplies. His problem was that it seemed cruel to rob them since they worked hard while receiving no breaks from Earth. The miners paid premium prices for everything. It could be said that the Martians worked equally hard. The environment on the face of the planet was, in some ways, even more dangerous than space. The lack of atmosphere and temperature would kill an unprotected human as quickly on Mars as in the vacuum of space.

The surface of Mars was subject to almost as much radiation as the ships in space. The other danger the Martians faced was in the form of wind storms. While the thin atmosphere did not lend itself to storms of hurricane levels, the wind could blow very quickly, and when it carried a load of dust, things could get bad.

Adam shrugged. It was regretful, but he couldn't afford to be concerned with the Martians. They had made their choice to work with Earth. Besides, the Feds would not let the Martians starve. There was too much money invested in the colony.

All of this meant only one thing. He would have to continue to raid the supply ships and fight the Federal effort to stop the piracy.

# 24
## SHIPS AND PLANS

THE VOYAGE BACK home had been uneventful. When they arrived, they found that Flynn was ahead of schedule. He'd finished with the Chance, cleared the debris that was left floating in the construction space, then moved the Nautilus II inside. Flynn's crew was just getting started on the renovation of their fourth ship.

"Captain, I don't want to complain, but we're short of pretty much everything. We don't have enough parts to finish the shield system, let alone build two more plasma cannons. We're so short of raw materials that we've taken to smelting metal out of the denser veins that are in the Bubble's walls."

Flynn was waving his arms as he spoke. The little Irishman was mercurial in temperament and couldn't seem to utter even a simple sentence without gesticulating. He eventually waved his arms too vigorously. This resulted in his foot coming unhooked from the edge of the built-in desk. He drifted toward the ceiling, looking exasperated rather than surprised.

Adam snagged Flynn's pant leg and pulled him back to the desk.

"I understand. We're just going to have to make the best of it. This last raid gave us some of the parts we need. It also produced enough food to last us for a while. We'll have to go out again. Lucky that the supply ships have to keep coming regularly. The Martians are already squawking about shortages as a result of our raids. I expect the Feds to increase the frequency of the supply ships."

"Aye, but won't they send a force to stop our thieving?" Flynn was holding to the edge of the desk, but he still managed to free one hand to wave in the air.

"I'm sure they will. They've tried sending Marines and LAWs. Both of those approaches have failed, although it's been more due to us being lucky than anything else. They've got to be planning on sending a squadron out here."

Flynn nodded. "Give me a couple more weeks, and we'll have the Nautilus armed. We'll have enough strength to fight off twice our number of Feddies then."

Adam wasn't so sure. The tactics he and Ngombe had worked out had yet to be tried in a combat situation. They might not be as good as he hoped. It would have been useful if he had studied such things in school. Of course, there were no texts or courses on space battle, but he could have possibly gleaned some ideas from atmospheric fighter strategies.

He didn't like that train of thought. In mild desperation, he changed the topic.

"You've been smelting your own ore, then?"

Flynn nodded. "Yes. We found some relatively pure iron and enough nickel and other metals to make some pretty good steel. What we need now is a carbon-based structural material. Oh, and there's a bit of copper now. We captured a small meteoroid about thirty meters across. The bloomin' thing was practically full of copper. I estimate we have enough to create a wire that would stretch from here to Earth if we wanted to lay a telephone line."

The other thing about Flynn was he couldn't speak without exaggerating. Adam mentally divided the quantity by one hundred. It was still a significant amount, and it meant that they would need that much less wire. Insulation for the wire was also required. That meant organic materials. It wasn't like he could order a couple of tons of plastic. They'd have to try and find raw materials somewhere.

"Look, Flynn, can you think of any way we can pick up enough gas from Jupiter to get the organics we need?"

"Hmm. Sure, given that we have enough materials, time, and men to invent and construct a cloud scoop that hasn't ever been invented yet. As it is, no. We might find some of what we need on a rock somewhere out here, though."

"How about a comet?"

"Aye. That might be possible. It would beat looking at stony meteoroids. There's more likely organics on comets, but, once again, how are we going to get 'em off?"

Adam shrugged. He couldn't think of anything else except more raids.

"We'll have to hope that the Feds send more parts and raw materials to Mars. I can see that we're going to have to interdict every single supply ship. I don't want to starve the Martians out, but we need to inspect each ship for the essentials we want."

Flynn nodded, then rather querulously asked, "Well, then, how about women?"

"Huh. What?"

"Listen, Captain, I know you're happy with Nile, but have you ever thought about the rest of us? We're almost all men. The two women we have are spoken for. Spacers are used to being alone, but if we're going to have a colony out here, we really need to have a colony. That means women. The men are going to get fed up eventually. Then you'll have a mutiny on your hands, maybe. Anyway, where you going to find 'em?"

He didn't know. "I'd hoped that the Martians would help in that department, but they only gave us men. Maybe we'll have to intercept a colony ship. There are bound to be unattached women on one of those."

NILE WAS OF the same opinion.

"You have to keep one of our ships out at all times. It will have to be ready to grab off every supply vessel that comes from Earth. Flynn's right, too. I've seen the looks the men give me. How can I miss them?" She laughed. "If we can grab a colony ship, that will solve our population problem."

She was right, but there was likely to be a complication.

"The Feds won't stand for an unlimited number of raids. They'll take more action. If they can get enough ships completed, they'll come out after us. They might even begin to arm the supply ships."

She didn't think so. "No. That's not likely. The supply ships are designed for one task only. They aren't particularly maneuverable, and they barely carry enough fuel to reach Mars' orbit. They'd have to be modified extensively."

"That's true. We could probably tell if they were modified. Their profile would change. They'd have to add some missile pods and point defense turrets. We can't be ambushed that way. We can lay off and inspect the ships before moving in, but they could still play really dirty. It occurred to me that they could load one of the ships with a nuke set to go off when the ship is boarded."

She looked stunned. Her face paled as she thought that over. "Nukes! That's going too far. It's...it's inhuman."

He laughed. "Not really. Humans built those things to be used. I just hope they don't think of it."

"What if we go after more miners? They have supplies."

"We could, but I'd rather have them come to us. I'm thinking of sending Ngombe out in the Chance to try and recruit. Some of those people have got to be fed up with the treatment they're getting from the Feds."

"Probably. Ngombe's crew and some of the scientists were ready to join us. Have you thought of organizing our enterprise on a share basis?"

He hadn't gotten that far. Thinking about organizing the colony was something for the future. Right now he had more immediate problems. Still, it was going to be necessary eventually.

"What do you mean?"

"Historically, English naval ships divided up money from prize ships among the crew. Every member got a share. The officers and captain got more, of course. We could organize the colony as a corporation and provide shares of stock as an inducement to get people to join us."

"Nile, I haven't got a clue how that would work. Would you look into it for me?"

She laughed and put up her hands. "I'm about as clueless as you, but I was talking to one of the scientists. Those guys are pretty well read. Dr. Edwards knows a lot about economics. I'll ask him to think about it."

"Okay. I've got more than I can handle just thinking about raids."

ONE OF THE things he was thinking about was improving the mining lasers as weapons. These were generally located on the bow of the mining ships with a simple mount that only moved in one direction. The idea was that the ship could nose into the target, take its time about aiming, then use the laser to slice off chunks of the meteoroid.

If they mounted two of the high-power lasers on a cannon turret, rather than the simple mount, the lasers could be fired one at a time as the mount tracked the target. The things required a short interval of downtime before they could shoot again. With two of them, the pulses would be nearly continuous, although the power requirements would limit their use. They'd have to give the capacitor bank time to recharge periodically.

Flynn had grumbled, but the new mounts were now being built using their own manufactured steel. Fortunately, each of the mining ships carried a spare laser. They'd have to get more, though, since they couldn't build the things. At least, not yet.

NGOMBE KNEW THE mining community well, having been a part of it for two previous voyages. The miners tended to stay away from each other since they competed for valuable finds. There were two exceptions to their enforced isolation. One was the requirement to assist other miners in need. This was viewed as a moral imperative.

None of the pirates really felt comfortable with preying on fellow miners. Despite their outlaw status, they still felt like they were a part of that community. Adam had stopped the two ships out of necessity. Even so, he and the crew weren't entirely at ease with their actions.

The second exception was due to the human desire for social interaction. Floating in space with the same small crew for a voyage that lasted anywhere from eighteen to forty months was difficult. The miners weren't selected for their easy-going personalities. In fact, they tended to be fractious. They felt they had a reputation to uphold and often got arrested between voyages, usually as a result of a bar fight.

To blow off tension, the miners sometimes arranged to meet at a designated location and time. There they would link ships so that they could trade, socialize, and party. Sometimes the parties got a little rowdy, but the general consensus was that it was all in fun. Any fights were quickly forgotten.

Over the last five years, these meetings had gradually morphed into a periodic rendezvous.

It had become a looked-forward-to event that now attracted dozens of ships to swap supplies, sometimes crew, and socialization. The social aspect had become the most looked-forward-to part, taking the form of a massive drinking party.

Ngombe and Adam had discussed the issue of their relations with the mining community at length. They'd decided that they should try to establish a working agreement. It wouldn't benefit them as much as the failed Mars trade agreement, but it would still help.

The miners might volunteer to become part of their effort to establish their own community. They would also provide a limited source of supplies, although they usually only carried enough for an extended voyage. They would be eager to trade surplus supplies if they were headed in. The Federal policy was to simply confiscate any extra supplies without paying the mining ship for them.

The miners were outraged by this action since they received no credit for returns against the cost of new supplies for their next voyage.

IT WAS AGREED that Ngombe would take the Chance and meet with the miners. The next meeting was only two weeks away, so he took the ship out, with a crew of four, and headed sunward toward the scheduled rendezvous.

Adam watched the Hell's Chance leave, hoping that it would return with much-needed help. Meanwhile, the rest of them would finish the additions to the Nautilus II. Once that was done, they'd take the Phoenix and the D-R toward Mars hunting for more supplies, while the Nautilus and a four-man crew were left to guard the Bubble.

# 25

# THE NEXT RAID

THE SENSOR SUITE alarm on the Phoenix went off exactly halfway through the alterday shift. Adam had it keyed to his bedside comm, and the shrill sound felt like a kick to his eardrums. He sat upright, then looked at Nile. She was already getting dressed.

He climbed out of the bunk, then bent to get his pants.

"You'd be quicker at that sort of thing if you'd been through boot camp, you know," she said, smiling as she finished adjusting the fit of her woven top.

"Yeah, I guess." He tugged his pants up, then turned to her. "But, I wouldn't be me, if I'd been to boot camp. I'd be someone else."

She laughed. "You're cute when you're sleepy, but you'd better wake up. You don't make any sense."

"What I meant was I'm just me, a non-military physicist in training, and all around nice guy. Now, I'm trying to figure out how to be a pirate. Wasn't there some military slogan years ago about being the best you could?"

"'Be all you can be' was a slogan used by Army recruiting until about 2006, I think. They replaced it with 'Army Strong,' a loser slogan. The Space Marines could beat that group every time." Her mood changed, and she frowned.

"What?" he asked.

"Just thinking about my mates. For a wanna-be pirate, you did pretty well against them, dammit." She paused, then added, "Sorry. I guess I miss the camaraderie."

He grimaced sympathetically. "I didn't mean to make you unhappy."

She came around the bed and placed her hand on his cheek. "Adam, you don't. You make me happy. I didn't think I'd find someone I like as much as you. Still, I miss the group sometimes. Promise me this. If we encounter more marines, let me talk to them. I know for a fact that many of them aren't too pleased with the way the government is changing. Maybe they'd jump over to our side."

"Really? I'd think that they would feel the same degree of duty that you did, er...do, or whatever." His statement trailed off into a kind of mumble. Now that he'd reminded her, he wondered if she would see things differently again.

"You have a way with words, you know. I still feel an obligation to the marines as an organization. There are some good people in that group. I'd rather not be shooting at them, and I most certainly don't want them shooting at us. They are too accurate."

She moved closer. Adam leaned in, and they brushed lips briefly. She pulled back almost immediately and said, "The alarm?"

"Oh, yeah. Got to go see what it is, but I'll bet it's the supply ship. It's about time for it to come into sensor range."

She nodded, silently.

He turned to the door. "Let's go shopping. The cupboard is nearly empty, and we need groceries, not to mention as many graphene sheets as we can get."

THE SENSOR ALARM had been silenced when they reached the bridge. One of the new crew members was watching the display.

"Captain. It's the supply ship, but it looks odd. It isn't the regular ship."

He looked at the display. There was little detail, but the mass-reading indicated a lower density profile than usual for the heavily-laden supply ships.

Nile exclaimed, "It must be a colony ship! Those have a large profile, but the inside is taken up by habitat and rooms. They never bring much in the way of material supplies, and only enough food for the colonists to reach Mars without having to resort to eating each other."

That was borne out over the next hour as the ship drew nearer. Nile had been correct. The question, Adam thought, was whether it was full of colonists, or a division of Marines. He'd prefer the colonists. They probably wouldn't put up much of a fight.

Either way, he was committed to intercepting the ship. Colonists would be welcome additions to the tiny community at the Bubble. If the ship held military, then he'd already promised Nile she could try to convince them to join up. If she couldn't, he could let it proceed on its way.

That was assuming, of course, that it wasn't some kind of armed warship. If that were what it was, they'd have a fight on their hands. He turned to the comm tech.

"Hey, Wilson. Signal the D-R to hold position until they hear our broadcast to the colony ship. Then they should approach on a quartering route until they're in cannon range. I want them to hold at that distance, and no firing, until I signal. Understand?"

Wilson nodded, then dictated the message into the signal laser system.

It would reach out to the D-R with an infrared carrier. Once the return laser was sensed, the message would be modulated on the carrier. Since the system was line-of-sight, there was no reason to worry that the colony ship might intercept the message. There was no sense alerting them that they were moving into a classic kill-zone ambush.

The nav comp beeped, drawing his attention. Nile was there, laying in the approach vector they'd discussed. It was nice to have someone that knew what to do without being told. Another reason to like Nile.

A vague thought formed in his mind. Did he just "like" her, or was there more to it than that? She'd never said how she actually felt about him. At least not in so many words. He mentally dragged himself back on topic. That could be dealt with later. Right now was business time. Pirate business.

Wilson made an inarticulate noise. "Arrgh. They've just launched a missile, no two missiles. We've got about thirty seconds."

Adam jumped to the cannon controls. The bow cannon was already pointing directly at the oncoming ship. He moved the aim slightly so the ship wouldn't be caught by the blast, then fired.

The lights dimmed slightly as the capacitors began to recharge. They could see the plasma bolt expand as it raced away.

He was pleased to see the oncoming missiles explode when they contacted the plasma cloud.

"Mr. Wilson, any more launches?"

"No, Sir. I've got the long-range video focused on them. It looks like they had two missile tubes strapped on. Maybe as an afterthought. They must have guessed we'd try to intercept the voyage."

Wilson leaned closer to the screen. "Wait a minute. There's something else. It looks like a gun turret of some kind. Not very big, though. Maybe a LAWS."

Adam moved to the newly modified mining laser system.

"Time to give this thing a try. Let's see if I'm as smart as I pretend to be."

That got him a disapproving glance from Nile. He ignored her and aimed the converted mining lasers carefully. As he did, he could see tiny flashes coming from the colony ship's side.

"They're shooting at us. Nile, is the shield at full strength?"

"Yes, Sir. It's up and showing between ninety-eight and ninety-nine point five percent of nominal."

Since the system never quite reached one hundred percent, that was what he expected.

"Okay. Stand by for incoming. We may get bumped a bit, depending on how good a shot that thing is. It won't last for long. I'm returning fire now."

The capacitor bank hummed, and the lights flickered. There was a brief pause, then the sequence repeated as the second laser fired. Then the first one fired again. Adam stopped shooting to check on the results.

The turret on the colony ship was slagged. There was a large hole in it, and it looked like the gun that had been firing at them was out of commission. The laser pulses had instantly heated the barrel white hot. That resulted in an explosion when the gun fired again a moment later.

"Mr. Wilson, give me the comm," Adam said, turning from the fire-control station.

He radioed the oncoming ship. The D-R would also hear the broadcast and begin its approach.

"Colony ship. Cease acceleration and prepare for boarding. We're coming alongside. Do not attempt to flee. We're faster. Do not attempt to fight. We can destroy you easily. Is that clear?"

Jem clicked the microphone button twice to signal his receipt of the signal, then the D-R began to move in. Almost as if fate were waiting for the signal three additional things happened nearly simultaneously.

Nile made a yelp, then exclaimed, "Missile burn. Coming right at us and it's too close to avoid."

Immediately after that, the colony ship acknowledged their hail. "This is the USS Colony Ship Asgaard. Who are you and what gives you the authority to haul us down?"

Hard on the termination of that query, Jem came on. "Sensor suite alert. There's a large ship approaching. We can just barely sense it, but it's about the size of another cruiser. What do you want us to do?"

Adam looked back and forth, stunned, then mentally took charge of himself. First things first.

"Nile, where did the missile come from?"

"Looks like the colony ship shot two as cover while they ejected a third. That one drifted away and just now activated. We're going to take impact in less than ten seconds."

Nothing to do, but hold on. He hit the take-hold signal. The other two had already buckled into their seats. He jumped into the third and slammed the belt together. As he did, the Phoenix jumped, then rang like a bell. The lights dimmed, flickered, then came back to full brightness.

"Damage control. Let's find out what happened. Now!" he yelled.

Nile was flipping through screen after screen, checking comp read-outs for the status of various systems. Adam glanced at Wilson. The crewman hadn't actually locked his buckle. He'd been flipped out of his seat and had slammed into a bulkhead. He lay in an unmoving heap near the door.

"Damn. Wilson's hurt. Nile, do you have anything?"

"Looks like everything is okay. No. Wait. Uh-oh. That's bad." She was leaning close to the monitor, reading.

"What's bad? Dammit!" Adam was turning the plasma cannon towards the vector that the incoming ship was taking as he spoke.

"The Em-Max is out. The hull is intact, but the shock broke one of the Em-Max anchors. The safety override kicked in. We can't move until the engine is tied down again. It's not safe to fire it when a mount is broken. It will create too much strain on the other mounts."

He was ahead of her. "Okay, what about the maneuvering jets? Tell me that we can still maneuver."

"Yes. That system checks out."

The intercom came on. "Crew is all okay. No injuries."

Good. The three remaining crew had escaped.

He called back. "Damage control in the engine room. One of the Em-Max anchors broke. Get on it. Repair parts are in bin 078, in the engine room locker. It should be simple, but call me if you get stuck. Be advised we may have to maneuver with the jets with little warning. I'll call, but keep a rope on and don't spread tools or parts all over. Keep them secured against movement."

"Yes, sir." Whoever it was sounded like they were calm and under control. That was good.

Now, the colony ship.

"This is the pirate vessel Phoenix. We took a hit from your third missile. Any additional tricks and we'll blow holes in your hull. We don't take your action lightly. I'm tempted to retaliate in a way that you won't enjoy."

The colony ship captain didn't lack courage. He responded immediately.

"You're wanted by the Federal Government. If you took damage, it's your own fault for waylaying us. We're not unprotected. The Federal Cruiser, Mt. Hood, is twenty light seconds behind us. You might escape if you leave now. They won't view it lightly if you damage us further."

Adam growled in his throat. Then shook his anger off.

"Captain, if you do not cease accelerating, you will be damaged irreparably. The Hood will not be able to prevent that."

The other man immediately flinched. "We've stopped accelerating. We've got six hundred and thirty-five colonists on board and a crew of twenty-five. You can't endanger them. They've done nothing to you."

He grinned at Nile. She shook her head negatively, then pointed at the sensor suite. The Hood was just starting to show up.

The laser comm was still aimed at the D-R. He swung to that system and sent a private message.

"Jem. Sheer off. Make it look like you're running. Don't accelerate too quickly, though. We're going to have to slug it out with the Hood. We can't accelerate. The engine's out temporarily. When you see their missiles launch, loop back. Come in on their back quarter and use the plasma cannon. Shoot to destroy. Be advised that we will be doing the same, so don't cross our line of fire. Once you shoot, deviate away from a direct intercept. Use both cannons, parallel them and keep firing. Confirm."

"Confirmed, Captain. D-R out."

Nile was actually laughing. "They're in for a surprise. Good thinking."

Back to the colony ship.

"Phoenix to colony ship captain. What's your name, please?"

"This is Captain Castenada. We're following your orders."

"Captain Castenada. I'm Captain Maxwell. You will stay on the same course, not accelerating. We have a small matter to discuss with the Hood. When we are finished with that discussion, we will board your ship. Follow our orders. We have nothing bad planned for you. We simply want to offer your colonists a choice. They can make up their own minds. Do not try to escape. Confirm."

"I understand, Maxwell. We will not accelerate. You're faster than we are and your laser weapons can cut us to ribbons. We're at your mercy."

Nile said, "They don't know about our plasma cannon or our damaged drive. They think the lasers are all we've got. You didn't notice, but they sent an encrypted packet on a sub-frequency. It was undoubtedly a message for the Hood. The cruiser captain will be prepared for our lasers, but not our main guns."

Adam replied, "I guess I can't blame Castenada. He's trying to survive. We're an unknown factor here. We'll have to treat them well, regardless of their decision. If it gets around that we're decent people, the next colony ship might just come looking for us, rather than trying to avoid us."

THE MT. HOOD was just about in missile range. If they had fired too soon, the missiles would run out of fuel. They would then coast along the course they'd been following. If the Phoenix moved just a few klicks, the missiles would slide by harmlessly.

The comm system beeped. The Hood was calling.

"Pirate ship, cease hostilities. This is the USS Mt. Hood. We're prepared to destroy you. If you surrender, only the captain will be charged with piracy. Stand by for boarding."

Adam couldn't resist responding. "Avast, ye scurvy swabs. This be the Pirates of the Asteroid Belt. Ya want ta board us, ye'll have to beat us first."

Nile snorted at him. "That's too corny, you loon. They won't take you seriously."

He grinned at her. "But, we're the pirates. They should be running."

"Not likely. They aren't going to back off. Now, watch out. They've launched their first salvo."

Adam could see the tiny white burns of the oncoming missiles. They were fast, but at the current distance, they would still take several minutes to reach the Phoenix. It would do no good to try to avoid them. At their relative velocities, given the fact that the engine was out, there was no way to escape.

"Let's hope our shielding is up to the task. Wait until they're about twenty seconds out, then burn them with a plasma burst. If we keep the missiles directly between the Hood and us, any remnants of the plasma that misses the missiles will strike the cruiser. We'll follow up with a second shot aimed directly at their ship. After that, I hope the D-R gets in close without being noticed."

She shook her head. "They'll see the D-R. Their sensor operator is too well trained to miss it. Let's just hope the captain is too shocked by our plasma to wonder what the D-R is doing."

She paused, then added, "But I wouldn't count on it. He'll undoubtedly shoot some missiles at them."

"I know. Here we go. The missiles are almost here. Fire when you have them targeted."

She made a quick adjustment, then the ship lurched, the lights flickered, and the system hummed. The plasma bolt closed rapidly with the oncoming missiles. The glowing high-energy gas spread out as it went. One of the missiles made an abortive attempt to avoid the bolt. Apparently, its guidance system had sensed something, but it was too late.

There was an intense series of flashes as the missiles detonated.

Adam said, "That's conventional high explosive. No nukes, at least."

She replied, "They'll eventually get around to using them. Never doubt it."

He nodded, then said, "Fire at the ship."

She complied. The Phoenix lurched slightly.

"Shot away. They've got a few seconds to swerve. No. They're not able to turn quickly enough. Oh! It's a hit. Look!"

The Hood had taken the plasma full on the bow. The stricken ship's hull was covered with sparks for a moment, then white-hot droplets of metal streamed away like rain.

Adam increased the magnification on the vid. The Hood had stood up remarkably well to the blast, but there were streams of condensing atmosphere shooting away from it. The Feds' hull was leaking in ten or fifteen places.

"Shoot 'em again."

She laughed, merrily. "Don't mind if I do, Captain One-eye."

He flinched, then grinned. She was getting into the pirate role. Besides, he couldn't take it amiss. He loved her.

He stopped, shocked. That was the feeling he had. He hadn't recognized it, but it was true. Funny how it took the stress of a battle to make him realize that he was in love.

He shook his head in amazement. Then said, "Nile, I love you."

She jerked, froze for a moment, then turned to look at him.

"You'd better not be fooling with me, Mister. I've heard similar stuff before. We can talk about it later, assuming we survive this goat-rope."

He laughed weakly. Her response wasn't what he'd hoped for.

"Ha. No fooling and this isn't a goat-rope, it's a historic occasion. The first space battle with more than two ships. Look."

He waved at the monitor. The D-R had just released a plasma blast, followed closely by a second.

Nile fired her second shot, then turned to the first cannon. It was almost fully charged by this time, so she adjusted the tracking until it was directly on the Hood.

The two close shots from the D-R struck. The Hood's hull wasn't as well armored on the rear quarter. The entire tail lit up like a firework, then ablated away in a stream of white-hot drops.

"That's got her engine. She's not going anywhere now," he said.

Nile started to reply but stopped as their last shot struck.

The Hood sparkled, then something in her exploded. There was a brilliant flash, followed by secondary explosions as the ship's store of missiles exploded.

The flashes dazzled Adam's vision for a moment. While he waited for it to clear, he thought of the debris cloud. He fumbled for the comm system.

"Colony ship. Captain Castenada, move your ship. The debris cloud will be on us in a few minutes. You're not armored well enough to survive it striking you. Move out of line as quickly as you can, then wait for us. You've seen what we can do, so don't get any ideas about running beyond avoiding the debris."

This time, Captain Castenada didn't argue. He'd seen enough to make him very respectful of the pirate threat.

"Yes, Sir. Moving now."

The colony ship gradually turned away from the oncoming debris cloud.

# 26
## RECRUITS

LIVING CONDITIONS ON the colony ship were horrid. Adam had initially been shocked at the miners' way of life, but this...this was inhumane.

There were six hundred and thirty-five colonists plus twenty-six crew, if Castenada was counted. He, at least, had a private cabin.

The crew had their own quarters, too, although their sleeping arrangements had to be shared a shift at a time.

The truly bad accommodations were reserved for the putative Mars colonists. They were confined to a large, converted hold. There were multiple banks of hammocks, a single communal toilet facility, which offered no privacy, and an open food prep area. Adam really couldn't call it a kitchen.

Now the colonists were assembled, waiting for him to speak. He looked around, scanning the area. People were hanging in hammocks along the walls in rows extending far above his head. The whole mess made him feel dizzy.

He took a deep breath, then coughed. That had been a mistake. The atmosphere recycling system was overloaded, and the air was just this side of putrid. He sniffed tentatively, then winced. It smelled like a combination of a locker room and a pig farm. Not good.

He looked around again, trying to think of something to say, then jumped as Nile poked him in the ribs.

"You gotta convince them. Start talking."

Sometimes she was remarkably unsympathetic.

He gritted his teeth. This was something he hadn't trained for in school. How was he supposed to convince...his mind leaped to a solution.

He was a pirate; a one-eyed pirate. As nervous as he was, the people watching him were probably terrified. For some reason, that thought gave him the needed confidence.

"People! Listen to me. You think pirates have captured you. The Feds think we're the Pirates of the Asteroid Belt."

He had their attention. He paused dramatically, then said, "And, we are! At least so far as they know."

"But! But, what we really are, is a group of miners who have been so mistreated by the government that we decided to build our own colony.

We control part of the asteroid belt, and we intend to expand our holdings. So far, the Feds have not been able to contend with us. You've just seen a graphic example of our power. The USS Hood is no more."

He looked around. Some of the nearer faces seemed pale and drawn. They were frightened.

"But, you...you poor people have no reason to be frightened of us. You've been shoved off Earth. Probably traded to Mars in exchange for something the government thinks is more valuable than you."

"You can become Martian colonists. It will be difficult and a lot of work. Conditions on Mars are almost as harsh as living in space. In some ways the life you'll find there will be harder to bear than you've been told. You're little more than slave labor to the established Martians. If you survive, and if you can accumulate enough credit, you'll eventually become citizens of Mars."

He looked at his audience. They were hanging on his words.

"However, you'll still be under the boot heel of the Federal government. They control Mars. They own the Martians. Without their good will, the Martians will die. They rely on supplies from Earth."

"We, on the other hand, need colonists. We value our workers and our freedom. If you decide to join us, I can promise you that your life will be hard and danger-filled. Living in the asteroid belt is not for the faint-hearted."

"The big difference, the thing that makes it worthwhile, is you will instantly be a free citizen of the Belt. You will have the opportunity to choose your line of work. You will be able to accumulate credits faster than on Mars. You will be able to invest your credits and possibly become wealthy. If you invest in a syndicated mining voyage, you will share in the proceeds. If the voyage discovers a real prize, say a meteoroid composed of rare metals, you might become fabulously wealthy."

He definitely had their interest. He glanced at Nile. Her mouth was slightly open, and she had a look of astonishment on her face. He mentally shrugged. He had been laying it on pretty thick. Now he had to figure out how to syndicate mining voyages. Well, someone had to figure it out anyway.

"People, we need colonists. We have a few ships now, but we plan to build our own. We have a nice place to live. Each of you can have your own private room. You'll have to help build your cabin, but there is plenty of space. The materials are available. Everything is waiting for your decision--on you."

He looked at Castenada. The man was watching him with no sign of resentment.

"I'm offering you a choice. You can elect to come with us and take control of your own life, or you can go serve your new masters on Mars. There your work will go to enrich the Feds. We've offered to trade with Mars. They are afraid. Afraid they'll anger the Earth government."

"They refuse to trade with us. That leaves us with no choice. It's true, we are pirates. We take what we need. The Feds are our enemy. Mars is afraid to trade and will soon become hostile since we will continue to capture their supply ships. We are all alone against the entire solar system, but we stand proud and free. We are the free pirates, but I'd rather call us revolutionaries. Just as the old United States was founded by revolutionaries, we are founding our own free state in the belt."

He paused again, raised his hands in an all-encompassing gesture, then said, "It's your choice. Join us or go to Mars. You have one hour to decide. I will require a list of those who want to come with us. That's all I have to say. Please think hard about your choice."

He turned, grabbed Nile's arm, and headed to the door to the bridge. Castenada followed quickly. Behind him, he could hear the conversation start, then multiply in volume.

The dull roar of sound faded as he turned the corner in the passageway and entered the bridge.

AS USUAL WITH humans, the colonists formed three groups. The smaller group, consisting of a little more than a third, was enthusiastic about joining the pirates. The others were either fearful that the government would disapprove or were outright hostile to the idea.

They seemed to feel that the pirates weren't playing by the rules and should be made to pay. The upshot was that they wanted to go on to Mars.

Adam listened to the two who had been appointed to represent the colonists with as much patience as he could muster. The woman who represented the "Originalists," as the ones who wanted to go on to Mars were calling themselves, was rude, loud, and in love with her own voice and opinions.

"You so-called pirates are nothing more than common criminals. You're almost all men, too, so you can't possibly have any idea about forming a law-abiding colony. That's a role for women and men who have been educated properly. The government sent us to Mars with good intentions, and it's up to us to follow their orders. Mars needs colonists. With our informed help, they will surely see that their governing structure is backward and should be changed. A modern approach is what is needed to make Mars a utopia in the heavens."

That speech was just so much wasted oxygen, Adam almost broke into laughter. Fighting back a grin and trying to look sober, he responded, "I think you'll find they have their own opinions on their government and the government of Earth. I've given you a choice to stay with the Feds or to form a new system with us. Based on what you've said so far, I'm increasingly tempted to rescind our offer. You should go on to Mars. You have some knowledge about the conditions there and know at least a little bit of what will be expected of you. I can't promise that."

He bit his tongue. He'd almost told her that he personally didn't want to see or hear her any longer than necessary.

The other representative was an older man. He'd remained mostly silent while the woman had spoken. Now he commented, "Captain, you're seeing the basic division in our group. Many of us were volunteered by the Feds to be colonists because they didn't like our independent attitude. We're intrigued by your offer, and I believe that we can contribute to your planned colony or state or whatever you end up calling it. The Federal government won't leave you alone, though. If they did, they'd suffer an embarrassing loss of face. They can't have that. It would make maintaining control more difficult. A lot of the population on Earth is becoming increasingly rebellious. We aren't alone in our desire for independence."

The man nodded to reinforce his point, and Adam nodded in understanding.

The woman started to speak again, but Adam held up his hand preemptively. "You've had your say. I understand your position. I want to hear more from Mr.?" He looked at the man, encouraging him.

"I'm Fitzgerald Hornsworth, but people just call me Fitzy." He frowned at the woman who was making an attempt to speak over him.

"Alice, I'd appreciate it, if you'd allow me to finish."

"No. I'm not hearing any more of this anti-federalist crap. It's treason. Both of you should be executed or banished." She stopped abruptly and looked upset. Apparently, she'd just realized that she, and those on her side, had also been banished.

Fitzy nodded and said, "We've all been banished. The Feds don't like your group any more than they like ours. You've been far too outspoken, Alice. They figured that either the Martians will shut you up or you'll be too busy trying to survive to keep bothering them with your ideas of Utopia."

He turned back to Adam. "As I was saying, Captain, we like the idea of independence. We want to join you, but we do have some reservations about government interference. Do you really think you can withstand the force they'll bring against you once they get organized?"

"I think we can, yes. You saw that the Hood could not cope with our weapons. At the moment we're better armed and better shielded than their ships. I expect this situation won't last forever, but we're working on additional innovations that may help us hold our advantage. Your group will find plenty to do, both building our habitat and working on new ships. We intend to become totally self-sufficient, but that will take time. For now--"

Alice interrupted with a shrill tone. "You're going to keep stealing the food from honest citizens? You're criminals, and you'll pay. I'm going to let the Martians know just how low you people are. I'm going to--"

She squealed and clapped her hands to her buttocks with a curse, then looked around. Nile was standing behind her, holding a wicked looking knife. The tip was red with blood.

Nile grinned evilly. "That'll be all we hear from you, Alice. You've communicated your group's desire to become slave labor on Mars. You can go back to them and let them know we understand their position."

Alice started to speak again, but Nile waved the bloody knife in front of her eyes.

"That's all you're going to say. Now, git! If you don't, I'll see you walk the plank!"

The woman sniffed, made a harrumphing sound, then left the room, still holding one hand on her punctured behind.

Nile smiled at Fritzy as she sheathed the knife. He smiled back.

"Thank you, young lady. That woman is unbearable. I don't think she really represents the other part of our group. There are some of the Originalists who do feel as she does. They think they're on some kind of rescue mission to save the Martians from themselves. The other people are simply more afraid of the unknown that you represent then they are of the bad conditions on Mars. It's that and the fact that they're so used to being oppressed by the government that they can't really bring themselves to think about an act of rebellion. Give me time to talk to them. I think more will decide to join you. Us, I mean."

Adam said, "Everyone you can convince is needed and will be welcome, but we're going to have to separate shortly. The loss of the Hood will force the Feds to send more ships to stop us. I expect to see them attack in force as soon as they can."

Fritzy paused, then asked quietly, "Do you really make people walk the plank? How?"

Adam started to laugh. "That's Nile. She's just trying to live up to the pirate role we've been given."

Nile snorted, and Fritzy chuckled.

THE NUMBERS CHANGED in the next few hours. Another ten percent of the group came over to the pirates' side. This was a mixed blessing. They really needed the help, but transporting that many people with their two ships was going to be difficult. The colony ship would be sent on to Mars. He had promised that those wanting to become Martians would be allowed to continue on.

Returning to Swift and unloading the Originalists, then taking the colony ship was tempting, but it was probably too risky. The Martians had passed on their opportunity and would now have to demonstrate their loyalty to the federal government. There was too great of a chance for an attack for him to risk the Swift base again.

The whole thing was a mess. He really wanted to take the colony ship, but that wasn't going to work out as long as he kept his promise to the Originalists. The people were packed like sardines in the large ship, even without those who had volunteered to come with the pirates.

The cargo hold of the Phoenix and the D-R's smaller one would barely hold the newcomers. The trip back to the Bubble would not be direct, of course. He still had to use a circuitous route. Protecting the Bubble's location was critically important.

THE COLONY SHIP was only visible in the Phoenix' long-range sensor. The Phoenix was moving slowly on a course that would exit the solar system on an obtuse angle to the ecliptic. The D-R had gone in a separate direction, moving quickly. The conditions on the smaller ship were worse than on the colony ship. The cargo hold was so packed that people had to take turns sitting down.

The D-R had to unload at the Bubble before its atmosphere handling system started to fail. That necessitated a more direct route at full speed.

Adam and Nile were watching the colony ship's approach to Swift. The vessel had entered Mars orbit and was maneuvering to match up with Deimos. As they watched, there was a flash, visible as a tiny point of light on the screen.

Nile exclaimed, "What the hell! Look at the sensors. Look!"

The long-range sensor wasn't showing any trace of the colony ship.

Adam looked at her. "Was that what I think it was?"

"Those bastards must have launched a missile. The colony ship is gone." Her eyes were huge.

It was gone. The Martians or possibly the federal officers had taken revenge for the Hood on the only available target. It was a vindictive strike that made little sense to Adam, other than to show him that the Feds were angry and would destroy his ships if they had the chance.

That was nothing different. He already knew that.

# 27
## BUILDING

THE SPACE AROUND the Bubble was congested. At least it seemed that way to Adam. He was simultaneously pleased and horrified by the presence of seven mining ships, in addition to his four. The eleven ships made the location stand out like a beacon. It would be easy to see if anyone were looking. The chance of someone looking was high, given how angry the Earther government must be.

On the flip side, Ngombe had been successful. The miners he'd contacted had eagerly agreed to participate in the rebellion. They were just as fed-up with their treatment as had been Captain Suarez. The opportunity to create their own independent nation was extremely attractive.

When the Phoenix had arrived, the miners and the colonists from the D-R were hard at work creating additional apartments inside the Bubble. There was plenty of room for everyone to have their own home. While the rooms weren't large by Earth standards, they were considered spacious by the spacers. Everyone was used to the restricted space on shipboard, so the rooms offered a welcome respite.

The Phoenix passed through the large lock and entered the Bubble. It was the easiest way to debark the colonists. There were not enough space suits for everyone, so that was not an option. The boarding tube would have taken a long time and exposed the colonists to unnecessary cold and low pressure, with the additional possibility of an air leak. Entering the Bubble with the Phoenix allowed the colonists to exit en masse through the cargo doors.

The process was simple. The colonists were acclimated to weightlessness, and the presence of an atmosphere allowed them to jump from the ship to the Bubble wall. Once there, they were given magnetic slippers and wristbands. With these, they could move freely on the largely iron inner surface since it was mostly iron.

Construction was proceeding apace. Everyone was enthusiastic, and a provisional governing council had been established. Adam was mildly hurt by that. It almost seemed as if he was no longer needed. After thinking it over, common sense prevailed. He concluded that he did not want to be involved in day-to-day operations. Governing democratically was not something he wanted to do, either. He was happier giving orders that would be carried out without any discussion.

Nile helped when she told him that his role was far more critical. He had to both acquire food and other supplies and to provide defense for the newly formed nation.

Things would work out however they worked out. He controlled four ships and would try to get more. The governing council could ask him to help, but they could not order him. After thinking about it, he was pleased with that situation.

The biggest worry was food. The miners had some hydroponics, but the capacity was not even close to what was needed. An algae-culture vat had been set up, and it was beginning to produce enough to feed everyone if the tasteless, cardboard-like wafers of pressed slime could be considered food.

Adam met with the mining ship captains, some of whom were near the end of their third voyage. Radiation exposure was their main worry, and they were desperate to get the plasma shield.

Adam waffled on that a bit. It offered him a considerable amount of leverage, but humane considerations dictated that he pass the knowledge on to others. The mining ships began to display the bumps of the plasma shield generators within twenty-four hours after he showed the miners how the system worked. It would not take more than a week before all of the mining ships were shielded.

He and Nile discussed the possibility of their technology leaking out to the Feds.

"Look, Nile, it will eventually end up in their hands. On one side, I don't want them to have it, because that would even out the odds in a fight, but on the other side, it is the right thing to do. Humans are going to be in space, and forcing them to die of radiation poisoning or to become earthworms again really isn't something for which I want to feel responsible."

She nodded. "I can see that. I agree we should give everyone the shield. On the other hand, the plasma cannon tech has to be guarded closely. We can give the miners the information about the laser weapons we've designed. Their ships all have mining lasers already. It's nothing to sync the things so they can be used as weapons. We just have to keep something in reserve."

He considered the problem. It wouldn't do to let the Feds catch up in the arms race. That would quickly lead to defeat. Given equal shielding and weapons, the government would build a large fleet and overwhelm their few ships. After a bit, an idea came to him.

"Nile, what do you think the chances are that the Feds will completely analyze the plasma shield equipment once they have a working unit?"

"Huh? I don't know. They might not if it worked and they needed it quickly. Otherwise, they'd eventually tear into it until they understood the principle underneath the shield."

He nodded slowly. "That's kind of what I thought." He rubbed his cheek, then explained.

"If they get to decide when to act, they can wait until they're totally ready to attack us. If we force the issue, they will have to respond and, if they're not ready, then maybe we'll have a better chance."

She sniffed. "Sure. That's obvious, but what advantage will it give us and what does this have to do with the shield system?"

"I was thinking of maybe changing the circuitry so that it would accept an external signal. The generators use infrared lasers to coordinate their emissions. The current circuitry only uses a very narrow bandwidth for the coordinating signal. The filter circuitry can be changed so that it responds to the original bandwidth and a harmonic. I can put in a circuit that will time-out when it senses the harmonic. The challenge is to incorporate it into the rest of the circuitry in such a way that it isn't apparent what it does. It has to look like it's necessary for the generator to function."

Nile shook her head. "Look, I'm just a space marine. Translate that to something I can understand."

"It's simple. We give them the shield generator. Make it so the Feds think they stole it without us knowing about it. Then we threaten an attack. They duplicate the generator as fast as they can and install them on all of their ships. They've got the shield, so they think they're ready to fight us. They attack. You know they want us in the worst way. We're making them look bad, and they can't take that."

She said, "Yes, but how does the harmonic help?"

He smiled. He understood she was playing the part of a foil to help him formulate his idea. It was a good strategy.

"The harmonic signal comes into play when we're in battle. We hit their ships with a laser that is tuned to that bandwidth.

They might not even notice it. It could be low power. Anyway, the filter passes it, the circuit overloads and times out. Voila! Their shields fail right at a critical time."

"I see. Would this critical time be just a moment before a plasma burst hits them?"

"Now you're getting the idea. If they haven't figured out the circuits, but have only duplicated them, they might not wise up quickly. Maybe they'll just think that the plasma cannon is too powerful for the shield. Maybe that will give us the advantage we need to beat them."

"The timing would have to be precise. The shield can't go down until right before the plasma hits them. Otherwise, they might let their other ships know their shield mysteriously failed. That would increase the chance of some bright scientist figuring out the problem."

"Yeah. I'm not sure how to build the circuitry, but it's something I'll work on."

THE ADVANTAGES THEY currently held were few. The shield was one, but he was practically ensuring that the Feds would get it if he followed his humanitarian impulse and gave it to the other miners.

The plasma cannon was the second. Given the shield technology, the plasma cannon was an obvious modification, although the use of the Em-Max principle to boost the plasma velocity wasn't something anyone else would think of as quickly as he had. His father had been the Em-Max expert, not only because of his modification of the device but also because he had an understanding of the device's working principle that no one else could match. He couldn't count on the enemy remaining behind in the arms race. It occurred to him that it would be terrible if the Earth scientists were working on something similar or even better. That was a grim thought.

The other two advantages the pirates had going for them were the carbon hull coating and the fact that the Feds didn't know where they were based. He couldn't count on that, though. It was only a matter of time before the Bubble habitat was discovered by the Space Navy. When it was, it had better be prepared to defend itself.

Now that was a better thought. Adam did some quick calculations. They showed that it would take a huge number of plasma generators to shield the Bubble. He revised his calculations, assuming more powerful generators. That was better since it couldn't take so many. He made a note to have some larger units built.

That in itself would be a problem. They needed so many of the standard size generators to protect all of the new ships, that it would use all of the production resources for months. Their manufacturing capacity had to be boosted. If he could put off the miners for a week, they could build a prototype of a larger unit. That would let him experiment. It could be paired with some of the smaller ones to create a shield to test.

The Bubble ought to have its own plasma cannons for defense. If the larger generator worked, it could be adapted to cannon use. That would allow a more massive plasma burst. Of course, that led to the necessity of having a bigger Em-Max to drive the plasma. He sighed in frustration. It seemed like everything depended on something else. Their industrial capacity simply had to be increased rapidly.

He needed resources for weapons and defense so the housing issue would have to take second place. People weren't going to be happy if they had to wait for an apartment. He had to convince them that it was in their best interest.

The issue suddenly became more urgent the next day. A large mining ship, The Star of Bethlehem, had arrived. It was a newer ship constructed by a private combine to their own specifications and operated by Captain Javid. Javid had heard about the Bubble from another mining ship. The word was spreading.

The big ship was fresh from Luna, and the captain had brought news that the navy was building twenty ships on Luna. Fifteen of these were of the cruiser class, but the other five were a new, larger model. It was only a matter of time before the Feds' space navy was going to be powerful enough to cause real problems.

The elected council formalized Adam's status. He was the Admiral of the Bubble Navy. It was a meaningless title, but it gave him a warm feeling, nevertheless. It would have been more meaningful if he had about a hundred more cruisers.

As Admiral, he had to plan for the common defense, and also arrange for additional provisions. The second part was going to be the most difficult.

Some of the new captains volunteered to contribute asteroid-based hydroponic gardens that they owned. It was an excellent strategy to have an automated garden that would grow vegetables. Some of the miners had started the trend, and now many had gardens. This was a source of food that he hadn't counted on, but it wasn't enough. They needed the Mars supply ships to keep their growing population fed.

Adam didn't like that much. The Martians would resent the loss, and that could cause problems in the future. A possible solution occurred to him. It was something they could begin immediately, even without the Martians' permission.

He delegated three of the new ships to the job of collecting ice. They would push ice towards Mars orbit. The Martians didn't want to trade with the pirates, but nothing prevented the pirates from dropping much-needed water on the red planet in exchange for looted supplies. It wasn't an ideal solution, but it eased his conscience somewhat.

Some other mining ships arrived. Some of them joined without hesitation. Others agreed to trade if they could get their ships shielded. Some of the groups joined the rapidly growing enterprise but did not want to live in the Bubble. A few had their own habitat, usually an inflatable dome located on a large asteroid, and they wanted to continue building their own small community.

There was nothing wrong with that, as long as they didn't decide the Feds made a better ally than the pirates. Adam spoke to the council about that.

Someone had come up with the idea of forming a confederation, and the articles were being hammered out. If all of the diverse groups signed up, they would have a framework for their interaction. That was something that a physics education didn't cover, and Adam was happy to let the older and "wiser" heads struggle with the details.

Meanwhile, the work had become more organized. Some of the new colonists had experience along those lines. The apartment construction slowed a little, but not much. Some of the workers had been assigned to shield production, and that was speeding up. The mining ships were sprouting generators right and left.

Another group had formed a private business that offered hull coating. They started with the carbon spray coating, but quickly increased their capability until they could provide a reflective layer. A ship that had the reflective coating was relatively immune to laser attack.

If the carbon coating was added, it made the space ship difficult to visually detect. It could still be seen with radar, but that required excess power. Most of the ships had a radar unit in their sensor system, but they didn't use it much due to the power drain.

The new company, the first based out of the Bubble, was almost overwhelmed with work. Every captain wanted the new tech.

A second group came to Adam with a proposition. If he turned the plasma generator manufacturing over to them, they would act as contractors to the council. This was attractive because having the manufacturing under his control bothered him. He wasn't sure how all of the activity would work out economically, but he had a gut feeling that it would be best to allow things to decentralize. The open market would provide a granularity of control that a central bureaucracy could never match. That seemed both obvious and desirable.

He turned the plans over to them and made them sign an agreement not to modify the system. He didn't want to risk having someone remove the over-load circuitry he'd woven into the system.

IT HAD BEEN weeks since Adam and Nile had been in space. They'd been too busy with details to even think about going out in the Phoenix or the D-R. They had been given a spacious apartment, courtesy of the council. It was a perk that went with the Admiral title. Adam wondered if he'd be allowed to keep it if he retired, but that even was so distant in his mind that it seemed unreal.

Two ships had been delegated to intercept the next Mars supply ship. They came back with full holds and happy crews. The ship had been an unmanned drone, and they'd had an easy time of it.. They took what they needed, leaving some for the Martians in accordance with Adam's orders.

Due to the raids, Mars was lobbying for more supply ships. They listened in to the radio communications as a matter of course. The ongoing conversation between Mars and Luna had never been encrypted.

That suddenly changed. The communication stream had been fully encrypted and they didn't have the computer resources to break the code.

The transmissions from Earth were still the same. The planet leaked electronic signals like a sieve. Commercial television and radio were mostly satellite-based, but the signals couldn't help but spread. The news was generally upbeat. The dictatorship's propagandists were working overtime. No one knew what the actual conditions on the surface were, though. The Feds had stopped sending out mining ships, so the information that the new miners brought had ceased.

Those actions were a bad sign. It was apparent that the Feds and Martians were preparing to do something about the pirates. Not only had the pirates had shown themselves to be dangerous and had caused a problem, but the new community had given the miners somewhere to go besides returning to Earth. Their discoveries and cargo had started to come to the Bubble. Most of them were not eager to return to Earth. They rightly suspected that they would not be allowed back on their ships and would end up in prison or worse.

Adam was pleased to hear that someone had built a large optical telescope. It was a one-meter compound reflector that floated in space. The builder hadn't bothered to ask permission. He had constructed and placed it far enough from the Bubble that it wouldn't be in the way of shipping. He'd stuck a beacon on the frame so that incoming and outgoing ships would know where it was.

It had gas maneuvering jets and solar power and could move enough to target various parts of the Earth-Luna system. The resulting pictures were studied carefully for evidence of shipbuilding around Luna.

The telescope showed that the twenty ship number had expanded to forty-three. The space navy was increasing the number of ships far more rapidly than seemed possible.

There were now ten of the larger ships orbiting Luna. The really disturbing news was the sighting of a massive ship under construction. It looked like it would be roughly ten times the size of the Phoenix.

When he heard about that, it made Adam almost frantic. The Bubble defenses were coming along, but not fast enough to suit him. The same situation held with the mining ships. Every ship had modified its lasers so they could serve as a weapon, but so far, he had kept the plasma cannon a secret. Now it looked like he would have to arm all of the ships. He had to if he were to have a chance at meeting the USS Navy on anything remotely close to even terms.

NILE JUMPED. ADAM had gasped and was now sitting upright. It was their night, and they were in bed, netted down with a soft cover. He had slid up and was sitting with the sheet holding his thighs down.

"What's up? Something bother you?" she asked as she turned the light on.

He took a deep breath. "I had an idea. I was dreaming, and we were in the Phoenix. We were fighting against heavy odds. The Feds had twenty ships that were closing in on us, and the missiles were thick. They had fired a lot of explosive shells, so we had to get out of the way. The missiles were coming in from all sides. It was a nightmare."

"Yes, but what was your idea? Did we get away? I mean, in your dream."

He looked at her, calming down from the intensity of the experience. His answer didn't seem to relate to her question at first.

"You know, every time we've fired the plasma cannon, the ship has jumped."

She sighed in resignation. He was going to be mysterious, and she'd have to wait for him to explain in his own fashion.

He continued. "The plasma cannon uses a stripped down Em-Max to boost the plasma. The Em-Max has never been shown to emit a mass, but the suspicion is that it somehow accelerates virtual particles in the quantum plenum. I believe that I've demonstrated the accuracy of that assumption by the plasma cannon. No one can argue that the plasma is accelerated by the Em-max."

She nodded, and he paused, then continued. "No one can argue that fact. I am sure that the virtual particles give it a hard shove. So, anyway, the cannon works so well that I've never thought about fine-tuning it. Nor have I thought about using it for anything other than a weapon. That was short-sighted of me."

Nile said nothing. It was apparent that she was waiting for him to explain.

He grinned a wolfish grin. "If I modify the cannon a little by using a more powerful Em-Max and by extending the cannon tube, the plasma will reach a higher speed, maybe even a significant fraction of light. There will be two effects. More energy will impact the target, and the ship will jump even harder."

She thought of a question. "Won't the shock of the recoil be dangerous? Could it damage the ship or hurt the occupants?"

"Well, that might happen. We'll have to make our ships more immune to acceleration. You see, on one level, the cannon can be viewed as a more efficient space drive. The plasma doesn't mass much, but it masses more than the virtual particles. It's reaction mass. No matter how powerful the Em-Max engine, the acceleration can barely be felt. There's just not enough mass ejected. That's why we accelerate so slowly. Now, we've seen that the cannon gives the ship a hard shove. A modified cannon will push it more. All I've got to do is to figure out how to feed the plasma continuously, and voila! We've got a plasma rocket. That will give us a great advantage in a fight. We can out-shoot, and now, out-accelerate the competition so we can out-maneuver them."

Nile's eyes were shining. "That is magnificent. I knew you were smart, but this is amazing."

She paused to pull him close. When their faces were inches apart, she said, "Adam, I am so in love with you. Will you marry me?"

He looked into her eyes. They were wide and deep, and he felt like he would fall into their depths. His breath seemed to have gotten lost and it took an effort to get it started again. He gasped, then became aware that his eye was watering for some reason. When he could speak, he said, "I thought you weren't interested in a long-term relationship."

She licked his ear lobe. "I probably gave that impression. I'm cautious, but I always told myself when I know that I'm committed, it will be for keeps. So, will you? Marry me, I mean."

Before he could answer, she looked closely at his face.

"Are you crying?"

"Uh. No. My eye is watering. I don't know why." He tried clearing his throat. Now his voice was unsteady.

"You are! Do I mean that much to you? Tell me." She licked his ear again.

He worked at getting control of his emotions, then attempted to answer. "It's just that I...I...Oh, hell. I guess I lost hope that I'd find someone. I've been happy since we've been together. When I'm with you, even our problems don't bother me." He paused, then added, "Well, maybe a bit."

He looked at her to see if she was going to laugh. She was looking at him with those huge eyes again, so he continued. "Nile, I didn't want to say anything or do anything for fear that you'd lose interest and dump me. My self-image is one of an eminently dumpable guy. Besides, I'm blind in one eye."

That last was a total non-sequitur, and it made him feel stupid. If he could just learn to make sense. Now that he'd botched his explanation, she probably would lose interest.

Nile pulled back and looked at him with a funny expression. After a moment, he recognized it as falling somewhere between love and tenderness.

She whispered, "That's why I love you. You aren't just some average macho pirate. You're a sensitive pirate." She kissed him. "And, a handsome one. Your eyepatch makes you look very dashing, too. So, answer me. Will you marry me? I'm not going to ask again."

He blurted, "Yes. Don't change your mind. I wanted to say yes, but I got confused and then embarrassed. You want a man who doesn't cry and..."

He paused, trying to get a grip on himself, then shook his head negatively. "That's who I am, I guess. Are you sure you want to marry me?"

Nile laughed. "You idiot. Why would I be asking you, if I wasn't serious? Of course, I do. I take this to mean that we agree?"

He nodded. "Yes. I'll marry you first thing when we get out of bed."

She snuggled close. "Let's turn out the light and get back to sleep."

She nuzzled his ear again. She knew that it made him crazy. Then she added, "Sleep or whatever comes up."

He felt an answering twinge. His blood pressure had just jumped about ten points, but there was something he had to do first.

"I'll turn out the light in a bit. Right now I've got to write some notes. I don't want to forget my dream insights."

She waited, her eyes on his profile while he scribbled on his tablet.

When he was done, he dimmed the light and turned back to her embrace.

# 28
## ANTICIPATED REPRISAL

ADAM'S RESEARCH ON his new space drive idea was progressing. The main problem was power related. Continuously operating the system drew more power than the standard mining ship reactor produced. This limitation meant he had to design and build a more powerful reactor, which was something he was not qualified to do. The alternative was to use the new drive as an emergency booster. That was the approach on which he was concentrating.

The probability of attack by the Feds was increasing daily. Everyone was aware of that, and it gave their daily work a sense of urgency. Defenses had to be ready, and ships had to be armed and battle-worthy.

Adam was pleased since he only had to explain what he wanted for others to take on the responsibility for the task's completion.

Several of the new Federal ships built at Luna had departed from orbit, only to be replaced by other ships being built. The vast ship being built at Luna was still in progress. Their telescope's pictures showed that it still had gaps in its hull. The general consensus was that the Feds were waiting until it was complete before they began anti-pirate activities in earnest.

The Mars supply ships were now escorted by a minimum of three cruiser class vessels. As a result, they had ceased raiding. The lack of food supplies had slowed them at first, but now there were several more hydroponic farms scattered on various asteroids.

ADAM HAD BEEN fine-tuning the boosters he'd installed on the D-R. He'd selected that vessel for his test platform since he felt he knew it marginally better than any of the other ships in the small fleet. The final adjustments had been completed, and the ship was ready for field testing.

Everyone was leaving the ship when he received a comm message from Nile.

"Adam, you'd better get to the comm center. A message has come in wrapped in your personal encryption. It's from Captain Javid." That was the captain and owner of the ship that was monitoring Mars-Earth communications.

He cycled through the airlock, grabbed a bottle of compressed air, and leaped towards the distant wall of the Bubble. They'd taken to using small bottles of compressed air to propel themselves from one side of the void to the other.

He opened the valve and jetted towards the far wall, noting as he did, that the general atmosphere in the Bubble seemed fresh and didn't smell. The new air recycling and scrubbing plant was working correctly. That had been a problem at first. No one liked stinky air, even if they did get used to it. Now that the space inside the asteroid was filled with air and heated to a reasonable temperature, moving around inside was a pleasure-almost like flying without wings.

Adam kept the valve open until he reached a velocity that was marginally safe, being careful to reserve enough to brake when he approached the far wall. A couple of the colonists had broken bones this way. It was better to be cautious and go slow than to miscalculate. That gave them a whole new appreciation for the phrase "hitting the wall."

Nile and Flynn were waiting for him along with various comm techs. They led him into a glass-walled room, shut the door for privacy, and expectantly waited while he keyed in his personal encryption key.

The comp immediately quit displaying the login dialog and replaced it with a vid of Captain Javid. The captain was obviously worked up.

"Admiral. I've encrypted this message for you only. I'm afraid that it might create an undue alarm if it leaks to the general population. The USSN ships that have been probing around the edge of the belt have moved into Mars orbit."

"They've formed up near Deimos, while they wait for the main part of the USSN fleet to arrive from Luna. The five larger ships and the single super large one are in that fleet. They somehow sandbagged us."

"The last pictures we saw from the telescope, showed the super ship in an unfinished state. Now we think they painted the hull with blotches that looked like open areas. They've had it ready to go for some time and were only waiting for it to be fully armed."

"We also found out that the ships near Deimos have requisitioned iron slugs from the Swift base. They specified the dimensions precisely. They won't accept anything that doesn't meet those specs."

"We believe the slugs are for use in some kind of mass driver weapons, probably railguns. That technology was close to being complete, the last time we were at the Ribbon. They may have rushed the development. If that's correct, we will have to face more than just missiles and conventional weapons.

Railguns can fire streams of projectiles at speeds faster than boosted missiles."

Javid looked worried. "Have the plasma shields been tested? Will they deflect a twenty-kilogram slug going at missile speed?"

Without waiting for an answer, he concluded his message. "I estimate that the USSN will be ready to begin operations against us within twenty-four hours of the big ships arriving from Luna. I hope you're ready. Out."

Adam looked up. The other two wore concerned expressions as they waited for him to speak.

"Well, it's not great news, but it's better than some of the things I've been imagining. The plasma screens have been reinforced and should provide partial protection against railgun projectiles. The problem is, we don't know the failure point. It depends on how many projectiles strike the same part of a shield and how quickly. They might overload the shield with rapid fire. However, we still have an advantage. We have plasma cannon and they don't. Besides, there's a good chance their shields will fail."

He was referring to the built-in overload circuitry. If the trick worked, it would be a big surprise to the Feds. But that was if it worked. No one knew whether the Feds had modified the circuitry. In fact, they didn't actually know when the Feds had acquired the shield generator tech. It might have reached them through a couple of different pathways, neither of which was reliable and both of which had disappeared and weren't reporting.

He wasn't going to mention the booster engines. They still needed testing. It wasn't likely that they'd be able to install them on more than a few ships, given the lack of time.

Flynn shrugged and said, "Reality is what it is. We have to be ready. We knew they'd be coming sooner or later."

Adam said, "They aren't here yet. I'd give a lot, though, to know where they'll head from Swift. Will they spread out, or stay together? Interesting problem, that."

Nile said, "They'll stay together. We've shown them that we can take individual ships. They won't want to split up and give us the chance to intercept them singly. Their strength is in numbers, but they might break into a couple of squadrons. That way they could cover more area as they search for us."

Flynn said, "That makes sense. Hey! I just remembered something that could help us. They've been escorting the supply ships to Mars, but they let them return alone. What if we grabbed them on the way back. We could use them for something, and it would keep the government busy replacing them."

Adam thought about that. It would build their fleet, and it would probably make the Feds angry enough that they would have to detail some of their force to fly back to Luna with each returning supply ship. That would help even the numbers a little. Even the larger colony ships flew back empty, with just their crew onboard.

Now that was a thought. If worst came to worst and the USSN fleet located the Bubble, it would be a good idea to have an escape plan. One of the colony ships, or even better, two of them, would provide a way to get people off the rock. Otherwise, it was likely going to be a massacre.

"Isn't it about time for another colony ship to be on the way?"

Flynn looked at the schedule they'd compiled through long observation. "It already arrived. It should be returning to Luna shortly. It will pass the Fed Fleet on about a week out from Swift. Why?"

He thought it out, then explained. "We can send some ships to intercept the colony flight. The Feds will be at Swift or heading wherever they decide to head. We can grab the colony ship behind their back. That should disrupt their plans a bit. We'll have to head way out and circle around to the Bubble. Once we've got that ship, we'll have a means of escape, if they find our location. I'd prefer to evacuate all non-combatants. I just don't know where we'll go if we have to relocate."

Flynn seemed amused at that idea.

Adam was a little disgruntled at the small man's attitude. "What is it, Flynn. Why is that so funny?"

"I know something you don't. That's what. One of the last mining ships to arrive has been poking around Uranus. There's a rock out there that's plenty big enough to hold a second city. It's not as nice as the Bubble, but it has a bunch of smaller caverns. Tunnels like. We could seal the entrances and build rooms inside. They didn't say if the caves had multiple openings or not, but we can cope with whatever is there. That's what we do, right?"

It was Adam's turn to grin. "That's what we do. What we have to do. Alright, let's find out as much about this new rock as possible, and also get a couple of ships launched to go after the colony ship. We need its capacity."

THE FEDERAL FORCE had arrived at Mars. The telescope showed a pretty picture of forty-three ships were arrayed neatly in two separate formations. The admiral in charge must have been determined to impress the Mars colonists with his fleet's precision.

The formation also impressed the pirates. Rumors were flying through the space inside the Bubble almost as quickly as ships flew through the void. The spacers were all realists. No one survived long in space without being grounded in practical matters. They were inclined to evaluate the potential life-threatening aspect of every development so they would be prepared.

It was a good habit to have. Practically speaking, every unexpected event was life-threatening. No accident in space ever brought a happy ending.

As a result, the rumors were all negative. It was becoming demoralizing and work suffered. The council issued several directives about rumors, but they had little effect. People were depressed and had little interest in work.

After two days, Adam realized he had to take action. The fleet was still in Mars orbit and had yet to commit to action. He had wanted to wait until the ships had left Mars and were, hopefully, headed out into the belt before his two ships grabbed the colony ship.

That ship was now approaching Earth space. The necessity to improve morale, and to get the ship before it was so close to Luna that it fell within missile range, meant that he had to act now. Accordingly, he had the order sent to attack and shortly after receiving an acknowledgment from the two pirate ships, he released the news to the Bubble population.

That was viewed as a positive, and the prospect of immediate action cheered everyone. Work resumed, and the engineers and construction workers showed an increased sense of urgency. They had wanted action to demonstrate that they were not going to be passive victims. Now that they had it, the impending conflict made their preparations seem more critical. Everyone worked like furies.

THE CAPTURE OF the colony vessel was too critical to be withheld, and Adam released it as soon as he knew their mission had been successful. The capture had gone down smoothly. The returning crew had surrendered rather than risk damage to their ship. The pirates' weapons had proven so effective in the past that they gave up as soon as they were hailed.

The transport's crew was reluctant to join the pirates. As much as they feared the pirates' weapons, they feared the USSN's treatment of traitors more. Ngombe classified them as prisoners of war and had them locked up for the duration of the voyage.

The three ships immediately headed out of the solar system, heading at an acute angle to the ecliptic. They would reenter the belt near Jupiter's orbit and then backtrack to the Bubble.

ADAM HAD SPOKEN to the captain who had discovered the cavern-filled rock near Uranus' orbit. The asteroid was an unusual one. It was a mix of metallic ore and stone. The caverns that extended throughout were partially filled with water ice. The object might have been part of a comet that was captured by Uranus' gravity, but there was no way of knowing.

It was important because of the caverns and ice. The combination made it as perfect a prospect for habitation as could be found in the outer solar system. Some members of the council had been enthusiastic about settling on Saturn's moon Titan. Others had proposed Europa or some of the other moons of Jupiter, but radiation from the planets paired with lack of magnetic fields made those locations less than optimal.

The major problem with moons was that human presence would be detected quickly by any astronomical research project. The satellites were under almost constant observation from both Earth and Luna, not to mention Mars.

The pirates had considered capturing the Feds' Ceres base, but that would make them even more of a target. Ceres was the most massive asteroid, nearly the size of a small moon, but it was a barren, rocky lump that held little promise. There were no caverns, so the base was a simple dome structure. Taking it didn't make much sense.

The other asteroids were less likely to be watched. That was how they'd gotten away with creating their base at the Bubble. Its location helped since it orbited beyond Jupiter and was often hidden from Earth by the giant planet. So far as they knew, their presence hadn't been detected.

The new asteroid was the logical prospect. Accordingly, they had planned a mission to create a bolt-hole there. Several ships full of tools and engineers, or people that passed for engineers, had been dispatched to the rock.

As soon as the colony transport arrived, it would be loaded with additional supplies to be taken to the new location. The council had set up a commission to create a list of the settlers and supplies that would be transported to the second location. Their job would be to take the work the first crews had started on to the next level and create a habitat that could hold the entire population, should they have to evacuate the Bubble.

THE CAPTURED COLONY transport had circled around and was inbound to the Bubble. It would take it another week to arrive, and the preparations for its arrival were in process. The shield manufacturing group had worked double shifts to produce enough generators to shield the transport. They wanted to have it ready to go within a few days after its arrival.

Adam and Nile were eating when his comm signaled. It was Jem.

"The USSN is moving. They've left Mars orbit and are headed into the belt. They're making no secret of their destination since they're flying directly towards Ceres. I expect them to make that their forward base. The base itself doesn't have much capacity, but they could make a missile storage facility there. There's plenty of space on that rock."

Adam and Nile looked at each other. This was not unexpected. The odds had been high that the Feds would head to Ceres. If they stockpiled missiles there, it would make the big asteroid a prime target for a raid.

The only ship they currently had with missile capacity was the Phoenix, and its racks were full. The desirability of adding missiles to the mining ships hadn't occurred to Adam.

"Nile, what about putting some missile racks on the smaller ships?"

She wasn't optimistic. "They don't have enough storage to carry more than maybe four extras. The missiles mass a little less than a thousand kilos each. You mount four on the outside of a mining ship and jam four in the cargo bay, and that's going to impact the acceleration. It will also impact maneuverability. You sure that you want to handicap them in a fight?"

"Well, maybe we mount four on the hull and don't give them any reloads. They could launch all four at the inception of a battle, then their specs would be almost normal."

"That might work, but what about the shields that the enemy now has?" She paused, then added somewhat sarcastically, "Thanks to us."

"We don't know if they've put them on all of their ships or even any. If they do have them, they might be tempted to let the shields handle missiles without using their point defense."

She got the point. "That'd be a big mistake. The shields go down just as the missiles arrive and boom!"

He nodded. "That's assuming our trick works. If they modified the generators, it might not."

"Yeah, but a direct missile hit will shake them up. Remember what happened when we took one. The hull rang, and a lot of stuff got broken. I'd hate to be inside when four missiles struck at the same time, even if the shields held."

"That's a given. The mining ships fire all four at once at the same target. Then they use the override signal just before the missiles impact. That should optimize the strategy."

Nile added, "Then they shoot 'em with the plasma cannon and clean up the pieces with the weaponized lasers. Right?"

He thought about it, then remembered the iron slugs. "They have the railguns. They'll be shooting as we approach. That might stop the missiles."

She shook her head. "No. The railgun slugs aren't fast enough at long range. They'll want to wait with those until we get relatively close. Otherwise, our ships can get out of the way before the slugs arrive. At the speed this is going to happen, those slugs will be almost like stationary obstacles."

He didn't answer immediately, so she added, "I guess they could throw a bunch of iron at the missiles, but that will help us too. They'll use a lot of energy and ammo blasting at the missiles. They're not so easy to hit, you know."

Adam agreed. "Anything that depletes their ammunition should help. What if we ambush them?"

That seemed silly to Nile. "How? They can see us coming."

"Yes, but if we dump a hold full of debris, rocks and such, on the way in, it could cause trouble for them."

"Only if it hits them. If they see it coming and move out of the way, it will have no effect. Besides, wouldn't it be chancy? What if one of our ships hit the cloud?"

"Yeah. That would be bad, but I don't know, it seems like rocks might help. I'm going to have some of the scientists think about it. Maybe they'll have an idea."

Nile somewhat hesitantly agreed that a debris cloud could possibly deflect or slow down some of the railgun slugs.

Adam finished by dredging up Moltke's insight. "Well, it's a given that no battle plan survives first contact with the enemy. I guess we'll just have to do our best."

# 29

# ENEMY ACTION

THE USSN FLEET rendezvoused at Ceres. It stayed near the planetoid for three days, then split into two groups and departed. The pirates kept a close watch, but the telescope lost sight of the smaller group after a day. The other detachment of twenty-five ships was not moving very quickly, but its course was clear. It was headed directly toward the Bubble.

Ngombe looked up as Adam came onto the bridge.

"Admiral. It looks like they know where we are. They're heading right for us."

"Ugh. That's too much of a coincidence to be coincidental. You must be right. What about the other group?"

Ngombe drew his lips back in a grimace. "We've lost them. They were headed off along the Jupiter vector the last we saw, but I'm suspicious. If they located us, that second group could be circling around to come at us from the side."

This was serious. "They could. I'm thinking that we don't have to worry about them trying to surround us.

They don't want to get in the direct line of fire from their own ships."

Ngombe wasn't so sure about the issue. "They can still effectively box us in a kill zone. We'd have to fight on two fronts, and it could be a real mess."

It was Adam's turn to snarl. "Yes, but we can prepare for that. How are the debris fields coming?"

Adam had turned the idea of launching debris over to a couple of the scientists. They'd modified the concept, and it had become a passive defense. They were placing cargo holds of rocks and metallic debris in space around the Bubble. The clouds overlapped with planned pathways that the pirates could fly through. Anyone who didn't know about the fields would have to approach slowly or risk damage.

"They have covered about a quarter of the sphere. I don't think they're going to finish in time. The Feds aren't coming quickly, but the debris clouds are taking longer than we thought."

Adam wasn't going to sit passively by and let the Feds destroy the Bubble. "Let's drop some missiles in the other quadrants. Have them modified for remote control. They'll be indistinguishable from normal rocks, and we can launch them once the USSN arrives. If we play it right, we can wait until they've passed the missiles before we launch. That will put a torch up their behinds."

Ngombe laughed. "Yeah. I can imagine. They might even think we have an invisible ship."

In point of fact, all of their ships were now almost totally invisible. Each silvered hull was covered with carbon particles, making them difficult to pick out against the blackness, except when the ship occluded a star.

"They will have difficulty seeing us. If they can't see our ships with optics, they'll have to use active sensors. That will remove our advantage since they'll find our ships. On the good side, it will allow us to keep track of them more easily, and we can target their signals."

The Nigerian shrugged. "We're so far outnumbered, I'll take any advantage I can get. What about a running battle? Should we send out a force to intercept them before they get here?"

That was something he'd been thinking about. It might mess up the enemies' plans, but it would also weaken their defenses.

"I don't think we should attack until they're massed here. We're going to send out four ships. They'll wait about a million klicks out, then accelerate back in once the battle is joined. They can reinforce any weak points."

Adam paused. "You know, Captain, this is all new to me. I'm not a military tactician, and I'm flying blindfolded."

Ngombe answered, "No one is experienced in space battle tactics. The closest humans have come to this is in aircraft dogfights, but I'm thinking it's more like a naval battle, only in three dimensions. The military historians will have a lot of fun tearing your strategy to bits for years to come."

"That's what I'm afraid of. That and the possibility that I'm going to serve as a perfect example of how to lose."

Ngombe grinned, apparently amused, but said nothing.

Adam added, "I'm hoping they delay until we get that empty colony ship here. I'd like to send as many people out to the new location as we can. That way..." He paused, thinking of the possibilities.

Ngombe said, "That way if they destroy the Bubble, we might barely have enough people to start over. The death toll won't be one hundred percent, just about half."

When put that way, it sounded horrible. They had to defeat the USSN force before the Bubble was destroyed. Now that the Feds had shown they knew where the pirates' base was located, there were only two possibilities. They could leave the Bubble to become a navy base, or they could fight and defend it. It would have to be heavily protected continuously for the foreseeable future. Its presence would serve as a constant reminder that the Feds didn't control everything in the solar system. Adam couldn't see them letting that reminder stand.

They'd heard that the North American population wasn't too happy about the new dictatorship. It seemed that there were still some people who loved their freedom more than the dubious benefits of an all-controlling government. The pirates had become something of a rallying symbol for the resistance.

The existence of a group that controlled their own destiny and didn't report to the government served to encourage the few citizens that hadn't given up their desire for self-rule. While the news they'd intercepted was obviously propaganda-laden, there had been some facts that leaked out via unauthorized transmissions from the few countries that were not yet assimilated under the dictatorship.

The situation was unstable, and the pirates' existence had become a black eye for the government. Adam was sure that the Feds would spare no expense to wipe them out. The question was whether the current force was enough to accomplish the task.

DURING THE WAITING period, the Bubble was a frenzy of last-minute activity. Every ship was loaded with four missiles and a disposable rack. The holds were filled with boxes of debris, rocks, and scrap metal, while the pulsed laser systems were synchronized. Adam had decided that the plasma cannon was too important a weapon to keep secret. He didn't want the Feds to find out about them, but it couldn't be helped, so they were mounted on the mining ships. The Bubble surface sprouted shield generators and plasma cannon emplacements, along with missile racks.

Morale was high. People were too busy to become depressed or fearful. Partly due to the Feds insistence on calling them pirates and partly because Adam had become hugely popular, the Bubble residents had taken to calling themselves Pirates of the Asteroid Belt. That was soon shortened to either Pirates or Belters.

The general consensus was that the USSN was flying into a trap. There were standing bets on how long the Fed ships would last.

Adam had reluctantly sent Nile off as commander of the four ships that were designated as a flanking force. They were to float silently in space a million kilometers off until the Federal Navy had joined battle with the defenders around the Bubble. Then they would advance and attack targets of opportunity.

She had wanted to stay and fight on the front line, but he had overruled that idea. In contrast to the general feeling, he had doubts about the outcome and believed there was a marginally better chance for survival in one of the flanking ships. If things were going poorly for the pirates, the flanking ships could slip away without engaging and rendezvous at the second asteroid.

THE GROUP'S SPIRITS were raised even more when the colony ship arrived, along with its escorts. The list of people to go to the second asteroid base had been posted for days, so there was almost no delay in loading for the voyage out.

Families and lovers were separated as the ship was loaded. Everyone who was staying knew that they were facing potential death. There was no sense in keeping the young ones at the Bubble, so families split up and sent their children and a parent outbound. The choice of which spouse was to go with the kids depended upon the respective skills of the two parents. Those who were needed to construct the new base were ordered to go. Those whose skills were more general, or who were required to handle the defense, stayed.

The colony ship renamed The New Hope, left within twenty-four hours. After a somber moment as they watched the ship accelerate, the remaining pirates returned to their defense preparations.

The oncoming battle group was closer to Ceres than to the Bubble, but it was evident that they'd detected The New Hope's departure. The pirates had not had time to spray The Hope's hull with nano-carbon, and it was unfortunately shiny, and easy to see.

Two of the USSN cruisers split from the battle group and turned to a heading that would align with the Hope's course. It was going to be a stern chase, but the cruisers were faster than the more massive ship and would eventually overhaul it.

That couldn't be allowed. Even if the cruisers didn't catch up with the Hope, their presence on its trail meant that it couldn't go to the new hideout. Fortunately, the flanking group was located near the Hope's course. Adam ordered Nile to split her four ships.

One was to intercept the cruisers and engage them. With luck, the superior armament of the smaller mining ship would destroy the cruisers.

One ship was detailed to escort the Hope to the second location. Adam specifically ordered Nile to take that role. She agreed although he thought she didn't argue enough. That was suspicious. Nile was nothing if not aggressive, and she didn't take kindly to being forced into what she viewed as a passive role.

The remaining two ships were to stay on station and fulfill their original flanking role.

The Fed battle group was reduced to twenty-three ships. It included the five larger vessels, which had tentatively been assigned the role of battleships, and the extra-large craft. The purpose of the monster ship was still unknown. Various ideas were floated, but none seemed to be correct. It could be a staff ship, or battle controller, a super-dreadnought, or possibly a carrier for small attack fighters. Small fighters were not known to exist, but they could have been under development for years, and none of the pirates would have known it.

The location of the smaller group that had split off and left Ceres early was still unknown. The optical scope, as good as it was, hadn't located the missing ships. Adam believed that the second group was circling around and would arrive at the Bubble at the same time as the main group. No other explanation made sense, especially in light of the slow approach of the main group.

The flanking group would have to travel much farther, to circle around. The telescope operators kept up a constant scan in an attempt to locate the missing ships, but to no avail.

The main battle group made no attempt to disguise their approach. They had arranged themselves into a formation that resembled a half-sphere. It seemed apparent that the commanding admiral intended to englobe the Bubble and attack from all sides.

Adam was discussing this tactic with Ngombe for about the third time when it occurred to him that the battle had been joined without any fanfare. Both sides were taking preliminary steps to set up for the impending clash.

Ngombe didn't think too highly of the englobing tactic. "Look, Adam, they'll have to watch where they shoot. A miss will pass us and endanger their own ships if they've surrounded us. Also, the formation is bone-headed, because they don't have enough ships to really do a good job of surrounding us."

"I can see that, but you've forgotten that they don't know about the debris fields and the missiles we've left for them. Their strategy would make more sense to you if you took our passive defenses out of the picture. They can surround us if they can get close. As it is and assuming that the debris field will cause problems for them, you're right. They don't have enough ships to cover a large sphere. I'm thinking that the second battle group will arrive at the same time and form the second half of the sphere. That's got to be what they're planning," Adam said.

Ngombe thought it over and agreed. "What would you think, if I took some ships out and met them head on?"

That was a possibility. They had fourteen mining ships, not counting the Phoenix. Adam had planned on using his small fleet to thrust directly at the center of the Fed formation. The ships would fly in pairs, and each pair would jointly target one of the Fed ships. Given the superior power of the plasma cannons, two simultaneous blasts should severely damage one of the enemy vessels.

He planned to blast through the center of the fleet and then spread out to attack from behind. The debris field would slow the enemy advance toward the Bubble. That way they would force the enemy formation to spread out, making them unable to concentrate their force.

Most of the time, he thought the strategy was brilliant. Only when he tried to sleep that it shifted into a total, idiotic disaster in which his entire force was destroyed.

"Ngombe, I know you'd like to harass them, but that's what the inactive missiles and the flanking ships are for. Let's stick to the plan we've got. I think there's a good chance it will work."

The other man sighed. "Well, no one really has any experience in space battles. If we can survive flying up their throat, your plan will break their formation into bits. After that, it will be a dogfight with every ship for itself."

# 30

# THE BATTLE OF THE BUBBLE

THE USSN BATTLEGROUP was approaching from Ceres vector and would arrive in twenty-four hours when the telescope crew radioed that they'd located the second Battlegroup. It was, as had been speculated, approaching from the opposite direction. It was slightly above the ecliptic and had apparently flown in a circle timed to arrive at the Bubble in time for a joint attack.

An hour after that, Adam received a report that the ship he'd ordered to intercept the Hope's pursuers was closing in and preparing for battle. The location was off along the Ceres vector. The two Fed ships had been accelerating at a slight angle to that vector, taking a course that was obviously intended to intercept The Hope on its trip to the new asteroid.

What the Feds didn't know was that the pirates were intent on concealing their bases. The Hope was not heading directly to the new location and would change vectors once it had exited the belt on the Jupiter side. The plan relied on that change not being detected by the Feds. It probably wouldn't, unless they were watching the larger ship continuously.

He had taken command of the Dire Rhea. Ngombe was in charge of the Phoenix. The other ships in their fleet were being flown by their respective owner/captains.

Adam sat down at the sensor console and scanned for the two USSN cruisers. They were barely detectable, and he could not pick up the smaller mining ship at all. He looked away in frustration, and the system chose that precise moment to beep in response to a sudden flash.

He snapped his focus back, wondering what had happened. All he'd heard was the beep.

It had been in response to a plasma burst fired by the intercepting ship. He wasn't sure who was in command. That had been Nile's choice.

There was another beep; another shot. Then the screen lit up with several flashes. Those must have been missiles, but whose? He became aware that he'd bitten his knuckle. The metallic taste of blood brought him to himself.

"Smith, check the comm. Can you get anything from our ship?" he snapped.

The crewman muttered to himself and fiddled with the system for a moment. "Nothing, Sir."

Adam jumped up. This was worse than being in battle himself. The sensor was still showing a confused mess. Both missile and plasma blasts tended to create residual echoes in the system.

The comm crackled, and a voice came through. "Mad Hatter to D-R. One killed, the other has no maneuverability left. We're returning."

The entire crew was in the bridge trying to find out what was happening and the message elicited a cheer. The Mad Hatter was one of the most recent additions to their fleet. It had been a last-minute addition to the ambush group. Adam hadn't thought it would be ready in time, but the engineers had worked their tails off to get it finished.

Adam was elated until he realized the voice was Nile's. She'd ignored his orders and had gone after the two pursuing ships herself.

The sensor beeped again, drawing his attention to it. There had been another flash. The comm sputtered, then Nile came on. "We've taken missile damage. They fired a final spread, and three of the four hit us. Shields down and Em-Max is not responding. We're stuck here."

Adam grabbed the comm mic. "Nile! Lay low. We'll send someone for you as soon as we can."

The two minutes it took for the comm to turn around seemed like forever.

"That's a Roger, Sir. They're dead over there. We're fine, just a no go on propulsion."

The sensor suite lit up in warning, alerting to the fact that the main battle group had launched a burst of missiles. The system reported thirty incomings at hypersonic velocity.

During the last phase of preparation, the plasma cannons on all of the ships had been linked to a newly installed targeting system. The computer provided instant firing solutions and allowed synchronization between ships. The firing system displayed the target acquired message an instant before To'afa's finger pressed the Fire button.

The D-R jumped backward as the plasma burst fired from the two guns. The visual screen showed a cloud of sparks as the massed shots of the pirate fleet flew towards the enemy. The sparks faded, then nothing.

To'afa said, "Wait. Any time now."

The screen remained blank for three breaths, then it lit up with explosions. Some of the incoming missiles had detonated. It was impossible to tell if any were still coming since the screen was still reacting to the disruption.

Something struck Adam as strange. He asked the room in general, "Where did the extra five missiles come from? They should have shot twenty-five, one from each ship. Someone over there fired extra missiles at us."

Smith had been watching the sensor suite closely. "Sir, I saw it. The other missiles came from one of their battleships. It fired seven at once."

To'afa interrupted. "Take hold! Incoming!"

The ship shuddered from a near miss, then the lights flickered, and the ceiling seemed to become the floor for a second. Adam found himself slammed against the floor on the rebound. He stood up quickly, wincing as he felt a lump on his knee.

"That second one was too close. Check the shield generators," he said.

"To'afa was strapped into his seat and hadn't been bothered by the violent shaking. He leaned over the shield status display.

"The shield is at eighty-nine percent and climbing. Now at ninety-five. Still going up. It's okay. The blast didn't hurt it."

Adam leaned over the sensor system, his chest pressing against the big man's shoulder. The system was clearing, and it showed one of the newer ships drifting out of formation.

"Smith, call the Rockhound. They're drifting. I want their status," he snapped.

He waited, listening to Smith trying to raise the damaged ship. His mind wandered for a moment. He was angry with Nile. She would be safely away if she'd obeyed his orders. Now she was drifting in space, closer to the enemy than to him. He was almost frantic about her situation. Concentrating on the business at hand was difficult.

Smith suddenly said, "They answered! They're alive over there, but their power generation is off-line. They're working to repair it, but it looks like it will be awhile."

The man turned to Adam, alarm in his eyes. "They're not going to be able to help us fight. We should disengage now. Those missiles are too fast. If they hit us--"

Adam interrupted him. "That's enough, Smith. The enemy won't allow us to disengage. We're about to hit them back in a way they won't forget. Now tend to your business."

One of the vid displays was directed toward the Bubble. There were two flashes from the metallic asteroid, and Adam assumed they were from missiles that had bypassed the ships. On the other side of the display, there was a flash as a late-coming missile exploded when it struck the debris field.

It was time to move the ships. They'd been firing at the battle group through an opening in the debris that had been left for expressly that purpose. They had not been able to fully stabilize the clouds of rocks, and the random motion of the separate layers of rocks was beginning to close the hole. He'd planned to move to an area where the rock layers were thicker to give them more protection against incoming missiles.

He was about to order the movement when he realized that the Navy battle group had continued to close. Their ships were close enough that the plasma cannon bursts would arrive a few seconds after they were fired. This was too good an opportunity to pass on.

He ran a quick comp on the missile speed. Their missiles were slower than those of the Feds, and the plasma burst speed far exceeded that of the missiles. The numbers showed a fifteen-second difference at the current range.

He grabbed the Comm. "On my count, fire two missiles at the Fed group, then stand by and wait for my command to fire plasma cannons. Pick your targets and lock on. Five, four, three, two, one. Launch!"

The ship lurched a little as the missiles dropped off and began to accelerate. The small swarm of missiles made a cluster of diminishing flames as they accelerated through the debris cloud and headed towards the Fed ships.

He continued to count mentally. At thirteen, he triggered the microphone and shouted, "Fire!" His vocal cords were so tense, the command came out in an unimpressive tenor tone.

To'afa's finger jabbed the trigger, and the D-R jumped as the guns fired. The visual display showed a stream of plasma bursts following the faint trail of the missiles.

The Navy ships responded as Adam had hoped. Their point defense pods lit up as they filled space with a metal barrier intended to destroy the pirate missiles. Phalanx fire was mixed with the blue-green beams of lasers. The lasers were more accurate than the bursts of cannon-fire but had to be held on target for twenty seconds or so before the beam melted through the missile casing.

The closer the missile, the quicker the laser would burn through. The Phalanx guns laid down a barrier that was intended to intercept missiles the lasers missed. Space around the USSN cruisers lit up as the missiles began to explode. Most blew before they were close enough to the cruisers to do any damage.

He'd continued to count down to himself. The plasma bursts were due to arrive in three seconds. It was time to activate the override signal for the Feds plasma generators, then bit his lip. This had better work.

The battle group was now about a half light second away. There was a perceptible pause, then the blue glow of the shields faded from every one of their ships. He yelled something incoherent.

Smith and To'afa cheered at the same time. The stratagem had worked!

Over in the Federal ships, the crews had to be working frantically to restore their shields, but it was too late. The pirate plasma bursts struck the unshielded ships with devastating effect.

Five cruisers blew up in quick sequence. First one, then three more, followed by the fifth. They drifted, lights out and sides split leaking a cloud of vapor and mixed debris. Six other ships developed holes that were serious enough to vent their interior atmosphere. Of those six, two continued to shoot, while four quickly went dark, apparently dead. The comm system crackled with cheers.

Adam got his excitement under control and issued the order to switch position. His small fleet accelerated to the pre-planned spot under a dense concentration of shielding rocks. The Federal ships launched another batch of missiles and then began shooting railgun slugs at what he thought was extreme long range.

It would take the slugs some time to arrive, but they would lose no momentum. The shield was not likely to handle too many high-velocity hits with that amount kinetic energy before it was overwhelmed and the ship was damaged. They'd have to move again before the slugs arrived.

He noted belatedly that the five battleships were launching their own streams of railgun fire. They probably had more power and bigger railguns. That was what he'd have built into them, at least. He figured the government arms experts were probably ahead of him, so he expected the slugs from the battleships to mass much more than those the cruisers shot.

The battleships ceased their railgun fire simultaneously. He thought for a moment they were out of ammunition, but then the reason for the cease-fire became apparent. The big ships launched a spread of ten missiles each. The railguns had ceased firing to allow the missiles a clear space to accelerate. Once the missiles were on their way, the guns began to fire again.

The incoming missile wave struck the debris field with a startling effect. Sparks and glowing pieces flew in every direction. It looked like fireworks at the climax of an immense holiday show. The crew watched the video monitor as the random motion began to transform into something else. Rocks hit each other and rebounded. The rocks absorbed momentum from the strikes and began to move, striking others in turn.

Smith breathed, "Look! It's a perfect Kessler avalanche."

It was true. The entire mass of debris was now moving, some of it headed outbound toward the enemy and some inbound toward them.

Adam jumped. He'd almost been hypnotized by the rapidly moving and changing scene. The incoming rocks were going to cause his ships problems if he didn't do something quickly.

"All ships back around the Bubble. When we're out of the way of these rocks, we'll move outside of the debris field, then come back around both sides of the Bubble to hit the enemy from two angles. That might confuse them for a moment. Use your plasma cannon and lasers as soon as they come in sight."

The ships turned and accelerated back around the Bubble. Everyone held on as the g-force grew as they raced the avalanche of rocks and debris. The Kessler event had not reached the far side yet, and the rocks were bouncing around between the Bubble and the enemy. Without gravity, the avalanche was moving around the asteroid slowly.

The late-arriving missiles didn't have a chance of penetrating the moving rock field. Their explosions added velocity to the remaining rocks, but the pirate ships had avoided the mess, except for a few random pieces that were destroyed by the shield system.

A few of the missiles survived the passage, coming out near the Bubble. Some of these struck the asteroid and some locked onto the retreating pirate ships.

The pulsed lasers were turned towards the approaching missiles resulting in additional explosions, but several slipped through the crossing lights. There were three explosions, followed by two more as the missiles struck.

When the video screen cleared, Adam could see that he'd lost three other ships. One was ripped nearly in half, while the other two had gaping holes in their hulls. If there were anyone alive in them, they would have to wait for rescue, assuming that there was anyone left to rescue them.

The weapons comp beeped, demanding his attention. A firing opportunity had just opened as the moving debris field thinned to non-existence for a moment. The ten battleships were moving closer, doubtless reloading their launching racks.

Adam nodded at To'afa. The big man was in perfect sync with his admiral and didn't have to be told what the nod meant. He triggered both plasma cannon. The guns on the other ships fired shortly after.

They watched as the plasma bursts traced a faintly glowing line towards the enemy.

The enemy ships started to turn, but there was no way they could accelerate quickly enough to avoid the hellfire that had been unleashed upon them. The plasma struck with a flash as external elements burned off the ships. An instant later, there was a violent explosion as one of the battleships blew.

Once again the vid broke up. Adam glanced at the sensors. They were still scrambled, but the radiation counter flashed into the red. The battleship had been carrying at least one nuclear device that had exploded.

The video rolled, then steadied. There was no sign of the battleship that had blown up, and four of the cruisers that had been near it were buckled and drifting. Whatever had been in that ship had been powerful.

There was another nearby flash of light as a late-coming missile struck the Chance. The mining ship was leaking smoke from a hole near its waist. Whatever was in there was on fire, but it started to fade quickly.

Space made a great fire extinguisher unless the burning material contained its own oxidizer.

The comm clicked, followed by a quick message from the Chance.

"Crew quarters on fire. We have to evacuate the atmosphere to extinguish the flames. We'll be back online as soon as we can get the fire out."

Before Adam could respond, two more of his fleet were struck by incoming missiles. He couldn't quite comprehend where the additional missiles were coming from, but then realized that there were still some of the enemy ships that were able to fight.

To'afa was on the comm now, asking for a status report. The remaining ships called in, most reporting disabling damage. Four were still operational, including the D-R and the Phoenix. The other two ships were captained by late-comers who Adam hadn't met personally. The Space Bunny and the Ferret moved closer, and the four ships began to shift to the far side of the Bubble.

Flynn came on the comm. "Admiral, better get ready. The remainder of the Feds has arrived over here."

Adam hesitated. Maybe it was time to bring the Bubble's plasma guns into play. He cursed himself mentally. His lack of experience was going to get them all killed. He had to concentrate better. He'd almost forgotten those guns. The pirates had managed to mount six plasma cannon spaced evenly around the Bubble. The guns were more powerful than those of the ships, courtesy of the big central reactor that powered their asteroid habitat.

He called the battery commander and ordered him to fire when he had targeting solutions.

"Thank you, Admiral. It's been rough waiting for the go ahead. The poor Bubble has been shaking like an earthquake, but we haven't lost any weapons so far."

"Good. Wait until you get a solid lock, then blow them out of space."

"Yes, Sir."

Three of the big guns flashed blue radiance within a second of the Commander's acknowledgment of the order. He must have been working on firing solutions constantly.

One of the big plasma streams shot near the four remaining undamaged ships, on its way to the enemy. Even though they knew it wasn't aimed at them, the men watching the vid flinched. It was impressive and frightening, even though it was there and gone in a fraction of a second.

The vid broke up again. Adam cursed, "Damn rotten technology. We've got to get someone to build a system that compensates for plasma bursts."

The other two looked at him but didn't respond. He suddenly remembered that he had been going to check on the Albatross, the sole remaining ship of the four that he'd sent out to flank the enemy.

A quick check showed their position was wrong. They'd started inward too late and too slow. Now it was unlikely they'd be near enough to affect the outcome on this side of the Bubble. He keyed an encrypted message into the laser comm system and shot it out, directing them to attack the second battle group of ships approaching on the other side.

They undoubtedly wouldn't survive the attack. So, this was what it felt like to send people to their deaths. It wasn't a good feeling, but there was no time to dwell on it.

The vidscreen cleared, taking his mind off the Albatross. The damage to the government ships was impressive. The powerful blasts had destroyed three of the six cruisers and two of the battleships. The five remaining ships included the monster ship. It had holes showing in its hull but seemed to be still operational.

More railgun slugs arrived, crashing into the remaining rocks. The things had been launched minutes before and only now were showing up. Many of them struck the asteroid surface, flinging pieces and drops of molten metal out into space.

One of the Bubble's cannons suddenly disappeared in a cloud of fragments. One of the battleships' big railguns had scored a perfect hit.

A missile rack folded in half on the underside of the Phoenix as a slug ripped through the support brackets. The slug or a piece of it went on to strike one of the damaged ships, creating a large hole in the bridge area.

Adam turned to To'afa and said, "How can we be so lucky? We haven't been hit."

As if cued by his words, the D–R rang as a slug struck. The comp started to beep, signaling a malfunction. Smith worked at the touch screen for a moment, then said, "Part of our shield is down. That shot hit right on a plasma generator."

He changed his view, then added, "Looks like C24 is out. I think we can route around it, but the shield won't be at full strength. The port front quarter section will be weak."

"Get it going as best you can. We'll have to keep that side away from the enemy, but we need our shields back immediately."

Smith went to work, keying in changes and muttering under his breath as he programmed the system to compensate for the missing generator.

Adam dragged his hand over his face. When would he learn not to tempt fate?

To'afa grunted, pulling his attention back to the situation.

The Navy's monster ship was changing. Its sides were opening, and it was extending multiple missile pods from each side. As Adam watched, the arms carrying the pods locked into place and a swarm of missiles launched.

Smith cried out in fear as the huge swarm accelerated toward their position.

To'afa said something inarticulate, then tried again, "The doggo mines."

What was that? Then he thought of the missiles that he'd ordered released to lie dormant in space.

"Fire those missiles now!" he shouted.

To'afa spun around and stabbed at the weapons console. The screen showed missile flares as the weapons launched, but the incoming swarm dominated the video.

The arsenal ship began to move as someone over there detected the launches, but too late. One of the drifting weapons had been relatively close, and it struck the big ship, slipping through a hold door that was beginning to close.

The resulting explosion made everything that had happened seem minor in comparison. There must have been thousands of more missiles in the hold, and some of them had nuclear warheads.

The just-launched missiles in the swarm were destroyed by the blast. The radiation released fried their circuits, causing them to veer into others. The resulting chain reaction of explosions took out maybe forty percent of the launch.

Adam fired the D-R's plasma cannons at the oncoming mass, then shoved the engine control to full power, firing the enhanced Em-Max boosters at the same time. They had to get out of the way. The Bubble was about to take a huge pounding, and there was nothing more his ship could do.

The Phoenix fired and accelerated beside the smaller ship.

Somewhere he'd misplaced the Space Bunny and the Ferret. He had no idea where they were now, but it was too late to give them orders. The gates of Hell were open, and they only had a few seconds to get out of the way.

The two ships raced away from the Bubble, heading through an opening in the debris cloud. As they flew, Adam noticed that the remaining battleship and the sole remaining USSN cruiser had sheared off. They were heading outbound on the Ceres vector. That reminded him of Nile. He had to go after her as soon as possible.

The Bubble's remaining guns fired at the oncoming missile cloud, lighting the entire region with explosions. White-hot metal flew everywhere, creating a spectacular and deadly storm of sparks.

The remaining missiles could not possibly have reliable guidance since there was just too much hot metal flying around. Some of them struck and annihilated pieces of debris, while the majority hit the Bubble.

The Space Bunny was close to the Asteroid. To'afa pointed it out to Adam. The small ship was using its pulsed lasers against the incoming missiles, but there were too many. One struck the ship and was deflected by the plasma shield, but then it disappeared as four other missiles hit it directly.

The missiles were still coming in, and a few had locked onto the two ships as they accelerated away from the Bubble. After a nervous moment, their flares wavered and died. They were out of fuel and coasting. The ships turned hard to avoid them and a moment later the last missile coasted by.

The Bubble defense control was on the comm.

"We've got a disaster. Cannons two, four, five, and six are gone. We can no longer defend ourselves on the Sol side. The airlock doors are damaged. Right now they're leaking seriously. There's a seventy percent chance they'll blow completely. The main generator is damaged, and we're losing power rapidly. All available ships are needed to help evacuate surviving personnel."

There were over five hundred men and women left on the asteroid.

Adam wondered how many were in airtight compartments or space suits.

All, he hoped. He couldn't bear the thought of his friends hemorrhaging out in the vacuum. If they weren't in a safe place, there was nothing he could do for them. Considering the state of his fleet, there weren't going to be any ships available for evacuation for some time, if ever.

The sensor suite alerted them that there was a single ship approaching from the rear. Smith checked and reported that it was the Ferret. The miner had survived the missile storm and was now rejoining the other two.

What was he going to do with three ships, no, four counting the Albatross, against the eighteen cruisers that were closing in?

Smith was trying to get his attention.

"Yes, Smith? What is it?"

"There's another ship coming around the edge of the Bubble, Sir. It's the Chance."

That was good news. "Call them, never mind the laser system. Use the comm. What's their condition? Can they fight?"

His question was unnecessary. The Chance was calling them to report as he asked it.

"This is Hell's Chance. We've got our fire controlled. We've taken damage to the starboard waist and our shield system is intermittent, but we can fight. Our guns and lasers are fine. We've still got two missiles and their onboard diagnostics say they're ready to fire."

Adam switched to encrypted mode and made sure all three ships were online.

"Form up with the other three of us. We're going to start out on the Mars vector, then turn and come back in. The Bubble still has some offensive capacity." He hoped that was true. "I'm going to ask them to engage the battle group. If they can keep the cruisers occupied, then we might have a chance to close before they respond. We'll come in with all weapons firing. Launch all missiles after the first plasma shot barrage."

The Bubble command center was difficult to raise. They took some time to respond to his signal.

"Bubble. Are you coming to get us?"

"Bubble, this is Maxwell. We have no available vessels to evacuate you. The Feds' second group is approaching you on the shadow side. Do you still have control of your guns?"

A different person came on after a minute. This was a woman, but Adam didn't recognize her voice.

"Admiral, we can fire the guns we have left. The shadow side is relatively undamaged. We have three plasma weapons and five pulse laser emplacements that are operational. We're not good for more than a few minutes, though. Main power is on its last legs and won't hold much longer. Placing a load on it with the weapons will make it fail even sooner."

He thought about that. There really was no choice. If they failed, the Feds would probably take all survivors back to Luna for a show trial followed by execution. They'd want to make an example of them to dissuade any other impulses to seek freedom.

There was a single desirable outcome. He had to defeat the second battle group. With that in mind, possibly condemning the people in the Bubble to slow suffocation, or a quick death in vacuum was the only option.

"Understood. We have to defeat the second group. If we live, we'll pick you up. For us to survive, I need you to engage the enemy with everything you've got. Keep firing until you can no longer shoot. I need you to keep their attention while we maneuver. Got it?"

"Affirmative, Admiral. We'll do what we can. The battle group is going to be in our range in two minutes. They've been firing missiles, but none have arrived so far. We estimate thirty seconds before the first ones strike."

"Start shooting now. Use the lasers on the incoming missiles, then fire your own missiles in response. Wait until they're closer before opening up with the plasma guns."

"Roger." The comm clicked making the acknowledgment seem curt.

To'afa looked back at him from his seat, and said, "There they go. Lasers firing. Uh. I've got multiple missile launches."

Smith asked, "From the Feds?"

"No. From the Bubble. Ugh. The Feds just launched in return. Looks like they shot everything they had."

The small group of ships accelerated away from the Bubble. If the enemy sensors detected them, Adam hoped they would think they were running. He'd taken a slight angle off the Mars vector so that they wouldn't occlude the sun. He was depending on the carbon particles to help them slip away unseen.

To'afa grunted again. "Ugh. There's another ship far back, behind the enemy."

It was the Albatross. The captain was executing Adam's orders in a way that Adam hadn't foreseen. The ship was coming in at full acceleration. It would have only one chance to shoot before it passed the enemy group. Then it would fly by the Bubble and be out of range. At that speed, it would take hours to turn and re-engage.

Adam gritted his teeth in frustration. He needed the extra guns, but he'd have to do without. Everything would be over by the time the Albatross got back. They might still play a role in evacuating survivors from the Bubble, provided he routed the Feds.

He keyed the comm. "Wait until the Albatross has fired, then loop back. They'll be caught between incoming fire on two vectors. They'll be busy, and I'm gambling that they'll miss our approach. As soon as you have a firing solution, take it. After the first burst, you're on your own. We'll see you on the other side."

There was a spark of light from the incoming Albatross. It was the flare of a missile launch, and it was followed by three more. They'd shot all their missiles. Things must be getting confusing in the cruisers by now. They couldn't have missed the rear attack, but they couldn't afford to weaken their frontal defense. The Bubble's missiles would arrive in seconds.

The Fed missiles were moving through the remains of the debris field. There were sporadic explosions as they struck rocks. The next thing to hit the Bubble would be railgun slugs, provided the cruisers had fired them. The slugs were difficult to detect. They were small and almost invisible, and the railguns didn't flash or give any indication of their firing.

The Albatross' missiles reached the battle group at almost the same time as those from the Bubble. The Fed point defense pods fired and kept on shooting, sending visible streams of hot depleted uranium slugs towards the incoming weapons. Missile after missile succumbed to the Phalanx fire, but the debris was still a formidable weapon. It struck the cruisers like a blast from a shotgun, destroying antennas, sensors, point defense radar domes, and damaging external missile racks.

Two of the cruisers fell out of formation. The debris had done enough damage to knock them out of the battle.

One other was struck head-on by a missile. The explosion wiped out the bridge area, and the ship veered towards some of the others, forcing them to avoid it. Their formation had become a mess of flying metal and ships moving to avoid each other.

At that point, the four missiles from the Albatross slammed into the Fed line, blowing up two ships entirely and damaging one more. They hadn't seen them coming after all. There had been no attempt to defend against the rear attack.

The Albatross was close when it fired both plasma cannons. One of the bolts missed entirely, but the other burned through the side of a fourth cruiser. Now there were eleven, but the Albatross did not escape unscathed from its firing run. It hit something, possibly a railgun slug, immediately after it fired. Pieces came off the small ship and accompanied it on its path away from the Bubble.

Adam took a deep breath. His group was closing rapidly. Should they brake, or do the same kind of flyby the Albatross had done?

The answer came when a wave of plasma from the asteroid-mounted cannons hit the remains of the battle group line. There was a massive flare of blue light mixed with the red of explosions. When the vid came back on, the Feds had lost five more ships.

The odds were now four to six. If they flew by, they would surely get at least half of the six. The remaining ships would probably turn and run, realizing that they had no hope of standing against the pirate ships when they returned.

The Bubble still had the laser guns firing. The power supply was holding out better than predicted. The people there would not be unprotected while he turned around and made his way back.

The four ships came on at full acceleration. None of their racks held missiles. Those were all gone long ago. The pulse lasers would be no good at this speed. They had to keep on target for a few seconds to penetrate. The plasma guns were the advantage that would decide the battle.

The Federal cruisers were in disarray, but starting to reform to continue toward the Bubble while Adam's group approached at high speed.

The cruisers started to turn towards the pirate group. They'd been seen, but before the railguns could be aimed, the four pirate ships had released a barrage of eight plasma bursts. The glowing blue radiance swept through the reforming Fed ships, wreaking havoc.

They were by and past so quickly there was no time to see what the result of the barrage had been. The vid took a few seconds to clear, then To'afa turned it to focus on the Battle Group.

It was no more. The eight shots had taken out four ships, two killed outright and two more holed with vapor pouring out. The remaining three ships seemed paralyzed.

They were starting to turn toward the two damaged vessels when a final cannon blast from the Bubble destroyed one of the derelicts. The three ships immediately turned and fled.

Adam's first thought was that he'd won, but that was submerged in a burst of rage. The Feds wouldn't leave them alone. He'd have to teach them that they'd be better off not messing with the Belter community.

He keyed the comm and shouted, "All ships! After them! No one escapes."

The Feds had made a slight tactical mistake. They had turned along the same vector that the pirate ships were on. This put them behind the fast moving ships, a situation that might have given them an advantage if they had been armed with plasma weapons. As it was, it meant that they were accelerating towards the now slowing pirate ships.

Adam realized he'd made a mistake in turn when it became apparent that the Fed ships would pass his rapidly slowing group at a speed that would make it difficult to get a firing solution. The USSN ships were moving so quickly by the time he'd figured out they were going to get away that, even with the Em-Max boosters, it would be a long stern chase if he were to catch them.

He cursed under his breath, then stiffened in anger as his expectations proved correct. The Feds shot by and the weapons comp proved unable to lock on the rapidly moving vessels. He reprimanded himself a second time when To'afa pointed out that the Feds would catch up with the Albatross in about an hour.

His mood had changed from triumphant to frustration. He wanted to finish the battle, and now he had to run the remaining ships down.

The D-R lurched as something contacted the plasma shield. It shrieked past, leaving a red light flashing on the boards. The Feds had shot at him as they went by and one of the slugs from their railguns had grazed his ship. The red light was from the waist cannon control unit.

A quick check showed that the horizontal aiming servos were not responding. The damage was a problem, and it added to his anger.

"All ships accelerate on their tail. We're going to finish this as quickly as we can, then go back to help the Bubble survivors."

Smith nodded and keyed in the command to increase the boost. The ship began to speed up again. After a moment, the other pirate vessels accelerated, following in a loose formation slightly behind the D-R.

The rate at which the fleeing ships were shrinking in the screen began to slow. They would catch up, but would the Feds spare the Albatross or shoot at it?

He ran some quick calculations. The Feds were going to catch up to the Albatross before he could get there. He'd arrive about five minutes after they intersected. The Albatross would have to defend itself if the Feds were going to shoot.

There was a slight flash in the vid that showed the drama happening ahead of the D-R. He bent to look closer. The Feds were firing lasers. That wasn't so bad since he'd made sure that all of his ships had reflective hulls under the carbon particles. A laser beam would bounce off after it burned the carbon away. The important thing was the Feds had started shooting at the slower ship. They weren't done fighting yet.

"Dire Rhea to other ships. Weapons status," he ordered.

The reports were not good. No one had any missiles, there were only three operational plasma cannon left, now that the D-R had lost one. The other two were on the Phoenix. Both the Chance and the Ferret were down to pulse lasers only. The odds were still in the Pirates favor, though. The plasma cannon were so superior that they changed the total equation.

That couldn't be counted on to last. There was an old rule that he'd read somewhere that said if you introduce a new weapon to the battlefield, your enemy will be using it within fifteen years. That had arisen long before space flight. The actual time would probably be less than a year. Now that the plasma cannon's superiority had been s demonstrated the government would doubtless devote massive funds to a research program to duplicate the weapon.

It wasn't such a huge discovery, Adam had only modified some of his research for the shield, then one thing led to another. There was no doubt that the Earth scientists were smart enough to figure his invention out, now that they knew it existed. Well, that was a worry for the future. Right now, they were nearly in range.

He was staring at the vid when the Albatross was hit by a stream of railgun slugs. The Fed ships must have been firing as fast as they could as they approached. The plasma shield flared, and sparks flew as it vaporized the first few slugs, then it failed and went dark. The remaining slugs tore through the Albatross' bridge area, ripping it open.

The ship went dark and began to spin wildly. The maneuvering jets were venting their gas randomly. The damage was bad, and he doubted there were any survivors.

To'afa swore under his breath, then said, "Get them. Let's make them pay for that."

Smith added, "They didn't have to shoot. They could have just gone by, and we could have let them escape. We still can. Do you think there are any alive somewhere in the ship?

It was an effort to speak. His words seemed to grate through his teeth. "We'll get the enemy first, then check for survivors."

As soon as he'd said it, the image of Nile came to him. God! He hoped she was okay. He had to finish this mess and go find her. The other ships could go help the Bubble, but he wasn't going back until he found her.

They were finally close enough, and he fired the remaining plasma cannon.

Two blue pulses came past to the port side, making him flinch. The Phoenix had shot at almost the same time. All of the shots were on target. One of the fleeing cruisers exploded. Holes appeared in the hull of another. The third seemed undamaged.

The comm chimed. It was the Chance. The makeshift repairs they'd done were failing, and they had to break off the chase to try to keep the ship going.

Adam radioed back, "Fix what you can. We'll see you back at the Bubble."

The answer came back, "Affirmative. Good hunting."

The remains of the Albatross were receding to their rear. Ahead the remaining two Navy ships were apparently out of railgun slugs and missiles. They were shooting back at their pursuers with lasers and the Vulcan cannons of the Phalanx point defense. Neither of those weapons bothered Adam much. It would take a lucky hit to damage his ships.

Both of the Ferret's plasma cannon were out of commission, and it was not shooting, but the Phoenix was ready to fire again. The capacitor banks charged more quickly in the bigger ship because it had an excess of reactor power.

That was something that should be fixed. The smaller ships would need to have upgraded reactors if they were to hold their own against the more powerful cruisers when the latter were armed with plasma guns. The more quickly the caps charged, the faster the guns could fire. Firing rate would make a critical difference in the future.

The Phoenix fired both guns before the D-R was ready to shoot. Again their aim was good. Another Navy cruiser flared and went dead, drifting off in a way that said it wasn't going to recover.

The last cruiser began to slow and ceased firing. That looked like they intended to surrender. Taking a prize would be good. They'd lost so many ships that a replacement was highly desirable.

Adam waved To'afa off. "Don't shoot. We can take their ship, so let's not damage it."

The Samoan grunted, "Uhh. They should die."

"Yes, I want to blast them, too, but as I said, we need their ship. We can make the crew work on repairs at the Bubble or something. We'll figure out how to make them pay."

The Fed ship had slowed, and they were closing quickly. Adam was still tempted. To'afa's urge to revenge the Albatross and all of the rest of their losses was very tempting. He moved to the weapons system and looked at the cannon trigger. It seemed to beckon his finger closer. He touched it, but then drew back slightly.

He was a good person. He'd always tried to get along in school and even before that. Everything had started going wrong for him when he'd met the Senator's daughter. In retrospect, she'd been the one who taught him that there were people who weren't actually interested in goodness as a character trait; people who lied and cheated to get and for revenge.

The captain of the Federal cruiser suddenly showed that he was one of those people. The cruiser had reserved some railgun slugs and fired three point-blank into the Phoenix.

The shots struck the bow and ripped through the hull. Flames shot out, and pieces flew into space, spinning wildly in all directions. The Phoenix' shields flickered and then went dead.

Ngombe was on the comm within a few seconds. "Admiral, we're hit bad. We've got to get out before the reactor blows. Can you pick us up?"

Adam was paralyzed. He'd wanted to be true to himself, but this was too much. He didn't think about the possible repercussions before his finger stabbed down at the gun trigger. The D-R lurched, and the Federal cruiser ceased to exist as a threat.

The close-range plasma bolt burned a hole lengthwise through the cruiser. Flames showed through the hole for a moment, then the ship exploded with incredible violence.

"What the hell?" To'afa exclaimed.

After a moment, Smith answered. "Radiation levels just peaked the meters. Shields are holding well, but the Phoenix..." His voice trailed off.

Adam was dismayed. The Fed cruiser must have held a nuke. He'd probably just doomed his friends on the Phoenix. Their shields were down. The radiation would have blasted through the hull almost as if there was nothing there. He looked down at his hands, trying to find a way to justify the plasma blast.

It was highly likely the cruiser would have turned its guns on the D-R next. That was some justification, but his conscience was screaming at him that it was not good enough. He waited for the vid to calm down. The close range blast had scrambled the silly thing.

When the vid screen had quit acting up, the D-R maneuvered close to the still burning Phoenix. Three small figures were crossing the intervening space. One of them towing the other two. Their progress was erratic. It was challenging to balance pulling two space-suited people while steering the jets of the maneuvering pack.

Adam said, "Smith, you go and meet them at the lock. It looks like two are hurt. I want to talk to Ngombe as quickly as he gets his space suit off." Then he thought to add, "If he's able to talk."

A FEW MINUTES later, he heard the clank of the airlock. Shortly after that, Smith called on the intercom.

"Admiral, they've been exposed to a lot of radiation from the plasma blast. Captain Ngombe is better than the other two of his crew, but he's not in good shape either."

Would his luck ever get better? He'd let his temper take over and blasted the treacherous cruiser, but in so doing, he might have condemned his friends to a slow and painful death.

To'afa said, "It couldn't be helped, Adam. You won a great battle, but there is always a cost to the victor."

Adam couldn't look at the big man. His eye was blurry. After a moment, he realized that he was crying. He wiped at the moisture angrily. He was a damned Pirate and an Admiral. Crying wasn't part of the image.

He started to turn away, then saw tears trickling down To'afa's face also.

Maybe tears were justified in this instance.

# 31
## SEARCHING

NGOMBE LOST ALL his hair and forty pounds, but he managed to hang on from day to day. His two crewmen weren't so fortunate.

Ngombe had been last out of the Phoenix and had been shielded from the direct radiation by its hull. The two crew had exited first and were in the open space between the Phoenix and the D-R when the plasma cannon burst hit the navy cruiser, and the warhead had gone off. They'd received well over a fatal dose of hard gamma rays. One died within ten hours and the other the next day. Ngombe was in pain and suffered a lot, but he kept breathing. Whether he would recover or succumb to the direct effect of the radiation was anybody's guess. Even if the direct radiation didn't kill him, it was a good bet that he'd eventually develop fatal cancer as a result of the exposure. They'd fed him all of the potassium iodide they had on board to try to avert that result, but it wasn't very much, and it might not work anyway.

Adam had been in a quandary over the ill men. On the one hand, he wanted to go after Nile in the worst way, but on the other, his sense of duty and compassion forced him to devote all of his time providing sick care. Once it became apparent that Ngombe was going to survive for longer than a few days, he turned the D-R to the Ceres vector. The Ferritt had long since headed back to the Bubble to provide what aid it could. That was assuming that there was anyone left there in need of assistance.

There had been a discussion about sending Ngombe with the Ferritt, but the smaller ship had no private cabin for him. The status of the Bubble facilities and the survivors was unknown. All told, it didn't seem like a good idea to send the sick man into a situation where he would be only a little better off and possibly worse than he was currently.

Captain Ngombe was confined to bed. Adam had given him his own cabin since it was the largest and most comfortable on the ship. That wasn't saying much since it was only about ten by ten, but the other quarters were smaller.

Adam had taken to spending his time on the bridge, even when he was supposed to be sleeping. He'd developed the habit of taking cat naps, dropping off for a few minutes at a time, then waking to check on the status of the ship, Ngombe, and whatever else had been haunting his most recent nightmare.

When Ngombe appeared to be over the worst of the immediate effects, the D-R began the search for the lost Mad Hatter and Nile.

The last contact with the Hatter had been when Nile reported a successful engagement with the two cruisers that appeared to be trying to intercept The Hope. She'd destroyed one and damaged the other, then reported that she was returning. After that, there had been nothing, and Adam had been too busy fighting to think much about it, although he remembered losing focus and thinking about her a few times.

Based on her last reported position, it was going to take them a calculated forty hours to arrive in that vicinity. During the interim, To'afa and Smith attended to Ngombe, rested, and helped Adam work on the plasma cannon.

One of the cannons had suffered a partial failure. The plasma generator had suddenly developed a glitch that slowed its recharge time and limited the amount of plasma it could create. The result was a gun that would fire smaller bursts at about half the rate it for which it was designed. Such a limitation wasn't automatically fatal for the D-R, but having both cannons at full operating capacity might make the difference in a fight.

The other problem was the damaged shield generator. Both systems needed work and, since Adam was having difficulty sleeping, he drove himself to get both fixed before they arrived at a point where they could reasonably expect enemy action.

Forty hours passed. The shield was back at full capacity, and the cannon was better than it had been, but not where it should be. They were approaching the point of the last signal, and the sensor suite was scanning for anything it could find.

"C'mon, Smith, surely you've got something by now," Adam repeated for the third time. He knew he was acting like a kid asking, "Are we there yet?" But he was impatient. Impatient, and scared. They were dangerously close to Ceres and the Feds might have left some ships there, or possibly one of their patrol ships was at the planetoid.

Smith didn't say anything. He shrugged and continued to watch the display.

That wasn't very satisfactory, and Adam started to say something else, but the system beeped, indicating that it had picked something out of the vacant space surrounding them.

"What is it?" Adam asked.

Smith studied the display and then answered, "I think it's a ship. It doesn't mass what it should, but it's definitely metal and not a metallic asteroid, either."

"Steel?" he asked.

"Yeah. And there's a radiation component. That might be from their power plant, don't you think?"

Adam did think. It might be. The problem was that the sensor suite was a relatively new addition to the ships and hadn't been tested in every possible circumstance. The inventor of the thing hadn't conceived of it being used to locate a damaged ship. It was intended to sort through various types of asteroids for ones with the most metal. It didn't differentiate between metals accurately, but it did indicate where they were to be found.

The D-R braked hard, then turned at a slight angle, pressing the humans on board against their seat restraints. Ngombe was strapped in a gimbled bed that would turn toward the acceleration, providing him the most comfortable ride in the ship.

The signal was stronger, indicating that they were approaching whatever it was. Adam's hope rose, then was dashed when they found the hulk of a USSN cruiser.

"This must be the one she blew. I wonder where the disabled one is located?" He was speaking mostly to himself under his breath, as he searched the vid for an optical view of the object they were approaching.

He made another pass across the minute of angle that contained the unknown object. Abruptly there it was.

They matched velocities and pulled slowly alongside the object. It was the destroyed cruiser, just as Adam had thought. There were holes burned completely through the other ship. It had died a quick death, and so had the compliment of humans that had been inside.

While it would make good salvage, the dead ship wasn't what he was here for. Nile was somewhere close by, Adam could practically sense her presence. It was possibly imagination, but he was greatly encouraged by the discovery of the dead cruiser.

They continued searching. The next object appeared off towards the spin direction of the planets. It was about four hundred klicks away, a tiny distance in the scheme of the belt. Adam turned toward the object, and the D-R moved quickly in that direction.

This time, they hit pay dirt. It was the Mad Hatter. This seemed like good news, but it was not to be. The Hatter had a hole that passed through the engine room. The Em-Max was gone. It looked like it had been a railgun slug that had done the dirty work. Someone had taken a shot at the mining ship against which it had been unable to defend.

The Hatter was dead with no power usage showing. Despite that, Adam insisted on going over himself and searching. The search was unproductive.

There was no sign of Nile or anyone else on board. The ship had been crippled, and everyone had been taken off or had jumped into the void to die a slow death of oxygen deprivation. In either event, the ship was empty.

Adam reentered the D-R with a heavy heart. There were no clues as to the whereabouts of the crew. He had found some of Niles personal effects and had grabbed a box of medals that she kept. He knew they were important to her.

He thought it was possible to tell what had happened by accessing the log and sensor suite records. He'd taken the time to recover the two chips that held that data before he'd returned to his ship. The next step would be to review the data to see if it contained any clue as to the disappearance of his beloved.

An hour later he was sitting in front of the comp, his head in his hands. The data told a disconcerting story. The Hatter had sustained some battle damage, and it appeared to have stopped the reactor, or maybe the reactor had been damaged and posed a threat. He couldn't quite tell. Either way, the crew had been in space suits.

That was a good thing. They wouldn't die quite so quickly, if there were a hull breach or if they had to leave the ship. That was what had apparently happened. The locks were closed indicating an orderly exit, but not secured against being opened from the outside. He took that second fact to mean that they had thought there was at least a chance of reentering the ship.

The recording from one of the external cameras showed the crew clustered around a spot near the reactor cooling vent, apparently working on repairs. They had been busy for a time, but then they stopped and turned to look as another ship, a USSN cruiser, approached.

He scanned the video quickly, slowing it and backing up to confirm his suspicions. The crew, his fellow pirates, had removed the plasma cannon at the waist of the ship and loaded it into the cruiser's hull. There was no sign of any navy personnel. No sign of compulsion and no weapons displayed. There was no radio chatter when there should have been.

He checked the settings menu, trying to figure out what was wrong. Someone had turned the comm recording function off. That was unusual, almost like the whole operation had been planned.

The only conclusion he could draw was that the crew had planned to turn over the plasma cannon to the Feds. Nile's loyalty to the Space Marines had initially been a problem for her, but he felt that he knew her well enough by now to know that she would never betray him in such an open fashion. If it wasn't her, then who was it? It was impossible to tell.

Once the cannon had been loaded, the airlock closed and the ship departed. It wallowed a bit as it turned, betraying the lack of finesse on the pilot's part. Perhaps they just didn't care, but he didn't approve of a sloppy turn like that.

The question he was contemplating was whether he should try to follow. The outbound vector was roughly towards Luna, and it was a safe assumption that was the ship's destination. They had such a headstart that, even with the advanced engines, the D-R wouldn't catch them before they arrived.

That was a good thought. The new engines! He scanned the Hatter's profile. The engines were all in place, and that fact didn't fit his suspicion. Whoever had arranged to turn over Pirate tech to the feds would have been remiss if they didn't bring an engine along also. The settings on the new boosters were complex and not easy to determine from an external view and a verbal description of the system.

They definitely should have taken one of the boosters. The things weren't even that difficult to remove. He'd had them mounted on a series of shackles. It would have been easy to unpin the unit, disconnect the control cable and take it.

It was a strange oversight, and it caused him to think of a variety of speculations, all of which led nowhere.

While he was thinking, Smith had received a direct beamed message from the Bubble. There were survivors. The Ferritt had arrived and had given them the D-R's approximate location and the bad news about the Phoenix. They wanted his help as quickly as he could get there. The status of their base was marginal, power was failing, and they had a grave shortage of oxygen, only enough to last for four or five more days.

Adam looked up and rubbed his unshaven face. There was no real chance to get Nile back, at least at the moment. He'd have to hope the Feds kept her alive and didn't merely space her the moment they found out who she was. As long as she was alive, there was a possibility that he could make himself such a thorn in their sides that they might ransom her to ensure that he left them alone. That was something to hope for, at least. Meanwhile, duty demanded that the D-R return to the Bubble and help in the rescue operation.

# 32

# REGROUPING

THE BUBBLE WAS a mess, both physically and organizationally. The sole member of the governing council whom Adam felt had been grounded in reality had been killed when the airlocks blew. The remainder of the group had divided into two different courses of action.

One group wanted to rebuild, while the other wanted to move to location two. The recriminations and backbiting were so severe that little constructive work had been done.

Some people had made an effort at rebuilding the airlocks, but since the foundry was under the control of the "leave group," they'd quit due to lack of raw materials. Altogether it was a dismaying and disgusting display of one of the worst flaws in human nature. The lack of cooperation had gotten so bad that there had even been some sabotage, apparently by the "leave group," in their attempt to convince the others that repair was impossible.

Adam settled into the power vacuum with only a little resistance from the divided council. Once he told them that a state of martial law existed, they quit arguing for the most part and followed orders. He was moderately amused by this since he didn't know if he had that authority.

Then he told himself that they were pirates, so why shouldn't the stronger party rule? As the captain of the only ship with working guns, he was the stronger party, barely, and until someone with more cannon showed up.

A thorough inspection of the Bubble showed that the battle damage was repairable. They had built the habitat from nothing but the promise of the cavern the first time, and there was no reason they couldn't fix the mess the battle had left. On the other hand, the Feds knew the location of the base precisely and could attack it at their leisure, once they'd rebuilt their fleet.

That was the one factor where the Earthers held an advantage. They could throw many more pairs of hands at rebuilding. The raw material advantage was on the side of the Belters. There was plenty of metal floating around waiting to be smelted, there just weren't enough hands to do it quickly.

What decided the issue was something that he hadn't considered. The North American government, under the control of now dictator Worthington, was encountering extreme resistance from various freedom-loving groups. Terrorism was on the rise, and many of the larger cities were becoming uninhabitable due to disruption of supply lines.

Some of the non-aligned countries had severed relations with the North American dictatorship. The balance of power was unstable, and it was anybody's guess how the players would align if it came to the point of taking sides.

That situation forced Worthington to take action. Since they were the foremost example of successful resistance, for both publicity and propaganda reasons, the Feds did their best to stir up anger against the pirates. Both the net and the vids were buzzing about the outrages committed by Adam's group. Most of the alleged dirty deeds would have surprised the Belters since the news flacks didn't hold back, instead they allowed their imaginations to run wild. The one-eyed pirate was personally accused of kidnapping an entire seventh-grade class on an excursion to Luna and hiding them in a secret asteroid base. Why this was and what he was supposed to have in mind for them was never said, but the implications were that he was either a cannibal or one of the worst kinds of deviant.

The less acute minded members of the North American population began to clamor for war with the belt. Those that had a degree of sense wisely kept silent. To speak against the popular cause was to court ostracism or violence.

The pirates were mostly ignorant of these developments. They weren't able to receive regular broadcasts from Earth. Most of the planetary news was now carried exclusively on fiber-optics. Unlike in the recent past, there were almost no broadcast radio signals. One factor that helped was the telescope.

It had miraculously escaped damage in the battle, perhaps because it was located far enough away that it hadn't been inadvertently struck by debris. Since it obviously wasn't a ship or weapons platform, no one had bothered to target it with a missile or to shoot at it.

The third day after the D-R returned, the staff manning the scope reported a massive series of launches from both the Ribbon station and the surface of Luna. The total was alarming. While the Feds had lost most of their spaceships, they had retained an enormous store of missiles.

THE DATA INDICATED that over a thousand had been launched. The launch vector left no doubt that the Bubble was the intended target. The only good thing about the attack was that it would take weeks to arrive.

They had time to take action. The attack crystalized Adam's thinking.

There was nothing to prevent the Feds from continuing to lob shots at their location. The constant necessity of defending the Bubble would make life difficult, if not impossible and there was always the possibility that the missile swarm was armed with nuclear warheads rather than conventional explosives. There had been some nuke armed missiles in the attacking fleet, although they didn't have the chance to use them.

The conclusion was clear. They had to move. On the other hand, he couldn't see any advantage in leaving the Feds the Bubble intact. If the oncoming missile swarm could be diverted, and it most likely could be, the Feds would then have a fantastic start on a second base. Between Ceres and the Bubble, they would control a huge swath of the belt.

He couldn't allow that to happen. It would be inconvenient, to put it mildly. Fortunately, not all of the nuclear devices had been destroyed in the battle. Salvage crews had been going through the remains of the Federal ships, and someone had found two intact missiles armed with nukes.

Exploding them inside the Bubble might not blow it apart, the asteroid was tough, and the walls were thick, but the radiation inside the cavity would make the vacant space unusable until far in the future.

The problem then became one of evacuating the residual population.

That was solved by the unexpected return of the Hope. It had successfully delivered the engineers to the second location, and they had begun transforming it into a usable base.

Finding himself without a necessary role in the transformation, Flynn had turned the New Hope around and returned. He'd guessed that the colony ship would be needed and his arrival was timed perfectly.

The Hope was loaded, and people said goodbye to their hard-built home. The bombs were placed, and the three ships retreated several thousand miles to watch the show.

The signal was sent. The Bubble ceased to be useful to humans in a spectacular explosion. The asteroid did not break apart. Instead, all of the force of the massive blast was channeled outward through the cavern opening.

Debris, vapor, dust, and flame shot out for hundreds of miles, and the asteroid began to move. The channeled blast had acted like a rocket, imparting momentum to the large rock. It didn't move quickly, but the motion was visible. The best part of the situation, Adam thought, was that the Bubble was now on course to depart the belt and, eventually, the solar system.

Everyone felt that it was a fitting end for their first home.

The small group of ships departed on a different vector, first heading toward deep space on the chance someone on Earth or Luna was watching. Their destination was location two.

Flynn had reported that the engineers had named the second asteroid. It had been referred to as location two from the beginning, but they had felt that wasn't a friendly name, so, in an excess of optimism, they'd renamed it Valhalla.

Adam couldn't quite reconcile the Viking reference with their identification as pirates, but he didn't try very hard.

The voyage to Valhalla took three stages. They flew out of the ecliptic, then turned and headed directly toward the Oort cloud, finally circling and coming back into their destination from behind Saturn.

HE WAS LOOKING at the computer display when Ngombe came into the bridge for the first time since the explosion. The screen showed the asteroids in the neighborhood of Saturn, along with the various moons of the ringed planet.

Ngombe approached silently and looked over his shoulder. Adam jumped when his friend asked, "Do you think you're going to find another Bubble in the display?"

He jumped, then turned. "Ngombe! You should be in your bunk. You can't be walking around."

The big man made an effort to laugh, but it came out as a pained groan. "Well, I'm not doing any good lying around, and I'm bored, so I thought I'd come here and bother you. It might not have been a good decision. I'm not feeling as well as I thought." He grasped the back of a chair, then spun it around and sat with a sigh.

Adam asked, "Better?"

"Yes. My endurance is way down. Lucky the gravity isn't much. I wouldn't be able to move around on Earth. Maybe not even on Luna."

He took several deep breaths.

"Now tell me what you're looking for. Take my mind off how bad I feel."

Adam marshaled his thoughts. "The second asteroid isn't as perfect as the Bubble based on the pictures I've seen. I'm not really happy with its potential. We can use it, well...anyway, I was just looking, wondering about Saturn's moons. Some of them are big enough to have a respectable gravity. There might be enough to hold an atmosphere, provided it was replenished periodically."

"Yeah. That might be possible, but we'd have to replenish it pretty often, but..."

"But, what?"

"The Feds undoubtedly have the moons on their list of places to visit and possibly exploit. They'll find us there for sure. The second asteroid might be more secure."

"There is that. I'm not sure we should assume we have to hide from them. If we're going to become the second power in the solar system, we can't continue to play that game. We can't allow them to intimidate us. We'll have to figure out a way to face them on an equal playing field."

Ngombe paused, pensively, then obviously thought of another point. He looked up, a frown on his face. "That would be fine with me, but they have too many resources for us to compete with. They can build thousands of ships. We can't."

Adam had already thought of that and knew it wasn't right. He shook his head negatively. "Look, my friend, they have more workers than we do. That is the main problem. Otherwise, they are at a grave disadvantage. We have far more metal than they do. One good asteroid will provide plenty of iron to build a thousand ships, other metals too. We have plenty of water and therefore, oxygen. Energy is not much of a challenge. We can get hydrocarbons if we develop a way to scoop gasses from the big planets."

He paused, and Ngombe started to answer, but Adam cut him off.

"Another thing is they have to operate with the huge handicap of their gravity well. Everything they build, every resource that comes from Earth, all their labor and supplies have to be boosted up from the surface. The Ribbon handles that pretty well, but if they become too much of a nuisance, we can cut it."

The big man's eyes widened. "But, that would be...it would be..."

Adam continued. "Yes, it would be tantamount to an act of war against Earth, but what have they done for us? They've made us outcasts, wanted, pirates. I can't see how we owe them anything right now."

He thought, then modified his statement. "The government, at least. The common people are suffering under the new dictatorship from what we've heard, but they could rise up and overthrow it."

"Don't be too sure. The majority of people are too fearful to rebel. They just want to get along and be left alone. As long as the dictatorship ignores them for the most part, they will keep their heads down."

He shrugged. "Well, they could grow a pair and stand up for themselves if they really wanted to. Maybe we can help. Our very existence shows them that freedom is possible. If we keep hacking at their forces, they will eventually give up. Besides, if they don't, we can drop a few rocks on the capital and other strategic points. A KEW or two will disrupt things to the point that the common people will have an opportunity to break free."

Ngombe wasn't convinced. "Well, maybe, but they might decide that you're are the real enemy. I mean, what kind of human would drop a rock on his home planet? Don't overlook the fact that they're masters at propaganda. They can have the entire population programmed into clamoring for war against the inhuman pirates in a heartbeat. I don't think we want to go there."

"Maybe you're right. Still, we could cut the ribbon and set them back a long way. Even make it look like an accident. We could start a rock moving from a long way out. If it were big enough, they probably wouldn't be able to divert it before it struck."

"Ugh. That's not likely. It's a good idea, but I don't think we can be accurate enough to ensure it clips the ribbon after traveling a couple of Aus. It could hit the planet, Luna, or miss. That's like trying to shoot a molecule at a thousand miles distance. We can't be that accurate."

Adam sighed. "It was just an idea. Doubtless, you're correct. I guess we'll have to fly in, shoot the ribbon in half, then let them blame us. We can always say we didn't do it. The population is so used to false flags that at least half of them will believe that we're telling the truth. Their media is controlled by Worthington's people. We can confuse the issue, and maybe that will be enough. The good thing is even if they want to start a war with us, they'll have to rebuild the ribbon first, and we can cut it again. I think we have an advantage there."

Ngombe nodded, then said, "Maybe you're right." Then his eyelids fluttered. He swayed, then steadied himself by leaning against the console. "I've got to lie down again. I guess I'm not as strong as I thought."

Adam was instantly concerned. He hadn't meant to tire his friend out.

"Let me help you back to your cabin." He pulled the big man up, aided by the weak gravity, then helped him down the hall. Ngombe mustered enough strength to assist by placing his hand on the wall whenever he staggered.

THE SHIPS WERE on their way inbound to Valhalla. They'd gone far out, almost past Uranus' orbit, then turned in a wide arc and headed sunward. The asteroid was only a couple of days ahead.

Adam's plans had finally solidified in his mind. While everyone in the small fleet was intent on what they'd do to make the new asteroid their home, he was thinking ahead.

The Bubble had been an almost ideal habitat, but the Feds had ruined it. Now that they'd fired a nuke off inside, it would never house humans again. The loss of their hard work and their homes had hurt everyone. The problem was that an asteroid, no matter how welcoming, was too susceptible to enemy attack.

Now that he thought about it, even the Earth could be severely damaged. All an enemy had to do was to shove a big enough rock up to a fraction of c, aim it correctly, and then go take a nap. When they woke up, probably all life on the planet would have been vaporized.

To him, this indicated that humans needed to grow up quickly. There had to be some kind of moral boundary beyond which people would not trespass. Unfortunately, humans had had such boundaries in the past and had never shown any significant reluctance in ignoring them. The only thing that really limited human behavior was the knowledge that there would be an unavoidable repercussion for whatever sin they committed.

This was all well and good back when everyone believed in a higher power that knew everything and punished every misdeed. That belief had primarily fallen away. Modern humans were wary of being caught and held to account by human-created laws, but otherwise, most of them, in Adam's experience at least, didn't give a fig about what they did to other people.

He was angry about that. If he had the power, he'd enforce a strict standard of behavior that limited aggression. At that point in his thinking, a little humor interjected itself. It was fortunately not in his power. He was neither omnipotent nor omniscient. He'd undoubtedly make a lot of mistakes if it were up to him to judge other people's behavior.

Despite that bit of humility, he decided that his musings had a good result. He'd have to make sure that his people, Belters, pirates, or whatever, were defended well enough that no one and that meant mostly the Feds, would dare to attack them.

Since Valhalla was a little smaller than the Bubble, it was more vulnerable. It was also more likely to be breached since the opening to the interior was much large. The airlocks would have to be larger as a result, and that meant they would be less able to withstand enemy fire.

This was not an ideal location. There was no doubt about it. He'd have to find somewhere else more attack resistant and then convince the council that it would be desirable to move most of their population to that location.

The problem was locating the somewhere else. Then he remembered the moons of Saturn. The close-in ones received too much radiation. The small ones were too small. Some of them rotated too quickly. Some had volcanic action. He would have to choose a larger one that was farther away from Saturn. He turned to the computer to look over the possibilities.

There were seven major moons. Titan was the largest, and it had the benefit of a nitrogen atmosphere. It was larger than Luna so it wouldn't pose a technological problem. The trouble with Titan was that it was the one moon that everyone always thought about when they thought about Saturn. The Earthers would get around to a colonization effort for Titan sooner or later. Maybe it was already in the works. He didn't know.

None of the other major moons seemed to work. For the most part, they were too close, and that meant they would be subject to higher radiation. He discarded that idea, then looked at the irregular satellites. Of these, Phoebe was the one that seemed most interesting. It was a little over 200 kilometers in diameter and had a higher density. Besides, it carried a lot of water ice and carbon dioxide, along with quite a bit of organic materials.

Phoebe was odd in that it had a retrograde orbit. Perhaps that was due to its origin. No one was quite sure, but it was thought to be a captured centaur object that had originated in the Kuiper belt. If so, it was a long way from where it started. He marked it as a possibility. It would have to be investigated to see if it would be suitable. The gravity was low, almost nonexistent, but they'd been doing reasonably well in the Bubble, and it had virtually zero gravity.

Thinking about it, it seemed a shame that humans didn't adapt to zero gravity better. He sighed. We're children of earth, so we're formed for its environment. Zero gravity brought challenges for human bodies. Proper exercise helped, but there was really no substitute for regular gravity. A space ship could be rotated or have a rotating ring, substituting centripetal force for gravity. They might eventually have imparted spin to the Bubble, but that was a closed option.

He switched out of the database with a tentative conclusion. He'd investigate Phoebe. It might serve as a small base, and it might also have resources they could use. It would not be suitable for a major population. Titan was the only possibility. If they Feds showed up, it would be too late. Titan would be the property of the Belters. The pirates would have to be prepared to defend the moon.

He rubbed his forehead with his hand, disturbing his eyepatch. The scar throbbed at times, and this was one of them. He rubbed it, then rearranged the patch.

That action brought Nile into his mind.

Really, she was never out of his thoughts. He wanted to drop everything and leave to search for her. He just didn't know where to look. She might be held by the USSN, but they'd sent no messages. She would, of course, keep her mouth shut. It would be almost impossible for the navy to know that she was important to him. They might not care if they did know.

The other possibility was that she had died. Something had happened to her ship, and the crew might not have survived. There wasn't any way to know.

An image of her frozen body drifting in her suit against the blackness of space kept creeping into his mind. He tried to force it out, but it kept coming back. It wasn't something he wanted to contemplate.

THE VALHALLA HABITAT was rudimentary. The people who had come first had worked hard, but it was apparent that the location would never be as appealing as the Bubble. The cavern wasn't as large. It couldn't be used as a dock or a ship assembly space. It was only suited to filling with closely packed apartments, and that was what was being built.

The good thing was that there was enough space to accommodate the passengers on the Hope. The additional bodies filled all of the available space and people had to double up, sharing beds on alternate shifts, but they fit.

Everyone was so glad to be off the ship, that they didn't complain much about having to share space. Besides more apartments were coming online daily.

Adam couldn't seem to get enthusiastic about their prospects. Perhaps it was due to his missing Nile, or perhaps he just wanted something better. The first few days there, he spent his time in meetings with the council and with various engineering groups. On the fifth day, he moved back into the D-R's captain's cabin.

Ngombe was in what passed for a hospital on Valhalla and was expected to eventually recover, although he would never again have any hair. He made light of it, saying that it would save him time since he wouldn't have to shave his scalp to fit into a space suit helmet.

That was silly, of course. Adam had allowed his hair and beard to grow. There was plenty of space in a helmet for hair as long as it wasn't allowed to compromise any of the seals.

Adam was alone on the D-R. Smith had moved in with a woman from the Hope. He had formally resigned from the D-R's crew and was intent on making a home and having a family as soon as feasible. To'afa was off somewhere with another woman. There had been a few Hawaiian's in the colonist group, and he'd found a woman that he fancied. He had assured Adam that he'd be back soon, though.

"My people come from a line of seafarers. We're used to making long ocean voyages. The women have to take care of themselves while we're gone. Besides, I can't take too much of her constant talking," he confided.

They were speaking on the comm. To'afa had called to see when the D-R would be outbound again.

"I understand the noise factor. I had to move back onboard for much the same reason. I've been isolated too long with just you, Smith, and Ngombe. The constant presence of all those colonists was just too much," Adam replied.

To'afa's deep voice came over the comm. "Agreed. I've about had enough here, myself. Are you going to go on a raid or something? Let me know. I'll be there."

He nodded to himself. That was all he needed. He'd been thinking of going somewhere and, if To'afa wanted to go, then that was enough encouragement.

"I'm thinking of exploring Phoebe. It might make a good base. From there, we probably should check out Titan. We can't land, but we can take a close look. Want to go?"

"Give me a day to get things settled here. Okay?"

"Okay. I'll give Flynn a call. Maybe he'll want to go. The council seems to be ready for me to leave also."

In fact, the council was more than ready for Adam to leave. He was so popular that their authority was compromised when he was around. People always asked him for his opinion on major decisions. It was uncomfortable for him. He didn't want to rule the group and felt strongly that council rulership was what they needed.

He actually hadn't thought about it much in the past, but now that he had involuntarily been placed in a position that competed with the council's power, he had become more concerned with the general organization of the group. It would be better, he thought, if he were out of the picture for a while.

Accordingly, he called Greg Barrett, the current council chairperson.

"Hey, Greg!"

"Hey, yourself, Adam. To what do I owe this call?"

Might as well present his voyage as something he was going to do, regardless of the council's opinion. "I'm going to do a little exploring. I think we should have at least two other locations as options. We'll outgrow Valhalla pretty quickly. I've been thinking about Titan."

"Hmm. Don't you think the Feds will have that on their list?"

"I'm sure they will, but what are they going to do, if we have already taken it? Attack? We've proven that we can defend against their strongest attack."

"So far. They could wait until they have a lot more ships to attack. We can't match them in productivity."

"That's possibly correct, but we have more resources easily available. I'm going to check out Phoebe for hydrocarbons and other resources, then go on to scout Titan. It would be pretty easy to put a base there. We can drop enough water ice to change the atmosphere. If there are hydrocarbons on Phoebe, we can use them for plastic manufacturing and other chemicals. They're a lot more convenient than boosting everything out of the Earth's well into space."

"Earth's got the Ribbon. It's not too hard to get stuff into orbit now."

"Look, Greg. I know you don't want to think about it, but we're basically at war with Earth right now. We're not going to destroy Earth and kill off humanity, but they are more than willing to kill all of us. I think that means that we're justified in taking rather extreme steps to ensure our survival. I'm talking about cutting the Ribbon. That would slow them down by years."

"God! You can't do that. It would kill millions of people on the surface. Why, when the Ribbon falls, it will wipe out the entire city at its base."

"It will, but we can make it clear the Ribbon is coming down. The people will have ample time to evacuate. You can't make an omelet without breaking eggs, you know. Anyway, we don't need to worry about that now. I'm simply talking about checking out two additional resources while I look for another location for a base."

"I guess you're right. We will need more space pretty quickly. Valhalla is okay, but it's no Bubble. If they attack us here, we'll have a lot harder time defending ourselves."

"That's true. The Bubble was almost impregnable. The airlock was the only vulnerable part. Here, half your buildings are hanging out in vacant space. A missile strike would wipe you out. Speaking of which, have you got the weapons and shielding in progress?"

"Uh. We're working on shielding at the moment. We need it most for the radiation, so we thought we'd do it first."

"That's alright, but you need to start putting in gun emplacements and a missile racks too. Might not be a popular use of resources, but if you have to defend yourself, it will be too late to install weapons, if you haven't already got them in place."

"That's what I've been arguing, but the other side of the table doesn't want to spend the resources."

By that, he meant the opposing council members. The council was composed of eighteen members, and at least seven of them seemed to be a little naive. They had expressed hope that Earth would leave them alone if they showed no signs of belligerence. Adam thought they were idiots but had avoided getting entangled in the dispute.

"You'll have to convince them to go along with the idea. You can use my name if you need to. Say that I've ordered it. They'll be reluctant to go against that, especially if you make it public knowledge."

Greg laughed, a bit hollowly, then replied, "You'd be a difficult opponent if you wanted to get into politics."

"Yes, but I don't. I think you're doing a great job of governing. It's not something that I care for myself. Just give me a ship and let me explore in peace. I'm happy doing that."

He thought that he'd be happier if he had Nile with him, but that wasn't worth talking about.

"You'd better be happy being in charge of our defense, Admiral. You can't ignore that part of your responsibility. You've proven that you're invaluable to us."

"Maybe. So use that against them. You can say that I ordered it or whatever, but get some cannons on the outside along with the shielding. Okay?"

"I'll try. How long do you plan to be gone on this exploration voyage?"

Ha! Greg had accepted that he had the right to go where ever he wanted.

"I think about three weeks. Maybe less. I want to do a thorough job of it. I'm going to take a couple of people with me, of course."

Greg grunted, then said, "Okay. Keep in touch and watch for Fed ships."

"There aren't many left to watch for. We pretty much wiped them out, but I'll be careful."

The next call was to Flynn. The little man was quite ready to go. He apparently had some gambling debts, and the people he owed were pressing him to pay up. The sooner he got off the asteroid, the better, as far as he was concerned.

The two men showed up the next day and settled into their usual routines. The three had been together off and on for long enough that they felt like a working crew immediately.

Their harmony was slightly disrupted when Adam discovered that one of the others had decorated his spacesuit with a pirate flag. The Jolly Roger was tied as a sash around the middle of the suit. He started to rip it off, then looked at it carefully. It was neatly stitched out of what appeared to be a couple of sheets, one dyed black. It was so nicely done, that he hesitated.

Once he'd thought it over, the idea was actually a little funny. He was, after all, considered the worst sort of pirate by the Navy. It wouldn't hurt to look the part, too. He rubbed his eye patch. Hell, he couldn't help but look the part. Besides, the Navy had taken Nile from him. He wanted revenge for that.

If wearing the flag made him look more fearful, that was all to the good. They'd better fear him.

It stayed in place on his suit.

# 33

## EXPLORATION

THE D-R PULLED out twenty-four hours later. They'd delayed to load some last minute supplies, and to allow Adam enough time to attend a council meeting where he started an argument by demanding that they install ten plasma cannon on the Valhalla's surface.

The council had debated it until Adam had lost his temper. At which point he stated that he wouldn't fight for them unless they cooperated in protecting themselves. The opposition folded instantly at that point.

He had returned to the D-R in ill humor, thought about removing the pirate flag from his waist again, but left it in place. The council opposition members had been mildly horrified at the flag. Videos of his arrival had been made available, and the flag had become a popular symbol almost immediately.

The skull and crossbones logo apparently inflamed a lot of people's imaginations. It had suddenly appeared in a lot of places: as graffiti, on people's shirts, and even some impromptu tattoos.

He couldn't imagine how it had become so popular overnight, but it had.

The council made an abortive effort to convince people not to use the symbol, but no one paid any attention to the morning announcement. The general attitude seemed to be that if the Earthers thought the Belters were pirates, they'd play the part.

THE D-R WAS only a half-light second or so from the asteroid base when the comm signaled for Adam. It was Greg.

The council chair looked worried, but that wasn't unusual. His message, though, made Adam worry also.

"There's been a disruption on Earth. Worthington was assassinated a day ago. This was relayed from Mars through a couple of mining ships that were in the area. Apparently, Mars has decided that they need to make nice with us. It looks like Earth isn't going to be much support for them."

Adam was startled out of his funk. "What happened? I thought Worthington was well protected." Then, after he realized what Barrett had said, he added, "We didn't hear anything on the comm. Was it a general broadcast?"

"No. The Mars signal was, I guess, but we didn't receive that. It was laser relayed through two of our associated ships, one was in close to Mars and picked up the broadcast, the other was midway through the belt and sent it on to us. The two ships are owned by a family and make an effort to keep close track of each other's location, so that's how the laser signal got through."

"Okay, but Worthington?"

"Yeah. From the story, he had taken a new mistress. Sounds like she wasn't willing, but that's never stopped him yet. Anyway, his valet was related to her somehow. They said possibly a cousin. He slipped a knife through the President's waistcoat while he was helping him dress. That's the minor part of the news."

Adam leaned forward. "What's the major part?"

"The President's daughter took immediate steps. She sent in a military division, and they arrested everyone who had any possibility of stepping into the void left by Worthington's death. They've been executing a lot of cabinet members and other public officials. Firing squads, apparently.

Elseth has taken power and is calling herself the new ruler. I believe she has chosen to call herself 'Queen,' but the big thing is the eastern block of non-aligns saw the power vacuum as a perfect time to attack.

They've got a full-out war going on down there. New York has been destroyed by a nuclear missile as has Colorado Springs and Miami. The Ribbon is still intact, and both sides are vying for control of it.

The Feds have just started dropping KEWs. We didn't wipe the navy entirely out. They have a handful of cruisers that were almost finished. They've been using these to throw GPS-guided iron ingots at their enemies. Both Beijing and Moscow have suffered multiple strikes.

The council has been in emergency session since we got the news and it was suggested that we needed your input. You've proven yourself to be an apt battle tactician. Does the current situation impact our status, in your opinion?"

That was a difficult question. He responded, "I'm still trying to get my head around the whole story. Do you know that I know Elseth?"

"No. How's that? We didn't know you traveled in such high circles."

"It was mostly an accident. She's responsible for me being here. She got me kicked out of University. I've no liking for her, or her disgusting father, either."

"He's beyond worrying about your feelings now. What do you think? Will the Eastern bloc of non-aligns win? If they do, will they leave us alone?"

"Ah. That's not an easy question. My gut feeling is that the Feds will have enough KEWs to batter them into a cease-fire. Have any of the cruisers been hit by missiles from the surface?"

"We don't have that information. Maybe there will be an additional report, but so far, no more than what I've said."

"I'm thinking that we stay out of the mess. At a minimum, it will keep the Feds too busy to think about us. That will give us time to consolidate our position and build some more ships. We need armed ships that can defend against another attack. I'd like to see us have a more powerful cruiser with more plasma guns."

"That's possible. I'll ask the engineers to consider your idea. They're mostly busy with habitat construction, but there are enough additional people, now that the Hope has brought the rest of the colony. We could possibly start on a ship. No promises, though."

That was irritating. Didn't the chair see that it was everyone's survival he was talking so casually about? It wasn't like Adam was some kid asking for a new toy. They needed offensive capability.

"Okay. You do that. But keep in mind that I can't fight without ships. If they come after us again, the best chance for the few remaining ships is to leave Valhalla to its own devices." He didn't really mean that, but perhaps it would shake Greg out of his complacency.

"You can't do that! You're the Admiral. You have to defend us."

"Greg, I've got zero chance of being successful without more ships. Now get started on building. I'm begging you. It's for your own good."

"I see what you mean." Greg paused, leaving the mic hot, then asked, "If the Eastern Bloc prevails, are they going to come after us?"

"I don't think they will. At least not immediately. They'll want to lick their wounds and consolidate their victory. That goes for the Feds, too, if they win. The problem is that the winner is going to have more resources to spend on expanding into space. When they get around to coming out here, they may have a lot more ships. We'd better be ready."

"Yes. You're right. I think it might take them a while to focus on us, though."

"Probably, but we can't be too sure. If they have additional cruisers that we didn't know about, they may think they can get resources from the belt. It would be easy to get KEWs out here."

"Well, yeah. We've got plenty of raw materials that they would call strategic resources."

"Just so. Here's what I think. You get as many hands as you can on the ship-building detail. I'm going to go ahead and scout Phoebe and Titan. We may need another bolt-hole, and I want to be ready. It was just luck that we had Valhalla when they decided to attack. If they ruin Valhalla for us and we don't have anywhere else, it will get nasty."

Barrett paused again. He seemed to have a habit of keeping the mic hot when he wanted to continue.

Adam could hear some discussion in the background, but couldn't make out what was being said. The microphone was designed to pick up close signals only.

After a minute, Barrett came back on. "So, it's decided. We'll do things your way, with the caveat that you will come directly back after looking over Titan. We need you here. Understood?"

It was time to let Greg feel like he won a point. He'd conceded on the shipbuilding, so he probably needed something in return.

"Okay. I'll return as soon as I check out Titan."

In point of fact, Adam had been trying to figure out how to land on the big moon. He wanted to get his feet on the surface. The problem was that the well was too deep to set the D-R down casually. The Em-Max drive by itself couldn't kick them off the surface.

Sure, he could land on Phobos. There wasn't enough gravity to worry about there. Titan was almost a planet in its own right.

Its mass was half again as great as Luna so landing and taking off would take a lot of boost.

The newly installed engines might work, but he wasn't sure. He hadn't had a chance to run the necessary calculations. That would have to be done, but he'd been concentrating on Phoebe first. There had seemed to be plenty of time to plan before he got there.

He signed off, then turned to the comp. Might as well get the calculation done now.

THE CALC INDICATED that landing on Titan would be possible, but marginal. The ship had skids on the belly. All mining ships did. They were typically used to ensure that whatever asteroid the crew was exploring did not accidentally ding the hull. The standard procedure was to orient so that the skids acted as a stand-off between the ship and the asteroid.

Rapidly rotating rocks were not approached that closely. The skids were only used when it was possible to touch the subject body without danger. Rotating asteroids could be sampled by using the lasers to create vapor samples that could be analyzed spectroscopically.

Mining rotating asteroids was difficult. A standard method involved slowing the rotation by boosting a smaller rock towards the rotating one. If the two collided accurately, the imparted momentum of the smaller one would slow the rotation, hopefully to a point where mining became feasible.

The skids could be used to land on Luna, but the thrust from the Em-max wasn't enough to kick the mining ship out of the weak gravity well. Conventional booster rockets were used for that purpose. Now that he'd added the plasma-enhanced boosters to the Dire Rhea, Adam believed that it would have enough acceleration to leave Titan.

He wasn't sure about that, though. He believed there was enough thrust, but there was an element of uncertainty about the plasma-Em-max combination that he hadn't quite been able to quantify. Landing would be possible, leaving might be...he thought about it...it might be interesting, for lack of a better term.

Phoebe, on the other hand, was no problem. The moonlet wasn't rotating particularly quickly. It completed a day every 9.3 hours, and since it was only a little over two hundred kilometers in diameter, that gave it an equatorial rotation speed of approximately seventy-two kilometers per hour.

Any competent ship driver could match that with one eye closed. He winced. He'd become so used to his one-eyed status that he often didn't remember it. He always had one eye closed.

That got him to thinking about Nile and how she hadn't flinched when he'd removed his eye patch. The scar wasn't pretty, but she hadn't cared. He wanted her back. The worst part was, he didn't know if she was captive, dead, or had just decided to go elsewhere. The 'not knowing' was, he concluded, the worst part.

No one was in the bridge at the moment, but he looked around with a guilty air. His eye was watering for some reason, and he didn't want anyone to see.

Another thought struck him. If the Feds were holding her captive and he found out about it, heaven help them. He'd teach them to fear the asteroid pirates. He ran through a couple of imaginary space battles in his mind just to reinforce his opinion of how deadly he could be, then dropped the exercise with a sigh. It wasn't satisfactory, and it did nothing to bring Nile back.

THE DAYS PASSED uneventfully as they headed toward Phoebe. Valhalla was currently far away from Saturn, so the shortest route was to cut inside Mars' orbit, passing close to Earth orbit, then to pass entirely through the belt as they approached Saturn.

The sun happened to be kicking up a bit of discharge. There were more sunspots than normal, and there'd been a vast coronal discharge. That meant that radio communications were spotty. They used the line-of-sight modulated laser system, but it wasn't accurate enough to reach Valhalla reliably, so there was a lack of news during the voyage.

The communication disruption turned out to be a grave problem. The first Adam knew about it was when To'afa summoned him to the bridge.

"Better get up here, Captain. The laser system is receiving, and you need to hear the message. I'm recording, but it isn't too clear. Maybe you can make something out of it."

He pulled on his pants and ran, barefooted, up the hall. When he arrived, To'afa motioned him close to the speaker.

The words were distorted as if coming through a long pipe. They echoed weirdly, and parts of the message were lost entirely. What Adam got was a distinct impression that the message was an infinite repeat loop. It seemed to recycle periodically.

After listening to the entire loop several times, he looked inquiringly at To'afa.

"That's it. Alls I could make out was they been pointing at Phoebe and hoping we'd hear. It sounds like they think there's a navy ship around here someplace."

Adam nodded. That was about what he'd understood.

To'afa wasn't satisfied with the message. "I mean I could understand it if we hadn't cleaned their clock so good at the Bubble. They hardly have any ships left from what I hear."

Apparently, the islander hadn't heard the story about the Feds' new cruisers.

"They've built some new ones at Luna. They've been using them to drop rocks on their enemies from low orbit. I think they're trying to settle with all opposition on the planet at once."

"Then there might be one out here after all. Maybe the guys at Valhalla are right. We'd better keep watch a little more closely."

The telescope hadn't been damaged in the battle. Leaving it behind wasn't an option, so it still had a small crew. The information might have come from them. Adam didn't know. What he did know was that the sensor array didn't show anything nearby except Saturn.

They'd nearly arrived, but couldn't see their destination. Phoebe was on the other side of the planet at the moment.

The rings were tilted at an acute angle due to their approach vector, which made for an artistic view. Adam thought the picture would make a great postcard, but then reprimanded himself. It wasn't like he had anyone to send a postcard to or any mail service for that matter.

He snorted in disgust. It was precisely this silly part of his personality that he wanted most to be rid of and it kept popping up at the worst times.

To'afa looked up at the sound. "What is it? You see something?"

He grinned, embarrassed. "No. I just had a thought, that's all."

"What is it?"

"What's the chance the Feds are poking around out here at exactly the time we're here? They've got the whole belt, hell, the whole solar system to fool around in. I'm wondering if they knew we were going to be here."

To'afa shrugged. "That's a good question. I'd say there's no way they could know. Unless..." He trailed off.

"Yeah. Unless. Unless they've got a spy planted with us. That's kind of unlikely, though. The sun is still kicking up a mess, and the comm system is hosed. How would a spy send them a message now?"

"I don' know, Adam. Maybe he sent it when we first left. That would make the timing better. They could just about get from earth orbit out here at the same time it took us to arrive."

"You've got a point. Use that big head for more than a place to hold your hair, don't you?"

To'afa snorted in turn. "Ha. Ha. I never told you, but I got a Masters degree in math. It don't do a man any good to let on about education out here, though."

That was a surprise. He hadn't known that, although it was true that the miners as a group tended to scoff at anything but learning through experience. Theoretical knowledge could get you killed too quickly. Practical experience was what counted. The longer a person survived in space, the more experience they accumulated, and the more likely they were to continue to survive.

"I didn't know that, but I'm glad to hear it. I'll keep it in mind in the future." He couldn't think of anything else to say in response.

# 34
## PHOEBE

THEY INSERTED THE D-R into Phoebe's orbit, then waited for the little moon to catch up with them. They were moving slower than it was and had to keep making orbital corrections as a result. The ship didn't want to stay at that orbit at a slower speed without some additional thrust.

Adam periodically fired the engine to adjust their altitude as Phoebe gradually approached. The final part of the approach involved a flurry of activity as he fired the maneuvering jets and the engine simultaneously.

When the action was over, the D-R was lightly resting on its skids on the dark surface of the centaur's body. The view was strange. The pirates were used to looking at asteroids, but this moon was an odd one.

The view showed what looked like dirty snow spread across a sharply curving plain which was accented by several impact craters. The small diameter of the moon made the horizon appear very close. There were no mountains or even significant hills, but the distant view was interrupted by large boulders or possibly lumps of ice.

The snow was thought to be water ice, but it obviously carried some additional organic components. It looked slightly greasy in addition to the dirty-grey-shading-to-black coloration. When one looked into the distance, just above the surface, there was a faint haze. Adam thought that might be due to Phoebe's plowing through some of Saturn's ring material. It wasn't thick enough to be a problem for them, even though the moon was moving in a retrograde orbit against the ring rotation.

To'afa was sitting right beside him, eyes glued to the display. He asked, "You think this thing is really a centaur and not a natural moon?"

Adam answered, "It's supposed to be from the Kuiper belt. The composition is odd for a moon. It's certainly not like the larger ones."

The big man glanced at the read-out from the chemical analysis. The sampling probe had already captured some of the material, and the auto-lab was busily testing the stuff.

"If there are organics in that gunk, we might be able to use them. We're always short," To'afa commented.

It was true. They depended on organics for the synthesis of all sorts of useful chemical compounds, from plastics to vitamins. The bulk of the asteroids were either rocky or metallic. Not many carried much in the way of organic materials, the odd comet remanent excluded.

Adam agreed. "Yeah. It would be nice if we had a source close to Titan."

To'afa looked at him. "You sound like you already made up your mind about a base there."

He had. It made perfect sense to him. Titan was the second largest moon in the solar system after Jupiter's Ganymede. It was larger than Mercury and massed more than Luna. Titan wasn't as good from some perspectives as Mars, but it had an advantage in that it had more atmosphere than the red planet.

If one ignored the cold, it was practically a garden spot. They'd be able to survive there in more comfort than the constricted Valhalla offered. He met To'afa's eyes.

"I'm going to push for a settlement there. The Earthers won't leave us alone unless we make them. To do that, we'll need more population. More population gives us more workers for industry, and that's what will make the difference. If we get big enough, we can build enough ships to have a fleet that will be able to keep the Feds at bay." He paused, visualizing the desired result, then added, "We have to have a big base. Titan is the only piece of suitable real estate around here. There's nothing else as good."

"What about the Feds? Won't they try to take it away from us?"

"We have to move quickly and get on the power edge of the curve. Make it too difficult for them to defeat us. I don't want to, but we could set them back a long way by cutting the Ribbon."

To'afa blinked. "That's a thought. They'd be furious, but it would slow them down, until they rebuilt, at least."

"Their problem and our advantage right at the moment are they seem to be at war with each other. If the North American dictatorship wins, that will be when they turn towards us. If the non-aligns win, it will probably give us more time. They usually can't even agree on what to have for lunch, let alone something as big as making war against us." He wasn't entirely sure about his logic, but it sounded right.

To'afa glanced at the sensors. A single light was flashing with a steady rhythm.

"When did that start? Something's set off the long-range detector," he said.

Adam inspected the display. Something was moving in their direction.

"Maybe it's a rock in the ring?" To'afa hazarded, his voice rising in inquiry, making a question out of the supposition.

The display numbers changed slightly. Adam studied them for a moment.

"I think we're going to have company. That looks like a ship, and it's headed this way."

The darker man pushed back and said, "I'll warm up the plasma cannon. Just in case." He grinned happily, then added, "Be a good idea to have a warm welcome for them."

Adam nodded. If it was a ship, it could be a miner or the Navy cruiser. He sighed. With his luck, it was undoubtedly the cruiser.

He thought of the shield. It was turned off. That wouldn't do if there were the potential for enemy action. The thing had to be off when they landed, otherwise it would overload from contact with the surface.

Flynn came trotting in at that moment. He'd been sleeping and was rubbing his eyes. "What's up? Can't a man get any effin' sleep round this madhouse?"

He wasn't in the best possible mood, but, then again, he never was, unless he was drinking.

To'afa answered, "Looks like a cruiser is coming for a visit. We got to get ready."

Flynn was instantly all business.

"I'll lift the ship. You get the cannon unlocked and ready. Adam, er...Captain, would you be so kind as to switch on the shield when we're off?"

Flynn hadn't gotten used to being second. He'd been in charge of his own ship, and that experience had seemed to suit him.

The comm buzzed. All three men turned and stared at the unit as if it was haunted.

Flynn swore under his breath, then added, "Now who in Finnegan's Tavern could be callin' us out here?"

"Obviously the USSN," Adam answered, trying not to be sarcastic. He continued, "I guess I'd better answer and see what they want. We can boost off as soon as they make their intentions clear. I don't think they'll shoot at us without warning. Otherwise, we wouldn't be getting a call. They'd have shot already."

To'afa reiterated the conclusion in almost perfect sync with Adam.

"They'd have shot at us already."

Adam spoke into the mic. "Unidentified ship, this is the D-R. State your intentions."

There was a momentary pause, then a slightly accented voice came through.

"This is the USSN Hartford. We are landing and want a face-to-face. I trust I'm speaking to Adam Maxwell. Correct?"

Flynn cursed again. "In the name o' the Trinity. Who the eff is that and how'd he know it was us?"

Adam was ahead of the curve on this one. "They've obviously got a spy planted on us somewhere. That's the only way they'd know we were out here."

To'afa objected, "But, how would they be able to get a message out? If they were at Valhalla, I mean. It's not like you can just get on the comm and call the Feds. People might get a little suspicious."

Adam shrugged. "Code, encryption in a message to a mining ship that could relay the message onward. I don't know, but we're going to have to find out. We can't have spies working against us."

He lifted the mic. "Come ahead. Land around the curve of the moon out of direct sight. Keep your missile pods closed. We won't stand idly by and allow you to shoot at us. Once you've landed, we can arrange things."

He turned to the others and said, "They've got something in mind. I wouldn't put anything beyond them. Keep an eye on the sensors. Let's make sure they don't have another ship sneaking in."

Flynn nodded, then asked, "Who's goin' ta meet with 'em?"

Adam shrugged. "It'll be me, I guess. I'll be armed. I'll tell them that only one man can come out. I can handle that."

To'afa shook his head negatively. "No, you can't. They'll sneak someone else out and snipe you from behind a rock. I'm getting dressed and getting my ax. I'll circle around and come up behind to keep an eye on things."

Adam nodded slowly. "Okay. Don't do anything unless I need help, though."

"Okay." The larger man got up and headed towards the space suit locker.

Adam looked at Flynn. "You got things here? If they start getting hinky, lift off and give them a sample of our plasma. Make sure they don't get away. Okay?"

Flynn nodded. "I wish we had something more effective than the plasma cannon. It usually kills 'em, but sometimes it's not definite enough for me."

Adam answered, "I've been thinking of another weapon. Came to me when I couldn't get to sleep. We'll see if it's practical once we get back to the base."

Flynn shook his head. "Bad timing. We could use it now. I can see they got something that looks a lot like one of our plasma cannons."

Adam leaned forward and looked at the highly magnified display.

"We couldn't expect them not to catch on. It's a relatively simple idea. Once they got hold of the shield generators, the cannon is the next logical step. It was coming sooner or later. I'll have to make my idea work, that's all."

IT TOOK THE Hartford the better part of an hour to match up and land. Whoever was flying the ship was apparently a novice at landing on asteroids.

There was a moment when the navy cruiser had the D-R directly in its sights, but it didn't fire. Instead, it continued maneuvering for a landing around the curve of the moon.

Once it was down, the same accented voice came on again. Flynn relayed the communication to the suit locker, where Adam and To'afa were donning their suits.

"He's callin' again, Captain. I'm switching it through to you."

The speaker clicked, then the navy ship's commander was on. He'd apparently been speaking and hadn't realized that he was being relayed. The comm came on mid-sentence.

"and we'll meet midpoint between the two ships. The Queen has instructed me to make you an offer you can't refuse. I've got an inducement for you, Maxwell. Cooperate, and you can have your girlfriend back. No tricks, now."

Adam jerked to attention with his helmet in his hands. He looked at To'afa to see what the big man's response would be. The islander was already dressed. As Adam watched, he bent and picked up his ax.

Adam answered, "What did you say?"

The comm clicked, and Nile's voice came through.

"Adam, it's Serge Rolfson. He picked me up when we had to evacuate the Mad Hatter. He --" Her voice stopped abruptly, then Serge came on again.

"That's right, Adam. It's me. Elseth sent me to bring you in. She's willing to forget your past actions if you help us defeat the non-aligns. Your country needs you. I'd never have thought that you'd turn out to be so good at fighting space battles, but I guess you never know. Right, friend?"

Adam gritted his teeth in anger. The last time they'd met, Serge hadn't been so friendly unless he thought pointing a gun at someone was a sign that you liked them.

"Agreed. No tricks. Bring Nile out with you. Just you two. I'll listen to what you have to say, but I'm taking her back with me."

Serge replied, "That's the plan. Elseth wants you to trust her. You follow instructions, and you can have Niley back. She's proven to be less accommodating than I like in a woman, anyway."

"You better not have touched her, you..." He couldn't think what to say.

Serge laughed in his superior fashion. Adam hadn't remembered how grating that was. It got on his nerves instantly.

"She's none the worse for wear, except maybe a few spots, but those will heal up nicely. We'll be out there in fifteen. I estimate that we're about two klicks over the horizon from you. It'll take maybe another five minutes for us to get in view. You wait out in the open. I want a clear look so I can make sure you're alone. Oh, and no guns. I'm not bringing one, and I don't care to be the only unarmed one."

Adam answered, "No guns. I agree."

He looked at To'afa and lifted Captain Suarez' cutlass down from its hook, then whispered, "I'll just wear this. I can arrange it so this crazy flag you guys stuck on my suit covers it, I think. It should give me an advantage."

Serge came back on. "No guns. If you're thinking of cheating, I warn you, Nile is going to be the first to suffer. I've rigged a Det charge on her helmet. It's not too big, but it'll crack the seal, and she'll die. I'm carrying the trigger, so don't get smart."

Adam was already at the lock controls. He slapped his helmet on over his hastily tied back hair and pulled the lock actuator.

# 35
## HOSTAGE RESCUE

ADAM LED THE way. They were ahead of Serge and Nile by a few minutes, and To'afa wanted to get in position. The presence of the Navy ship meant that they couldn't use their comms. Instead, Adam touched his helmet to To'afa's. The sound came through faintly.

To'afa said, "That boulder over there by the crater. It's got a patch of deep shadow. I'll wait in there."

Adam said, "Make sure they can't see you. I'll hold my left arm straight out to my side when I can't see you. If I don't raise it, move into a darker place. Okay?"

To'afa said, "Sure. Likewise, raise your left arm straight up, if you think you need help. I'll come as quickly as I can. He won't know what hit him."

"I hope that won't be necessary. Remember the Det charge. I want Nile back alive. Understand?"

"Yeah. I'll be still unless there's a real problem. You better get the trigger off him before you separate. He could blow it just for spite."

Adam had been thinking of nothing else. "Have you got any vacuum tape in your kit? My pouch is empty."

The big man dug for a moment, then handed a tape dispenser to Adam.

"Thanks. If her helmet is cracked, maybe I can patch it quickly enough. It's worth a try."

To'afa didn't answer. Instead, he turned and bounded off towards the patch of shadow.

Adam watched him go. The greasy snow kicked up in spurts as To'afa bounded across the open space. That was bad. He was leaving a trail.

Adam moved forward quickly. He wanted to get as far away from their tracks as he could. Maybe Serge wouldn't notice the second set of footprints if they met far enough away from where the two had separated.

HIS FEET WERE getting cold. The suit's heating element was working full out, but the conduction loss where the suit touched the snow was sucking the warmth out of his toes. He hoped the meeting would be over soon enough to keep him from getting frostbite.

He rearranged the flag. His cutlass had slipped partway into view. When he looked up, the heads of two space suits were just visible coming over the horizon. One seemed to be lagging slightly behind the other. From the smaller stature, he thought it was Nile.

His heart seemed to be beating faster than it should, and his vision was a little blurry. He shook his head. No time for that now. He couldn't afford to be distracted.

The two approached and stopped about three meters away. Adam gave Serge a cursory glance, observing that he'd grown a beard since they'd last met. The thin man didn't seem to be carrying a weapon, just as he'd promised. Then his eyes went to

Nile. Her dark complexion didn't show bruises easily, but he could see that she'd been brutally beaten.

One of her eyes was swollen half shut, and her nose looked as if it might have been broken. A trickle of blood leaked from one nostril in mute evidence of recent violence. She made a hesitant effort to smile at him, but her lips were so severely damaged that the right side did not curve up, turning the smile into a sneer. Adam could feel the blood suffusing his face. He was barely able to contain his horror and anger. No matter what she'd done, she didn't deserve that kind of brutal treatment.

Serge had been silent, watching Adam's eyes betray his shock. Now he spoke. "Captain Maxwell, I presume? I just love those old trite lines, don't you? You'll have to excuse your girlfriend. She can't speak. Oh, I mean she can, even though her lips are a little messed up, I've disabled her comm unit. She can hear us, but she can't tell you anything. That way I can dominate the conversation. I find that it's better, not having a woman interrupting all of the time, and she wouldn't shut up. Not at all."

Adam interrupted, "You filthy animal. I'll--"

Serge kept speaking as if he hadn't heard Adam or possibly as if whatever Adam had to say was so unimportant that it wasn't worth attending to.

"You've caused Elseth no end of trouble, you know. First, you were helpful, and we owe you for that."

"How was I helpful?" he gritted.

"Oh, you created so much of a stir in the deplorable part of the population, that the good Senator had to crack down. That caused a lot of resentment, so no one really bothered to investigate when Elseth arranged for his assassination. It was a clever thing, a thing of real beauty. You know he had a thing for young women? Elseth allowed him to see her maid and he had to have her. She was a pretty young thing and the sister of one of the domestics who had access to Worthington's suite. Jose killed Worthington after he found Alissandra's body. You probably didn't know that the Senator played that rough, but this wasn't the first time. Jose didn't take it well. Stuck a pair of scissors through Worthington's larynx. He strangled as a result. Good riddance, I say."

Adam wasn't really tracking the conversation. He was still focused on Nile.

"What? Wait, Elseth arranged that?"

"She did. With my help in planning, I must add. So, when the Senator was killed, we hung Jose as an object lesson, then Elseth used her military lap dog to take control of the Capitol. Then it was a simple step to proclaim her Queen and get the media to gush over it. They've never truly loved the country, and you know that Americans always seem to love royalty. It was a masterstroke."

Adam nodded. This time, he'd been listening carefully. A part of his mind had stepped in, calmed the anger and outrage, and was now guiding him with relentless intent.

"So, Elseth is Queen? She'd like that. She always acted like she could barely tolerate the Deps. I never quite knew what she saw in me, but then, I found out that she only wanted to use my expertise. I suppose I should thank you for that."

Serge sneered mockingly. "Thanks accepted. It was a pleasure. You should have seen your face when I pulled that pistol. What a laugh! You, a Dep, thinking that the Senator's daughter could be interested in you."

Adam just nodded slightly, his lips held tight.

"Then you had to make such a pest of yourself, you and those absurd miners, or are you calling yourself pirates now, like the media says?" His eyes strayed to the Jolly Roger wrapped partially around Adam's leg.

Adam answered. "We're Belters. This is our space, and we intend to keep you and the Earthers out of it. If you're nice, we might trade with you eventually, but you're not welcome out here at the moment. Now, get to the point."

"My, my. Touchy, aren't we," Serge sneered again. "Okay. Here's the deal, as simply as I can make it to suit your limited comprehension. You come back to Earth. Elseth makes you the new Admiral in charge of the USSN. You defeat the non-aligns and enforce her rule in space. That means Earth space, Luna, and even out here." He held up his hand before Adam could say anything.

"Oh, don't worry about your precious miners or pirates or whatever. We have no intention of imposing on you. We simply want to ensure that there are no further attacks on our Martian colony. That's all."

He waved his hand in a dismissive motion, then reconsidered. "You also get to keep this bit of baggage." He motioned towards Nile. "Although why you'd want to, I can't imagine. There's plenty of available females on Earth, and you'd be in a position to have your choice or," He hesitated dramatically. "All of your choices. At once, if you so desire. So what will it be? Deal?"

Adam composed himself, then answered. "You make it sound as if it will be simple and easy."

Serge nodded. "Yes. Yes, you do understand at a rudimentary level, after all."

Adam grinned savagely. "Your sarcasm isn't appreciated. Here's what I understand: I have no interest in seeing Elseth again or in becoming her pet admiral. You can solve your own problems on Earth, although I warn you, if you get too obstreperous and we decide that you're doing too much damage to the population of any nation, aligned or non, we'll stop you. Finally, since you've been kind enough to bring Nile out here to me, I'll overlook the way you treated her long enough for you to get back on your ship and leave. After that, if I ever see you again, you will regret it."

He moved his right hand casually against the flag that was draped at his waist, slipping his thumb under the edge of the flag and around the hilt of the sword.

Serge said, "That's about what I thought you'd say, so I prepared."

His hand dipped into the suit pouch and came out with a small pistol that he pointed casually in Adam's direction.

"This isn't much of a weapon, but then, it doesn't have to be. We're in a near vacuum. One hole in your suit and you won't make it back to your ship, regardless of whether the bullet does any damage to your body. You're coming with me, so start walking."

At the same time, the thin man waved his left arm, then said, "Come on in and help me control this fool."

Adam snarled, "You lied about the gun, and you've also got someone out there, hiding. That's about what I thought you'd do."

There was a sudden burst of static over the comm, followed by To'afa's voice. "There was one sniper, Adam. I got him."

Serge looked startled, then raised the pistol, but it was too late. The cutlass whirled around, catching the glint of the distant sun on its blade as it arced down. It struck the little pistol on the slide. The gun flew away and disappeared in the snow.

Adam lunged forward, grabbing at Serge's left hand which was fumbling at something clipped to his belt.

"No, you don't," he shouted, wrenching the hand away from the trigger device.

Serge shoved him hard, but Adam maintained his grip, dragging both of them backward. His rear foot regained traction, and he pushed back, then thrust the cutlass against Serge's helmet. It glanced off the hard material, sliding between Serge's neck and the air supply.

Adam twisted, simultaneously pulling back. The sharp blade cut through the line as he withdrew it.

Serge's eyes bulged in fear, then agony. His mouth silently worked as he reached behind his neck, groping for a solution as his air whistled out into the vacuum.

Adam stepped back and put his arm around Nile. She'd dashed around the two struggling men and had been standing behind him.

Serge went down on his knees, his face pale and his eyes bulging. With the last spasm of his arms, he toppled over, face down in the dirty snow.

Adam saw To'afa coming around the shadowed boulder.

"Come on. Let's get back inside. My toes are freezing."

The big man began to bound in the direction of the D-R in response.

Nile leaned forward, touching helmets with Adam.

"The crew of the cruiser will start shooting at us. We've got to get under cover," she said.

Adam grabbed her arm, and the two began to move quickly after To'afa.

They were nearly back to the D-R when the comm broadcast a message from the cruiser.

"Captain, we haven't heard from you for three minutes. We're executing the emergency directive in twenty seconds. Respond."

Adam glanced back, but there was no sign of the cruiser. It was around the curve of the planet. The two kept moving.

A few more seconds and they were inside the airlock. The door slid shut and the atmosphere equalized with a sustained hiss.

Adam wrenched at his helmet as To'afa opened the internal lock.

He shouted, "Flynn, get her up. Now! They're going to start shooting."

The Irishman must have had his hands poised over the controls. The D-R leaped, then accelerated away from Phoebe's surface, turning as it went.

The sudden movement slammed the three against the wall, and they slid in a heap into the nearby corner. Flynn's belated, "Take hold!" warning came too late.

The lights dimmed as the capacitor bank fired. From their tangle in the corner, Adam could hear the deep-throated hum as the power plant took the load and began to recharge the cannon. Flynn's voice followed with a wild yell of elation.

"That'll teach you, you scurvy dogs! Ya don't go messing with the Pirates of the Belt!"

# 36
## NILE, AGAIN

ADAM MOVED HIS arm carefully. He didn't want to wake Nile. They were tightly wedged in his small bunk, and he had to go urgently.

She moved, then groaned. "Agh. My ribs hurt. That bastard thought he was a big man, beating a tied-up woman."

"He had you tied up?" he asked.

"Yep. I kicked him in his unmentionables when he started in on me, so he got help, and they tied me. From that point on, it was just trying to endure. He wasn't so tough, though. Not like basic training, anyway. I'll be better."

She paused, then turned towards him with a funny expression.

"You make me better. Have I ever told you I love you?"

Adam's knees felt weak. "Yes, but I'm not tired of hearing it. It's mutual."

She replied, "Well, I do, and I'm going to hold you to your promise to marry me."

Adam leaned down and kissed her gently. "I'm glad you brought that up. I was planning on holding you to it."

She smiled, a faint shadow of her usual smile, then said, "When I rest a bit more, I'll want some food. Then I've got to tell you about the mess on Earth. We'll have to do something soon. That ex-girlfriend of yours--"

He interrupted. "Don't bring Elseth up to me. It was a mistake. I was a stupid kid, and..."

Nile said, "Not like now. Now you're a stupid pirate. Get your business done and get back in bed with me. Your warm body against my aching back is better than a heating pad."


The End

# ABOUT THE AUTHOR

Eric Martell has a doctorate in experimental Psychology. He says that the primary benefit of his graduate degrees was that he learned to learn.

He is the author of three science fiction series and a number of short stories for various anthologies. He is a longtime student of the spiritual, holds a black-belt in Tae Kwon Do, is a licensed Heart Math™ provider, and has been trained as a Quantum Energy Healer and medical intuitive. Eric also plays guitar. His taste in music runs from Country through Reggae and Rock to Jazz and New Age.

Eric stumbled into real estate after a successful stint in software that covered everything from early childhood education to military training and consulting. He has 30+ years of experience in real estate investment.

Eric's passion is writing novels and short stories that are intended to both entertain and give readers material for thought. He makes the science in his stories as close as possible to that of the real world given the constraints of the plot. His stories are realistic and, although he does not go out of his way to offend, he sometimes uses difficult or sensitive topics to advance the plot.

# BLOG INFORMATION

If you enjoyed this book, please follow my Author Blog at EricMartellAuthor.com for information about my other books. You'll find free short stories there, occasional preview pages for new novels in progress, and blog posts about things that I find interesting (most lately Artificial Intelligence).
I welcome comments and enjoy discussions with readers.


You can also follow me on Facebook at ESMartellbooks. My Twitter handle is @emartell. You can email me directly through my Author Blog.


Please consider leaving a review. That is the way I know you enjoyed my stories. It also provides me with motivation to write more about a particular character.

# LINKS FOR THE TIME-EQUATION STORIES

*Heart of Fire Time of Ice*
http://bit.ly/HeartofFire
*Paradox: On the Sharp Edge of the Blade*
http://bit.ly/ParadoxBlade
*All the Moments in Forever*
http://bit.ly/MomentsinForever

# LINK FOR THE GAIA ASCENDANT TRILOGY

*The Time of the Cat, Second Wave, & Confederation*
http://bit.ly/GaiaAscendant

# LINKS FOR THE CYBER-MAGIC STORIES

*Cyber Witch-The Origin of Magic*
http://bit.ly/Cyber-Witch
*Nano-Magic*
http://bit.ly/Nano-Magic

9 780999 898059 1